Tom Holt was born in London in 1961. At Oxford he studied bar billiards, ancient Greek agriculture and the care and feeding of small, temperamental Japanese motorcycle engines; interests which led him, perhaps inevitably, to qualify as a solicitor and emigrate to Somerset, where he specialised in death and taxes for seven years before going straight in 1995. Now a full-time writer, he lives in Chard, Somerset, with his wife, one daughter and the unmistakable scent of blood, wafting in on the breeze from the local meat-packing plant. For even more madness and TOMfoolery visit www.tom-holt.com

Find out more about Tom Holt and other Orbit authors by registering for the free monthly newsletter at www.orbitbooks.net

By Tom Holt

TOM HOLT

HOLT

Snow White
and the
Seven Samurai

www.orbitbooks.net

ORBIT

First published in Great Britain by Orbit 1999
This edition published by Orbit 2000
Reprinted 2000, 2001, 2002, 2003, 2004, 2005, 2006, 2007,
2008, 2009

A CIP catalogue record for this book
is available from the British Library.

ISBN 978-1-85723-988-1

Printed and bound in Great Britain by Clays Ltd, St Ives plc

Papers used by Orbit are natural, renewable and recyclable
products sourced from well-managed forests and certified
in accordance with the rules of the Forest Stewardship Council.

Mixed Sources
Product group from well-managed
forests and other controlled sources
www.fsc.org Cert no. SGS-COC-004081
© 1996 Forest Stewardship Council
FSC

Orbit
An imprint of
Little, Brown Book Group
100 Victoria Embankment
London EC4Y 0DY

An Hachette UK Company
www.hachette.co.uk

www.orbitbooks.net

For two very different Thompsons –
the much-enduring Pete
(who sold me the bloody computer)
and the entirely imaginary Cronan
(who only exists inside it)
– and for Dave Sparks, on general principles.

CHAPTER ONE

Once upon a time there was a little house in a big wood.

Not all little houses in big woods are quaint or charming, or even safe. Some of them are piled to the rafters with stolen car radios, others house illegal stills used for making moonshine (so called, they say, because one carelessly dropped match could lead to a fireball that'd be visible from the Moon). Some of them are the lairs of big bad wolves dressed as Victorian grandmothers, not that that's anybody's business but their own.

But this particular house *is* quaint. Roses scramble up the door-frame like young executives up a corporate hierarchy. Flowers bloom radiantly in its small but neat garden, and for once they aren't opium poppies or coca plants or commercially exploitable varieties of the mescal cactus. Just in case there's any doubt left in the onlooker's mind, it has a shiny red front door with a big round brass knocker, which in these parts is a sort of coded message. It means that if you go inside this house, the chances are that you won't be strangled, stabbed, smothered with a pillow or eaten, although you may easily die of terminal

1

cuteness poisoning. If you're particularly observant, you can probably deduce more about the people who live there from the seven brightly coloured coats and hats hanging just inside the porch, and the fact that the lintel of the door-frame is only four feet off the ground.

The conclusive evidence is round the back, where the occupants of the little house put out the trash. No need to get mucky rummaging about in the dustbin bags; shy, timid, razor-clawed forest-dwellers have ripped the bags open, and the rubbish is scattered about like confetti on a windy day. There are approximately three hundred and twenty empty beer cans, forty-nine squashed styrofoam pizza trays, roughly half a pound of cigarette butts and ash, some slabs of cheese with green fur growing on them, several undergarments that were obviously worn too long to be cleanable and were then slung out, some crumpled balls of newspaper still smelling strongly of vinegar, and a thick wodge of the kind of newspapers that have small pages, big pictures and not much news inside them.

In this little house in the big wood, therefore, seven small men live on their own, with nobody to look after them. Nobody to clean and tidy; nobody to make them lovely home-cooked, low-fat, low-cholesterol meals with plenty of fresh green vegetables and no chips or brown sauce; nobody to remind them to take their muddy boots off before coming inside; nobody to throw away their favourite comfy old pullovers when they aren't looking. How sad. How terribly, terribly sad.

Don't worry, though. All that's just about to change; because any minute now, a poor bedraggled girl will come stumbling out of the bramble thicket twenty-five yards due east of the front door. She'll see the friendly-looking cottage with its cheerfully red front door and she'll make straight for it, like a piranha scenting fresh blood. And in a week or so, you won't recognise the place. It's inevitable; it has to happen. No power on Earth can stop it.

Surely . . . ?

*

Beautiful.

Stunning. Breathtaking. Fabulous. Gorgeous. Out of this world.

Satisfied that there had been no change since the last time she looked, the wicked queen turned away from her reflection in the mirror, slid back a hidden panel in the wall and switched on the power. The surface of the glass began to glow blue.

She frowned and tapped her fingers on the arms of her chair. For some time now she'd been trying to summon up the courage to upgrade her entire system, which was virtually obsolete; lousy response time, entirely inadequate memory, all of that and more. All that could be said for it was that she was used to it and it worked. Just about.

Somewhere behind the glass, mist started to swirl. She watched as it slowly coagulated into a spinning, fluffy ball, which in turn resolved itself into a shape that gradually became less like a portion of albino candyfloss and more human. The queen yawned. In theory she should be used to the delay by now, but in practice it irritated her more and more each day. She fidgeted.

The ball of mist had become a head; an elderly man, white-haired and deeply lined, with cold blue eyes and a cruel mouth, but with an air of such dreadful loneliness and despair that even the queen, who had put him there in the first place, never liked looking at him for too long. At first he appeared in profile; then his face moved round until his eyes met hers.

'Running DOS,' he said. 'Please wait.'

He vanished, and his place was taken by a brightly coloured cartoon image of a spider spinning a web. Originally she'd meant it to signify cheerful patience, but now it was getting on her nerves. At least she'd had the good sense to disable the jolly little tune it used to hum when she first set it up. If she insisted on driving herself mad, there were far more dignified and interesting ways of going about it.

Just when she was beginning to think there must be something wrong with the mirror, the spider abruptly vanished and the old man was back. He gave her a barely perceptible nod. Good. At last.

The queen cleared her throat. With a system as painfully inflexible as this one, it was essential to speak clearly; otherwise there was no knowing what she'd get.

'Mirror, mirror, on the wall,' she enunciated, in a voice that would have secured her a job as a newsreader on any station in the universe, 'who's the fairest of them all?'

The old man sneered. 'Bad command or file name,' he said. 'Please retry.'

What? Oh yes. Damn. She'd said *who's* instead of *who is*. She scowled and tried again, and this time the old man looked at her steadily and replied:

'Snow White, O Queen, is the fairest of them all.'

The wicked queen lifted her head sharply. 'Repeat,' she snapped. Instantly the head shifted a few fractions of an inch, back to the position it had been in just before it made its previous statement.

'Snow White, O Queen, is the fairest of them all.'

The queen sighed. 'Diary,' she commanded, and the head turned seamlessly into a cute graphic of an old-fashioned appointments book, with a two-dimensional pencil hovering over its pages. She snapped her fingers twice and the pages began to turn.

'Stop,' she commanded. Next Tuesday, she saw, was almost completely free, apart from lunch with Jim Hook and an entirely expendable hairdresser's appointment. 'Insert new diary entry for Tuesday the fifteenth,' she said. 'Ten-fifteen to twelve noon; murder Snow White, end entry.'

The moving pencil wrote and, having writ, dissolved into a scatter of random pixels. She snapped her fingers, and the old man reappeared.

'All right,' she said, 'that'll do. Dismissed.'

The old man nodded. 'This will end your Mirrors session,' he said. 'Okay or Cancel?'

'Okay.'

There was a soft crinkling noise and the mirror seemed to blink; then all the wicked queen could see there was her own flawless, immaculate face. She studied it for a moment as she reached for her powder compact; then, having dabbed away a patch of incipient pinkness, she stood up, snuffed out the candle and stalked melodramatically out of the room.

Although it was dark now, the mirror continued to glow softly; a common occurrence with such an outdated model. In the far corner of the room, something scuttled.

'We're in,' whispered a tiny voice.

Three white mice dashed across the floor, in that characteristic mouse way that makes them look as if they haven't got any legs, and are being dragged along on a piece of string. They scampered up the curtain, abseiled down the tieback cord, swung Tarzan-fashion and landed on the mantelpiece, directly under the mirror.

'We're in luck,' whispered a mouse. 'Silly bitch has left the power on.'

All three mice twitched their noses. 'Are you ready for this?' one of them hissed. 'We could get ourselves in a lot of trouble.'

The other two treated the coward to a look of distilled, matured-in-oak-vats scorn. 'Pull yourself together, will you?' squeaked the mouse who'd spoken first. 'After everything we've been through to get here, this is hardly the time to get cold feet.'

'Paws,' interrupted the third mouse. 'Come on, guys, stay in character. Just out of interest,' it added, 'why *mice* for pity's sake? I hate mice.'

'Because it was the only way to get in. Look, either we're going to do this or we aren't. Let's have a decision on that right now, before we go any further.'

'Fair enough,' muttered the apprehensive mouse. 'I'm not

saying we shouldn't, I'm just saying we should think about it.'

'I've thought about it. Come on, Sis, where's your sense of fun?'

'In this costume, there isn't room. And before you ask whether I'm a man or a mouse, I'm neither, remember?'

The other two pointedly ignored that last remark. 'Come on,' said the first mouse, 'let's get it over with. Show of hands?'

'*Paws.*'

'Show of hands. All in favour? Right, Sis, that's two to one. We do it.'

'I still don't see why it had to be mice, though,' the third voice whispered in the gloomy silence. 'Yes, I know we had to hotwire a nursery rhyme or a fairytale or something like that in order to feed ourselves into the system. But why couldn't we be something a bit less – well, small. And furry. And, come to think of it, completely and utterly defenceless.'

The first mouse sighed impatiently. 'Not just any nursery rhyme,' it explained. 'Had to be an *appropriate* one, something with sneaking furtively about and getting into forbidden places. So, fairly obvious choice, three blind mice—'

'Three *blind* mice? Now just a damn minute . . .'

'It's all right, I fiddled the code a bit, so now we're three *colourblind* mice. A small price to pay, I thought . . .'

For a brief moment the mice were perfectly still, as if composing themselves. Then the first mouse reared up on his hind legs, waggled his forepaws like a small furry boxer and squeaked, 'Mirror.'

They waited breathlessly until the cotton-wool effect slowly began to extend inwards from the corners of the glass. The head appeared.

'Too easy,' muttered the mouse called Sis. 'I think we should . . .'

The head opened its eyes and stared straight ahead; then it

frowned, looked from side to side; then, its frown deepening, downwards.

'Um, hello.' The first mouse twitched his nose twice, unhappy with the way the face was looking at him. He could feel tiny spores of panic beginning to germinate in the back of his mind, but for some reason he found it impossible to say anything else. The head's eyes seemed to be dismantling him, taking the back off his head and probing around in the circuitry.

'What's the matter with you?' Sis whispered urgently. 'That thing's *examining* us and you're just sitting there doing paperweight impressions. Say something to it quick, before it eats our brains.'

'I can't,' the first mouse hissed back. 'I think it knows who we really are. Sis, I'm frightened.'

'I can see that,' Sis snarled. 'Get out of the way and let me handle this.' She pushed past him and sat up. 'Mirror,' she said.

The head looked at her, and she imagined that she could feel icicles forming on her whiskers. 'Mirror,' she repeated. The head studied her for a moment, during which she realised just how long a moment can be, namely three times as long as a life sentence on Dartmoor and not quite so nice.

'Running DOS.'

The head vanished and was replaced by the spider; only it wasn't the friendly, cuddly little spider the queen had summoned. Instead it was big and black and hairy, one of those particularly unpleasant South American jobs that eat small mammals and move faster than a photon that's late for an appointment.

'It's different,' muttered the first mouse. 'It wasn't like that when she did it.'

'It's not sure it likes us yet,' Sis replied, trying to sound matter of fact about it all. 'Once it's decided we're friends it'll be all right, you'll see.'

The other two mice didn't seem so sure; at least, they

shuffled round behind her, forming a short, fluffy queue. She ignored them and carried on looking straight at the mirror. Inside, of course, she was absolutely petrified, which shows that she still had the sense she was born with.

'Look,' breathed the third mouse behind her shoulder. '*He's* back.'

Sure enough, the head was there again. He didn't look appreciably less hostile, but he nodded. Sis took a deep breath and curled her tail tight around her back legs.

'Mirror, mirror, on the wall,' she managed to say; then she dried. Because it was all a bit of fun, because they'd never expected to get this far anyway, they'd never got around to working out what it was they were actually going to *do*, once they'd hacked their way into the wicked queen's magic mirror and all her incalculable powers were theirs to command. *This is embarrassing*, Sis muttered to herself. She knew she had to say *something*, or otherwise the mirror would get suspicious again. She didn't know what it was capable of doing to them if it finally came to the conclusion that they had no right to be there, but she was prepared to bet that it went rather further than the threat of legal action. On the other hand, breaking into the palace and hijacking Mirrornet just to play a couple of games of Lemmings seemed somehow rather fatuous. *Think of some magic, quick,* she commanded what was left of her brain.

She thought of something. It was nothing special, but it was all she could think of, 'Mirror,' she said, in as commanding a voice as she could muster, 'show me the man I am to marry.'

The head looked at her as if she had chocolate all round her mouth. 'Bad command or file name,' it sneered. 'Please retry.'

'You're a mouse, idiot,' the first mouse whispered in her ear. 'You can't marry a man if you're a mouse. Think about it.'

'Oh right. Mirror, mirror, on the wall, show me the *mouse* I am to marry.'

The head's brow creased. 'Bad command,' he said doubt-fully, as if he wasn't quite sure of himself. 'Error. Incorrect format. Ignore or Cancel?'

'Cancel,' Sis replied firmly. Somehow she felt better now that she'd seen the head looking worried. She decided that the only way to deal with this was not to let the wretched thing see that she was afraid of it; no, there was more to it than that. The answer was not to be afraid of it at all. It was, after all, only a Thing, and she was a –

Mouse. Well, a mouse strictly *pro tem*. For the first and last time a mouse. Even if she was a mouse *right now*, that was still several dozen rungs further up the evolutionary ladder than a sheet of silver-backed glass in a plaster frame. 'Mirror,' she said calmly, 'listen to me. I want you to—'

'Bad command or file—'

'Shut up,' she said; and when the head promptly stopped talking, somehow she wasn't surprised. 'I want you to turn us back into human beings. Now,' she added sternly.

'Sis,' the first mouse hissed furiously, 'what do you think you're . . . ?' Before he could complete the sentence, he wasn't a mouse any more. He was a teenage boy, dressed in jeans and a T-shirt and sitting, rather to his surprise, on a mantelpiece several inches too narrow for his backside. He slid off and landed on the floor.

'Ouch,' said his younger brother. 'Damien, you're sitting on my leg.'

The three ex-mice untangled themselves, and as soon as he was sure which arms and legs were his, Damien scrambled up and scowled horribly at his sister.

'What the hell did you do that for?' he cried.

'I'd had enough,' his sister replied. 'Mirror, turn Damien back into a mouse. He's not fit to be a human.'

'Sis . . .' the mouse that had very briefly been Damien landed on its back, squirmed round, scrabbled for a foot-hold and was lifted up and dumped unceremoniously into Sis's cardigan pocket. Her other brother gave her a look of mingled terror and respect and wisely said nothing.

'Right,' she said. 'Now at least I can think straight. I hate mice,' she added, with a slight shudder. In her pocket something wriggled and squeaked. 'That's why I'm glad,' she went on, 'that we've got a cat.'

The wriggly object in her pocket suddenly became terribly still. She patted it affectionately and turned back to face the screen.

'Now then,' she said. 'Mirror, are you still there?'

The head nodded. It was, she noticed, looking at her oddly; almost as if it had never seen a human turn her brother into a mouse in a fit of pique before. There was something else in its eyes besides surprise, though; she gave it a long, curious look and worked out what the something else was.

Respect.

Ah, she said to herself, *now we're getting somewhere.* She took a deep breath and made a conscious effort to relax, letting the fear and tension melt out of her like ice cream through the disintegrated tip of a cone. In charge. In control. Now you can do anything you like.

'Mirror,' she said, 'first I want a million pounds. Next, I want a big house in Malibu and another in Chelsea, and a ski lodge in Switzerland and a Porsche with a personalised number-plate and . . .'

She froze; someone was coming. Her brother Damien yelped, leapt out of her pocket and scrambled under the table and into the Interface, the incomprehensible lash-up of technology that her other brother Carl had improvised to bring them here. He slid through like a jellied eel through a well-greased letterbox, but unfortunately, being a clumsy boy, he caught the edge of the Interface door with the tip of his tail . . .

'*OhnoforGodsake!*' Carl screamed, as the door snapped shut.

'Quiet!' Sis whispered furiously.

'But he's shut the *door*!' Carl wailed. 'We can't get back without it. *He's* safely back on the other side and we're stuck here.'

'What do you mean can't get . . . ?' Sis faltered. Regrettably, the words *can't get back* weren't what you'd call ambiguous. 'You mean, like marooned?'

'Yes.'

She looked round frantically for another exit; if not out of this crazy scenario, then at least out of the room, before anybody came. Not out of the window; this is a castle, remember, so out of the window would mean a long fall into a stagnant moat, and that's if she was lucky. Only one door. Nowhere to run and nowhere to hide. Oh . . .

'Mirror,' she said. 'Hide me, quickly.'

The head looked at her, and in its eyes there was enough raw contempt to keep the book reviews page of the *Guardian* fully supplied for a year. 'Bad command or file name,' it said disdainfully. 'Please retry.'

'Mirror!' she repeated imploringly, but the face vanished abruptly and was replaced by a pattern of slowly revolving geometric shapes, the one that makes your head spin if you watch it for too long. Whimpering, she tugged the curtain away from the wall and slipped behind it, just as the door opened and the wicked queen burst in, with an electric torch in one hand and a heavy Le Creuset frying pan in the other. She surveyed the room slowly and carefully, and sniffed.

'Mirror,' she commanded, 'where is she?'

The geometric shapes vanished and the head came back. 'She's hiding behind—' it began, but got no further; because behind the curtain, Sis had found the power switch and turned it off.

You can't blame her, of course. You could even say it was really rather resourceful, in the circumstances. And, also in her defence, it's hardly likely that she knew about the quite terrifying possible consequences of pulling the plug on an antiquated system like this one. After all, not many people do know that the principal drawback of Mirrors 3.1 was the very real risk of crashing the whole thing if you tried to shut it down without going through the proper procedure.

Suddenly, everything vanished.

Which is a rather melodramatic way of saying that there was a major systems malfunction, and all the information stored in the wicked queen's magic mirror was tumbled out of its drawers on to the floor, painstakingly jumbled up and then shovelled back at random; the kind of complete and systematic random it takes a computer to achieve. That, of course, is going to the other extreme, since it gives the impression that all it's going to take to get it all sorted out is the intervention of a pasty-faced young man with glasses, a beard and a packet of watchmaker's screwdrivers, probably called Dave or Chris. Sadly, not so. The difference is that all the little bytes and snippets that live behind the glass of the wicked queen's mirror aren't mere electrical impulses and digitised items of data; *I am not a number*, they could all say, and they'd be absolutely right.

For example –

Once upon a time, there was the same little house in the same big wood. And it still had a rose racetrack up one side, and a miniature Wisley seething away out front, and a garishly red front door with a vulgar brass knocker. But this time there's a note pinned to it, and it says –

> *Falling snowflakes*
> *Melt on the cherry blossom.*
> *This place is a pigsty.*

Or, while we're on the subject of pigs: a little way off in the same wood there's another house; bigger, rather less quaint and unmistakable because of the moat, drawbridge, razor wire entanglements, caltrops, mantraps and signposts reading MINEFIELD and BEWARE OF THE DRAGON that occupy about ninety-five per cent of what should have been a fair-sized front lawn. The house itself shines in the morning light like an American bodyguard's sunglasses.

The pigs in question are up a scaffolding tower, welding a searchlight bracket to the side of the house. There are three of them; and the smallest, having replaced a 5/8″ Stilson wrench in his toolbelt, wipes his snout on his foreleg and gazes with satisfaction at his trotterwork.

'Right,' he says. 'Just the perimeter fence to wire up, and we're done.'

The middle pig nods. 'Trotters crossed, lads,' he says. 'We've tried straw, sticks, brick, breezeblock, stone, kevlar-reinforced concrete and now molybdenum-steel-faced ceramic armour. If this doesn't do the trick, we're going to have serious credibility problems with the insurance company.'

'It'd help if we knew how he does it,' mused the biggest pig, pushing up the visor of his welding helmet and un-clipping the crocodile clip. 'I don't care what the forensic boys say, you're not going to convince me it's nothing but sheer lungpower. The last lot was better protected than the basement of the Pentagon, and how long did it take him? Thirty seconds, forty-five at the most, and all that hard work and expensive materials turned into so much second-hand Lego. If that's an example of what huffing and puffing can do, I reckon Oppenheimer and his mates were wasting their time.'

The middling pig grins; even the ring in his nose sparkles merrily in the early morning sun. 'He might just be in for a surprise this time,' he says. 'On account of the seventy-gigawatt interactive forcefield generator I've got hidden in the coal bunker. Just let him so much as sneeze near that and he'll suddenly find out what's meant by lethal feedback.'

The smallest pig, who'd been scanning the horizon through an infra-red viewer, scuttles down the scaffolding towards his companions. 'I hope you're right,' he mutters, 'because here he comes, the bastard. Right, positions, every-one. Desmond, you work the console. Eugene, the remotes. I'll do all the rest.'

In the distance there's a small grey four-legged shape. As it gets nearer, the three little pigs can make out the lolling tongue, the small round black eyes.

'Incoming,' Desmond snaps. 'Big bad wolf at bearing three-three-zero-mark-five-Alpha.'

Julian, the small pig, just has time to wire up the last few connections and throw the lever as the wolf reaches the outer perimeter of the security zone. Like all wolves, he doesn't look such a big deal when viewed from a distance; just a grey, long-haired Alsatian with a long nose and sad eyes. (And, by the same token, Australia looks like it might be a nice place to live, when seen from space.)

'Standing by,' crackles the intercom in Julian's trotter.

Julian takes a deep breath. He can't clench his trotters because trotters don't clench; but he folds them back as close to the knuckle as they'll go. 'On my mark,' he mutters. 'Steady. And, *activate!*'

Suddenly the air is alive with blue fire. The humming from the wires all but drowns out the wolf's all-too-familiar little speech. On the cue *blow your house down*, Desmond flicks the toggle that controls the remotely operated traverse of the Planetcracker-class laser cannon. There's a flash, like a fuse blowing in Frankenstein's laboratory, and –

'Missed,' Desmond growls under his breath; then, into the intercom, 'Julian, I've forgotten. How d'you set this thing for a wide-dispersal beam?'

'Red dial on the instrument panel, three full turns clock-wise,' the intercom crackles back. 'Get a move on, will you? He's through the fence, God alone knows how. I wish someone'd explain to me how he manages to do it.'

'Search me,' Desmond admits, 'I wasn't watching. Must have got under it somehow. It's all right, though, he's walking straight into the Claymore field.'

'Aha!' At his command post, Julian clasps his front trotters over his head in a gesture of triumph. 'This time he's for it. All right, commencing remote detonation procedure on my command. And go!'

The Earth shakes; then it starts raining divots. Then, as the smoke clears, the three little pigs are just able to make out the shape of a vulpine tail wagging on the edge of the drawbridge.

'I don't believe it,' Julian howls. 'That's *impossible*. An anorexic gnat could just have squeezed through on tiptoe if it'd had a copy of the minefield layout. All right, Desmond, turn on the cyanide gas. He'll soon realise he's just making things harder for himself.'

Desmond reaches for the dial; but before he has a chance to twist it, the wolf takes a deep breath. A huff, even.

'I don't like this,' Eugene mutters, not looking up from the long bank of monitors in front of him. 'I knew we should have spent the extra money and laid on air-to-surface support.'

'Try calling Strategic Air Command just in case,' Julian replies. 'You never know, there may still be time . . .'

The wolf exhales, letting out just enough breath to shift a small, lightweight leaf or project a very thin smoke-ring halfway to the ceiling.

'Oh Christ,' Eugene groans. 'He's about to puff.'

Julian growls. 'All right,' he says grimly. 'All power to primary deflector screens. Eugene, shut down the weapons systems if you have to, but keep those screens . . .'

Puff. The ejected carbon dioxide buffets against the side of the house like a half-hearted assault with a limp feather duster. The wolf breathes in –

'Exactly like the last time,' Julian observes. 'Hey, Desmond, why're you taking so long with that damn gas?'

'Should be through any sec—'

This time, thanks largely to the steel cladding, at least it was different. When the wolf blew out, instead of simply collapsing in a cloud of dust and flying masonry, the house crumples and twists like a squashed beer can. At first the metal stretches; then it begins to tear, and razor-edged seams unzip from the footings right up to the top storey windows, until the whole building peels back like a banana skin. Fortunately for them, the three little pigs are thrown clear at an early stage. They land, with more velocity than dignity, in their own moat, more or less at the same moment as the roof hits the ground.

'Woof,' says the wolf cheerfully.

Wearily the pigs roll onto their fronts and piggy-paddle their way to the bank of the moat.

'It's precisely this sort of thing that puts you off owning your own home,' Desmond grunts bitterly, hauling himself up out of the water. 'Mortgage interest relief is all very well, but maybe this time we should seriously think about renting somewhere instead.'

'How about an underground bunker?' Eugene says. 'Even *he'd* be hard put to it to blow it down if it was underground.'

'He'll find a way, don't you worry,' Julian replies, picking a needle-sharp splinter of steel out of his ear. 'What I want to know is, why? What harm have we ever done him? Is he just psychotic, or is he the Dirty Harry of the local planning department?'

'Planning permission we got,' Desmond points out. 'They know me so well down at County Hall, I've even got my own mug with my name on it. No, I reckon the only course of action left to us is a bloody hard pre-emptive strike. Unless we want to be doing this for the rest of our lives, we've got to waste the bastard.'

Julian lifts his head sharply. 'You know,' he says, 'you might just have something there.'

'Why not? We've got precious little to lose, after all. And there's three of us.'

'Tell it to the chipolatas.' Julian shakes himself, spraying water in all directions. 'This isn't something we can do ourselves, you know. Think about it; if we can't nail that overgrown granddad-of-a-terrier with laser cannon and Claymore mines, then creeping up on him while he's asleep and hitting him with a big stone's probably not going to work either. No, if we're going to do this, we'll have to hire someone.'

Eugene's little piggy eyes widen. 'An assassin, you mean? A hit-pig?'

Julian nods. 'Something like that. Only probably not a pig. And not an assassin. Villains hire assassins and we're the good guys. Good guys hire champions.'

'Ah.' Desmond wrinkles his snout, a symptom of increased mental activity. 'What you're saying is, we need to hire an odd-numbered company of adventurers and soldiers of fortune, each of them a rough diamond with a heart of gold who'll claim they're only in it for the money but who nevertheless are revealed as having a deeply felt vocation to right wrongs and fight for justice, freedom and the rights of the underpig. Yes?'

'You got it,' Julian says. 'Took the words right out of my snout.'

Eugene rubs his ear against a large stone. 'Why do I get the feeling,' he says mournfully, 'that the word *magnificent* is just about to feature in this conversation?'

Julian looks at him. 'You're way ahead of me,' he says. 'What we need is the Seven.'

Desmond and Eugene ponder this suggestion for a moment. 'You're sure?' Eugene asks. 'You really think they'll be up to it?'

'Oh yes,' Julian says confidently. 'Just so long as they stand on a ladder.'

'*Mirror!*' screamed the wicked queen.

The mirror looked at her.

The face was gone. In its place was a nightmare of jumbled components; as if Baron Frankenstein had dropped the drawer he kept all the bits of face in, and by some random, million-monkeys-with-typewriters fluke they'd fallen in a pattern that wasn't quite a face, but almost . . .

'Bad command or file name,' it croaked offensively. 'Trees reply.'

She sighed, and switched it off again. Then she slowly turned her head and gave the girl a long, long stare.

'Well,' she said.

The girl looked at her shoes. 'Sorry,' she mumbled.

'You're sorry,' said the wicked queen. 'You invaded my house, sabotaged my magic mirror and crashed the operating system for this entire dimension, and you're sorry. That's all right, then.'

'I said I'm sorry.'

'Yes, you did. Curiously enough, that doesn't seem to have solved anything. I expect you're feeling hard done by because I haven't turned you into a frog. Sorry; I would if I could but I can't.'

Sis's face burnt red. 'So what do you expect me to do about it?' she snarled wretchedly.

'Oh, let me see. How about putting right all the damage you've done? That'd help.'

Sis winced. 'You know I can't do that,' she objected. 'I don't know how your silly mirror works.'

'No, you don't, do you? Neither do I.'

Sis stared. 'You don't?'

'Not a clue. I just use the thing. I switch it on and it works. Or rather it worked. Important distinction there, don't you think? One instance where grammatical accuracy isn't just me being pedantic.'

'Oh.' Sis consulted her shoes again, but they were staying out of it. 'So what're we going to do?'

'I don't know,' the wicked queen replied, sitting down and rubbing her nose with the heel of her hand. 'I can give you a fair idea of what we can't do. We can't run the system. As a result, the entire dimensional matrix is going to tie itself up in knots. And just in case you don't know what a dimensional matrix is, it means that everything out there is probably going wrong. Everything,' she added, with a little smile. 'What fun.'

'What about Carl?' Sis suggested. 'He might know what to do.'

'Carl.'

'My brother. He's the one who hacked into your system in the first place. He knows all about computers.'

'Oh, how splendid. Where is he, by the way?'

'I –' Sis looked round, suddenly alarmed. 'I don't know. He was here a moment ago.'

The wicked queen nodded. 'He was here a moment ago, when you crashed my mirror. The other one got away, but I'm sure Carl was left behind. And now he's vanished. Wonder why.'

A look of horror passed across Sis's face. 'You mean he's been caught up in—'

'Yes, I do. Didn't it ever occur to you to wonder exactly *why* smashing a mirror brings you seven years' bad luck?'

'But we've got to do something,' Sis squealed urgently. 'We've got to get them back, *now*. Before—'

The wicked queen smiled. 'Before your mother and father get back from the office party and start asking what's become of the two siblings they left in your care? Ah yes. Let's all panic and declare a state of emergency. Just think; if you don't find Carl and Damien in time, they might cut off your pocket money.'

'Don't be horrible,' Sis replied angrily. 'And don't just sit there. You're the stupid old wicked queen. You've got to—'

'Do something, I know.' The wicked queen clicked her tongue wearily. 'There's all sorts of things I *could* do—'

'Told you so.'

'Unfortunately, none of them would help, except by way of easing my anger and frustration. We could try that, if you wouldn't mind holding still for twenty minutes.'

Sis backed away. 'Can't you phone somebody?' she asked. 'You know, a helpline or something.'

'Phone somebody. All right, I'll give it a try. Just as soon as you tell me what with.'

'Sorry?'

'Show me the telephone in this room.'

Sis looked round. 'There isn't one,' she said.

'Magnificently observed. Not in this room, this castle, this kingdom, this whole dimension. Remember where you are.'

'But surely—'

'No phone,' said the wicked queen, checking off on her fingers. 'No fax. No computers. Just a magic mirror. Don't you just love fully integrated systems?'

'Oh.'

'Now then,' continued the wicked queen briskly, 'this is the point at which any teenager worth her salt mumbles an excuse and departs, leaving someone else to clear up the mess after her. And I'd be only too delighted to see the back of you, if only it were possible. But it isn't. Integrated systems. I'm stuck with you. Isn't that jolly?'

'You mean I'm stranded?' Sis's eyes grew round with horror. 'But that's not *fair*,' she wailed. 'There must be—'

The queen chuckled. 'What're you going to do, call the Embassy? Walk home? I'm terribly sorry, my sweet, but this time you're going to have to face up to the consequences of your actions. Who knows,' she added, 'you might enjoy it. You'll never know until you've tried it at least once.'

Sis raised her head and scowled. 'Well, I don't see how you being horrid to me's helping either,' she said. 'Not very *constructive*, is it?'

The queen sighed. 'Very true,' she said. 'I imagine it's some sort of Pavlovian reaction, what with you being young and blondely cute and me being a wicked queen.'

'Pavlovian?' Sis queried. 'Isn't that ice cream and meringue?'

The queen winced. 'In a sense,' she replied. 'You're right, though, gnawing bits off each other isn't getting us anywhere.' She sat quietly for a while, picking at a loose thread on her sleeve; then her face lit up like the jackpot on a complicated pinball table. 'I'm an idiot,' she said. 'Water.'

'I beg your pardon?'

'Bucket of water.' She stood up, lunged across the room and came back with a heavy-looking oak pail, out of which water slopped on to her ankle and the floorboards. 'Mother Nature's laptop,' she explained. 'It's what we in the trade call backing up to sloppy.'

In the cartoon version, a light bulb starts to glow above Sis's head. 'Oh I see,' she said. 'You mean you made a copy, and it's stored . . .'

'In here.' The queen nodded. 'The memory's not up to much and the response time's lousy, but it's better than nothing. Right then, let's see.' She pulled her hair back from her face, leaned over the pail and looked at her reflection. 'Here goes. Mirror, mirror, in the bucket, are you reading me? Oh f— fiddlesticks.' She scowled, dipped her finger into the water and fished out a tiny, struggling fly. 'The slightest thing, and it refuses to play. Mirror,' she repeated sternly.

The water rippled, although the air in the chamber was still. Almost imperceptibly, the queen's reflection began to mutate –

'I hate it when it does that,' she commented, wrinkling her nose.

– Until it had become the image of a young man, comprising a small stub of nose sandwiched between an enormous pair of glasses and a bushy black beard.

'Bad command or file na—'

'Quiet,' the queen snapped. 'And take that gormless expression off your face, or I'll feed you to the dahlias. Display all systems files, and look sharp about it.'

The surface of the water rippled again, and just underneath the meniscus Sis thought she could see a pair of two-dimensional fish tracing geometric patterns. 'I know,' muttered the queen, following her line of sight, 'it'll send you potty if you look at it for long enough. One of these days I'm going to replace it with something that's not actually pernicious.'

The fish snapped out of existence, and a thick mass of symbols and equations glowed dully blue on the surface of the water. The queen studied them for a while and then shook her head.

'Doesn't mean a lot to me,' she confessed. 'It could be all the little cogs and gears you managed to trash just now, or it could equally be the thing that numbers your pages for you.' She thought for a moment. 'Do you really think this brother of yours could make sense of this?'

'I don't know,' Sis replied. 'He says he knows all about this sort of thing. It's worth a try.'

'Display our available options in table form, and it'd be at the top,' the queen replied with a sigh. 'And the bottom as well, seeing as how it's the only one. Right, let's give it a go. Mirror, locate – what did you say his name was?'

'Carl.'

'Of course. Mirror, locate Carl.'

Ripple, ripple. A crude graphic of a frog hopped off an equally rudimentary lily-pad. Then the face came back.

'Path Carl not found,' it replied sheepishly. 'Retry or Can—'

'Oh, be quiet.' The queen rubbed her hands together, as if trying to remove something distasteful. 'I know what's happened,' she said. 'When you bent everything, your wretched brother must have got renamed somehow. He's out there, but the mirror thinks he's called something else.'

'Oh.' Sis opened her mouth and closed it again. 'So what do we do?'

'I wish you'd stop asking me that,' the queen replied. 'I'm the wicked queen, remember. It's hard enough for me not to be poisoning you or having you taken off to be murdered in the woods without listening to you drivelling as well.'

'Queen,' Sis said, biting her lip, 'what *do* you think's happening out there?'

The wicked queen shook her head sadly. 'I only wish I knew,' she said.

★

The shiny red door of the quaint little cottage in the clearing opened, and a man stepped out on to the garden path. In a sense, he struck an incongruous note, dressed as he was from head to foot in lacquered black and red armour, with big rectangular shoulder-guards and a bulky helmet decorated with a shiny black upturned crescent. He was holding a rake, with which he proceeded to mark out a delicate pattern of semicircular sweeps in the thick, evenly laid gravel of the garden path. As he worked, he chanted:

'Softly blowing
Wind-stirred leaves of maple.
To our work we journey,
Hi-ho, hi-ho.'

Above him, a tousled head of golden hair appeared through an open casement. 'Yoo-hoo,' trilled a silvery voice. 'Hello! Mr Suzuki!'

The man looked up, saw the head and bowed politely. If there was in his eyes the faintest tinge of fear, it could only have been visible from a few feet away.

'Mr Suzuki,' the silvery voice continued, 'have you been cleaning your armour with my dusters again?'

The man bowed his head.

'I wish you wouldn't do that,' said the silvery voice. 'Dusters are for dusting, Mr Suzuki, not that you'd know much about *that*, of course. If you must clean your silly old armour in the house, there's a shoebox full of old socks and things in the cupboard under the sink. All right?'

The man nodded, head still bowed, unable to meet her clear blue eyes.

'Oh, and while you're there,' the voice went on, 'I'll just get you to nip into the hall and change the light bulb. It's gone again.'

(And before you ask, how many samurai *does* it take to

change a light bulb? Easy; seven, of course. One to change the bulb, six to commit ritual suicide to expunge the disgrace of the old one having failed. In this household, however, ritual suicide's on the forbidden list, along with Zen archery practice in the front parlour and walking on the kitchen floor in muddy wellies.)

Having blown down the little pigs' house, the big bad wolf glanced up at the sun, noted its position and calculated his estimated time of arrival at his next appointment. Then he dropped his head (aerodynamic efficiency) and broke into a trot.

Grandmama's cottage lay in a clearing in the south-western sector of the forest; a pretty hairy place for a big bad wolf to have to go into, what with the woodcutters and the Free Foresters, not forgetting the dreaded Greenshirts. Although he knew he was well behind schedule, the wolf slowed down. Any bush or briarpatch in this neighbourhood could be hiding a disgruntled timber worker with an axe or a string-happy archer, or any one of a number of talking farm-yard animals with an innate grudge against wolfkind. Futile to pretend he wasn't scared droppingless, but he'd figured out long ago that true courage is the ability to throw fear out of focus just long enough to get the job done. Through these mean glades a wolf must trot, and that was all there was to it.

When he saw the cottage, he stopped where he was and lay down under a bramble-bush, his chin on his forepaws, watching. His wet, delicate nose tasted the air, searching for traces of scent that shouldn't be there: human sweat, the delicate tang of fresh sap on a steel blade, beeswax on a newly cleaned bowstring, fresh earth where a pitfall trap had just been dug. But there was nothing except what he'd expect – week-old human spoor and woodsmoke, the stench of newly baked bread and lavender bags. Nothing unusual.

But in field operations such as this, the unusual is so usual as to be virtually compulsory. There *should* be other smells, he realised: fresh squirrelshit, the reek of newly sprouted mushrooms, a dash of unicorn pee and dissolving tree-bark. Something was wrong, and although he couldn't quite put his paw on it, he knew it was there.

Set-up.

Abort the operation and get out of there, his instincts screamed. But he couldn't do that, could he? Go back to Wolfpack HQ and explain that he'd abandoned his mission because everything seemed normal. Wolves who did that sort of thing found themselves pulled off active service and assigned to retrieving foundling human babies from riverbanks before their paws could touch the ground. At the very least he had to get close enough to see what form the trap took.

One thing they teach well at Wolfpack Academy is stealthy crawling. Gradually, his ears flat to his skull, his tummy brushing the dirt, he edged slowly forward, pausing every yard or so to taste the air. A small voice inside his head told him he was wasting his time. Elementary tactics demanded that the trap would be sprung close to the cottage, where there was little or no cover and a clear field of fire for archers hidden behind the chintz curtains of the upper storey. Between the edge of the underbrush and the front door there was an open space twenty-five yards wide that he'd have to cross, and while he was in the zone he might as well have a target-boss embroidered on his back in yellow, red and blue fibre-optic cable. Which left him with only one course of action. Stage a diversion.

Oh yes, piece of cake. With no backup and no resources, that was an order so tall they'd have to festoon it with coloured lights to stop aircraft flying into it. In his mind's eye he could picture his Academy instructor, wagging his tail and saying, 'Think, Mr Fang. What would Hannibal have done?' And never once, back in those dear long-ago days, had he pointed out the obvious fact that the recommended technique was fatuous, since Hannibal was never a wolf. Easy enough to guess what Hannibal would have done: he'd have encircled the cottage with his heavy infantry, made a feint attack with his light cavalry to draw off the enemy strikeforce and then sent in the war elephants to finish the job. Simple. Problem solved. Give me a thousand legionaries, five hundred horse archers and a dozen trained elephants and I'll be through here in a jiffy.

Think, Mr Fang. What would *you* do in this situation?

The wolf breathed in deeply, as if trying to inhale inspiration. And so he did, in a manner of speaking, because a moment later he made a lightning-fast grab with his left forepaw.

'Gerroff! You're squashing my ears!'

The wolf eased off the pressure slightly, and the gossamer shadow under its claws stopped squirming. 'Well now,' the wolf growled softly, 'what a surprise. And what's an elf doing in these parts, so far from the Reservation?'

The elf spat. 'That's Indigenous Fairylander to you, *Fido*,' she hissed. 'And you got five seconds to get your goddamn paw the hell off me, or you gonna wish you lived in a kennel and fetched slippers in your mouth.'

'Easy now,' Fang replied calmly, not letting go. 'You don't need me to tell you you're in no position to make threats. Instead of trying to scare each other, why don't we help each other out?'

The elf sneered. 'And why'd I want to help you, Mister Dog?'

'Because otherwise I'll eat you,' Fang replied cheerfully. 'Now shut up and listen. I've got to get in there and do a job of work, but I have the feeling I'm expected. So I need someone to stage a diversion.'

'Man, you can stage a Broadway revival of *Oklahoma!* for all I care. I ain't helpin' no wolf. What's in it for me?'

'Bread,' the wolf replied temptingly. 'Also milk. And a chance to get one back on the Yellowhairs. Interested?'

'Bread?' the elf repeated.

'Bread,' Fang confirmed. 'And milk. And I'm not talking

about the poxy little saucerfuls they deign to put out for you every once in a blue moon. I'm talking loaves and pints here. All the bread and milk you and your people need for a month, for just five minutes' work. And no shoemaking.'

The elf squirmed restlessly under his paw. 'Say, how do I know I can trust you?' she said. 'Wolf speaks with long pink tongue. You could be setting me up.'

The wolf yawned, making the elf shrink away instinctively. 'Why should I bother?' he said. 'Wolfpack's got no quarrel with you guys, even if you are thieving little scum. After all,' he added, 'it wasn't us who cheated you out of your ancestral lands in exchange for beads and firewater.'

'All right. First, you get your paw off me. Then we talk.'

Fang raised his paw a sixteenth of an inch; there was a faint gossamer blur, and the elf shot like a bullet into a patch of stinging nettles. 'Shit,' she muttered.

'Happier now?'

'Okay, Mister Wolf,' said the elf, 'you got yourself a deal. What you want me to do?'

Carefully the wolf explained, and a few minutes later the elf broke cover and whizzed in vertiginous zigzags across the open ground. When she was ten yards or so from the front door she changed course and started running round the cottage, whooping and yelling and shooting arrows from her tiny bow. It worked; almost immediately a gang of axe-wielding wood-cutters burst out of the hydrangea bushes and let out after her, swinging wildly and chopping divots out of the lovingly mani-cured lawn. When the pursuers and the pursued were safely out of range, the wolf got up and trotted casually to the front door, which had been left ajar. He jumped up, put his forepaws against it and pushed until it swung open. And that, of course, was as far as he got. In the fraction of a second between the searing flash of blue light and the completion of the process of turning into a frog, the wolf had just enough time to reflect that not all old women who live alone in isolated cottages deep in the forest are kindly old grandmothers.

CHAPTER TWO

They called him the Dwarf With No Name.

Where he came from, nobody knew, although since the same was true of all dwarves that didn't really signify. Nobody cared much, either. But when he swaggered into town and strolled in under the swinging doors of the Buttercup Tea Rooms, small cuddly animals dived for cover and pixies dashed back to their workshops and started roughing out tiny coffins.

'Milk,' the dwarf growled, flinging a handful of chocolate money on the bar top. 'Gimme the bottle.'

Mrs Twinklenose, the elderly hedgehog who'd run the Buttercup since the first prospectors struck treacle south of the Rio Gordo, picked up one of the coins, bit it, swore, spat, took the gold foil off, bit it again and slid a pint bottle along the polished surface of the bar. Without looking, the dwarf reached a hand up above his head, caught the bottle just as it cleared the edge, stuck a thumb through the foil and drank messily.

'Another,' he muttered, wiping milkdrops from his ginger beard. 'Keep 'em coming till I say when.'

Mrs Twinklenose shrugged. 'You got it, mister,' she said. 'There's a couple of pigs been in here looking for you.'

The dwarf looked up. 'Pigs?' he repeated. 'I don't know no pigs.'

'Reckon they know you,' the hedgehog said indifferently. 'If you're Dumpy the dwarf, that is.'

The dwarf reached up and balanced a half-empty milk bottle on the edge of the bar. 'I ain't heard that name in a long while,' he said thoughtfully. 'In fact, I ain't never heard it this side of the Candyfloss Mountains. Who did you say these pigs were?'

'Just pigs,' Mrs Twinklenose answered, polishing a glass against the plush fur of her tummy. 'Never could tell them critters apart, and that's the truth.'

'Gimme another milk.'

Business was quiet in the Buttercup that afternoon. Customers who drifted in – thirsty ladybirds with trail-dust caking their wing-cases, fluffy pink bunnies from the treacle mines, the occasional stoat and weasel newly arrived on the riverboats and looking for some action, all the regular extras you'd normally expect to find in an alphabet-spaghetti Western – tended to swallow their drinks quickly and leave as soon as they set eyes on the dwarf. The heaped plate of currant buns grew staler by the minute, and the ice-cream cake melted into a sticky pool. The dwarf didn't take any notice; he stayed where he was, slumped under a bar stool, methodically gulping down the house semi-skimmed by the pint. Several times Mrs Twinklenose tried to suggest politely that since there weren't any other customers, she'd quite like to close up for the day, but the dwarf proved resolutely hint-proof and silent. It was nearly dark when he looked up, pushed his hood back and said, 'These pigs.'

'Yeah?'

'Did they happen to mention when they'd be back?'

Mrs Twinklenose shook her head, accidentally impaling a dozen sticky buns on her neck spines. 'Never said nothing to me. You could maybe ask over at the hotel or the livery stable.'

'Nope.' The dwarf tilted back his head, drained the last drop out of the bottle and licked a few white globules out of his moustache. 'Reckon I'll stay here, in case I miss them. You got any better stuff than this? This ain't fit to go on a pixie's cornflakes.'

Reluctantly Mrs Twinklenose reached under the counter and produced a pint of gold-top, the condensation misting its sides. 'Full cream's extra,' she said without hope. The dwarf nodded and tossed her some more coins, but she could tell by the thunk they made on the bartop that they were phoney; solid gold, not chocolate at all. She sighed and dropped them in the spittoon.

The dwarf sniffed, his nose wrinkling; then he drained his milk, wiped the tip of his nose and stood up. A moment later the door swung open. Trotters pecked tentatively at the floorboards. Someone snuffled and cleared his throat.

'Excuse me, sir,' said the smaller of the two pigs, 'but are you Dumpy the dwarf?'

The dwarf turned slowly round, his thumbs tucked inside his belt-buckle,. 'Maybe I am,' he drawled, 'and maybe I ain't. Who wants to know?'

The two pigs exchanged nervous glances. 'He's taller than I thought he'd be,' whispered the bigger pig.

'Doesn't matter,' his colleague hissed back. 'And for crying out loud don't let him hear you say . . .' The pig glanced up, then down, and realised that the dwarf was staring at him. 'I'm sorry,' he stuttered, 'you've got to excuse my brother, he's only ever lived with pigs, he doesn't know how to behave around regular people.'

'Who're you callin' regular, friend?'

The pig became pinker than usual, until he looked like a ten-year-old girl's idea of a chic colour-scheme. 'Look,' he said, 'can't we please start again? My name's Julian, this is Desmond, we've got another brother called Eugene. We live out on the other side of the Big Forest. Can we buy you a drink?'

The dwarf leaned against the side of the bar and folded his arms. 'Reckon you can, at that,' he said affably. 'Milk.'

Mrs Twinklenose produced another bottle and slid it across the counter. 'Hey,' she said. 'Because they're with you, it's okay. But usually we don't serve his kind in here. Except,' she added meaningfully, 'as scratchings. Just so as you know.'

'They're with me,' the dwarf grunted, spearing his thumb through the foil and spurting milk up his nose. 'All right, boys, what can I do for you?'

Julian swallowed. He felt as if he had an apple in his mouth. 'Well,' he said, 'it's like this.'

'Does anybody else live here,' Sis asked, 'or is it just you?'

The queen sniffed. 'That, my young pest, is a good question. I suppose it mostly depends on when. Sometimes, you just can't move for extras – you know, halberdiers, courtiers, pages, flunkies. Do you know what a flunky actually does, by the way? I've been trying to find out all my life, but nobody seems to know. The rest of the time, it's deserted. Just little me. In fact, I'm not even sure it actually exists when I'm not here.'

'Ah,' Sis replied noncommittally. 'It sort of depends on context, does it?'

The queen nodded. 'Everything does, in these parts. Mostly, you see what you expect to see. I imagine that if I were to shout for the guards to come and drag you off to the dungeon, the door would fly open and there they'd be. But if we tiptoed out of this room and went looking for them, there wouldn't be any. It's just the way it works. Or worked,' she added sourly, 'before a bunch of young idiots . . .'

'So we're probably completely alone now,' Sis said with a shudder. 'I see.'

'Not necessarily.' The queen stood up and stretched, like a cat. 'If I'm making any sense at all of what I can see in the pail there, all the usual functions haven't been switched off or blown away. They've been jumbled up, any old fashion.

Which is, of course, worse,' she added. 'Much worse.'

'Oh.'

'If it was simply a case of the mirror having been wiped, you see,' the queen went on, 'we could just reinstall it all from the bucket. But we can't, because it's all still there. Do you see?'

'No,' Sis admitted. 'But it sounds awful.'

'Doesn't it ever,' the queen said, grinning. 'Still, it doesn't do to sit around all day moping. There's something I want to try, just in case it works.'

'Ah,' Sis replied hopefully. 'Do you think it will?'

'No. But I can't think of anything else, so I'm going to do this. Ready?'

Sis nodded and took five steps back, until she bumped into a carved oak table. The wicked queen, meanwhile, had opened a cupboard and taken out a broom.

'Not my prop, really,' she said. 'More your sort of witch's broom, hence the little sticker on the back that says *My other broomstick's an Addis.* Personally I think this whole escapade's doomed to failure from the outset, but we'll soon see.'

She sat down on the floor, the broom in one hand, the other resting on the rim of the pail. 'Mirror,' she said.

The usual ripples; and then the beard-and-glasses face appeared. Before it had a chance to get further than 'Ba—', the wicked queen lifted the broom up over her head and dipped its bristles in the water. There was a sizzle, like frying sausages, and a puff of hot steam.

'I think this is going to be a *disaster*,' said the queen cheerfully. 'Oh well, never mind.'

'What are you trying to do?' whispered Sis, from behind a footstool.

'The idea is to slave the broom to the bucket,' said the queen, who was now almost entirely hidden by the cloud of steam. 'The bucket takes control of the broom, the broom scoots off and finds Carl, Carl fixes the mess, job done. It'd be a good idea if only there was a hope in hell of it working.'

Sis peeped round the edge of the stool. 'It's doing *something*,' she said.

'Very true,' the queen replied. 'But doing *something* and doing anything useful, or even not actively harmful, ain't always the same thing. Ask any government. Oh dear, I think it's starting to go terribly, terribly wrong.'

The broomstick had pulled itself out of the queen's hands and was balancing itself on the surface of the water, like the Messiah of All Brooms, and glowing cobalt blue. There was also a humming noise that Sis didn't like the sound of one little bit, and a faint but obnoxious smell.

'At this point,' said the queen, 'I ought to grab the broom and try to pull it out before things get out of hand. But I won't, because I know full well it'll only shoot sparks at me and throw me across the room.'

'It'd do that?'

'That's what it usually does. I told you this idea was doomed from the start.'

The broom sank an inch or so into the water. Then it began to twitch slowly from side to side, in the manner of a loose tooth when you jiggle it about with your finger.

'Here we go,' said the queen. 'If I were you I'd climb up on something, quick.'

With a sharp, hard-to-follow movement, like speeded-up film of a roving triffid, the broom hopped out of the bucket and started waddling across the floor, leaving behind it a trail of what looked strangely like soap-suds. The queen jumped clear just in time to stop her shoes from getting soaked, and pitched on a low chair.

'What on earth is it doing?' Sis whispered.

'Ah,' replied the queen. 'Looks like the broom's slaved itself to the bucket okay, but the bucket's failed to override the broom's default programming. Which means,' she continued, as the broom started shuffling backwards and forwards across the floor in a pool of suddy water, 'the broom's reverting to doing what it was primarily designed for, namely cleaning floors. Like I said,' she added glumly. 'Disaster.'

'Is it? Surely it can't do any harm just . . .'

'Are you ignorant or just plain stupid? Think, girl. It's going to carry on doing that indefinitely, and there's absolutely no way of switching the wretched thing off.'

'Oh.' Sis's eyes became very round. 'You mean like the Sorcerer's—'

'Yes.' The queen had become rather red in the face. 'Exactly like that. Again. Other people learn from their mistakes, but not, apparently, me.'

'You mean *you* were the—' Sis stopped, swallowed a giggle and went on. 'But I thought the um, apprentice, was a boy.'

'Some kind of chauvinist bigot, are you, as well as everything else? Let me give you a tiny scrap of advice. If you were planning on making a career for yourself in the diplomatic service, now would be a good time to explore other options.'

The broom had already covered half the floor in an ankle-deep carpet of suds. Sis hopped up on to the footstool and swayed out of the way to avoid the waving broomhandle. 'So now what do we do?' she shouted.

'Stop asking me that.'

'But what did you do the – the last time?'

'Waited for the sorcerer to come home and turn it off. Unfortunately he's dead –' A strange look passed over the wicked queen's face '– Sort of; so that's not a realistic option. Have you got any ideas?'

'No,' Sis replied, 'none at all. But then, *I* wouldn't have set the horrid thing off in the first place.'

The queen hitched her skirts up to her knees as the suds flecked her legs. 'The only thing I can think of is knocking over the bucket,' she said. 'That'd probably stop the broom, but we'd lose all the stuff saved in it.'

'What, the water?'

'The backup from the mirror. All gone, for ever. And without that—'

'We'd never find Carl.'

'We'd never fix my system, more to the point.' She looked down at the rising tide of suds, then very cautiously started to clamber out on to the arms of the chair. 'In the words of the late Oliver Hardy—'

'Why don't we just run away?' Sis interrupted.

'Another fine me—What did you say?'

'Run away. Just leave it and go. We could take the bucket with us.'

The wicked queen thought for a moment. 'You mean, buzz off and leave someone else to clear up the mess?' she said.

'It's always worked for me.'

The chair wobbled, and the queen made a yelping noise. 'All right,' she said, 'why not? Instead of being responsible for all this chaos, let's be irresponsible for it.' She hopped off the chair, which fell over, and landed on the floor with a splash and an explosion of soapy spray; then she grabbed the bucket, yelled, 'Come on!' and headed for the door. The two of them just made it through the door before the broom could catch them.

'Rivet,' said the big bad wolf. 'Rivet rivet rivet.'

The owl, seconded to Wolfpack by Avian Intelligence, translated. 'What he's trying to say,' she chirped, 'is that he's going to, um, croak and wobble his cheeks in and out and then he's going to blow your house down.' She paused and pecked at her pin-feathers with her beak. 'At least, I think that's what he said,' she added doubtfully. 'Look, you in the bunker. Is any of this making sense to you guys? My frog's a bit rusty.'

Inside the bunker's command centre, Eugene made a great effort and forbore from making the obvious reply. 'I get the message,' he said. 'You tell him from me he can save his breath.' He frowned, reflecting that under the circumstances, he could have phrased that a whole lot better. 'Frogs don't frighten me,' he went on firmly. 'Who ever heard of a frog who—?'

Later, in hospital, once he'd come round from the coma, Eugene reckoned that the method the frog had used must have been something like blowing the yolk of an egg through a pinhole in the opposite end of the shell. He explained it to his brothers in those terms.

Julian closed his mouth, which had flopped open like the tailgate of one of those lorries they transport cheap televisions on. 'A *frog* did that?' he whispered.

Eugene nodded, as far as the neck restraint would allow. 'Small green frog, about the size of an apple. Julian, what's going on? This is all beginning to get out of trotter.'

Julian sat for a while, fidgeting with his nose-ring. 'I don't know,' he finally admitted. 'From time to time I think I'm starting to see a bit of the big picture, and then it all goes fuzzy on me again. Rather than understand it, let's try doing something about it instead. I tracked down that dwarf.'

Eugene raised his eyebrow, the one that wasn't trussed up in splints. 'You mean the dwarf with no name?'

Julian nodded. 'Actually, his name's Dumpy. Anyway, he's agreed to help us out, and he's recruiting the other dwarves he says he'll need.'

'Uh-huh.' Eugene sighed. 'This is going to be expensive,' he said.

'Probably. But don't worry, we'll cope. You concentrate on getting better. You got any idea how much it's costing us per day having you in here?'

'It's not exactly a fun place to be,' Eugene replied bitterly. 'It's full of horribly mutilated people. One guy they brought in yesterday, he was so badly smashed up he came in six separate carrier bags.'

'Jeez,' Desmond muttered. 'So what happened to him?'

'Fell off a wall, so I heard. It was so bad they had to call in a specialist team of surgeons from the military. They got him fixed up, though, eventually.'

Julian looked up sharply. 'They did?' he asked.

'That's right. Wonderful job, by all accounts. That's him,

look, over there at the end by the wall. Big egg-shaped guy with no head.'

'The one having his temperature taken by the polo pony?'

'That's the one. You know him?'

'Heard of him,' Julian replied. 'I think.' Doing his best not to be too obvious about it, he turned his head and took a long look. 'Certainly seems to be in one piece now,' he conceded, and the edge to his voice was sharp enough to cut rubber. 'How about that?'

The patient in the next bed, who'd noticed Julian's interest, grinned. 'One hell of a show,' she whispered. 'He was in the theatre sixteen hours, so Sister told me. At one point they had a whole battalion of the Royal Engineers and seventy polo ponies in there working on him with rubber bands and glue. Wonderful, the things they can do now.'

Julian nodded, frowning. 'Wonderful,' he said. 'Excuse me, but don't I know you from somewhere?'

'I doubt it,' the patient replied, 'unless your line of work brings you in contact with hydraulic engineers, because that's what I do. The name's Jill, by the way. Pleased to meet you.'

'Likewise.' The pig looked away, then swivelled back sharply. Jill's head was heavily bandaged. 'Sorry if this sounds a bit personal,' he said, 'but do you work with somebody called Jack?'

'My business partner. You've heard of us?'

'I think so. Looks like a pretty nasty knock you've got there,' he observed neutrally. 'How d'you do it?'

Jill pulled a wry face. 'Fell down a hill, of all the silly things to do. Jack was all right, but I wasn't so lucky.'

'*Jack* was all right . . .'

'Oh yes. As in "I'm all right, Jack", only the other way round. Why do you ask?'

'Oh, no reason,' Julian answered unconvincingly. 'Just curious, that's all.'

Not long afterwards, Sister came and slung the visitors out. As they walked home, Julian was unusually silent. Desmond, who'd been outlining his plan for a mobile home slung from the underside of a helium-filled airship ('Away, yes. Away we can handle. Down, no.') stopped dead in his tracks and waved a foreleg in front of Julian's snout.

'Julian?' he said. 'Snap out of it. You look like Uncle Claude just after they'd finished inserting the sage and onion.'

'Sorry.' Julian sighed. 'I was just thinking about what Eugene said; you know, about things getting out of trotter. He's right. Something very odd's going on.'

'So? Around here, it sort of goes with the territory.'

'Maybe. I guess I need to think it through a bit more.' He twitched his nose and sniffed, as if he'd just sensed truffles. 'Suddenly I'm beginning to see things that probably aren't there. You know, conspiracies and paranormal phenomena and cover-ups and everybody acting as if everything's perfectly normal. There's a word for it when you start doing that.'

'American?'

'Paranoid. Maybe I'm getting paranoid.' He shook his shoulders. 'The hell with it,' he said. 'Come on, I'll buy us each a turnip down the Swill and Bucket.'

There was a new note on the front door of Avenging Dragon Cottage. It was written on scented pink notepaper, and it read:

> Spring winds stir the willow,
> A distant star flickers.
> Empty the dustbins.

'Marvellous way with words she's got,' observed Mr Hiroshige, idly straightening the petals of a wind-blown flower with his mailed fingers.

Beside him, Mr Miroku nodded. 'I particularly liked the way she used the image of spring, the time of renewal in nature, to suggest the need for a new dustbin bag. Whose turn is it?'

'I did it last time,' young Mr Akira pointed out. 'And the time before that.'

The other two considered this. 'In fact,' pointed out Mr Miroku, 'you already have considerable experience in emptying dustbins.'

'True,' said Mr Akira.

'Expertise, even.'

'I suppose so. Not that it's all that difficult.'

'To you, maybe not,' said Mr Miroku gracefully. 'Likewise, the trained ivory-carver has no difficulty creating a perfect netsuke out of a tiny scrap of waste bone, whereas you and I wouldn't know where to start. I expect your children will find it easier still, and so on down the generations.' He smiled. 'You carry on,' he said. 'You don't mind if we watch, do you? It's always inspiring to watch a craftsman at work.'

Mr Akira shrugged and went off round the side of the cottage. A little later he came back holding two densely stuffed black plastic bags.

'Observe,' said Mr Hiroshige thoughtfully, 'how he's holding one in each hand, so as to equalise the weight distribution. The boy's clearly got a flair for it.'

Mr Akira couldn't help simpering a little with pride. They were, after all, fully accredited adepts in the Way, whereas he was little more than a novice. As he shifted his grip on the left-hand bag a little, there was more than a touch of conscious *élan* about the movement.

'Correct me if I'm mistaken,' said Mr Miroku, stopping him with a courteous gesture, 'but isn't this the point where you put the plastic bags in the big PVC dustbin up by the garden gate?'

'That's right,' the young man replied.

'How do you do that, exactly? It must be ever so difficult.'

'I wouldn't say that,' replied Mr Akira, frowning a little. 'At least, I've never had a problem with it. I just lift the lid and put them in.'

The two older men exchanged glances. 'He's just lifts the lid and puts them in,' Mr Hiroshige repeated. 'Like the archer who, on the point of releasing the arrow, closes his eyes and entrusts its flight to the harmonies of the universe. It's like what I've always said: the more apparently complex an act, the more vital it is to search until you find its inner simplicity. May we watch? We promise not to make a noise.'

'Feel free,' said Mr Akira, with a slight bow. 'This way.'

They followed him up the path and stood at a respectful distance while he dumped the bags in the bin and put back the lid. The other two dipped their heads in respectful admiration.

'Likewise,' said Mr Hiroshige, 'whereas even the most skilled worker in jade could never produce a really convincing facsimile of a leaf, with all its endlessly complex veins and textures, a tree puts forth new leaves without a conscious thought. Thank you. That was –' He paused, took a deep breath, and let it out again slowly. 'Beautiful.'

'Oh. Good.'

'And yet,' interrupted Mr Miroku gently, 'it would be presumptuous to congratulate him on a skill that comes not from within himself but from the essential forces of the cosmos. After all, one compliments the painter, not the brush.' He turned and gestured politely towards the bin. 'Would you mind terribly doing it again?'

Mr Akira raised both eyebrows. 'All right,' he said. 'If you like.' His brows furrowed for a moment like trysting earwigs. 'This is a Zen thing, isn't it? Like doing the ironing or unblocking the sink trap.'

Mr Miroku's smile was beatific. 'All things are Zen, my son,' he said. 'When you've truly grasped that, you will at last be one of us.'

'Oh. Gosh.' Mr Akira took the lid off the dustbin, pulled out the bags, put them back again and replaced the lid. 'Did I do that all right?' he said.

The other two nodded. 'Remarkable,' said Mr Hiroshige.

'You put those bags in almost exactly the same place as you did the last time. Now if you'd tried to do that on purpose, measuring the clearances and the distances and measuring the angle at which the bags were inserted, I'll wager you wouldn't have achieved anything like the same level of precision.'

'Quite so,' Mr Miroku agreed. 'But by subordinating your conscious self to the forces of the natural order—'

'Ah.' Mr Akira beamed with pleasure. 'Now I see. There's just one thing, though,' he added apprehensively. 'With the very greatest respect—'

'Feel free to speak, my son.'

'All right. It's just,' Mr Akira went on, 'I'm probably being very dense here, but how exactly is putting out the dustbin bags and all the other housework you kindly let me do going to help me to become a superbly trained master swordsman?'

The other two exchanged a gentle smile. 'Show him,' said Mr Miroku.

'No, no. You do it so much better.'

'You're very kind.' Mr Miroku composed himself and closed his eyes; then, in a single fluid movement, so swift and smooth that it was almost impossible to follow, he reached to his left side, drew the great two-handed *katana* broadsword and brought it down with devastating force on the dustbin, slicing it into two exactly symmetrical halves without even disturbing the lid. There was a moment of sublimely perfect stillness; then he opened his eyes and gave the blade a little twitch, whereupon the two halves of the bin and the precisely bisected bags within opened like the pages of a book, slowly toppled over and slumped on to the grass.

'Gosh,' said Mr Akira.

'It was nothing,' Mr Miroku replied. 'Or rather, it was a power so great, so universal, as to be far too vast for our weak minds to grasp. One might as well try to contain the sea in a teacup.' He performed *chiburi*, the seemingly effortless flick of the wrist that shakes the blade clean, and sheathed the sword with a graceful flowing movement. 'But please observe this, because it's very important.' His face suddenly became grave. 'Because within the Way all is as one, your act of putting the bags in the bin and my act of cutting the bin in half were fundamentally one and the same act.'

'So if anyone asks . . .' Mr Hiroshige added.

Mr Akira nodded twice, very slowly. 'I think I'm beginning to understand,' he said, as the wind gently ruffled the pages of a precision-sliced newspaper. 'Thank you. Thank you very much.'

Mr Miroku made a tiny gesture with his hands. 'Think nothing of it,' he said. 'What nobler calling could there be than to guide another's footsteps along the Way?' He started to walk towards the cottage, then looked back. 'One last thing, though.'

'Yes?'

With the merest quiver of a single finger, Mr Miroku indicated the sprawl of garbage, which was being gradually dispersed by the gentle breeze. 'Get that mess cleared up, would you?'

'I don't think it's following us,' the wicked queen panted, leaning against an apple tree as she caught her breath.

They looked back at the castle. There was something white and fluffy oozing out of all the upper storey arrowslits, and the moat looked like a bubble-bath. The queen breathed a sigh of relief and rested the bucket carefully on the ground.

'I spilt some,' she said, 'but not too much, I don't think.' She peered at the surface of the water and nodded. 'Looks like all we've lost is some of the naff graphics and the Spell Check.'

'Spell—?'

'Don't ask. It never worked anyway. Well now,' she went on, 'here we both are, with the bucket and the clothes we stand up in and not a lot else. Any ideas?'

Sis just shrugged.

'It wouldn't be a problem if the system was still running,' the queen went on, taking off her shoes and sitting down. 'Normally, we'd have just enough time to catch our breath before a wizened old crone or quaintly humorous hunchback came by offering to tell us everything we need to know. Marvellous feature of the program, that was, when it was working okay.'

'Don't look now,' Sis muttered, 'but there's two men under that tree over there staring at us.'

'Are there?' The queen lifted her head. 'That's interesting. You never know, maybe that part of the system's still running. Let's give it a try, shall we?'

Sis looked doubtful. 'They don't look terribly nice,' she whispered. 'Wouldn't it be better if we—?'

'No.' The wicked queen stood up and waved her shoe. 'Hello! Yes, you there. Are you Help?'

The men who'd been watching them started guiltily, looked round just in case the queen had been talking to somebody else, then slowly walked towards them. It was easy to see why Sis hadn't liked the look of them. Where she came from their sombre grey suits, sunglasses and bulging left armpits could only mean one thing: they were some sort of Them.

'Sorry?' one of them said. 'Can we help you?'

'That depends,' replied the queen briskly. 'By rights, you should be a little old man with a long white beard or a gnarled old peasant woman bent double under a heavy load of firewood, which we would proceed to carry for you.' She paused for a moment, then continued. 'If this is making absolutely no sense to you, then you aren't who I think you are.'

The elder of the two cleared his throat. 'Actually,' he said, 'we know what you're driving at, but we aren't who you think we are.'

'We aren't even here,' added his colleague, with a rather mimsy grin.

'Not officially, anyhow,' the elder man said. 'This is supposed to be covert surveillance.'

'Then you're not very good at it, are you?' the queen replied. 'Come to think of it, I *do* know who you are. You're the Grimm boys, aren't you?'

The Brothers Grimm smiled sheepishly. 'So much for blending into the crowd,' said the elder. He elbowed his brother in the ribs. 'Told you we should have dressed the part.'

'We'd still have stuck out like sore thumbs,' the younger Grimm replied. 'And it's bad enough having to tell people you collect fairytales for a living without having to dress up in all that ridiculous schmutter.'

'I know you,' the queen repeated. 'You're the official observers, aren't you? From where *she* comes from.'

The Grimms noticed Sis for the first time. The younger specimen hauled out a complicated-looking scanning device, waved it in Sis's direction and looked down at the readout. 'Gawd, she's right,' he said, 'she's one of ours. How in hell's name did she get here?'

'Good question,' the queen growled. 'Anyway, wasn't it lucky I bumped into you two creeps when I did? You can take her back with you.'

Sis was about to protest, but the Grimms did it for her. 'No can do,' said the elder Grimm, shaking his head. 'Not our pigeon, repatriations. We're just . . .'

'Observers,' the queen finished for him. 'All right, observe this. Either you can get her out of here, now, no pack drill, or else your bureau is going to be hearing from my lawyers about a claim for massive disruption to my systems caused by one of your strays hacking into it and crashing the damn thing. Now, shall I wrap her or will you take her as she is?'

But the Grimms shook their heads again; this time, more or less in unison. 'Still not our pigeon,' the elder replied. 'Cost us our badges, that would. Of course, we'll report back to Immigration soon as we get back, but that's all we can do. Sorry.'

'But you've got to help,' Sis burst out. 'My brother's lost in here, somewhere, and *she's* not doing anything to find him.'

The Grimms exchanged glances. 'Awkward,' said the younger specimen.

'Very awkward,' agreed his brother. 'Don't know what we're going to do about that. I mean, it could be abduction, which'd be State Department business—'

'Or mythological asylum,' put in the younger Grimm. 'That'd come under Political.'

'Might even constitute an act of war,' added the elder, 'which'd mean bringing in the military. Sorry, no, can't touch that with a ten-foot pole.' He shook his head once more, just in case Sis and the queen hadn't been looking the first couple of times. 'While we're on the subject, though; when you say crashed the system, what exactly . . . ?'

The queen gave him a stare you could have put in a gin and tonic. 'Oh no you don't,' she said.

'But if you're having, um, technical difficulties,' the elder Grimm said solicitously, 'I'm sure our people would be only too pleased to offer technological support and backup. It'd be the least . . .'

'You want me to let your spooks come poking their noses into the workings of my system,' the queen translated. 'Whereupon you'd download everything you think you'd be able to use back where you come from, and then bugger off. Probably,' she added, 'leaving behind a few little mementoes of your visit buried deep down among the cogs and wheels, all ready to go bang! and blow a hole in the operating system whenever the bunch of paranoid psychotics you work for decide we constitute a threat to your dimensional security. Oh, come on, boys, I wasn't written yesterday.'

'You're being very unfair,' muttered the elder Grimm. 'And that's just going to make it harder for us to repatriate our, um, errant citizen here.' He stripped all vestige of expression from his face, and went on: 'I do take it you want rid of her?'

The queen snarled. 'You're calling *me* unfair,' she said. 'And somehow I don't believe you'd actually do that, abandon one of your own in an alien dimension. If word ever got out, you'd be flayed alive. And, unlikely as it seems, sooner or later *someone's* going to wonder what's become of this one and her two noxious siblings.'

The Grimms grinned. 'Quite so,' said the junior partner. 'And guess what. Anybody who so much as suggests that the reason for their disappearance is that they've been kidnapped by the fairies is going to end up wearing one of those funny jackets with sleeves that don't let you look at your watch. Forget it, your Majesty. We've extended the hand of friendship and you've thrown it back in our face—'

'Interesting mental picture,' the queen interrupted. 'Sorry, do go on.'

'You want our help with one problem,' the elder Grimm said, 'you've got to accept our help with the other. Simple as that. You think it over, and in the meantime we'll just go about our business.'

'Observing,' added Junior.

'I know, anything that isn't nailed down.' The queen breathed out through her nose in a manner that suggested a dragon or two in the back lots of her genetic matrix. 'I'll have you for this, don't you worry. Not immediately, perhaps, but eventually. And when I do—'

The elder Grimm smiled placidly. 'Tell it to the hobbits,' he said. 'Remember, our people know we're here. And when we're expected back. And right now, it doesn't look to me like those automated defence systems of yours we've heard so much about are in any fit state to cope with a sudden dose of Reality. Think on, Highness. Ciao.'

The queen snorted; fortunate for her that some things don't run in families, or she'd have roasted her own toes. But the Grimms turned their backs and walked away. When they'd gone fifty yards or so, the queen distinctly heard a snigger.

'Wonderful,' she said. 'Now it looks as if I'm stuck with you long-term. All this is beginning to get on my nerves.'

Sis glowered at her. 'That's right,' she said, 'blame me for everything. If you hadn't been so rude to those men, they might have helped us to fix your rotten system and find Carl and Damien.'

'Oh, be quiet.' The queen sat down again and pulled on her shoes. 'Well, I don't think we're going to meet any funny old men or informative wizened crones, so we might as well make a move before those idiots think of something else to threaten me with and come back. I think I might have difficulty staying serenely regal if they were to do that.'

'So where are we going to go? Or are we just going to drift about aimlessly carrying this stupid bucket and getting our shoes wet?'

The wicked queen scratched an itch at the very tip of her perfect nose. 'You clearly haven't understood how things work here,' she said. 'It's a whole different attitude to cause and effect. If you've got a problem, you don't go out and look for an answer. Heaven forbid. You might find the wrong one, and then where'd you be? No, you keep going till the answer finds you. It will.'

Sis wrinkled her nose in distaste. 'Oh, really?' she said. 'You mean, you'll just happen to bump into an adventure that'll put everything right. And in the meantime, you just roam about the place smelling the flowers.'

'More or less,' the wicked queen replied. 'After all, if someone's been to all the trouble of putting us into a story, it stands to reason they've got work for us to do.'

'And suppose we wander off in the wrong direction and the right adventure can't find us? Or is there a convention, like you always wander North or something?'

The queen smiled indulgently. 'Oh, the adventure finds you all right, don't you worry, just like a cat can usually be relied on to find a mouse inside a small cardboard box. That's what the system's . . .' She tailed off. 'Was for,' she added.

'Exactly.'

'Before *you* crashed it.'

'Yes, all right, you've made that point already.' Sis sighed and sat down on what she thought was a tree-stump, though in fact it was a giant mushroom. 'Point is, we can't rely on this silly old system of yours. In fact, any adventures that do come along are likely to be the wrong ones anyway. *That*,' she added, 'is the law of probability. Or don't you have it here?'

'Not in the way you think,' the queen admitted. 'Around here, if you find yourself captured by a bandit chief and he's about to slit your throat with a great big knife, you know it's your lucky day, because it's a dead certainty he's your long-lost brother and you're in for a half share of the year's takings. It's getting so it's hard to find people who're prepared to be bandits these days. Too expensive, they reckon.'

Sis sniffed, as if she could smell toast burning. 'This isn't getting us anywhere,' she said. 'Now then, think. Who is there apart from my brother Carl and your dead sorcerer who might know *something* about your horrid old system?'

'Don't think there's – Just a moment, though.' A smile leaked out over the wicked queen's face. 'There *is* someone who might just be able to help. Mind you, it's highly unlikely—'

'Good.' Sis nodded firmly. 'Then by your reckoning it should be a sure thing. Which way? You explain as we go.'

'I –'The queen looked round. 'To be truthful I'm not sure. Usually, you see, there'd be this little old man—'

'Or an old crone carrying firewood, I know. Come on, *think*.'

'All right, I'm doing my best.' The queen closed her eyes, turned round three times, pointed at random and opened her eyes again. 'That way,' she said.

'You're sure?'

'Absolutely positive,' the wicked queen replied, freeing the hem of her skirt from a stray bramble. 'Come on, then, don't dawdle. And I think it's your turn to carry the bucket.'

CHAPTER THREE

'You again,' snarled the elf. 'Don't you people ever give up?'

The frog dilated its cheeks. 'No,' it croaked. 'It's a little thing called duty. Not something I'd expect your kind to know anything about.'

'That's where you're wrong then,' jeered the elf. 'I know lots about duty. It's seventeen per cent on gin, whisky, rum and tequila, twenty-eight per cent on cigars . . .'

'Forget it. Now, this time it's going to be different.'

'You bet,' grumbled the elf, squirming ineffectually between the frog's long, flexible toes. 'For a start, I'm not having anything to do with it.'

'That's what you think, is it?'

The elf looked up into the frog's round, yellow eyes. 'Be fair,' she said. 'If you want to go around eating grandmothers, be my guest. Go for it. Just so long as you leave me out of it, because it's not my war and I don't want to get involved. When it comes to the irreconcilable conflict between man and beast, our role is strictly confined to robbing the dead. Okay?'

'No,' replied the frog. 'Now, when I give the word . . .'

The elf planted her feet against a green toe and pushed with all the strength of her legs. It wasn't enough. 'Just think, will you?' she said. 'What makes you think it'll work a second time? They may be woodcutters, but they aren't stupid.'

'Maybe, maybe not,' replied the frog. 'Actually, I have a theory that constant exposure to fresh sap rots their brains. There's only one way to find out.' He blinked twice with disconcerting rapidity. 'What it comes down to is: who are you more afraid of, them or me?'

The elf subsided. 'Go on, then,' she muttered. 'What's the big idea?'

'Better attitude. Now, on my mark I want you to run about and start yelling at the top of your voice *The wolf is coming, the wolf is coming!* Can you manage that, or would you prefer it if I tattooed your lines on your knees?'

The elf scowled. 'I should be able to manage that,' she said. 'But what's it going to achieve?'

The frog grinned. 'Because, my one-thirty-second-scale friend,' he said, 'that way they'll be looking for a big bad wolf, not a frog. Simple, isn't it, when you think it through.'

'You're the boss,' replied the elf. 'Okay, ready when you are.'

It worked. As soon as the elf broke cover, the woodcutters leapt to their feet and hurried off in the direction she'd just come from, allowing the small green frog to hop unmolested out of the bushes and squeeze itself through the crack under the door.

Wonderful! He was in.

Now all he had to do was eat the grandmother.

In front of him was a huge black thing, like a low hill. Further reconnaissance proved it to be one of Granny's shoes. It was then that the frog realised that perhaps, when he was planning the mission, he'd focused a little too intently on getting in and hadn't given as much thought as he should to what came after that. With a lot of effort, a little luck and a week to do it in, he might just manage to eat one of Granny's toes.

Then the ground began to shake. He tried to hop, but something huge and burning hot caught him and lifted him high into the air. Involuntarily he closed both eyes; when his conscious mind had recognised that self-induced blindness wasn't likely to be the editor's choice for Survival Trait of the Month and had sent word down his cheapjack amphibian synapses to belay that last order, he was staring into a vast pink –

Face.

'Hello, little frog,' said a girlish voice that reverberated from one end of the galaxy to the other. 'I'm Little Red Riding Hood. I think you're cute. Have you got a name, little frog?'

The frog wanted to snarl, lay his ears flat to his lean wedge-shaped skull and bare his teeth; the best he could do was croak 'Rivet!' very weakly and kick into thin air with his back legs. The giant red-hot human let forth a silvery laugh that threatened to bend the sky.

'Oh you're so sweet,' said the voice, 'I think I shall call you Sugarplum and keep you in the pocket of my apron. Wooza itta bitta pretty liddle frog, den?'

The face came slowly down on him, like nightfall on a man condemned to hang at dawn, and the frog could see an opening beginning to form in the sheer rose-red wall of flesh. It was opening its mouth.

Poetic justice, thought the frog, *I'm going to get eaten.* In a way, it wasn't such a bad way to go at that. Looked at from the right angle, the food chain's more like a party conga, winding in and out through the discarded paper trays and slices of cake ground into the carpet and taking everybody with it. He braced himself; then couldn't help a spasm of terrified pain as the burning hot surface membranes of the all-enveloping mouth made contact with his skin. There was a ghastly slurping sound –

And then, nothing. He hadn't been eaten after all.

Not *eaten*.

Kissed.

That was when things really started to happen. It was as if he'd topped off a meal of beans, onions and garlic with a large primed bomb, and his skin was stretching under the force of the blast. He was also falling – the girl had dropped him – and his ears were deafened by her little gasp of surprise. He landed, but found he was going *upwards*, and standing on his hind legs at the same time. He was growing, dammit, and at a terrifying rate. He was –

There happened to be a mirror on the wall opposite. The mere fact that he was tall enough to look in it should have been enough to warn him that things had just defied the laws of physics and got worse. He looked into it. 'Oh, shit a brick!' he moaned.

'Language,' Little Red Riding Hood warned, wiping her lips on the back of her hand. 'If Grandmama catches you swearing, she'll rip your ears off.'

He'd turned into a handsome prince. 'Turn me *back*!' he yelled hysterically, staring at the mirror. 'That's *awful*! I don't *want* to be one of those *things*!'

'Tough,' replied Little Red Riding Hood with a grin, and as she advanced towards him, she produced from the pocket of her dainty scarlet cape a pair of handcuffs and a nasty-looking hypodermic. 'That's the way it goes, buster. And you'll have the satisfaction of knowing it's all in aid of medical research.'

'Uh?' Fang goggled at her. 'What are you drivelling about?'

'Medical research,' the girl replied, making a grab for his arm that he only just managed to avoid. 'The nasty old authorities banned us from using frogs for our –' (horrible grin) 'experiments. But we found a way of getting round that, as you can see. Just turn the frog into a cute boy, the cute boy gives his consent to the experimental treatment programme, and Bob's your uncle. Now if you'll just hold still . . .'

A last tiny drop of adrenaline flopped from his pineal gland and gave Fang the little spurt of energy he needed to dive between the girl's legs and bolt for the door. 'Spoilsport!' she screamed after him; then she threw the handcuffs, which hit him behind the ear and raised a nasty bump. Fortunately, he still had enough of his wolf mindset left to prompt him to jump into a tangled thicket of brambles, where a mere human wouldn't dare follow for fear of being horribly scratched.

A short while later, he remembered that he was a mere human now, and later still spent a thoroughly miserable couple of hours picking thorns out of all sorts of places, many of which wolves don't even have.

In fields, mushrooms; in high streets and shopping precincts, video libraries, designer greetings cards vendors and small, eternally hopeful shops stocking silver jewellery, aromatic oils and CDs of traditional Tibetan music; here, castles. They pop up out of the ground, bloom, burgeon; then, when the story's finished with them, they vanish without leaving so much as a scar in the grass.

This castle, at the other end of the forest from the wicked queen's rather more substantial pad, is the #2 Enchanted Kingdom set. Its graceful coned roofs and swan-necked towers imply that it's happy-ending compatible, but the absence of rosy-cheeked peasants and bustling market-stalls outside the gates suggests that the happy ending's still a reel away, or even that the story hasn't started yet.

There were two halberdiers in fancy dress armour in front of the castle gate when Dumpy, the Dwarf With No Name, slithered awkwardly off his Shetland pony and tethered it to the guard-rail. He looked at the halberdiers, and they at him.

'You're a dwarf,' said one of them nervously.

'So?'

The halberdier fidgeted with the handle of his spear. 'And there's just the one of you, right?'

'Reckon so.'

The two halberdiers exchanged glances. 'Pass, friend.'

'Mighty obliged to you.'

He chuckled to himself as he crossed the courtyard and started to climb the spiral staircase. How dwarves had acquired this extraordinary reputation for blind savagery and skill at arms he didn't know. Among the empty cardboard boxes and string-tied bundles of old newspapers in the cellar of his memory was a vague recollection of a time when it hadn't been this way; of having to scamper out from under the feet of contemptuous humans in the streets, of the sting of sand kicked in his face on a hundred beaches right across the dimension, of jeering references to fishing-rods and dinky red hoods. Since the furthest back he could remember was last Thursday (or Once Upon A Time, local designation) this wasn't saying a great deal in absolute terms. Around here, people simply didn't remember things for very long. A gold-fish, which forgets where it's been in the time it takes to swim a circuit of its bowl, could have made a good living in these parts as a database.

In which case, he mused as he rested halfway up the ver-tiginous stairs of the tower, how come he seemed to remem-ber a time when he was able to remember back to a time he'd since forgotten?

Must be a reason. He scratched his head. If there was one, it had slipped his mind. Couldn't have been important.

There were more halberdiers at the top of the stairs, stand-ing on either side of the doorway that led to the royal apart-ments. They looked at him and flinched.

'It's okay,' he said, in a tone of voice implying the exact opposite. 'Just put down the halberds where I can see 'em, nice and easy, and nobody's gonna get hurt.'

The guards did as they were told, laying their weapons down as if they were spun-sugar tubes filled with warm nitro-glycerine. 'Beat it,' Dumpy growled. They fled.

And another thing. Why am I talking in this most peculiar way?

Doesn't sound like the way I'd have imagined I usually talk. Sure does seem mighty odd. Yeah, sho' nuff.

The door wasn't locked; after all, it was only the door to the king and queen's private apartments, why the hell should it be? As he reached for the handle, he heard voices on the other side. He listened for a moment or so, then smiled. Yup, he'd come to the right place.

'Valdemar?'

'Nope.'

'Vernon?'

'Nope.'

'Victor?'

'Nope.'

'Vincent?'

'Nope.'

'Well, that's the Vs. Okay. Walter?'

'Nope.'

'Wilbert?'

'Do me a favour.'

'William?'

'Nope.'

Dumpy pushed the door open. Inside the chamber it was dark, lit only by the few skinny photons that had managed to squeeze through the loopholes in the wall, but he could see the King (must be the King, because he's wearing a crown), his young wife, the baby hugged protectively in her arms, and a short, hunchbacked man squatting on the clothes press and swinging his legs.

'Say,' he demanded. 'You the dwarf?'

The little man looked up and scowled. 'No, I'm Arnold Schwarzenegger, but they washed me without looking at the label first. Would you mind waiting outside, whoever you are? I'm in a meeting.'

Dumpy ignored him, ducked under a footstool and strode into the room, not failing to notice the way the King and Queen shrank back as he approached. 'I was told there was a dwarf in this here castle,' he said. 'Reckon as how you'll fit the bill, friend.'

'Jolly good. Now, if you'd care to wait outside . . .'

Dumpy folded his arms across his diminutive chest. 'They call me the Dwarf With No Name,' he went on. 'I . . .'

He stopped abruptly. The Queen had made a funny squeaking noise. Dumpy spun round and glowered at her, then faced the little man again.

'Do they?' The little man glowered back. 'What a co-incidence.'

Dumpy's eyebrows puckered. 'Don't say you're a dwarf with no name too,' he said. 'That'd sure make things mighty complicated.'

'I should say so,' replied the little man. 'Actually, to be fair, it's not so much that I haven't got a name, more a case of—'

Dumpy reached out and lifted the hem of the hood that overshadowed the little man's face. 'I know you,' he said. 'You're Rumpelstiltskin.'

The Queen made a loud yipping noise and started dancing round the room, while the King clenched both fists, punched them in the air and shouted 'Yes!' For his part, the little man gave Dumpy a look that would've poisoned a reservoir.

'Oh thank you,' he said. 'Thank you ever so much.' He slid off the clothes press, swivelled round and kicked it savagely. 'Have you got any idea how long it's taken me to set up this gig? Six months of hard work, sitting up all night spinning straw into gold, and thanks to you it's all just gone down the toilet. You blithering . . .'

He broke off, mainly because Dumpy had grabbed him by the lapels and lifted him off his feet. 'I'd think twice about calling me names, pal. That's how come I ain't got one. I guess,' he added, suddenly uncertain. He put Rumpelstiltskin down again.

'All right,' said the other dwarf. 'But that works both ways, you know.'

'Yeah,' Dumpy growled remorsefully. 'Guess I owe you an

apology, at that. Shoulda guessed you might still be pulling that old name scam.' He frowned. 'Another thing I forgot,' he added to himself. 'C'mon, let's git,' he said, pulling himself together. 'I get the feeling these folks ain't feelin' too friendly.'

Sure enough, the King and Queen were beginning to fidget in an ostensibly warlike manner. The two dwarves headed off down the stairs.

'Why were you looking for me?' Rumpelstiltskin asked.

'I'm looking for good dwarves,' Dumpy answered, as they came out into the castle courtyard. It was deserted, and the only sound was that of hurriedly closing shutters and bolts being slammed home on doors. 'Dwarves I can rely on. They gotta be smart, mean and fast with a—' With a what? Suddenly he realised that he couldn't remember what dwarves fight with. Something small, presumably, and capable of being used to devastating effect against the ankles of their victims. 'Fast,' he repeated. 'Real fast.'

'I see,' Rumpelstiltskin said thoughtfully. 'Smart, mean, fast, reliable dwarves. What's this for, a cut-price pizza delivery service? One where you just carry the pizza in under the door without waiting for the customer to open it?'

Dumpy shook his head, trying to recall what the job was. 'Fighting a wolf,' he said, suddenly inspired. 'I been hired to keep this wolf from preying on three little pigs.'

'And so you want reliable, quick, clever, stingy dwarves. Sorry if this sounds rude, but the logical connection escapes me.'

'Not stingy,' Dumpy explained. '*Mean*. Like in, you know . . . mean.' Dammit, he *knew* there should be a better word, a word that'd mean what it meant, but somehow he couldn't think of it. It was as if there was a big fat policeman standing outside the door of his memory, refusing to let him in there unless he could produce the necessary permits. He knew he was capable of expressing himself in something more lucid than this strange idiom and this horrible drawling accent, which he knew for certain had never been spoken by any *real* person. 'Mean,' he repeated. 'Don't you understand Dwarvish?'

They reached the gate. The two halberdiers on duty took one look at them, dropped their weapons and jumped in the moat. 'What was all that about?' Rumpelstiltskin asked.

Dumpy shrugged. 'Folks is just scared of dwarves, is all,' he said.

'Oh. Why?'

'Because we're mean, I guess.'

'Ah. I can see where that might be annoying, like if you've gone out for a meal together, but not frightening, surely.'

Dumpy concentrated. A stray shard of memory was loose in his mind, but it wouldn't stay still long enough to be identified. 'You saying that where you come from, folks *ain't* scared of dwarves?'

Rumpelstiltskin nodded. 'It's more or less the other way around, in fact. At least, I think so. Thought so. You know, it's sort of slipped my mind.'

'Where you come from,' Dumpy repeated, 'dwarves are scared of regular folks?'

'I think so. Or at least they try to stay out of their way. Partly I imagine it's unthinking bigotry and size-hatred, but mostly it's because they tend to tread on us without realising we're there. That's why we're shy, retiring creatures who live deep in the forests and hide when the Big People come clumping by.'

Dumpy was shocked. 'We do?'

'Apparently. Hard to credit, isn't it?' Rumpelstiltskin frowned, and the frown hardened into a scowl. 'Can't be right, though. I mean,' he went on, straightening his back and letting his chin jut out, 'we're *dwarves*, dammit. How come we let those big guys push us around? How come they don't show us no respect?'

'Too darned right,' Dumpy confirmed. 'You ain't got respect, partner, you ain't got nothin'.' He jutted his chin out too, so that the pair of them looked like a bonsai granite outcrop. 'C'mon, let's go out there and kick us some ass.'

'Sure thing,' replied Rumpelstiltskin, punching the palm of his left hand with his right fist and wincing slightly. 'Mind you, we may need to stand on something in order to reach.'

Dumpy bristled. 'Forget that kind of talk, mister,' he said. 'Dwarves bend the knee to no man.'

'Well, quite. Wouldn't be a great deal of point. Still, let's get out there and teach the suckers a thing or two.' He grimaced horribly, knowing that for some reason it was the right thing to do. It hurt his face, and he stopped.

'Sure.' Dumpy rubbed his chin. 'Though of course we ain't gonna go around terrorising innocent folks.'

'No? I'd have thought they'd be easier. For beginners, that is.'

'Hell, no. We don't do that kinda stuff. We're *good*.'

Rumpelstiltskin blinked. 'We are?' he said. 'Oh.'

'You betcha. We're the goddamn *heroes*. Okay, maybe we gotta throw our weight about from time to time, punch out a few guys who don't show us no respect, but deep down we're the best. In a land torn apart by anarchy and oppression, we are the law.'

'Oh joy,' muttered Rumpelstiltskin, without enthusiasm. 'What I always wanted to be when I grew up.'

'Somewhere,' muttered the queen, a shoe in each hand, 'near here.'

Around their ankles, the mud of the swamp seethed and gurgled like a casserole neglected in a hot oven. Wisps of thick grey fog wound in and out of the skeletons of dead trees. In the distance, swamp gas occasionally flared into torches of lurid orange flame. Overhead, some kind of huge, slow-moving bird wheeled and circled, watching them with a more than passing interest.

'Somewhere near here,' the queen repeated. 'Usually, of course, he comes to see me.'

Sis groaned, and shifted the bucket across to her left, marginally less blistered hand. Something in the mud around her ankles was nibbling at her toe. 'Who are you talking about?' she asked.

The queen pulled aside a curtain of lank reeds, shook her head and let it fall back. 'My accountant,' she said.

'Your *accountant*?'

'That's right.' She turned her attention to a dead tree, its heart eaten out by time and some indeterminate form of blight. 'Hello? Anybody home? Oh well.'

'Your accountant.'

'You seem surprised.'

'Sorry. It just seems a bit unlikely, that's all.'

The queen raised an eyebrow. 'Not a bit of it. Oh, your heroes and dragonslayers and knights in shining armour are all right for fetching and carrying and basic pest control, but when you're in serious trouble what you need is sensible, level-headed professional help. And this chap we're going to meet is so level-headed you could play snooker on his hat. Given a choice between him and your average heavily armed leather fetishist—'

'I see what you mean,' Sis replied. 'It's just that my uncle Terry's an accountant, and his office is over a chemist's shop in a suburban high street. This doesn't look . . .'

'Different strokes, girl,' the queen said patiently. 'In these parts, this *is* a suburban high street. I wish you'd said you were an accountant's niece. I'd have taken you a bit more seriously if I'd known that.'

'I—' Sis would undoubtedly have said something worthy of her ancestry if she hadn't chosen that moment to step on a chunk of green, slimy log and topple over. There was a horrible-sounding *glop!* noise, and she disappeared into the mud.

'Oh God,' the queen said, hauling her out, 'the bucket . . .'

She looked round. Being lighter than a fairly well-nourished adolescent girl, the bucket hadn't sunk into the mire; it was sitting, or floating, on the scummy surface at an angle of about forty-five degrees. There was a newt swimming in it.

'Hell,' the queen said. 'That's another chunk of data we've lost. Much more of this and we might as well forget the whole thing. Why couldn't you look where you were going, instead of . . . ?'

Sis wasn't listening. Rather, she was staring at something behind the queen's back and pointing. 'Over there,' she said.

'Hm? Oh good Lord, right under our noses and we didn't see.'

The base of the dead tree had swung open, revealing a carpeted staircase apparently leading down into a tunnel under the mud. Having carefully unglued the bucket, the queen waded across, looked in vain for something to wipe her feet on, then squelched down the stairs and out of sight, leaving Sis to follow as best she could.

The staircase was long, narrow and dark, and the slippery condition of her shoes made the journey an interesting one. When she finally emerged into light and air, she found herself in what looked unnervingly like a warm, bright, enchantingly dull waiting-room. There were the usual plastic chairs, the usual table with dog-eared copies of ancient magazines, the usual gaunt-looking avocado plant in a too-small pot; and behind the absolutely standard receptionist's desk sat a nice, cosy-looking middle-aged –

'Hello,' the leprechaun was saying to the wicked queen. 'Have you got an appointment?'

''Fraid not,' the queen replied. 'If he could spare me a minute or so, it'd be greatly appreciated.'

The leprechaun beamed. 'I'll let him know you're here,' she said, and pressed a button on her desk.

'I'll regret asking this,' Sis muttered while the receptionist was making her call, 'but isn't that—?'

The queen nodded. 'They all are. Logical choice of profession, given their experience in hiding pots of gold under rainbows. Don't stare, it's rude. She's not staring, and you're a whole lot weirder in these parts than she is.'

By the time Sis had thought that one through, the connecting door had opened and a – dammit, yes, a funny little man with sparkling eyes behind round spectacles and a long white beard was shaking hands with the wicked queen and asking after the health of some carefully memorised relative. Sis felt better; that *proved* he was an accountant, for all that he was four feet tall and dressed in red and yellow slippers with bells on the toes. Any minute now, she thought, he'll press the tips of his fingers together and say 'Let's just run through those figures again, shall we?' and then she'd *know*.

She followed them through into the leprechaun's office, which was even more reassuring. There was the desk; one comfy chair behind it, two chair-shaped instruments of torture in front. There were the filing cabinet, the rows of loose-leaf reference books, the files neatly stacked on the floor with Dictaphone tapes balanced on them ready for the typists, the obligatory framed photograph on the desktop with picture of generic wife, small child and dog (look closely at some of those framed photos; wherever you go, sooner or later you'll notice they're all of the same woman, child and dog). The only thing missing was the VDU and where it should have been there was a free-standing grey-plastic-framed mirror.

'So,' the leprechaun said, nodding them into the punters' chairs, 'what can I do for you?'

The wicked queen settled her face into that expression of charming helplessness that can sometimes draw the fangs of even the most hard-bitten professional adviser. 'I'm afraid I've done something awfully silly,' she said, 'and I was wondering if you could possibly help me.'

The leprechaun smiled. 'That's what I'm here for,' he said. 'And I'm sure it can't be as bad as you make out.'

The queen simpered back; Sis had done enough pocket-money work for Uncle Terry during the school holidays to know it was tactically quite sound, but that didn't stop her wanting to be noisily sick. 'It's like this,' she said. 'We – that's her and me – we've managed to crash the Mirrors network for the whole kingdom and all that's left is what's in this bucket, and we've spilt quite a lot of that. Also, her two brothers are missing out there somewhere, nothing seems to work at all, and we haven't a clue how to put it right. Do you think you could suggest something?'

'Um,' the leprechaun replied, looking as if he'd just found a sea-serpent coiled round his soup spoon. 'All due respect, but that doesn't really sound like an accountancy problem. I'm sorry if that sounds negative,' he added quickly, as the queen's face fell like share prices after a spring election, 'but the tax advantages of a total systems wipeout aren't all that great. Of course,' he went on, 'it's all a bit of a grey area, and I'd need to take another look at the figures—'

(*Ah*, whispered Sis to herself. *I believe*.)

'Actually,' the queen interrupted, 'the tax thing isn't absolutely uppermost in my mind right now.'

The leprechaun looked at her and blinked. 'It isn't?' he said.

'Well, no.'

'Oh.' Something in his manner suggested that where he came from, people had been burnt at the stake for less. 'So how can I help?'

The queen smiled and pointed at the mirror. 'I seem to remember you saying that your, um, one of those ran off an independent network, and I was just wondering if I might possibly—'

The leprechaun looked at her gravely, as if she'd just asked if she might borrow his mother for a little experiment. 'I'm not sure,' he said guardedly. 'What did you have in mind?'

'Nothing drastic,' the queen assured him. 'For starters, I was wondering if we could use your mirror to translate my, um, bucket. You see, it's all jumbles of silly letters and symbols and things, and I haven't the faintest idea what that's all about. It certainly isn't any use, how it is. If we could somehow load it on to yours, we might be able to get things running again.'

The leprechaun leaned back in his chair and fiddled with the stem of his spectacles. 'Of course I'd love to help in any way I can, you know that,' he said. 'But there are sensitive personal files relating to my clients' financial affairs—'

'I won't peek, honest,' the queen cooed.

'Quite so.' The leprechaun hesitated, patently torn between his obligations to his paying customers and his loyalty to his queen. 'Unfortunately, the rules of the profession are very strict. After all,' he added, sensing that he'd hit on a winning argument, 'you wouldn't want me letting all and sundry look at *your* file.'

For some reason, the queen suddenly looked thoughtful. 'Fair enough,' she said. 'You do it, then. You probably know far more about these gadgets than I do anyway. Don't suppose it'd take you more than a minute or so.'

It was the accountant's turn to look thoughtful. On the one hand, he was saying to himself, my mother didn't raise me to be no systems analyst; on the other hand, for his usual hourly charge, paid cash, quite likely in advance, he'd cheerfully do handstands in the street, sing serenades under young girls' windows while accompanying himself on the mandolin (hire of mandolin extra), escort inconvenient female relatives to social functions or clean out a blocked sink. 'Certainly,' he said, plastering a smile onto his face and then wiping it away before it set hard. 'I shall do my best.'

'Oh good,' the queen said. 'That's a weight off my mind. Here's the bucket.' She hauled it up and placed it carefully on the desk; she didn't spill a drop, but the mud on the bottom made an awful mess of a thick wodge of paperwork. 'Do you want us to wait in the waiting room, or shall we go away and come back, or what?'

The leprechaun peered down into the bucket, wiggled his

ears, and sat down in the general direction of his chair. When he spoke next, there was a curiously shellshocked tone to his voice.

'This may, ah, take some time,' he croaked. 'Perhaps you'd better go away and come back later. Better still, I'll call you when it's ready.'

The wicked queen raised an eyebrow; it was a gesture that suited her, and she knew it. 'How?' she asked sweetly. 'With everything being offline all over the kingdom.'

'Oh.' The leprechaun looked up, his mind clearly else-where. 'I'll, er, send a messenger. You're going back to the palace, presumably.'

The queen nodded. 'That's very kind of you,' she said. 'I feel ever so much better now.'

Once the door had closed and the sound of footsteps on the stairs had died away, the accountant got up, drew the curtains, checked under the mat and behind the picture frames, took off his red and yellow stripy jacket and loosened the staid, demure tie he wore hidden under the vestments of his trade. Then he looked into the bucket again. Then he grinned.

'Hold all calls,' he barked into the intercom, 'and cancel all my appointments for the day. Something's come up.'

'Well?' Julian demanded.

'Nearly finished,' Eugene replied, his mouth full of bolts. 'Just got to tighten up this last nut and . . . There, all done. What d'you think?'

Julian looked up and saw a dear little cottage, with roses around the door and chocolate-box windows curtained in flowery chintz, suspended twenty feet in the air from the belly of a huge balloon. 'I see the logic behind it,' he said eventually. 'I'm just not sure about how you've put it into practice.'

'What's there to see?' Eugene shouted back. 'It's pretty simple, really. The next time the bastard starts huffing and puffing, all we do is cut the anchor cable and then just ride out the blast. Okay, so perhaps we end up a hundred miles away, but I've fitted a couple of rocket-powered motors, so we'll be back home within the hour. It'd damn well better work,' he added with feeling. 'I got a carrier pigeon from the insurance company while you were out, and they're not happy. Somehow I feel that threatening to take our business elsewhere isn't keeping them awake at nights any more.'

'Come down,' Julian said. 'Sorry to sound downbeat, but I don't think that thing's safe.'

Eugene gazed up at the balloon. 'It'll be all right,' he said. 'But I'm coming down anyway. Press that red button on the instrument panel, would you? It works the elevator.'

'Which red button? There's two of them.'

Far away in the distance a dish and a spoon, each carrying two suitcases, a flight bag and a yellow duty-free carrier that clinked as they moved, paused to look up at the strange grey sausage that seemed to have a house hanging from it. A passing cat started to play 'Fly Me To The Moon' on the violin.

'The one marked Lift,' Eugene shouted back.

'Lift-off?'

'No, Liiiiiift!'

'Sorry,' Julian yelled, as the balloon abruptly tore away from its moorings, wrenched loose by the explosive force of the rocket motors. 'I think I may have pressed the wrong button.'

On the distant hillside, the cat lifted the bow clear of the strings and corrugated her brows into a pensive frown. 'I thought it was meant to be a cow,' she said.

''Scuse me?'

'Taking part in the moonshot,' the cat explained. 'I read about it in the paper, *Daisy Set To Be First Cow In Space*. And that thing hanging out of the upstairs window is either a very small pink cow, or it's a pig.'

'Don't ask us,' replied the spoon, 'we're tableware.'

★

Snow White threw open the quaint old leaded window of her bedroom, leaned out over the sill, took a deep breath of crisp morning air and thought, *Yes!*

Most of the time, life's hard for a girl living on her wits in the Big Forest. The dividing line between predator and prey blurs. Wolves wear sheepskin, fashionable sheep wouldn't be seen dead in anything but one hundred per cent pure wolf, three quarters of the lucky breaks turn out to be menacing cracks, and come Happy-Ever-After time, you're only ever as good as your last scam.

Not this time, Snow White reflected, giving thanks to the patron goddess of her vocation. Just this once, she'd fallen on her feet instead of her head or her butt. She had the house, in a neighbourhood where there was no chance of bumping into any of her old associates. She had the story, perfect in every detail. Most of all, she had the marks; a prime set, all complete, first editions, collector's items every one. Seven dreamy otherworldly Orientals, gentlemen and scholars all, already eating out of her hand and doing precisely what they were told, automatically and without question. It went without saying that they were wealthy; all Japanese were. Give it just a few weeks more, time enough to reel them in without any risk of arousing the slightest suspicion, and then it'd be time for the first fleeting hints about the gold mine her poor dead uncle had just left to her and the wonderful investment opportunity it offered. Hell, fish in a barrel were the Viet Cong compared to these poor fools. It was perfect; raining Schrodinger's cats and Pavlov's dogs.

She left the window, with its heartstoppingly lovely view of the glade, the clearing and the mist-wrapped treetops, and inspected the contents of her wardrobe. There was the plain white frock, the homely cute gingham with the designer patch on the left knee, the blouse-bodice-skirt combo she'd arrived in and the black leather jumpsuit that represented the last resort when the going got really tough. Not going to need *that* on this job, she reassured herself smugly, which was good; it was hot as hell in that thing, and wearing it always made her feel like toothpaste in a hostile tube.

She decided on the gingham, as being most appropriate for what was on the day's agenda. So far she'd won their sympathy, their trust and their affection; now she had to launch Phase II and convert that useful groundwork into the fierce avuncular protectiveness that experience had taught her was the best preparation for the sting. When they've rescued you from death and Fates Worse Than a couple of times, hung around your bedside waiting for you to open your pretty little eyes and look up at them with love and trust, all that really remains is to administer the final *coup de grâce* while making shortlists of what to spend the money on.

She adjusted the dress in front of the mirror, straightened the neckline, lifted her skirt and tucked into her garter elastic the dainty little nickel-plated .25 automatic that had more than once proved to be a girl's best friend in a tight spot. Not that she saw herself having any need of it here; God, but these marks were a joy to work with, so much easier than the riverboat gamblers and treacle miners she'd cut her teeth on back in the old days . . .

She frowned. She could remember the old days quite vividly, but only as a sort of big screen memory, all perfectly lit, beautifully framed and in needle-sharp focus. It was almost too vivid to be real, because surely memory doesn't work that way, in sweeping panoramic shots of atmospheric saloons and archetypal levees beside a cobalt blue river. Too perfect, too perfect by half. She had the feeling that if she were to be fatally injured and have her past life flash before her eyes, there'd be an usherette with a torch to show her to her seat.

She unclenched the muscles that shaped the frown and ordered herself to quit being so damn paranoid. Everything was going to be just fine; fairytale ending.

There was a knock at her door. Quickly she shut the wardrobe, checked the line of her skirt, knocked her voice back into little-girl mode and chirped, 'Come in.'

She relaxed. It was only nice Mr Akira, with her break-fast tray: toasted muffins, fresh milk, apple, this morning's *Financial Times*. She smiled; he blushed, bowed low, nutted himself on the rustic latch and withdrew.

Once she'd had something to eat and had run her eye down the closing prices, she composed her thoughts and began to formulate her plan. In order to tighten her grip the last few essential degrees, she needed to be saved by the marks from some awful fate, preferably an aggressive act by an outside agency. Rescued from wolves? Worth a try, except that she'd never had much luck with wolves in the past; they tended to steer clear of her, though whether from fear or pro-fessional courtesy she'd never worked out. A human assailant would be better, if she could find one. Wicked stepmother? Jealous rival?

Wicked queen . . .

Perfect. Just the right overtones of sex and politics. No bother at all to cook up a tale about being a dispossessed orphan princess on the lam; it'd appeal to the rich vein of aristocratic snobbery that these great feudal lords undoubtedly indulged towards mere parvenu royalty. All that remained was to find one at short notice. That might present problems; wicked queens aren't something you can express-order from the Inno-vations catalogue. But in a place like this, there was bound to be one within a small radius. At least one; which meant she'd be able to take advantage of good healthy commercial com-petition and shop around for the best deal. Even at the best of times, the wicked queen racket's a cut-throat business.

Just in time, she remembered that she'd forgotten to do her face. With a sigh and a curse, she pulled the chair away from her dressing table, sat down in front of the mirror and dabbed at her nose with a powder puff. When she'd restored enough girlish pinkness (memo to self: lay off the radishes and the garlic bread) she paused for a moment to look at her reflection.

Beautiful.

Stunning. Breathtaking. Fabulous. Gorgeous. Out of this world.

But she knew that already. There was something else about the image that faced her in the glass this morning that she couldn't quite place. She looked again and began eliminating the impossible.

It wasn't her, it was the mirror itself. It was *looking* at her.

'Mirror?' she whispered.

Her reflection regarded her coolly. Its perfect lips parted.

'Running DOS,' it said. 'Please wait.'

Snow White's eyebrows shot up; their counterparts in the mirror stayed put. What was going on? And what in blazes was DOS? And why did she feel this urge to ask . . . ?

'Ready,' said the face in the mirror.

'All right.' She drew in a deep breath. 'Um. Mirror, mirror, on the wall, who is the fairest of them all?'

The reflection's lips flickered for a tiny moment in a mocking smile. Then it went back to the perfect stone face, and made its answer:

'Thou, O Snow White, are the fairest of them all.'

CHAPTER FOUR

'Hell fire and buggery,' said the elf, with a barely suppressed snigger. 'Exactly what happened to you?'

The handsome prince snarled. 'You think it's funny, don't you?' he said bitterly.

The elf shrugged. 'Poetic justice, maybe. Actually, you should see yourself, it suits you. Better than the frog outfit, anyway.'

'Get stuffed.'

The handsome prince took a step forward, staggered and grabbed hold of a tree to steady himself. It had been bad enough being turned from a wolf into a frog, but at least the leg count had remained fairly stable. The sudden jump from quadruped to biped was something quite other.

'I guess that's what's meant by an identity crisis,' the elf went on unkindly. 'If you ask me, you're headed for really major problems if you keep this up. Not that you haven't got plenty of those already,' she added fairly. 'It's just that they're pimples on the bum compared to what's in store for you.'

The handsome prince levered himself upright and

extended a leg. His instincts were screaming at him that this was all wrong; walking on two legs was just a party trick, not the sort of thing any self-respecting wolf would even attempt to do while sober. He ignored the siren voices in his head; there was work to be done, he was way behind schedule, his recent performance record was looking pretty abysmal and he had his quarterly management assessment looming on the middle-to-short term horizon. Wolfpack didn't listen to excuses or tolerate failure; they didn't make allowances if you got turned into something nasty, because getting turned into something nasty in itself implied a whole subcategory of failures. He knew exactly what his superiors would say: if you're dumb enough to allow yourself to get turned into a handsome prince, you're just going to have to compensate as best you can. We are not an equal opportunities employer.

'Come on, you,' he grunted at the elf.

She ducked behind a nettle. 'You leave me out of it,' she said. 'Both times I've done my bit; *you're* the one who keeps screwing things up. Anyway, this is nothing to do with . . .'

Before she could complete the sentence, the handsome prince grabbed, closed his hand, snarled in triumph and then resorted to intemperate language as he discovered the hard way that human beings don't like the touch of nettles on their bare skin. The elf wriggled and squirmed like a cabinet minister on a chat show, but it didn't do her any good.

'This is kidnapping,' she squeaked. 'Also assault, intimidation and discriminatory treatment of an ethnic group.'

'Yes,' replied the handsome prince. 'Now shut your face and keep still.'

After half an hour or so of rubber-legged staggering, he'd reached the stage where he could reliably go more than three yards without falling over. Since he was in a forest, with lots of trees to hang on to, it wasn't so bad. He ought to be able to deal with the next item on his agenda.

Eventually, after a lot of effort and a great amount of un-intentional comedy (imagine John Cleese doing funny walks in zero gravity on a highly polished floor) he reached the edge of the forest and peered through the screen of low branches at the plain beyond. He saw what he was looking for, and chuckled.

He was looking at something which at first sight could have been taken for a giant windmill. It had huge, carefully shaped sails forming an X on one side, and stood on a circular plinth, which in turn was cemented into the ground. The upper section, which looked like a salt cellar designed by an illiterate giant, was clearly intended to revolve, turning with the wind. Where it differed from the average windmill was in having searchlights, .50-calibre machine guns and a barbed-wire entanglement.

You had to give the little buggers credit for trying.

He lurched, limped, wobbled and staggered out of the wood, across the plain and up to the gate in the white picket fence that surrounded the whole installation. A porcine head poked up out of a kevlar-reinforced skylight, took one look at him and vanished. Klaxons began to blare and red lights flashed. Under the ground there was a rumble of hydraulics as the ground fell away at the handsome prince's feet, revealing a deep trench lined at the bottom with savagely pointed stakes.

The handsome prince stooped, picked up a pebble and tossed it lightly against one of the steel-shuttered windows.

'Hello?' he called out. 'Anybody home?'

He stood still and listened carefully. The afternoon air was still, and he could make out the sound of raised voices inside the tower, made audible on the outside as they vibrated off the stiff steel plate of the shatterboards.

'It's him,' hissed a voice. 'I know it is.'

'Rubbish. It's a human.'

'Yeah,' replied the first voice irritably. 'And last time he was a frog. Can't you see it's another damn trick?'

'You can't be sure of that.'

'Can't I? Watch. And load the fifty-cals. I'm going to blow him apart where he stands.'

The handsome prince took off his hat, with its cheerful feather sticking out of the side, and waved it. 'Can you hear me in there?' he called out. 'Hello?'

'Yes, but if he *is* a prince and we gun him down in cold blood—'

'Oh get real, Eugene. If he's a prince I'm Noel Edmonds. Now get out of the way of my rangefinder. All I can see is your fat backside, and I know how far away that is.'

The handsome prince stood on tiptoe. 'I'm looking for a pig called Julian,' he called out. 'Anybody of that name live here?'

The nose of a surface-to-surface missile poked out of a loophole at the top of the tower, followed by the tip of a pig's snout. There was a flash as the sunlight caught the nose-ring.

'Who wants to know?' called out a voice from the loop-hole.

'You don't know me,' the prince shouted, 'I live the other side of the forest. But I met this talking wolf back along, and he asked me to give you a message.'

The snout vanished and reappeared a few moments later. 'So why couldn't this wolf carry his own messages?' it demanded.

'He was caught in a beartrap at the time,' the prince replied. 'Wasn't looking all that chipper, to be honest with you. Lost a lot of blood. In fact, I'd say if he isn't got to a vet in the next ten minutes, he's had it. That's why I want to use your mirror.'

The pig's head went away again, and the handsome prince started to count to ten. Just when he'd reached eight, the head popped out again.

'Assuming you're telling the truth,' it said, 'we've got nothing to be afraid of. But why the hell should we want to help that sucker? He does nothing but blow our houses down. Let the bastard rot.'

The handsome prince frowned. 'That's not a very nice thing to say, is it?' he said.

'True. What of it?'

'Fair enough,' the prince replied. 'I just thought there was rather more to you pigs than that. I was wrong. I'll try somewhere else. It's all right.'

Silence from the tower; then, 'Oh, the hell with it. Okay, we're winding back the ditch cover now.'

Reprise of the hydraulic hum, this time with feeling. The plates slid back over the spike-filled trench, and a doorway opened through the wire. The handsome prince waved his thanks and walked up until he was within fifteen yards. Then he took a deep breath –

Once he'd gone and the dust had started to settle, Julian climbed out of the lavatory cistern he'd been cowering under and looked around at the wreckage of what was supposed to be his home.

'Eugene?' he called out. 'Desmond?'

Something moved under a near-intact sheet of plasterboard. 'Has he gone?'

'I believe so, yes.'

When the first gust of air from the handsome prince's lungs (call it the huff) had hit the sails, they'd begun to turn; at first slow and graceful, gradually picking up speed, until the humming sound they made became unbearable. The tower had moved all right; more than that, it'd spun like a top round the concrete base as the forward momentum of the sails had tried to drag it out. It was quite a sight.

Then the handsome prince had started off Phase II; puffing. It was at this point that a lot of the shutters and other projecting features that didn't lie flush against the outer skin of the tower were ripped away and flung through the air like autumn leaves. The hum of the blades became a searing scream, and their axles started to glow red hot.

The third attempt was better. More dramatic. Brought the house down, in fact.

First, however, it lifted it up, with a horrible snap and the groans of overstressed metal. The blades were now little more than a molten blur, and the shriek and whine of the slip-stream on the curved aerofoils had been loud enough to boil a man's brain. And still the handsome prince had gone on blowing, until something structural had given way with an earsplitting twang, and quite unexpectedly the main body of the tower had lifted clear of the pedestal and launched itself into the air, lifted up by the action of the four 'foils. For a second and a half, maybe two seconds, it hung in space like a huge dandelion seed, until gravity and entropy reminded it that this was no way for a building to behave and escorted it back to the ground. It landed the wrong way up and flew to bits.

'I knew it was him,' growled Desmond. 'I told you, but you wouldn't listen. All that stuff about expecting better things from us because we're pigs; what human would ever have said that?'

Julian avoided eye contact. 'What I want to know is,' he said, 'how's he doing it? First a wolf, then a frog, and now a human. What the hell is the creep going to show up as next?'

Desmond spat out a chunk of concrete. 'A JCB, maybe. At least that'd be *honest*. Now what *I'd* like to know is, where the hell were those two hired dwarves of ours when we needed them most? How much again did you say we were paying them?'

'Off recruiting,' Julian said. 'Just our luck. I honestly didn't expect to see him back again so soon.'

'Underestimating the enemy,' Desmond complained. 'You keep doing it, and we keep ending up ham-deep in rubble.' He sighed and shook himself, dislodging a dust-cloud that enveloped him completely. 'Look, I know you're going to bite my head off for being defeatist, but why don't we just move on? Up sticks and go somewhere else where he isn't going to bother us? It'd be so much easier—'

'Sure,' Julian replied. 'Until the next one of his kind shows up and it starts all over again. Face it, Des, sooner or later we'd have to stop running and stand and fight. Better to do it here and now and get it over and done with.'

'You know something, Julian? I can't wait to see you with an apple in your mouth. It'd stop you talking garbage, for one thing.'

Julian shrugged. Matter of opinion, presumably. It had felt like the right thing to say, but maybe Desmond was right; perhaps it *would* be better to clear off out of the forest altogether, or go back to living in a sty with all the other non-uppity pigs, where they belonged . . .

'Come on,' he said, kicking away a strip of tangled steel with his hind legs. 'We've got work to do.'

'More power!' roared the Baron.

Fearfully, Igor obeyed, throwing his weight against the huge lever and driving it forward. Livid blue sparks like fat, sizzling worms cascaded from the contacts. Somewhere a fuse overloaded, but the failsafes and backups cut in immediately; a fine piece of work, though the Baron said it himself, continuity of power supply guaranteed no matter how recklessly he abused the system. He bent down over the Thing strapped to the bench and peered hungrily at the dials on the control panel.

'More power,' he repeated.

Igor's eyes widened like an opening flower in stop-motion. 'The resistors,' he screeched. 'They're at breaking point as it is. They just can't take any more!'

'More power.'

Oh well, muttered Igor to himself, he's the boss, presumably he knows what he's doing. And if he doesn't – well, in years to come Katchen and the children would take a picnic up to the ruined tower on the top of the mountain, and Katchen would bring them into the burnt-out shell of the laboratory and point to a man's silhouette appliquéd onto the flagstones and say, 'See that? That's your Uncle Igor.' Immortality, of a sort. And it was better than working in the cuckoo-clock factory.

He edged the lever forward, and at first nothing happened. Then somewhere behind the massive screen of lead bricks, something began to hum, and a moment later a tremendous surge of power began to burgeon and swell, like the wave of a surfer's lifetime on Bondi Beach. Little silver beads of molten lead glistened like dewdrops in the interstices of the shield.

A few inches away from the Baron's nose, the needle on a dial suddenly quivered. 'More *power!*' he roared, slamming both fists down on the console and sending his coffee-mug (a birthday present from Igor, thoughtfully inscribed *World's Best Boss*) flying to the floor. Igor closed his eyes, mumbled the first four words of the Ave Maria, and thrust the lever all the way home.

Raw power sprayed out of the circuits like fizzy lemonade from a shaken-up bottle. One of the minor transtator coils dissolved instantaneously into a glowing pool of molten copper; but the backup took the load, and the meter hardly wavered. You could have boiled a kettle on top of the main reactor housing, if you didn't mind drinking luminous green tea.

'Yes!' thundered the Baron. 'Igor, it . . .'

Before he could say exactly what, a gunbarrel-straight shaft of blue fire burst from the mighty lens poised a few feet above the bench and enveloped the Thing completely. The Baron screamed and threw himself at the fire-shrouded form, trying to beat out the flames before they utterly consumed his creation; but before he even made contact, a tremendous force hauled him off his feet and slammed him against the far wall. Igor ducked under a table as a cyclone of distilled energy ripped circuit-boards and clamps and conduits out of the benches and juggled them in a spinning maelstrom of blinding heat and light around the glowing outline of the Thing. It was incredible, awesome, terrifying; Spielberg let loose in the effects laboratory with a blank cheque signed by God.

Then, as suddenly as it had begun, it was over. All the lights snapped out and the laboratory was shrouded in darkness, except for an ice-cold blue glow from the bench where the Thing had been. The smoke cleared, and there was silence except for the sizzle-plink of molten copper slowly cooling.

'Igor?'

'Baron? Are you all right?'

Cautiously, both men stood up and stared at the bench and the source of the unearthly blue light. 'Did you see what happened, Igor?' the Baron whispered. 'That fire . . . Is there anything left?'

Igor shrugged. 'Search me,' he said. 'I was hiding.'

Together they approached the bench. The blue fire danced on the scarred surface of the oak like the brandy flare on a Christmas pudding, and in the heart of the glow, where the Thing had been, there was a shape; humanoid, certainly, with the correct number of limbs and in more or less the right proportions, but . . .

'My God,' whispered the Baron. 'Igor, what have we done?'

'What d'you mean, *we*?' Igor whispered back. 'I just work here, remember?'

Where there had been a seven-foot frame of carefully selected muscle and bone, painstakingly put together from raw materials taken from the finest mortuaries in Europe, there was now a short, stocky child-shaped object with a small, squat body, sticklike arms and legs and a head that was too large for the rest of the assembly. It was wearing brightly coloured dungarees, an Alpine hat with a feather in it and shiny black shoes. It was made of wood and had a perky expression and a cute pointy nose.

'It's a puppet,' the Baron growled.

'So it is,' Igor replied, trying to keep the grin off his face and out of his voice. Despite all the melodrama of the last half hour, he couldn't help liking the little chap.

'A puppet,' the Baron repeated. 'A goddamned wooden puppet. What in hell's name am I supposed to do with that?'

He broke off. The puppet had winked at him. 'Did you see that?' he gasped.

'See what, boss?'

'It winked at me.'

Igor craned his neck to see. 'You sure, boss?' he said. 'Can't say I saw anything myself.'

'It moved, I'm sure of it.' The Baron sat down heavily on the shell of a burnt-out instrument console. 'Or maybe the radiation's addled my brains. I could have sworn . . .'

'Hello,' said the puppet, sitting up at an angle of precisely ninety degrees. 'Are you my daddy?'

The Baron made a curious noise: wonder, triumph and deep disgust, all rolled up in one throaty grunt. 'It's alive,' he croaked. 'Igor, do you see? It's alive.'

'Oh sure,' Igor replied. 'We got ourselves a walking, talking, moving, breathing, living doll.' He closed his eyes and opened them again. 'When you go back and tell the investors about this, I want to be there. Can I have your lungs as a souvenir?'

'You're my daddy,' said the puppet. 'I love you. My name's Pinocchio and I'm going to live with you for ever and ever.'

The Baron groaned and buried his face in his hands; which surprised the puppet, because he'd imagined his daddy would be pleased to see him. A safe assumption to make, surely? Maybe not. There was so much about this wonderful new world he didn't know, and wouldn't it be fun finding out?

Deep inside his wooden brain, a tiny voice was squeaking *Hang on, this isn't right, it isn't fair, let me out! My name is Carl and I'm a human, and where's my sister and brother?* But the grain of the wood soaked up the last flickers of neural energy, and the dim spark drenched away into the cold sap. 'My name is Pinocchio,' the puppet repeated; and if its nose grew longer by an eighth of an inch or so, nobody noticed.

'You sure this is the right place?' Rumpelstiltskin asked.

'I reckon . . .'

A chair crashed through the front window of one of the saloons on Main Street, making a hole through which something small and human-shaped followed it shortly afterwards. The chair didn't travel much further than the saloon's front porch, but the small humanoid object, being lighter, travelled further and made it as far as a muddy puddle in the middle of the street.

'. . . so,' Dumpy concluded.

The swing doors of the saloon opened and a large, burly, bald-headed man in a barkeep's apron flung a tiny hat out on to the porch. It was sort of conical, like the narrow end of an egg. It was made out of an acorn-cup.

'And stay out,' the barman explained.

The two dwarves waited till he'd gone back inside, then strolled over to the puddle, across which the tiny creature was doing the breaststroke.

'Howdy,' Dumpy said.

'Get knotted.'

Dumpy shrugged. 'Only being sociable, friend. You Thumb?'

'Who wants to know?'

Dumpy rested his hands on his knees and leaned over. 'If you're the Tom Thumb who's got a $50,000 reward on his head in Carabas for cattle rustling and grand fraud, then I got a job for you. If not, then screw you.'

'A job? What kind of job?'

Rumpelstiltskin nudged his colleague in the ribs. 'Sorry if I'm missing the point,' he hissed, 'but isn't this one a bit too small to be of any use to us?'

Dumpy grinned. 'When you bin in this business as long as I have,' he whispered back, 'you'll learn that good things ain't all that come in small packages. This here is Tom Thumb, the meanest son-of-a-gun who ever got agoraphobia in a shoebox.'

Rumpelstiltskin shrugged. 'Up to you, I suppose. D'you want me to grab him?'

'Don't even think about it, partner,' Dumpy warned.

'Okay, he's small, but so is five ounces of plutonium. Also, what with him bein' a bit on the small side, he'll be able to do things we can't. Y'know, like crawling down ventilation shafts and overhearing secret plans. Talking of which, ain't it ever struck you as odd the way the bad guys always choose to have their tactical meetings plumb underneath a vent grille? I ain't complaining, mind; just strikes me as curious, is all.'

'Hey, you.'

Dumpy looked down. 'You talking to me?'

'Yes, you. The tall bastard.'

'Hey.' Dumpy scowled. 'Ain't nobody ever called me that before. Not as is still alive, anyhow.'

'What, you mean "bastard"?'

'Hell no. Tall.'

'Quit making wisecracks and go get my hat.'

Dumpy raised both eyebrows. 'You givin' me an order, Tiny?' he muttered softly.

Tom Thumb sighed. 'It's for your own good. Go on, get a move on. Or are you standing around waiting till you evolve into a sentient life form?'

Before Dumpy could make an issue of it, Rumpelstiltskin fetched the hat and handed it over. The tiny man grabbed it and jammed it hard down on to his head.

'That's better,' he sighed. 'There's an integral sound amplifier/universal translator built in to the hat. Means you can talk to me without shouting, and you can hear what I'm telling you. All right?'

'Reckon s—'

The tiny man winced, as if Dumpy had just stubbed out a cigarette in his eye. 'Not so loud, for God's sake. This is sensitive equipment here.'

Rumpelstiltskin nudged his colleague in the ribs. 'Brilliant combination we've got here,' he whispered. 'Aggressive, foul-tempered *and* a wimp. What's he supposed to be for, then? Lulling the enemy into a true sense of security?'

'Shuttup,' Dumpy growled back, 'you ain't helping.' He

leaned forward and grabbed; the little man tried to get away, but Dumpy's forefinger and thumb closed on his leg. He yelped as Dumpy picked him up, in the manner of a man removing a cranefly from a bowl of borscht, and let him dangle for a few seconds before dropping him into an empty matchbox and sliding it shut.

'Like I always say,' he sighed. 'If you ain't got their respect, you gotta earn it.'

It was disconcerting, to say the least, to hear a loud, raucous voice coming from inside a matchbox; enough to make at least one passerby freeze in the act of lighting a cigarette, stare at the match he was about to grind against the side of the box, think hard and put it carefully away with a mumbled apology. Dumpy, meanwhile, was counting to ten.

'All right,' he said to the box. 'You quit making that awful noise and I'll let you out.'

The matchbox replied in language that was certainly forthright. A little match girl, who had been huddling in a shop doorway looking pathetic and doing a brisk trade as a result, stood up in a marked manner and walked away. Dumpy tossed the matchbox up in the air, caught it lefthanded, tossed it up again, backhanded it with his left hand into his right, shook it vigorously and let it fall to the ground.

'Ready yet?' he asked pleasantly.

'Okay. You win.'

Dumpy picked up the box. 'You were right,' he said to Rumpelstiltskin. 'A wimp.' He slid back the lid and shook the tiny man out into the palm of his hand. 'You want the job or not?' he asked.

'Do I have a choice?'

'Nope.'

'Persuasive bastard, aren't you?'

Dumpy smiled. 'Guess it's my naïve charm,' he replied. 'Welcome aboard.'

*

'Do you trust that man?' Sis demanded as they squelched out of the swamp into the trees.

'Depends,' the wicked queen replied, 'on what you mean by trust. If you mean, am I sure I know what he'll do next, then yes. And that's all that matters, surely.'

The forest floor was carpeted with fallen leaves, which stuck like wallpaper to the portions of portable swamp they had on the soles of their shoes. It was also getting dark. Sis shivered, not entirely because of the slight chill in the evening air. 'This is probably a silly question,' she said, 'but do you know the way home?'

The queen shrugged. 'Depends on what you mean by know,' she replied. 'I can navigate pretty well by narrative patterns, but my geography's lousy.'

'Don't you ever give a straight answer to a simple question?'

'Depends what you mean by straight.'

Sis sighed wearily. Her legs were painfully tired and what she wanted more than anything else was a nice hot, foamy bath, but she was realistic enough to recognise that her chances of finding one in this context were roughly those of winning the lottery without actually buying a ticket. So, as much to take her mind off her poor feet as from any desire for knowledge, she asked the queen what she meant by navigating by narrative patterns.

'Easy,' the queen replied. 'As I said, in this neck of the woods, things – adventures, that kind of stuff – happen so reliably and regularly that you can navigate by them. Or at least,' she added wistfully, 'you could if the system was working. For example, by now we should have run into one crooked old man handing out magic wishing-pennies, three old crones gathering firewood who'd have told us what comes next in the story, at least two lots of highway robbers and a unicorn. So if we'd wanted to give directions to someone following us, we'd have said something like *straight on past the old man, at the third crone turn left till you come to the second bandits, then follow your nose till you reach the unicorn, then sharp right and you can't miss it.* The joy of it is,' she added, 'you can tell the time as well as work out where you are. You know, if that's the lion with a thorn in its paw, it's got to be 12.07.'

Sis shivered. 'Lion?' she asked apprehensively.

The queen smiled. 'Not in this part of the forest. Just wolves.'

'Wolves,' Sis repeated; as if on cue, the air was torn by a long, faraway howl. Sis squeaked and hopped up in the air.

'Relax,' the wicked queen told her. 'No wolves in this part of the story.'

Sis nipped smartly in front of the queen, then turned and pointed. 'What's that, then?' she asked. 'A copy-editing mistake? Lousy spelling?'

Sure enough, half hidden behind a tree some fifty yards away stood a large, slate-grey wolf, with small red eyes and a collection of teeth worth a five-figure sum to a tooth fairy. The queen gave it an unconcerned glance and nodded slightly. 'It's all right,' she whispered to Sis as the wolf nodded back, 'one of ours.'

'Really?' Sis muttered nervously. 'How can you tell?'

'I'll show you an easy test.' She held out her hands. 'Count those,' she said.

'Two.'

'That's how you know it's one of ours.'

Sis nodded. Logical. Depends on what you mean by logic. 'So what do we do now? Go back to the palace and wait, like he said?'

'Not on your life,' the queen replied, unhooking a bramble from her sleeve. 'That's the last thing we want to do.'

'Oh?'

'Believe me.'

'And why's that? No, let me guess. Narrative patterns.'

The queen half nodded her head. 'Narrative patterns have got something to do with it, admittedly. Mostly, though, it's because by now the whole palace'll be twelve feet deep in soapsuds. Or had you forgotten?'

Sis bit her lip. 'All right,' she conceded. 'But what are you going to do about that? Does this mean we're on our way to whatever passes for an estate agent in these parts to look for somewhere else for you to live?'

The wicked queen shook her head. 'Of course not,' she replied. 'As soon as the system's back on line I'll be able to deal with that sorcerer's apprentice thing and that'll be that, except for a few tidemarks in the curtains. Life goes on, you know, even in make-believe.'

'So what *are* we going to do?' Sis demanded. 'Just wander round in circles in this horrid wood until we bump into a wolf that isn't one of ours? I thought taking the bucket to your accountant was meant to *solve* something.'

'That remains to be seen,' the wicked queen replied absently. 'The trouble with you is, you're all linear.'

'Uh?' Sis scowled. 'Is that an insult or a compliment?'

'As in linear as two short planks,' the queen explained. 'You think in straight lines, instead of graceful curves. That's not going to get you very far, I'm afraid.'

'Huh.' Sis pouted. 'I'd rather be linear as two short planks than curved as a hatter.'

They had reached a small clearing, and for the first time in what seemed like ages, Sis could see a patch of blue sky between the branches of the trees. 'Where's this?' she asked. 'Don't tell me, it's somewhere narrative.'

The queen nodded. 'You're getting the hang of this,' she replied. 'If I've got my bearings right, this is a brief but significant adventure which ought to bring us out on the main narrative drag. Sort of a short-cut.' She peered round, obviously looking for something. 'Which with any luck'll save us at least two unnecessary plot developments and a couple of setbacks. Tell me if you spot anything that looks like a humble cottage, will you?'

Sis was about to say that she'd be hard put to it to miss something like that when she realised that she was staring at a small, picturesque house at the far end of the clearing. Ludicrous to say that it hadn't been there a moment ago, because unless it was built on the back of a Howard Hughes among tortoises, it didn't look capable of scurrying about the place. She just hadn't noticed it, that was all.

'You mean like that one?' she said.

'Just the ticket,' the queen replied cheerfully. 'Now then, let's just hope this works.'

Immediately, Sis felt hairs on the back of her neck standing to attention. 'What if it doesn't?' she asked.

'We get eaten. Come on, don't dawdle.'

When they reached the cottage the queen knocked at the white-painted front door, counted out loud up to twenty, pushed the door and went in. Apparently, nobody in this neighbourhood locked their doors; possibly, Sis speculated, for the same reason that spiders don't lock their webs. As soon as her eyes had become accustomed to the light, she looked round.

'Oh no,' she said, backing away. 'Don't say we're where I think we are.'

Three chairs: one big, one middling, one small. On the table, three wooden bowls (ditto), three wooden spoons (ditto), three mugs (ditto).

'Upstairs,' Sis whispered. 'Three beds?'

'Large, medium and small,' the queen confirmed. 'We're in luck.'

'Yes, but what sort? It comes in two kinds, remember. In luck up to our necks is the way I'd describe it.'

'Don't be such a misery,' the queen replied. 'My old master the sorcerer used to say that a problem's nothing but an opportunity wearing a funny hat, and inside every disaster there's a triumph struggling to get out.' She smiled nostalgically. 'Full of stuff like that, he was.'

'Quite,' Sis replied darkly. 'Full of it sounds about right. You never did say what happened to him in the end.'

'You don't want to know,' the wicked queen said quickly. 'Come on, this is your chance to be a star.'

'*My* chance? Now wait a minute . . .'

Before Sis could protest any further, the wicked queen

grabbed her by the shoulder and marched her up the stairs. Three beds, as anticipated; one large, one medium, one small with obligatory pink bedspread and matching pillowcase. On top of the pillow lay a rather dog-eared, obviously much-loved button-nosed humanoid doll. It was dressed in a jacket with tiny lapels, tight straight trousers and sunglasses, and its black hair was slicked into a kiss-curl. *Ah*, thought Sis, who'd seen something similar on the television, *a teddy*.

'What are we doing here?' she demanded.

'Gatecrashing,' the queen replied, kicking off her leaf-encrusted shoes and flopping on the medium-sized bed. 'What else would we be doing in the Three Bears' cottage?'

'Yes,' Sis insisted, 'but why? And if you say narrative patterns, I'll make you eat the curtains.'

'You and whose army?' the queen yawned. 'Sorry, but a better example of narrative patterns would be hard to come by. Just think for a moment, instead of whining. In this –' She waved her hands in the air. 'Well, for want of a better word we'd better call it a dimension, though of course it's nothing of the sort. In this dimension, things don't just happen in the messy, haphazard way you seem to favour where you come from. Things here happen because there's a slot or a hole precisely their size and shape in a story. And it's a well-known fact that once you've skimmed off all the tinsel and water-cress, there's only about twenty stories; all the rest are just the same ones with added bells and whistles. Accordingly, everything here has got to fit into its proper story, or else there's chaos. That's why you and your repulsive little siblings crashed my beautiful system; there wasn't a slot for you, but you came in anyway and that blew a huge hole right through the middle of everything. So, first things first, until we can find a way of getting rid of you, we've got to try a little damage limitation and find a slot to put you in. So; I thought about what you've done here so far – barge in uninvited, treat the place like you own it, break things, spoil things; in addition to which you're a cute little girl –'

'*Hey!*'

'– So the choice was obvious. You're a Goldilocks. An absolute natural for the part. What else could you possibly be? And here we are.'

'I am *not* cute.'

'I wouldn't bet the rent on that if I were you,' the queen replied with a nasty grin. 'If they weren't all down at the moment, I'd suggest you look in a mirror. You wouldn't know yourself.'

Sis clutched instinctively at her face. It felt the same, more or less; but since she'd never spent hours lying in the dark feeling her own face, that didn't mean a lot. But (now that the queen mentioned it) she could feel an unaccustomed tugging at the roots of her hair on either side of her head; she felt gingerly and discovered –

'Plaits,' she groaned.

'With big pink bows,' the queen confirmed maliciously. 'You've also got big blue eyes, freckles and a great big golden curl right in the middle of your forehead.'

'Yetch!'

'You should worry. You're not the one that's got to look at you. Honestly, if this was a Disney film you' be chucked out on your ear for excessive cuteness. Not to mention blondness with intent to nauseate.'

'Shut up.'

'But there,' the queen sighed, turning her head away in an ostentatious manner, 'it's very bad manners to mock the afflicted, so I won't say another word.' She stretched her arms and legs like a cat, then sat up on the bed and put her shoes back on. 'That's enough here,' she said. 'We'd better go down and start smashing furniture.'

It helped Sis to be able to take her feelings out on a dear little chair, and by the time she'd finished with it there wasn't enough of it left to provide a packed lunch for an infant woodworm. The cold porridge didn't interest her nearly as much, even though it was a long time since she'd had anything to eat. She forced down a couple of spoonfuls just to stop the queen nagging at her, spilt milk all over the tablecloth, and trod on a little wickerwork donkey she found on the mantel-piece. The last, the queen pointed out, wasn't exactly canonically correct, but Sis maintained that it was essential to her reading of the part. Then they sat down on the two surviving chairs to wait.

They were deep in a discussion of the state of Mummy and Daddy Bear's marriage – separate beds, the queen felt, was a sure sign that the whole thing was on the rocks – when the door opened. Which of them was more surprised, Sis and the wicked queen or the three little pigs, it'd be hard to say.

For what little evidential weight it carries however, it was Julian who spoke first.

'Oh, for pity's sake,' he complained. 'It was bad enough when he was a handsome bloody prince. The bimbo outfit's going beyond a joke.'

The wicked queen opened her mouth to say something but decided against it. Sloppy thinking, she chided herself. A failure to think things through to their logical conclusion before taking action. Of course, what with the system being down and everything being in a state of narrative flux, the last people you'd expect to see in the Three Bears' cottage would be the Three Bears. And, come to that, the deceased system's fatally Boolean logic, unable to locate the Three Bears, would automatically revert to the nearest available match, namely the Three Little Pigs. Spiffing.

'Told you,' Desmond muttered, shifting the pad of his crutch under his arm. 'Told you it was pointless running away to this godforsaken backwater and trying to hide from the bugger. I say we do Plan B and that'll be an end to it.'

Julian stared at him. 'Plan B? That's a bit drastic, isn't it?'

'No. Let's do it now, get it over and done with.'

The wicked queen cleared her throat. 'Excuse me,' she said.

'Shut it, you,' Desmond snarled. 'Oh, you think you're so damned smart, don't you, with your shape-shifting and your disguises and everything. Well, we're going to show you this time all right. This time, it's our turn. Eugene, where's that remote?'

Julian tried to protest, but Desmond and Eugene scowled him down. 'Des's right,' Eugene said, handing his brother a slim black plastic box with red buttons on the top. 'Let's end it right now. Okay, so the house goes up in smoke, us too, but at least we'll take this bastard with us. At least he won't be able to terrorise other pigs the way he's terrorised us.'

'Excuse me,' the wicked queen repeated urgently. She could feel sweat in the palms of her hands; a sure sign that (as her old mentor the sorcerer would have put it) a bloody great big opportunity was descending on her from a great height. 'I think there's been some sort of mistake.'

Desmond only laughed. 'Too right, wolf,' he said grimly. 'And you just made it. Eugene, stand in front of the door, just in case he tries to make a run for it.'

The wicked queen recognised the key word; a short, un-ostentatious little grouping of letters, easily overlooked in the rough and tumble of dialogue: *he*. 'Sorry to interrupt,' she said sweetly, 'but I'm not a he, I'm a she. So's she. Two shes.'

'Nuts,' replied Eugene contemptuously. 'You're a wolf. In she's clothing,' he added ineluctably. 'Prepare to die, sucker.'

'Now wait a minute.' Sis stood up, missed her footing, wobbled and grabbed the table for support. 'I don't know who you are or what you're planning to do, but it's nothing to do with me, okay? I'm just an innocent civilian. I don't even belong here. You want to do something horrible to *her*, be my guest, but . . .'

Julian was listening; the other two weren't. Desmond in particular was devoting his entire attention to the buttons on the remote control in his left trotter. 'Armed and ready,' he said harshly. 'Plan B laid in and ready to roll. It's a far, far better thing . . .'

The rest of his apt if predictable quotation was drowned out by the noise of the explosion.

CHAPTER FIVE

'**A**gain.'

The face in the mirror flickered, resetting itself to the position it had been in a few seconds earlier. 'You, O Snow White, are the fairest of them all.'

'I thought that's what you said,' Snow White replied. 'Still,' she went on, 'it does no harm to check these things. Who the hell are *you*, anyway?'

'Bad command or file name,' replied her reflection austerely. 'Please retry.'

Although her reflection stayed poker-faced, Snow White herself grinned like a thirsty dog. 'Dear God,' she said joyfully, 'don't say I've managed to hack into that bitch's system. That'd be *cool*. You there, identify yourself.'

A minuscule flicker of disapproval moved a muscle in the reflection's jaw. 'Currently running Mirrors 3.1, incorporating Magic for Mirrors and SpellPerfect 7. Warning: this program is protected by international copyright. Any unauthorised reproduction or transmission of this program may render you liable—'

'Enough.' Snow White took a deep breath and let it go gradually. Never in her wildest dreams had she ever imagined herself in a position like this; the Wicked Queen's legendary Mirrors system literally at her fingertips, enabling her to control the whole virtual-make-believe construct that made up the world she lived in. *Wow*, she said gleefully to herself, *cyberpunk comes to Avenging Dragon Cottage*. With a grin on one of her faces and a po-faced stare on the other, she leaned back in her chair and wondered what she was going to do next.

Where to start? Ask a silly question.

'Right, you,' she said briskly. 'First, I want you to open me a numbered account at the Credit Suisse and pay in – let me see, deutschmarks or US dollars? Let's make it dollars for now. Fifty million dollars, please. Next—'

'Bad command or file name. Please retry.'

Anger creased Snow White's lovely (fairest of them all) face. 'You what?' she snapped. 'Don't mess with me, dreamboat. One: fifty million dollars. Two—'

'Bad command—'

'Shut your face.' Or should that be, *shut my mouth?* Irrelevant. All that mattered was that she was in command here and the mirror had to do what she told it to. 'Why can't I have the money?'

'Requested operation out of character. Path not found. Retry or Cancel?'

'Bugger.' Hadn't thought of that. In order to be able to use the wicked queen's system, she had to become the wicked queen . . . Interesting dilemma for someone who really only wanted the money, rather than the power, the glory, and her head on the stamps. And if you're going to be a wicked queen, having your head on the stamps isn't necessarily a good idea. The citizens end up not knowing which side to spit on.

Not that that, in itself, was enough to deter her; but there was something to think about here, clearly. 'Pause,' she said;

the image of herself in the mirror faded and was replaced by the usual eye-bending mobile geometric shapes. She stood up and walked to the window.

Below, in the garden, Mr Miroku, Mr Hiroshige and Mr Nikko were standing watching young Mr Akira weeding the turnip patch. Snow White frowned; there was something about the set-up here that she couldn't fathom, and it bothered her. If only she could remember how she'd come to be here in the first place . . .

'That's right.' Mr Miroku's voice, carried up to her by the breeze. 'Now you've got it. *Be* the hoe.'

If I'm going to be a wicked queen, Snow White mused, stands to reason I'll need some trusty henchmen. Fat lot of good it'd be being a queen and having to do my own henching. Would these guys be up to the job? They prance around in armour with whacking great swords, so presumably they're qualified in that respect. It's just that they're so . . .

She shook her head, sat down at the dressing table and gave the mirror a tap with her fingertip. The reflection reappeared.

'Mirror,' she commanded, 'who am I?'

'You, Snow White, are the fairest of them all.'

Snow White nodded. 'Right,' she said. 'Now we've sorted that out. Am I right in thinking that I'm now the wicked queen?'

'Identity confirmed. Access available to all systems.'

Yes!

'In that case,' Snow White continued, 'what's become of the bi— I mean, who's Snow White?'

'Bad command or file—'

'All right, yes.' Snow White looked up and rested the point of her chin on the knuckle of her forefinger. She didn't need to ask the question. She knew. 'Never mind all that,' she said. 'How do we get this show on the road?'

The reflection didn't lighten up exactly; it still glowered at her like the proprietor of an expensive restaurant from whom she'd just ordered egg and chips. But there was a slight thaw, as if the mirror was acknowledging that there was now a possibility that they'd be able to work together.

'Running DOS.'

'Whatever.'

– Because if Mirrors was now back on line, by rights it ought to reconfigure all the buggered-up settings. Snow White would once again have seven dwarves, instead of seven Japanese master swordsmen. Since she was no longer Snow White but the wicked queen, that didn't affect her. Whoever was now Snow White would be the one with the dwarves. Find the dwarves and you'll find Snow White. Provided, of course, that she felt the need; after all, why bother? True, it would be in character for her in her new persona to send her seven henchmen to bring her Snow White's head on a sharpened pole, but that wasn't her personal style. So long as the kid didn't mess with her, she had no quarrel with a fellow professional. This forest's big enough for the both of us.

'Mirror,' she commanded, 'locate Snow White.'

'Ba—'

'Mirror,' she warned.

'Locating.'

Ah. That was good. She'd got the mirror frightened of her. Essential first step in the control of technology is the establishing of a state of permanent mutual distrust.

'Snow White currently located at Three Bears Cottage, The Forest.'

'Thank you. Show me the location of Three Bears Cottage.'

The usual clicks and crinkles; then the reflection more or less leered at her.

'Three Bears Cottage no longer exists.'

'Who's been sitting in my chair?' asked Baby Bear, holding up a fragment of chairleg.

'You know,' replied her father, poking around in the

rubble, 'right now, I figure that's the least of our problems.'

Baby Bear nodded, her snout wet with tears. Of the quaint, cosy little cottage in the woods, all that was left was a heap of scattered masonry and a few charred timbers. It did rather put a squashed chair and molested porridge into perspective.

'Who the hell do you think it was?' Mummy Bear asked, retrieving a miraculously unbroken sauceboat from under a fallen roof timber. Daddy Bear shrugged.

'All sorts of people it could have been,' he said. 'Pixie Liberation Organisation. Gnome Rule activists. Does it matter which particular bunch of nutters? Come on, let's see if we can salvage enough linen to rig up a tent.'

Mummy Bear sighed. 'You read about it,' she said, 'but somehow you never think it'll happen to you. Oh God, my mum's teapot.' She held up a chipped handle, sniffed and dropped it. 'Never mind,' she said bravely. 'It's all just things. Nobody got hurt, that's all that matters.'

The three bears poked about a little more. 'Good Lord,' cried Daddy Bear, brandishing a blue cup with a rather wobbly picture painted on it. 'My coronation mug. That's something, I suppose. My Uncle Paddy gave me that when I was just a cub.'

Mummy Bear clicked her tongue. 'Might have guessed that'd come through unscathed,' she replied. 'Fifteen years I've been trying to get that thing to meet with an accident. It must be made of cast iron.'

'Oh.' Daddy Bear looked hurt. 'You mean you don't like it?'

'Never could stand the horrid thing, since you ask. But you never did, so I never said anything.'

Daddy Bear shrugged. 'Well,' he said, 'at least we've got one cup left. There's poor starving bears in Antarctica who've got absolutely nothing at all.'

'Tell 'em they can have your coronation mug, then. They're welcome to it.'

Behind a clump of bushes at the extreme edge of the

clearing, the three pigs watched the forlorn search and tried not to feel as guilty as hell.

'Could have sworn it was our house,' Eugene whispered.

'Shut up and keep still,' Julian replied, adjusting a knot on the makeshift sling he was attaching to Eugene's arm. 'I'll admit I was fooled too, though,' he conceded. 'That's the trouble with these rotten little design-and-build jobs, they all look the same. Anyway, we know what it's like to have a house blown down around our ears, and it's not the end of the world. Just for once, it wasn't us after all. Be grateful for that.'

'And we've got rid of the wolf,' Desmond added brightly. 'Copped the full force of it, he did. No way he could have survived that.'

'Yes, that's true,' Julian said. 'Looks like Old Mr Silver Lining's finally been flushed out into the open. Hey, lads, if that's *not* our house, has anybody got any ideas where our house has got to?'

Eugene shrugged. 'It's a quaint little cottage in a clearing in the heart of the forest,' he replied. 'That narrows it down to about fifty thousand possibles.'

'Bit of a turn-up, though,' Desmond continued. 'I mean, it being us who wrecks the cottage. Role reversal, I think the technical term is.'

'Maybe it's something to do with all the weird stuff that's been happening lately,' Julian suggested. 'You know, like that business in the hospital with Humpty Dumpty and Jack and Jill. Like lots of things are getting stood on their heads all of a sudden.'

His brothers looked at him.

'Does that mean we're going to have to go around blowing down people's houses?' Desmond asked plaintively. 'Because I don't think I've got the puff for that.'

Julian thought for a moment. 'I don't know,' he said. 'Might be. I'm not all that sure how these things actually work. Adds a new terror to self-defence if it does.'

'Huh?'

'If someone attacks you and if you kill them, you've got to take their place,' Julian explained. 'If that's the way it's going to work from now on, I think I'd rather hold still and be eaten. Which,' he added thoughtfully, 'is the same thing in reverse, surely, since you are what you eat, though you don't necessarily eat what you are. Am I burbling?'

'Yes.'

'Sorry, I'll stop. There,' he said, tightening the last knot on the sling, 'how does that feel?'

'Bloody awful.'

'Oh well, never mind. It'll have to do for now. I suggest we wait here till nightfall and then try to find our house.'

The other pigs shrugged. 'Might as well,' Eugene muttered. 'Nothing to hurry home for, after all.'

'What's that supposed to mean?' Julian enquired.

Eugene frowned thoughtfully. 'It's just occurred to me,' he said. 'If we really have managed to snuff the wolf, what are we going to find to do with ourselves from now on? For as long as I can remember, we've been building houses for that creep to blow down. If he's gone—'

Julian stared at him. 'You're not saying you *miss* the bugger, surely.'

'I don't know, do I? I'm just asking a simple question, that's all. Personally, I reckon I'm too old and set in my ways for a radical career change.'

'He's got a point,' Desmond agreed.

'So has an almost bald hedgehog,' Julian replied. 'What of it? Nothing to say we can't carry on building houses just because there's no one to blow them down any more. Think of it. Building houses that are still there in the morning. I'd have thought you'd all have liked the idea.'

'It has a certain novel charm,' Eugene conceded. 'Though whether it'll catch on remains to be seen. There's such a thing as gimmickry for gimmickry's sake, you know.'

Julian made a vulgar noise. 'Don't you see,' he said angrily, 'we've done it. What we've been trying to do since I can't remember when. What we're *for*. We've killed the big bad wolf, and now we're free to go. Happy ever after. That's how it works, isn't it, in stories? Well, isn't it?'

The other two looked at him as if he'd just fallen out of the sky at their feet. 'What's he talking about?' Desmond whispered. 'I don't like it when he starts talking all funny.'

Eugene shrugged. 'Comes of being the youngest, I suppose,' he replied. 'You know how it is with litters, the run— I mean, the youngest isn't really even supposed to survive. Makes 'em a bit weird in the head sometimes.'

'Hey!' Julian glowered at his brothers, who smiled sweetly back at him in a manner that suggested that the only reason they weren't trussing him up in a straitjacket was that they didn't have a straitjacket. 'Do you mind,' he went on. 'I'm still here, you know.'

'Of course you are,' Eugene replied. 'Anything you say. Or maybe,' he added in an audible aside, 'it's just a bang on the head or something. That can turn people funny, and sometimes they get better.'

Julian thought for a moment. His mind was full of strange things, none of which had been there a while ago, though it felt as if they'd always been there. It was like going up in the loft for the first time when you've been in the house five years, and finding a whole lot of cardboard boxes left behind by the previous owners. In this case, Julian got the impression that the cardboard boxes had things like GELIGNITE – HANDLE WITH CARE stencilled on the side, which didn't exactly help.

Somehow he'd suddenly become aware of the fact that he was in a story. What a story was, or what being in one actually meant in practical terms, he wasn't exactly sure; there were little bits of information stuck to the insides of his mind like the shreds of paper that come off on your windscreen after you've pulled off a sticky-backed car park ticket, enough to make him realise that there was something important here to know, but not enough to make sense of any of it. It was as if he'd known the story once, but forgotten ninety per cent of it; fairly significant bits, like the beginning, the middle and the end. If he'd had any say in the matter he'd have deleted them at once, but that was out of the question. It was a bit like having someone tell you who the murderer is about halfway through a detective story you're really enjoying; you wish you didn't know, but you do and that's that.

And then he thought: *detective story? What's a detective story?* And it was almost as if he could see fragments of the memory rushing past him and gurgling down the plughole of oblivion, winking maliciously at him as they vanished.

This is silly, he muttered to himself. Get a grip. Pretend it isn't happening. Otherwise, at the very least, these two are going to have you put away in the bewildered pigs' home. At worst, that might possibly be the right thing to do.

'Sorry,' he said, 'just thinking aloud, don't mind me. All I was trying to say was,' he went on, sneaking a surreptitious glance over his shoulder to check that the way was clear if he had to make a run for it, 'why don't we carry on building houses, for now, and wait and see what happens? I mean, something's bound to turn up. Something always does.'

Eugene and Desmond looked at each other warily. 'I think he's trying to say he isn't crazy,' Eugene said. 'I'm not sure I believe him.'

'Nor me,' Desmond replied. 'I reckon we ought to tie him up in a sack and have him seen to. You know, take him some-where where they know about these things. A fair, or whatever.'

'A fair?'

Desmond nodded. 'Heard about it once. There's people at fairs who know all about pigs. They can even tell you how much you weigh just by looking at you. They'd know what to do, I reckon.'

Still smiling, they advanced, and Julian started to back away. At precisely the moment when Eugene, having assured him that it was all for his own good, made a grab for his hind legs and Desmond, explaining that they were only trying to help, tried to knock him silly with a chunk of wood, he darted between them, dodged their flailing trotters, and ran for it.

The accountant sat down and stared into the bucket.

He'd taken all the precautions he could to make sure he wouldn't be disturbed (and caution comes as naturally to an accountant as fleas to a rabbit); he could take his time, do the job properly, as it ought to be done. Opportunities like this, he knew, only come once in a professional lifetime, and it would be sheer folly to waste this one by rushing it.

He closed his eyes, took a deep breath and let it out again, but it didn't work; he was still tense and jumpy, not at all the right frame of mind for tackling such delicate work. He needed something calming, familiar, soothing, soporific. He opened his eyes again, reached up to a nearby shelf, and pulled down a volume of tax statutes at random.

'One of the characteristic features of Schedule D case III,' he read aloud, allowing his tongue to caress each solid syllable, 'is the provision under sections fifty-two, fifty-three and seventy-four of the Taxes Act 1970 for the deduction and collection of tax at source from the payer. The payee will receive a net sum from which tax has been deducted at source . . .' Better; much better. He could feel a sort of benign numbness creeping upwards from the junction of his neck and shoulders, a sort of delightful narcosis; now he'd have to be careful he didn't drift into that unique kind of half-sleep that anybody who has much to do with tax legislation spends so much of his life in, somewhere in the middle of a triangle formed by boredom, sleep and death. He needed to be relaxed, but not that relaxed.

When he felt the moment was right he closed the book carefully and laid it down slowly on his desk, taking great care to line the edges of its cover square with the desk-top; then, with the slow deliberation of an hourly paid sleepwalker, he took another deep breath, exhaled and leaned over the bucket.

'Mirror,' he said.

His own face, a Spitting Image caricature of a living prune, blinked back at him, stifled a yawn, twitched its nose and mumbled 'Running DOS' in a soft, bleating voice before closing its eyes and sliding forward an inch or so on its neck. For a moment, the accountant felt a deep-seated sense of confusion, as if acknowledging that the face in the water was rather more like him than he was himself. Then, as the reflection began to snore, he tightened the muscles of his throat and produced a tiny dry cough. The reflection opened its eyes again, looked up at him as if to ask why he'd thought it necessary to spoil such a beautiful dream (*I know that dream*, the accountant thought sympathetically, *it's the one about offsetting the costs of a sale of associated property against gains incurred on a series of linked sales of business assets spanning two consecutive fiscal years*) and mumbled, 'Please wait.'

A tiny spurt of excitement flared inside the accountant's brain, but he called on a lifetime of professional training and suppressed it, in a way that only an accountant could. The effects of excitement and emotion are about as desirable among members of the profession as a hungry rat in a mortuary, and the majority of their long, gruelling apprenticeship is spent learning how to prevent them. It's often said that the only way to get an animated reaction out of an accountant is to kill him and attach two electrodes to his feet; what's less well known is that when accountants say it, they do so with pride.

He waited as he'd been told, and just as he was about to nod off himself, he noticed a minute degree of movement on the surface of the water; tiny ripples, as if a little splinter of gravel had fallen in the bucket, except that these ripples started at the circumference and moved inwards, instead of the other way round. The circles gradually closed up, until the rings dwindled into a dot in the very centre of the meniscus, where they stopped, formed themselves into a minuscule water-spout, hung in the air for about two and a half seconds and then slowly subsided, sending another series of ripples back across the surface, this time proceeding in the conventional manner. When this process had repeated four or five times, the accountant nodded, muttered *screen-saver* under his breath, put the tips of his fingers together and settled down to wait.

'Ready.'

The accountant jumped; the words had summoned him back from the place where the good accountants go before they die, and for a moment he couldn't quite remember where or who he was. Then he caught sight of the reflection and sat up a little straighter in his chair.

'Mirror,' he said.

The reflection looked at him, expressionless.

'Mirror,' he repeated, 'compile a database of all financial records relating to the following. One: Ali Baba. Two: Aladdin. Three: Babes in the Wood, The. Four –'

It was a long list; but eventually he reached the end, double-checked and then triple-checked against the hand-written ledger entries, cross-checked the list against another list he kept locked in the top drawer of his desk, checked once again for luck and one last time because he didn't believe in luck, and then whispered the words 'Delete files.' There was another slow outbreak of ripples, a gurgle and a faint *plop*, and then the reflection sighed, bobbled its head sleepily and murmured 'Done.' The accountant asked for confirmation, received it, and allowed himself the luxury of stretching his arms and legs until the joints creaked. Then, with a smile of modest satisfaction at having removed every last trace of his most valued clients' affairs from the records of the Revenue Service, he leaned forward over his desk, cradled his head on his elbows and went to sleep.

The reflection stayed where it was. It didn't appear to mind; staring vacantly into space seemed to suit it very well. It was just about to dissolve into the pretty ripples effect when something disturbed the surface of the water. The face changed; it was no longer the reflection of the accountant, but a cute little face, a bright pink, shiny, painted face, with two black dots for eyes, a daubed line for a mouth and a length of wooden dowel radiused at the end for a nose. As the head swivelled from side to side, its movement was awkward and somehow mechanical. It wore an Alpine hat with a feather stuck in it.

'Help,' it said.

Nothing happened. The face looked round with that same artificial movement.

'Help,' it repeated.

The accountant twitched and grunted in his sleep. In his dream, someone was telling him to do something he'd prefer not to, and when he asked how much whoever it was had in mind for a suitable fee, there was no answer. He grunted again and his lips moved.

'Help,' said the face a third time; and the accountant made a snarling noise and sat up, eyes still closed, still fast asleep.

'Please wait,' he grumbled.

The wooden face's range of expressions was necessarily limited, but he was able to register joy by waggling his head from side to side. 'Oh come on,' it said. 'I haven't got long, and those two loonies could come back any minute. *Please* hurry. *Please.*'

But compassion's a hard enough commodity to get out of an accountant when he's awake, let alone asleep; in terms of difficulty of extraction, somewhere between his teeth and his money. No dice.

'You've got to help me, really,' implored the face. 'My name is Carl Wilson and I don't belong here, really I don't. I'm stuck actually *inside* this wooden puppet thing in this horrible laboratory, like something out of a bad horror flick, they've been connecting me up to the mains and electrocuting me, and all I did was try to hack into a computer game for free.

Not even *Microsoft* do that to people. And really it was my sister's idea, not mine, so if anyone should be in here . . .'

'For Help topics,' the accountant said in a flat, droning voice, 'select the appropriate mirror or press *f*1.'

'Oh right,' wailed the little wooden face, expressing exasperation and despair by waggling its head from side to side in the other direction. 'You tell me how, with no mouse and no keyboard.'

'For Help topics, select the appropriate mirror or press *f*1.'

'Oh *no*, I haven't got time for this,' the little wooden face snarled. 'No, wait, all right, let's try something. Execute voice prompt.'

The accountant didn't move. 'To execute voice prompt, select the appropriate mirror or press *f*9.'

The face waggled so furiously that its feather nearly came loose. 'Yes, but *how*?' it demanded. 'Oh go on, give me a break.'

'Bad command or file name.'

'All right, all right.' The face leaned over sharply to the right to convey Concentration.

'Let's start with the obvious. Select appropriate mirror for voice prompt.'

The accountant's lip curled half a millimetre before it replied. 'Error,' it intoned. 'Path not found.'

'You lousy—' The face twisted round through 180 degrees, a manoeuvre that would have snapped a human spine; then it swivelled back. 'They're coming,' it hissed. 'The Baron and his creepy friend. Come on, you've got to . . . Oh, exit Mirrors.'

The face disappeared with a *plop!* and the surface of the water slowly filled with more ripples; first one way, then the other, like the tides of the oceans of a tiny flat planet. The expression on the accountant's face softened into something approximating to a smile, while a tiny spider, dangling from the end of a long gossamer thread, dropped into his ear.

*

More so than the frog, the human itched.

Also, Fang muttered to himself as he stared balefully at his reflection in a puddle, it looked silly. There were of course times, he admitted to himself, when any self-respecting animal found it useful to stand on his hind legs; pushing open a door, or reaching things dangling from the lower branches of trees. But a species that spent its entire life reared up on its back paws was a gimmick, pure and simple, as contemptible as the circular teabag – some marketing executive somewhere deciding that since it hadn't been done yet, it was probably worth a try. It'd be bad enough if he were some naturally dim-witted, demoralised kind of creature, such as a bird or a fish; but for a wolf of all creatures to be violently and unexpectedly sewn up in a monkey suit and condemned to waddle about on half the proper number of feet was nearly unbearable. Although he knew it wouldn't work, he had a terrible desire to jump in the puddle and roll around just to see if the Human would wash off.

So: priority number one, get rid of it. And to do that, all he had to do was find a witch.

Hah!

It was typical, Fang reflected as he trudged sullenly and bipedally along the dusty road. Under normal circumstances, you could hardly move for witches in this neck of the woods. Shake any tree, and a witch'd fall out. Spit, and a witch'd get wet. It was that easy. Now, when he was actively looking for one, were there any? Were there hell as like.

Then, as he turned a bend in the road and found himself facing a spindly, rather run-down-looking tower that slouched among the trees like a spaceship playing at being an ostrich, the vestiges of his lupine sense of smell detected a faint but unmistakable flavour on the breeze. A rich, musty, unpleasant smell; stale cooking fat, unwashed human, iodine, cat-pee, onions and something from the cheaper end of the Giorgio Armani range of fragrances, all mixed together to produce something that, in concentrated form, was eminently suitable for use in trench warfare. Witch.

Fang breathed in deeply, then sneezed. Another definite black mark against human bodies was their truly awful sense of smell; to get any useful data at all, you had to breathe in enough air to float a large balloon.

The witch was up in the tower; and the tower, needless to say, was locked. Craning his neck, Fang looked up to see if there were any accessible windows, conveniently placed drainpipes, fire escapes, even (let's not forget the blindingly obvious) an open door, anything he could use to effect an entrance. Nothing doing; the lowest window was five storeys up and the heavy oak shutters were resolutely shut. Ah well, Fang told himself, there's plenty of witches but I've only got one neck. He shook his head sadly and was about to trudge on when something fell down the side of his tower and hung level with his armpits. A rope.

Now that was more like it; except, why would any sane witch throw down a rope when she could quite easily come down and unlock the front door? Laziness? A macabre sense of humour? He glanced up and saw that the rope was hanging from the very topmost window; it would be a dreadfully vertiginous ascent, and he wasn't absolutely sure that as a human he knew how to climb ropes. Also, there was something peculiar about the rope itself. Instead of the customary coarse hemp fibres it appeared to be made out of some kind of very fine sandy-yellow thread. Or hair, even.

A rope made out of hair; well, witches are a funny lot, not to mention not terribly well off as a rule. It was also worth bearing in mind that anybody who lived in a small chamber at the top of a very tall, locked tower might well have nothing better to do all day than weave hairdresser's salvage into a long, blonde rope. That would explain the composition of the rope itself, but not why it had suddenly descended right under his nose. Another factor worth considering was the old Wolfpack adage that if your enemy offers you a means of transportation, leave it well alone because it's bound to be a trap.

Prudence dictated that until he saw evidence to the contrary he should assume that any non-wolf he met was more likely to be an enemy than a friend. Just out of curiosity, however, he reached out a paw and gave the rope a sedate little tug.

'Ouch!'

The voice came from far up above, and it didn't sound in the least like any witch that Fang had encountered before. It was young and girlish and silvery, so presumably its owner was likely to be about as much use to him as a cardboard car-jack. What he wanted was something ancient and wrinkled and extra crone, not some long-haired kid.

'Sorry,' he yelled back.

The rope started to climb the wall; obviously its owner didn't trust him not to yank it again. He looked up to watch it go, and was thus in an ideal position to observe the contents of the porcelain vessel that a pair of unseen hands tipped out of the window as they sailed down and landed on his head. Wet, and didn't smell very nice. Eau de toilette, in a sense. He closed his eyes, swore, and started to walk away. An apple missed him by inches as he turned, closely followed by an old shoe and a coffee-mug. Taken together, they appeared to constitute a hint.

'All right, already,' he shouted, as the hint was reinforced by a half-brick and a week-old portion of macaroni cheese, 'I'm going . . .'

'*Help!*'

The second voice froze him in his tracks; fortunately, as it turned out, because whoever it was who threw the old saucepan that narrowly missed him in front had obviously included a nicely calculated degree of forward allowance in the throw, and if he'd still been moving he'd have been clobbered silly.

'*Help! Help!*'

Now that, Fang grinned to himself, sounds a bit more like it. A harsh, cracked, wheezy, gnarled old voice, not just extra crone but extra crone *plus*; the owner of that voice had to be a hundred and five if she was a day, and could easily be the Playmate of the Month from the current number of *Witch* Magazine. Ducking instinctively to avoid an egg so old it could easily have been laid by an archaeopteryx, he doubled back towards the base of the tower, where the overhang would afford him some degree of cover from the flying household ephemera, and he could formulate a plan of action.

'Sod off,' shrieked the first, silvery voice. 'Get out of it before I set the dogs on you.'

Of course, said Fang to himself, she isn't to know. That's all right then.

'I'm warning you. All right, then. Here, Buttercup, Popsy, Snowdrop! Kill!'

A yard or so to his left, the door creaked open and three large Rottweilers bounded out, ears back, tongues lolling. Fang let them get right up close and then, in his best parade-ground voice, barked out, 'Atten-*shun*!'

The dogs skidded to a halt, lifting divots with their out-stretched claws. By the time they came to rest, they were sitting up ramrod-straight, chests out, chins in, Oh-God-what've-we-done expressions engraved on their stupid canine faces. Fang counted to five under his breath and said, 'At ease,' whereupon the dogs snapped like lock-components into a triangular crouch.

'All right, as you were,' he murmured, and the Rottweilers sloped hurriedly off into the tower. Fang had plenty of time to slip in after them before the doors clanged shut.

'You there,' he grunted. 'Where's the witch?'

The nearest dog clicked back to attention, raised its offside front paw and pointed to a spiral staircase. Fang nodded, murmured, 'Carry on,' and bounded up the stair before any of the trio of feeble doggy minds had a chance to evaluate the recent exchange. Bred-in-the-bone instinct was one thing, but personally he wouldn't trust a dog called Snowdrop as far as he could sneeze it out of a blocked nostril.

Perhaps justifiably; somewhere near the top of the stairs, Silveryvoice was yelling, 'Buttercup! Popsy! What are you *doing* down there, you pathetic animals?' with such venom that, if he were a dog (even a dog called Snowdrop), he'd obey its commands without a moment's hesitation. Time, he decided, to get to the bottom of all this, find the witch and get out of here fast.

He turned a corner and found himself out in daylight again; and dead ahead of him, just turning away from the parapet, was the most beautiful girl in the world. Slim as a wand, with startlingly blue eyes, rosebud lips and golden hair that cascaded around her shoulders like the crystal waters of a mountain stream –

Instinctively, Fang threw himself sideways, lunging for the slight cover of the doorframe. If he'd had to rely on purely human reflexes, he'd never have made it; as it was, he was showered by chips of flying stone as a twenty-round burst from the girl's Uzi turned the frame and lintel of the doorway into gravel. Then there was a click, followed by a clatter as the discarded magazine hit the stone floor. Fang was up and out of the doorway before she had time to rack back the bolt, but he was still too slow. He could see her sweet face, and the snub barrel of the gun, behind the bowed shoulders of the ugly, wrinkled, hook-nosed, shit-scared old crone his tardiness had allowed her to use as a human shield.

'Back off, Fido, or Granny gets it,' the girl snarled. Then she lifted the gun and squinted down the barrel at him; he had a fleeting glimpse of a cornflower-blue eye along a runway of blued steel before his training and survival instinct sent him scampering back the way he'd just come.

Spiffing, he muttered to himself, as another fusillade of shots chiselled shrapnel out of the stonework inches from his head, *a hostage situation. One fuck-up, and it'll be the teddy-bears' picnic all over again*. He forced himself to stay calm. She had the hostage, the gun and the benefit of knowing the layout. Plus any other wee surprises she might have stockpiled up there, such as grenades. He, on the other hand . . .

. . . Had a matchbox.

Yes. Well. Put like that, it wasn't exactly mutually assured destruction. But a matchbox, under these circumstances, was at least a three hundred per cent improvement on nothing at all. He fumbled in his pocket, found the box and slid open the lid, praying as he did so that in his recent displays of acrobatics he hadn't contrived to squash its contents flat.

'Get lost,' hissed the elf.

'Shut up,' Fang reasoned, 'and listen. Up there, there's a fairytale princess with a machine gun. She's holding a witch hostage. I need your help.'

From inside the recesses of the box came an unpleasant snickering noise. 'I agree you need help,' said the elf, 'but since I don't have a degree in severe personality disorders, probably not mine. Now bog off and leave me alone.'

'I –' Fang's next few words were drowned by the ear-splitting roar of the Uzi, as its hail of lead sheared away another slice of the doorway. 'I'll make a deal,' he said. 'Do as I say and we're quits. You can·go. Free and clear. How about it?'

From inside the matchbox came a small, clear rude noise. Fang lost patience and knocked the box out over his open palm, somersaulting the elf into the fork between his index and middle fingers.

'Ouch,' screamed the elf, 'you're squashing me!'

'I know,' Fang replied, 'but not nearly as much as I want to. Now listen.'

While he was telling the elf what to do, another clatter on the stone floor informed him that the fairytale princess had slammed in a new clip and was ready to resume demolition. 'You got that?' he hissed; then, without waiting for a reply, he straightened his fingers and blew hard. The elf was buffeted into the air like a fragment of gossamer and floated away, shrieking curses at him, out of sight.

'You in the doorway,' called out the silvery voice, 'you got one chance. Come out now with your hands where I can see 'em, and—' The silvery voice broke off and turned into a fit of coughing that suggested that she was on at least forty a day; whereupon Fang hurled himself out of cover, lunged forwards, barged the witch out of the way and made a grab for the Uzi. He managed to get hold of it easily enough, but in the process –

'AAAAaaaaaaaaaaaah!' said the silvery voice; and then there was a dull thud from somewhere down below. Laying the gun carefully on the floor, Fang stuck his head over the parapet and had a look, just in case she was hanging from a ledge doing Doppler-shift impersonations; he needn't have worried. Far below he could see what looked like a Barbie doll that'd just been run over by a Mack truck. Fair enough, he muttered to himself; the cuter they are, the harder they fall. He turned back, and –

'Oh for pity's sake,' he complained, as the crone prodded him in the tummy with the barrel of the Uzi. 'I just rescued you, you senile old fool.'

'True,' the witch conceded, 'which explains why I ain't shot you. Yet,' she added, tightening her arthritic forefinger on the trigger. 'But you'll have a reason for doin' that, I dare say. Handsome princes don't do nothing 'cept for a reason.'

'All right,' Fang sighed wearily. 'Stop poking me with that thing and I'll tell you.' He nodded towards the parapet. 'Or we can do this the hard way,' he added meaningfully.

The witch shuddered. 'Ain't no need to go making threats,' she squawked. 'I'm just a lonely, defenceless old woman tryin' to take care of herself.' Her eyes flicked towards the edge, and then back to Fang. 'Say,' she said, 'how *did* you do that?'

Fang shook his head and grinned. It wasn't such an impressive grin, now that he had a toothpaste-ad smile where a row of foam-flecked upper canines used to be, but he could still make it fairly unsettling. The old lady cursed and lowered the gun, though she didn't hand it over.

'I had help,' Fang said. 'Now there's something I'd like you to—'

'Not so fast,' snapped the witch. 'What kind of help would that be, exactly? Only . . .'

'This kind, stupid!' said a tiny shrill voice somewhere in the vicinity of Granny's ear; and while she was looking frantically round to see where it had come from, Fang was able to reach across and take the gun away from her. Smirking, the elf hopped down off the top of her head and flitted like a small, tawdry moth on to Fang's wrist. 'You owe me,' she said blithely. 'Again. When this is all over, you're going to have to buy me Unigate.'

'I might just do that,' Fang conceded. 'Now then,' he continued, hoisting the Uzi over his shoulder by its sling, 'let's stop clowning about and get some work done. You're a witch, right?

'Nothin' wrong with that,' grumbled the crone. 'Used to be a decent living in these parts before—'

Fang looked at her closely. 'Before what?'

The witch thought for a moment, then shrugged her coat-hanger shoulders. 'Search me,' she said. 'You get to my age, you forgets things.'

Fang frowned; there was something tapping at the inside of an eggshell inside his mind, but he couldn't locate it. He let it go. 'Anyway,' he said, 'you're a witch. You can do turning people into things?'

Another bony shrug. 'Sure,' the witch replied. 'For a moment there, I thought you was goin' to ask for something difficult.'

'Big bad wolves?'

'Easy as pissin' in a pot,' the old lady replied. 'You ready?'

'When you are.'

The witch nodded. 'All done,' she said. 'There. Told you there wasn't nothin' to it.'

Fang looked down at his feet, then along his arms, then at his tummy. 'I'm waiting,' he said. 'When are you going to—?'

'Woof.'

He spun like a top. There beside him, glaring up at him with baleful red eyes, was the biggest, darkest, most sinister-looking wolf he'd ever seen in all his life. At the same moment, he realised that the elf was no longer perched on his wrist.

'Oh,' said the crone. 'You meant turn *you* into a—'

'Here's the deal,' growled Fang, as he jerked his head towards the parapet. 'You turn her back into an elf and me back into a wolf, and in return I postpone your flying lesson. All right?'

'All right,' the witch grumbled. 'I'll do the elf first, they're easier. You,' she snarled, pointing a long and disgusting fingernail, 'quit being a wolf. See?' she added, as the wolf was suddenly sucked back into a tiny elf-shaped packet, like fifty cubic feet of grey jelly being squidged out through a broken window in a pressurised airliner cabin. 'No sweat. You'll be that bit harder, of course, but— Just a minute.' The old lady was staring at him closely. 'I know you,' she said. 'You're him, aintcher? You're *the* big bad wolf, I'd know them nasty little eyes anywhere. What you doin' dressed as a handsome prince anyhow?'

Fang sighed. 'Believe me, I wish I knew. But what's that got to do with—?'

The witch took a step backwards. 'See you in hell first,' she hissed, reaching up for her black pointy hat and pulling out a four-inch hatpin. 'I ain't doin' no deals with no Wolfpack finks.' She swept off the hat; and from under it cascaded an enormously long braid of hair, all the colour of ripe corn (except that the roots needed doing) 'So long, copper,' she hissed, as she quickly looped the end of the braid round a free-standing gargoyle and secured it in an elegant timber-hitch. 'I may be a wicked witch, but I ain't that wicked.'

Before Fang could do anything about it, she'd hopped up

on to the parapet, both hands full of the braid. He tried to make a grab at her but missed; so instead he caught hold of the braid and began hauling on it to pull her back. Too late; the fine-textured rope slipped through his hands, burning them painfully, and just as he'd managed to get a more secure grip and was about to try again, he heard from below the sharp metallic sound of a pair of scissors closing. When he tugged on the rope, it came up at him like a jumping salmon, with nothing on the end except a black velvet toggle and some dandruff.

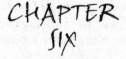

CHAPTER SIX

In her more morbid moments, Sis had occasionally speculated about what death would be like, and had managed to come up with some fairly revolting scenarios; but nothing she'd managed to dream up was nearly as depressing as what was (apparently) the truth, namely that death is just like life, only more so. She wasn't happy with the discovery. Apart from being a horrendous nightmare, it was a rotten swizzle, presumably part of some cheese-paring economy drive. Hopelessly short-sighted and doomed to failure, she couldn't help feeling. Care and rehabilitation in the community might work for some kinds of physical handicap and mental illness, but expecting it to sort out death was going a bit far.

'Eeeek!' she therefore said; and also, 'Yuk!' Then she opened her eyes again.

The view was more or less identical to the last thing she'd seen before what she'd taken to be her last moment on Earth; a messy, debris-strewn crater where the Three Bears' Cottage had been before it got blown up, with herself and the wicked queen in it. No past life flashing in front of her eyes, no long dark tunnel with a bright light at the end, absolutely zip special effects; and here it all was again, the only apparent difference being the camera angle (she was looking down on it, though apparently from no great height) and a feeling of giddy dizziness which she sincerely hoped wasn't permanent.

'There you are,' said a voice below her.

'I hate this,' Sis replied without looking down. 'I want a transfer. Either send me somewhere nicer or let me go back. And,' she added, remembering a tactic that always seemed to work for her mother, 'I demand to speak to the manager, at once.'

'What are you talking about?'

It was then that she realised that the voice was familiar. 'They got you too, then,' she said gloomily. 'No offence, but I really hope that doesn't mean we're going to be stuck here together for ever and ever. I mean, I'm sure you feel the same way too, so if we both file a formal complaint to whoever's in charge here . . .'

'Oh do be quiet,' sighed the wicked queen, 'you're starting to get on my nerves. And get down out of that ridiculous tree. I'm getting a crick in my neck just looking at you.'

Carefully Sis played back the last few sentences of the conversation, finally reaching the conclusion that the most important word in them, quite possibly the most significant word she'd ever heard in her life so far, was 'tree'. Then she looked up.

'I'm not dead, am I?' she said.

'Not unless they've changed the entrance requirements since I last read the prospectus,' replied the wicked queen. 'While you're up there, see if you can't spot a left-foot bright red court shoe with a small brass buckle and a two-inch heel. It's got to be around here somewhere, unless of course it was totally vaporised in the explosion.'

As soon as the news had seeped through the insulating layer of shock and befuddlement that seemed to be wrapped round her brain, Sis yipped with joy. 'We survived the blast,' she said. 'Isn't that amazing? I was absolutely sure I was dead.'

'Another thing you've got wrong, then,' the queen said, resignedly taking off her one remaining shoe. 'When finally you do die, be sure to bequeath your collection of bloody silly mistakes to the nation. It'd be a shame if they all got split up and sold off separately.'

'How do I get down from this tree?'

The queen snorted in exasperation. 'For the last time,' she said, 'I am not a set of encyclopedias. How should I know? Try wriggling around and leaving the rest to gravity.'

'I can't do that. I'll fall and hurt myself.'

'And what a tragedy that would be, to be sure. Look, if it's any help, you appear to be hanging from a branch by the belt of your pinafore. Now you're in full possession of the relevant data, surely the rest of it ought to be easy.'

Sis didn't seem to think much of that; she waved her arms, realised that that wasn't a sensible thing to do and started yelling 'Help!' very loudly. The wicked queen was about to throw the other shoe at her when a thought tiptoed across her mind, leaving in its wake a big smile.

'Something's just occurred to me,' she said. 'Do you like it up that tree?'

'What? No, of course not. Don't be *silly*.'

'So being up that tree is causing you unhappiness, yes?'

'Yes.'

'And another word for unhappiness,' the queen continued, clapping her hands together joyfully, 'is distress. So that's all right,' she added, sitting down and making herself as comfortable as the circumstances allowed. 'Now all we have to do is wait.'

Sis stopped yelling and shot her an unpleasant look. 'Wait?' she said. 'What, for the tree to die and fall over? Or are you expecting a herd of kindly giraffes?'

'Stop wittering and use your brain,' the queen replied sternly. 'In distress. A damsel. You. Someone ought to be along –' She paused, looked up at the sun, and calculated. 'Any minute now,' she concluded cheerfully. 'And with any luck, that'll carry us on to the next stage in the story. Credit where credit's due, my less-than-stoical little friend, just for once you've done something useful.'

'What are you –? Oh, I *see*.'

The queen nodded. 'Narrative patterns,' she said. 'Every time there's a damsel in distress, there has to be a hero to rescue her. Newton's second law, as modified for a narrative environment. The only conceivable way it might not work is for you to fall out of that tree before he gets here, so for pity's sake keep still. Though,' she added confidently, 'even if you were to fall out of the tree, you'd be sure to break your leg, which would also qualify as distress, so it wouldn't be a complete disaster, at that.'

A quarter of an hour later, the queen said, 'Won't be long now.'

Half an hour later, the queen said, 'He'll be here any minute, I'm sure. The hold-up must be something to do with the systems being down . . .' Her words tailed away as the painfully obvious flaw poked its head up through the hole in her logic and stuck its tongue out at her.

'Absolutely,' Sis said. 'The systems are down. More than that, as far as I can see most of them are back to front. Which means,' she went on, 'that somewhere out there in the forest there's a knight in shining armour standing on a kitchen table waiting for us to come along and shoo away a mouse. It's all cocked up, isn't it?'

'Not necessarily,' the queen replied, with rather more optimism than conviction. 'There's really no way of knowing. All we can do is be patient and . . .'

At the dreaded word *patient*, Sis began to squirm and wriggle, more from half an hour's backlog of fidgets than any sincere belief that it would help. As she did so, two things happened: the spur of branchwood that was supporting her weight gave way; and a knight in shining armour, galloping out of the trees and into the clearing in headlong flight from a small but compact dragon that was gaining on him fast, shot under the tree and flashed past the wicked queen like a stainless steel lemming over a clifftop. Accordingly, when the spur snapped off and Sis plummeted out of the tree, there just happened to be a nice bouncy-necked dragon directly underneath her to break her fall.

Her fall wasn't all that got broken, either.

'Now look what you've done,' groaned the wicked queen. 'You've killed it. Oh hell, that's all we needed. You'll just have to pretend it was worrying sheep or something like that. Look out, here comes the wretched thing's owner. You'd better leave this to me.'

She stood up and did her best to assume an indignant-livestock-owner expression; but she needn't have bothered. The knight, who had reined in his steed at the edge of the clearing, rode straight past her without even noticing she was there, vaulted off his horse and knelt beside Sis, who was still lying across the thoroughly dead dragon and watching a spectacular virtual-reality fireworks display. The knight doffed his coalscuttle helmet, laid it down on the grass beside him, and tenderly lifted Sis's hand to his lips.

'My heroine,' he murmured.

'You must be kidding,' Rumpelstiltskin whispered in horrified fascination.

Dumpy gave him a long, hard stare. 'Do I look like I'm kidding?' he growled, as he slammed the knocker against the brightly painted door.

'No,' his colleague admitted, 'but you know me, a born optimist. You can't really be going to recruit a – well, one of *them*,' he added, in a low voice. 'It's just not—'

'Shutup.'

'All right,' Rumpelstiltskin said meekly. 'Just don't blame me, that's all.'

Dumpy ignored him and lifted the knocker, then checked his hand as the door swung open, revealing a small, furry, whiskery muzzle bracketed by a pair of bright and hostile round black eyes. 'Children and animals,' Rumpelstiltskin mumbled under his breath, but Dumpy pretended not to have heard.

'Howdy,' Dumpy said, extending a hand. The mole looked at it, sniffed and shrank back a little.

'I mean,' Rumpelstiltskin went on, 'whatever else he is, he isn't a *dwarf*, no matter how you look at it. And I thought the whole point of the exercise, assuming it does have a point . . .'

'I said shut up,' Dumpy snarled. 'Say, partner,' he continued to the mole, who was looking at him quizzically, as if speculating as to what on earth he was meant to be for, 'I'm looking for the mole. Would that happen to be you?'

The mole twitched its snout and scuffled with its claws in the soft, fine earth. Rumpelstiltskin let out a deep sigh.

'It can't talk, you idiot,' he said. 'It's an animal, can't you see that? And animals can't talk. Well-known fact, that.'

'Ahem. Excuse me!'

'Don't interrupt,' Rumpelstiltskin snapped; then he realised he'd just been talking to the mole. He did a quick double-take, then stooped down. 'You just talked,' he said accusingly.

'All right, so I talked,' the mole admitted. 'So did you.'

'Yes, but . . .' Rumpelstiltskin made an effort to keep his mind clear, or at least on the translucent side of opaque. 'I thought you couldn't talk,' he said.

The mole twitched its nose at him. 'Didn't have anything much to say,' it replied meekly. 'Except *help!* but I sort of got the impression that that wouldn't cut much ice with your friend here. What is it we're all going to do, exactly? If you don't mind my asking, that is. This is all terribly exciting.'

'We're gonna save three little pigs from the big bad wolf,' Dumpy replied. 'If'n you want to ride with us, we'll be glad to have you.'

'Why, for God's sake?' Rumpelstiltskin interrupted. 'Look at it, it's pathetic. Oh God, it's started to cry now.'

'I'm s-sorry,' the mole snuffled. 'And you're quite right, of course, I'd probably only be a hindrance to you. It's all right, really, I quite under—'

'It can dig,' Dumpy said firmly. 'Reckon that might just come in handy. Now, are we gonna stand around here all day jawing, or are we gonna get on and do the job?'

'Oh, why not?' Rumpelstiltskin sighed. 'After all, it isn't as if I had a living to earn or anything better to do.' He hesitated and thought for a moment; it was true, he hadn't. 'After all,' he added, slightly more cheerfully, 'who's afraid of the big bad wolf?'

'Well, actually—'

'Let me rephrase that. Apart from the mole, who's afraid of the big bad wolf? Anybody? Right. Let's go get the sucker.'

'Yeah.'

'Right.'

'Well, if *you're* all going to go . . .'

'That's decided, then,' said Rumpelstiltskin. 'So let's—'

Dumpy scratched his chin thoughtfully. 'Just a minute,' he said. 'There should be seven of us. What about the other three?'

Rumpelstiltskin shrugged. 'Knowing our luck,' he said, 'we're bound to pick up three more dea— I mean, three more colleagues on the way. And if we don't, we'll just have to deputise the pigs. Make them honorary dwarves.'

'We could saw 'em off at the knee,' Thumb suggested. 'That ought to bring them down to our level.'

'Quite,' Rumpelstiltskin said. 'What's the loss of a few limbs compared to companionship and solidarity? I'm sure they'll come round to our way of thinking if we threaten them enough. And then we can go in there, get the job done and then,' he concluded, with his eyes closed, 'go home.'

'Yeah.'

'Right.'

'If you say so. I have absolute confidence in your judgement.'

It occurred to Rumpelstiltskin as Dumpy led the way back into the forest that they could achieve more or less the same result if they skipped the intermediate stages and just went home anyway, but he decided not to raise the point. For one thing, he suspected Dumpy wouldn't be entirely sympathetic. For another . . . He wasn't quite sure what the other was, though he had a nasty feeling it had something to do with narrative patterns, whatever in hell they were.

Probably, he muttered to himself, a sort of Paisley.

The accountant sat up.

'Running DOS,' he said, in a flat, toneless voice. 'Please wait.'

The face in the bucket made an impatient tutting noise. 'Oh, get on with it,' she said. 'You're even slower than the other one.'

If the accountant had been able to notice such things, he'd have detected a subtle change in Snow White's appearance. She was still the fairest of them all, no doubt about that. Her eyes were still the colour of summer skies, her lips were still the deep red of Valentine's day roses, the sort you get embarrassingly given when you have a working lunch with a female business colleague on 14 February. But there was something about the interplay of light and shadow around the contours of her face that made her look – older? Hardly; still that schoolgirl complexion that only exists here and in soap advertisements. Wiser? More knowing? Possibly. It looked as if she was wearing make-up, heavy eyeshadow and mascara, but she wasn't.

But all that was lost on the accountant, who was sitting bolt upright in his chair making little fast clicking noises with his tongue. If ever there was a man whose face advertised valuable warehouse space to let directly behind his eyes, there he was.

'You must be ready by now,' muttered Snow White's face in the still water. 'Right then, here we go. Mirror, mirror. Hello? You look as if you've gone to sleep.'

'Bad command or file name.'

'Well, at least that proves you can hear me. Well now, what are you doing sitting in that bucket, you enigmatic little system? You're a backup, aren't you?'

'Confirmed.'

Snow White frowned. It was, of course, an enchantingly lovely frown. Goes without saying.

'Sneaky cow,' she said. 'And I suppose her big idea was to wipe off everything else and then reinstall the system out of you. Except she doesn't know how to do it, which is where you come in. Yes?'

'Confirmed.'

Those lovely lips set in a hard, thin (but gorgeous) line. 'Well, now, we can't have that. Where's the bitch right now?'

'Path not found. Unable to create socket.'

'What? I'll assume that's the gibberish for Don't Know. I'm warning you, though. If you're trying to cover up for her, I'll take great pleasure in pouring you into a kettle and boiling you. Is that clear?'

'Bad com—'

'Oh, boo to you too.' Snow White sat quietly for a moment, thinking; meanwhile, a spider crawled out of the accountant's ear and gingerly scuttled down his neck and into the top pocket of his colourful jacket. 'All right,' she went on, 'here's what we'll do. Presumably she's going to come back sooner or later to see how you're getting along. Now, I think it'd be a good idea if you report back to me the moment you see her. Got that? Splendid. What a clever little bucket you are. I'd never have thought you had it in you, no pun intended. And of course we've got to make sure she can't actually use you to wipe off the system and reinstall, so how'd it be if I order you not to allow access to the system files without hearing the password first? Good idea? Glad you approve. All right, the password is – Oh, drat it, why can you never think of a password when you need one? – the password is *Meltdown*. Got that? Meltdown. It seems appropriate enough, and I don't suppose it's the sort of word that crops up in the course of ordinary conversation. Now then, bucket, you can run along and play. Bye for now.'

'This will end your Mirrors session.' Even as he said the words, the image on the surface of the water faded out into the accountant's own reflection; and at that moment, he seemed to wake up with a slight start. He blinked, shook his head a little and yawned hugely.

The spider, seeing its chance, scrambled out of the pocket, abseiled down the accountant's tie and scuttled across the desk, finally taking cover behind an empty coffee cup. There was the usual sticky brown ring surrounding the base of the cup, and two of the spider's feet caught in it, but it managed to pull them free.

'What—?' asked the accountant, of nobody in particular. Then he took a deep breath, yawned again and caught sight of his reflection in the bucket. *Hm*, he said to himself, *need a haircut. And that tie simply doesn't go with the shirt. And what's this bucket of water doing on my desk in the first place?*

He thought for a moment; then he flipped the intercom.

'Nicky,' he said, 'why is there a bucket of water on my desk?'

'You mean the one the wicked queen brought in?' said the intercom. 'Search me.'

The accountant sighed. 'Well, take it away, it's seeping all over my papers. Put it out in the woodshed or something. On second thoughts, better not. God alone knows what she wants it for, but if she comes back and asks for it, we'd better have it ready and waiting. Put it in the corner of the waiting room with a cloth over it.'

'Righty ho.'

'And bring me another coffee, would you? Black, no sugar. For some reason, I'm feeling a bit sleepy.'

Having collected the bucket and the empty coffee-cup, the receptionist went through to the kitchen to make the coffee. When she got there, however, the water pitcher was empty. The receptionist sighed; it was a long way to the well, and she was behind with her work as it was. Then a thought occurred to her. It must have been an unworthy one, because she bit her lip and frowned while she was processing it. Then she picked up the cup, slipped through into the front office and lifted the cloth off the bucket she'd just slid under one of the chairs. She glanced round to see if anyone was looking, then dipped the cup into the bucket, filled it and pulled it out again. Then she went back into the kitchen to fill the kettle and put it on. She didn't look back, and so didn't notice the spider, which had got itself stuck to the side of the cup and was now doing a frantic eight-legged version of the doggy-paddle in the middle of the bucket.

'Nicky,' the intercom barked at her as she returned to her desk, 'this coffee tastes horrible, like there's something in it.'

'Sorry,' she said. 'Would you like me to get you another one?'

'What? Oh, no, don't bother. Just don't buy that brand of coffee again, all right?'

'Right you are,' she replied sweetly; then she said something disrespectful under her breath and carried on with her work.

'The Way,' explained Mr Miroku, peeling an orange, 'is like a flower, which – just a moment, I think you missed a bit.'

Mr Akira paused, paintbrush in hand. 'Did I? Where?'

Mr Miroku pointed vaguely with a handful of orange segments. 'That bit there,' he said helpfully. 'Like I was saying, the Way is like a flower, which . . .'

'And that bit there, just under the sill,' added Mr Hiroshige, kicking off his shoes and putting his feet up on the sofa. 'Strive for perfection in all things, the sages teach us, for if there is a flaw in the One there is a flaw in the Whole.'

Mr Akira frowned. 'Sorry?' he said. 'Shouldn't that be the other way round?'

There was a moment of puzzled silence while the two adepts worked it out. 'Oh, I see,' muttered Mr Hiroshige, 'a *whole* in the *flaw*, very amusing. I'd concentrate on the job in hand if I were you.'

Properly speaking, it should have been Mr Hiroshige's job to paint the windows, just as it ought to have been Mr Miroku's job to strip off the old wallpaper and Mr Suzuki's job to emulsion the ceiling, while the roster pinned to the kitchen door had Mr Funiyami, Mr Kawaguchi and Mr Wakisashi chipping out the old putty in the windows. But they had, with characteristic generosity, allowed their young colleague to further his education in the Way by performing these simple exercises, while they sat around making sure that the significance of it all wasn't lost on him. It was, after all, the traditional method of teaching the finer points of philosophy; they'd all had to do it when they'd been Mr Akira's age, and now it was their turn, as they saw it, to put something back into the didactic process. For his part, Mr Akira was honoured, he supposed, and flattered, presumably, to be allowed to perform these tasks in the names of his elders and betters. They were, after all, entrusting him with their honour; if he left a grey patch on the ceiling or put his foot through a window, it'd be Mr Suzuki or Mr Kawaguchi who'd have to commit ritual suicide to expunge the disgrace. Of course he'd have to commit ritual suicide too, to expunge the disgrace of having caused the disgrace that Mr Suzuki or Mr Kawaguchi was having to expunge, but that wasn't the point, was it?

'This is fun,' muttered Mr Suzuki, a quarter of an hour or so later. 'Sitting watching paint dry. My favourite.'

'Watching paint dry,' replied Mr Miroku reprovingly, 'is of course a recognised exercise designed to instil in the novice the virtues of patience and the ultimate self-awareness that can only be reached through intensive meditation. It's only when you can look at a wet skirting-board and see in it a microcosm of the slow but relentless unfolding of the Triple Path that you ever really come to appreciate the Oneness of Being and the merits of non-drip gloss.'

'I see,' said Mr Akira, dabbing a spot of spilt paint out of the carpet with a cloth dipped in white spirit. 'And what does non-drip gloss stand for?'

'You'd be amazed,' replied Mr Hiroshige, stifling a yawn. 'Perhaps later, as and when you've advanced far enough in the—'

'He means there's the ceiling in the outside lav to do next,' Mr Suzuki explained. 'And when you've done that, the garden gate could do with another coat.'

Mr Akira's shoulders sagged a little. 'I see,' he said. 'And all this painting and decorating's going to train me to shatter a hundred bricks with one blow of my hand, is it?'

'Of course,' said Mr Miroku, wiping orange juice off his hands on to his trousers. 'At least, it ought to open your eyes to the fundamental principle that all actions are interrelated, and that the fall of a leaf from a cherry tree in Kyoto is every bit as significant in the Great Scheme as the death of an emperor or the fall of a mighty empire. In fact, I'd go as far as to say that if you're looking for an all-round exercise in cosmic awareness augmentation, it's the best there is, bar ironing.'

'Ironing?'

Mr Miroku nodded. 'Ironing,' he said. 'A more graphic demonstration of the interplay of hard and soft and hot and cold would be difficult to imagine.'

'Whereas washing up,' Mr Suzuki pointed out, 'exactly reproduces in miniature the cyclical nature of death and rebirth, with the washing-up liquid neatly symbolising the purifying effect of Enlightenment. Watch out, you're leaving hairs in the paint.'

Before Mr Akira could ask about the symbolic meaning of moulting DIY store bargain brushes, the door opened and Snow White strode in.

The important word there is 'strode'. True striding is a dying art, and unless you've been bred to it and practised assidu-ously since childhood, you'll find it difficult to carry off with any conviction unless you pull a hamstring or wear tight, heavily starched stretch jeans. Up till now, Snow White had shown no signs whatsoever of striding; if she'd tried it, she'd probably have tripped over the hem of her cute little gingham frock and fallen flat on her face. But this time, the samurai couldn't help noticing, she wasn't wearing the cute little gingham frock.

'You lot,' she said. 'I've got a job for you.'

The samurai tried not to stare. True, skin-tight black leather suited her, in a faintly bizarre kind of way, but Mr Miroku couldn't help wondering if it wasn't a bit hot and sweaty on a fine spring day. As for young Mr Akira, the fact that he'd put his foot in the tin of non-drip gloss and hadn't apparently noticed told you all you needed to know about his reaction.

'About time you started pulling your weight around here,' Snow White continued, and her seams creaked disturbingly as she folded her arms across her hitherto unsuspected chest. 'Right then, you lot, bring me the head of the wicked queen. Oh, come on,' she added, as the samurai stared at her in bewilderment, 'you're trained professional killers, and it's not as if I'd asked you to do anything difficult. Or do you want a diagram with a dotted line marked "cut here"?'

'Um,' said Mr Miroku, quickly chewing up an inconvenient mouthful of orange, 'I'm not quite sure that I understood you correctly. You want us to, er, *murder* someone.'

'That's right.'

'A defenceless woman.'

'You could say that, I suppose.'

'A defenceless woman who's also our rightful queen-empress.'

'That's her. Look, if it's the beheading bit that's bothering you, I'll settle for a quick strangling and a duly notarised copy of the death certificate, I'm not fussy about tradition and stuff like that. Just so long as she's dead, I couldn't care less.'

'Excuse me,' Mr Akira interrupted, looking pointedly at a mark on the wall an inch or so above Snow White's head, 'but are we supposed to do stuff like that? I thought our job was more along the lines of protecting the weak and oppressed and generally going around being helpful and nice.'

Snow White sniggered unkindly. 'Get real,' she said, 'you're samurai. In case nobody told you when you joined up, that means you're feudal warriors, duty bound to kill your overlord's enemies without question or hesitation. Or did you think the bloody great big swords were in case you were ever called on to open a six-foot long envelope?'

Mr Suzuki closed his eyes, opened them again and licked his lips, which had become unusually dry. 'I think the point that my young colleague is trying to make is that we're only supposed to use our formidable fighting skills in a noble and worthy cause. Contract killing, on the other hand—'

'You,' Snow White growled, 'shut up. Now, all of you,' she added, 'get your armour on and get moving, or I'll chop you into bits and feed you to the goldfish. All right? Good.'

When she'd gone, the samurai gazed at each other with the same befuddled look as Moses might have worn on discovering that he'd made a mistake in reading what it said on the tablets and that he was now committed to leading his people forth into the Threatened Land.

'There's something funny going on,' Mr Hiroshige said at last. 'But I'm blowed if I know what it is.'

'Yes,' agreed Mr Akira. 'We haven't got a goldfish.'

There was a bleak silence; then Mr Suzuki shrugged his shoulders. 'Maybe it's some kind of loyalty test,' he said. 'After all, the sages tell us that in order to appreciate the ambivalent nature of the Way—'

'Oh, shut up,' the others chorused.

CHAPTER SEVEN

The knight introduced himself as Sir Agravaunt.

He explained that he'd been going about his business in a quiet, inoffensive way, hanging out his washing between two convenient trees in a shady, peaceful part of the forest . . .

'Washing?' Sis queried.

'That's right,' said Sir Agravaunt. 'And then this horrid great big dragon—'

'Doesn't it rust?'

Sir Agravaunt looked at her oddly. 'How do you mean?' he said.

'Your, um, washing,' Sis replied, trying not to stare at the knight's shining armour. 'Wouldn't you be better off with a can of oil or metal polish?'

The knight's forehead corrugated, then relaxed. 'Not that sort of washing, silly,' he said. 'Sheets and pillowcases and table napkins and things. Anyway, along comes this tiresome dragon—'

'You do your own laundry?' Sis interrupted.

'Well, of course I do. Doesn't everyone?'

Sis, who had the same degree of passive understanding of how a washing machine worked as she had of the operation of the solar system, shrugged and said, 'I suppose so. But I thought you people had – well, servants and things.'

The knight shook his head. 'Not likely,' he said. 'Domestic service is a barbaric and outmoded institution, equally degrading for both servant and master. And besides,' he added ruefully, 'they'd want to be paid.'

Sis caught sight of a patch crudely spot-welded onto the left elbow of his armour and a run in a chainmail stocking loosely botched up with fusewire, and nodded tactfully. 'Quite right,' she said. 'You're very, um, enlightened. For a knight, I mean.'

Once again the knight shot her a curious look. 'You haven't met many knights, have you?' he said.

'Well, no, actually,' Sis admitted. 'Not actually met them, face to face. Er, face to visor. Whatever. I've read about them, of course,' she added quickly. 'You know, the knights of the round table, that sort of thing.'

'Round table,' Sir Agravaunt repeated, obviously mystified. 'Can't say that rings a bell. Are you thinking of Sir Mordevain, by any chance? He's got a circular Swedish pine table in his kitchen-dinette. And,' he added with a hint of venom, 'a bead curtain over the doorway, and a fur-fabric toilet-roll holder shaped like a cat in his downstairs loo. It only goes to show, there's absolutely no accounting for taste.'

The wicked queen coughed meaningfully. 'I don't want to hurry you,' she said, 'but there are a few things we ought to be doing. You know, setting the world to rights, darning the fabric of the space/time continuum . . .'

The knight, whose eyes had momentarily lit up at the words *darning* and *fabric*, sniffed disdainfully. 'Huh,' he said. 'Girl talk. I'll leave you to it. Thanks anyway, for saving me from the dragon and so forth.'

As he clanked away into the shadows of the greenwood, Sis scratched her head. 'That knight,' she said.

'Hm?'

'Are they – well, all like that?'

'Not really,' the queen replied. 'Or at least, they weren't. Knights were bold, fearless, courteous, a little bit on the psychotic side but nothing that hiding from them in a deep cellar under a pile of old sacks couldn't cope with. I think the word I'm looking for is *manly*.'

'Ah.'

'On the other hand,' the queen went on, 'ever since I can remember, knights have been exactly like that one we just met, if not more so. You want your living room redesigned or your wardrobe co-ordinated, you send for a knight. I wouldn't mind,' she went on bitterly, 'if it was one followed by the other, but it isn't. It's simultaneous, and that's what really makes me want to spit.'

Sis tried to make sense of it, but it was like trying to make one picture out of pieces from four different jigsaw puzzles. 'Please explain,' she said.

'I'll try. You see, there's the way it ought to be, which is how it was before you crashed – sorry, before the system went down. All right, so far?'

'I think so.'

'Good. There's also the way it is now, as a direct result of the system going down. If you care to think of it geometrically, let's say everything's at an angle of roughly sixty degrees to how it should be. Hence, for example, all that business with the three little pigs. I take it you know the orthodox version.'

Sis considered. 'Let's see. Pigs build house, wolf blows house down, pigs start again, build another one. Is that the one you mean?'

The queen nodded. 'And sure enough,' she said, 'the three little pigs built a house, and it did get blown down. Or rather up. The difference is that it didn't get blown up by the wolf, they did it themselves. Same approximate net result, different chain of events leading up to it; that's what I meant by an angle of sixty degrees. It's confusing and a horrid mess, but at least it ends up the same way. The narrative patterns are bent but not broken. It's the third one that's worrying me.'

'Well?'

'The third way is where things actually get swapped round with their opposite numbers, like the knight being saved from the dragon by the damsel. Now that's not just a phase modulation shift in the epic sinecurve, that's somebody deliberately mucking things about. And that's why I'm worried.'

'Oh,' Sis said. 'Have you any idea who it might be?'

'Oh yes. In fact, I'm morally certain I know exactly who it is. You see, I have this bad feeling that you and I together are in grave danger of becoming Snow White.'

Sis didn't know how to react to that. Her first reaction was to make a face and feign nausea; then it struck her that –

'If we're Snow White,' she said, 'who's the wick— I mean, who's being you?'

The queen grinned painfully. 'Go figure,' she said.

'Snow White? Snow White's turning into you?'

'Logical, to the point of dreary inevitability. And the problem is, if she's me, and she can somehow get the system working again—'

Sis swallowed hard. 'You mean she'll be out to get us?'

'Of course. It's what I'd be doing. What I probably am doing,' she added, clenching her fists in frustration, 'assuming I'm right, of course, and we are changing places. The nasty bit is that she'd be in complete control of the Mirrors core, which means she'd be able to change the rules. Like,' she added, shaking her head sadly, 'turning everything upside down.'

'You mean she's already started? Like with the knight and the dragon stuff.'

'You've got it,' sighed the queen. 'And that's where everything happening at once comes into the picture. That's what's complicating it so horribly, you see. It'd be bad enough if the three versions happened one after the other, but the wretched truth is that they're all happening at the same time.'

Sis was really at a loss to know how to deal with that. Nobody could accuse her of panicking, of falling to bits as soon as the going got weird; so far, she reckoned she'd coped admirably, largely by telling herself it was all one of those strange dreams soap-opera writers fall back on when they need to bring back to life someone who's been dead for the last hundred episodes. But even they'd never gone this far.

'Explain,' she said.

The wicked queen looked at her, then giggled. 'You should have seen your face when you said that,' she said. 'It was as if that bloke in *Alien* had had a bunch of primroses jump out of his tummy instead of the little wriggly treen. I know it sounds goofy,' she went on, with a sigh. 'Unfortunately, that's how things work around here. Your friend Sir Whatsisface, the knight; somewhere or other there's a story with him in it, right? Otherwise he wouldn't be here, he'd be somewhere else, probably working in a library or a fabric shop. In that story, you can bet your life that he's the one who kills the dragon, and the damsel in distress is the one who gets saved. Seem reasonable to you?'

Sis nodded. 'That's the way I'd expect it to be,' she said. 'Otherwise,' she added, 'why'd he be a knight in the first place?'

'Exactly. You're getting the hang of it now. What he is determines who he is. I must remember that,' the queen added, 'it's very good. Now, then. That story must *be* somewhere – in a book or a film or a cartoon strip, or even just inside the heads of everyone who's ever heard it, right?'

'Sure. I mean, why not?'

'So far, so good. Now think what happens when the system goes down and everything's thrown out of synch. The stories are all still there, but somehow some of the people have got into the wrong stories. Like what happened back there, with the three little pigs somehow winding up in the story of the three bears. That's pretty bad – a bit like a plumber suddenly finding himself doing brain surgery while the surgeon's been whisked away and wakes up to discover he's turned into an airline pilot. Get the picture?'

'In a sense.'

'Okay. Now think about someone deliberately screwing up the stories. The original story's still there, in a book or between someone's ears. Then there's the sixty-degrees-skewed version; well, we know that's running, because we're in it. Finally there's the deliberate fuck-ups, which seem to be precisely targeted to cause as much grief as possible. And they're all going on at the same time. If you want proof, ask someone. You'll find that their long-term memory's either completely gone or they're living with an entirely different set of memories from the ones they had this time last week. Fun, isn't it?'

Sis made one last effort to understand what she'd heard; but it was a lot to ask, the equivalent of expecting a one-armed man to empty the Pacific into the Atlantic using a tablespoon. 'So what do we do?' she asked.

'If you say that once more, I'm going to tie you to a tree and leave you there. For the last time, I don't *know*. Where you get this idea that I'm some sort of extra-brainy tactician from I don't know. What sort of bedtime stories did your mother tell *you*, for pity's sake?'

'But . . .' But the wicked queen *always* knows what to do, Sis nearly said; or at least, she always has a plan. Then it occurred to her that she already knew what the answer would be. 'Oh, all right then,' she said. 'How'd it be if we just stay where we are and wait for something to happen?'

'What a splendid . . .' The queen broke off, smiled, turned through forty-five degrees and pointed. She didn't say anything, because there was no need.

Sis followed the line of her finger, and saw a tall, fat man with a long white beard, dressed in what looked like a red towelling-robe with furry white trim, running very fast out of a fuzzy patch of undergrowth. Since she was not entirely without compassion, she had filled her lungs with a view to yelling, 'Look out,' but before she could do so, the fat man ran straight into a tree and fell over. Sis started to move towards him, but the queen grabbed her arm; and a moment later, a milk-white unicorn with a silver horn appeared from the same clump of shrubbery that had produced the fat man. It caught sight of him, whinnied savagely, lowered its horn and charged; at which point the fat man woke up, saw the unicorn heading towards him, made a shrill yelping noise and shinned up the tree with a degree of skill and dexterity that made Sis want to clap her hands and shout 'Bravo!' The unicorn made a couple of futile attempts to climb the tree after him, then dropped back on to four hooves and squatted down on its haunches, breathing heavily through its nose.

Smiling, the queen folded her arms and sat down on a boulder. 'About time, too,' she said.

'It's all right,' Eugene said. 'We aren't going to hurt you.'

Julian poked his head above the barricade of straw bales and nodded. 'Too right you aren't,' he replied. 'Not through any lack of effort on your part, but simply because I'm up here, you're down there and I've got the ladder. Now bugger off before I start dropping things on your heads.'

He had, his brothers had to concede, got a point there. It was their fault for letting him get such a good head start on them; by the time they'd tracked him down to Old Macdonald's barn, he'd had plenty of time to build himself an impromptu fortification out of straw bales.

'You've got five minutes,' Desmond said. 'Then we're coming in after you. Understood?'

'It's for your own good,' Eugene added.

'Yeah. And when we've finished with you, you'll wish you'd never been born.'

In his straw castle, Julian did his best to stay calm. Bluster, he assured himself. Huffing and puffing. Without the ladder, there was no way they could scramble up the sides of the hayrick. After all, he was the brains of the family, always had been, ever since they were piglets together . . .

Why are they doing this?

'Four minutes,' Desmond called out. 'Say your prayers, little brother, 'cos we're gonna *get* you.'

Piglets together . . . Ever since he could remember it had just been the three of them, pitting their plump little bodies and their agile wits against the lean, cold, mercifully stupid big bad wolf. And now, apparently, the wolf was dead and gone, all their troubles were over . . . And his brothers were laying siege to him as he cowered in a house of straw, wheedling and threatening him in turns while they prowled up and down –

Hang on. Just a cotton-picking minute. Play back the edited highlights of that train of thought.

- Huffing and puffing
- House of straw
- Three little pigs

'You think just because we can't get up there, you're safe,' Desmond went on. 'Well you're wrong, little brother, you couldn't be wronger. 'Cos—'

'Shouldn't that be "more wrong"?'

'Quiet, Eugene. 'Cos if you aren't out of there in three minutes, we're gonna set fire to the straw and burn you out. You copy?'

'Desmond—'

'Shut up, 'Gene, I know what I'm doing. Three minutes, sucker, and then it's roast pork. You got that?'

'Desmond—'

'I said shut it, little brother. This is no time to get sentimental. I mean yes, you've got to admire his tenacity. The pig's got balls. And quite soon they're gonna be served in batter with sweet and sour sauce. Now then, where's those matches?'

Extraordinary, Julian thought, with a shudder that started just behind his ears and kept going right down to the last twist of his tail. They're not just as bad as the damn wolf, they're worse. What *is* going on here? 'Look, you two,' he shouted back, trying to keep his voice steady, 'what's got into you? You're acting crazy, both of you. Just stop and listen to yourselves.'

'Two minutes, loser. You got any last requests? Favourite recipes?'

They won't actually do it. It's just bluff and bluster. Huffing and puffing –

He heard the rasp of a match, then a crackle. Instinctively he twitched his wide, sensitive nose and smelt smoke. Panic hit him, like a very large truck hitting a very small hedgehog.

'Desmond, what do you think you're . . . ?' Eugene broke off in a fit of harsh coughing, as ominous blue wisps started to curl round the lip of the straw-bale barricade. Julian had heard somewhere that once straw starts burning, there's next to nothing that can stop it; the flame leaps up inside the hollow stalk, finding inside it the oxygen it needs for a really keen burn, and even a sudden heavy downpour simply can't saturate the straw fast enough to stop it flaring up and blazing. His trotters shaking uncontrollably, he tried to pig-handle the ladder over his head and set it down against the already smoking parapet; but the shakes were too bad, he let go –

'For God's sake, Julian, mind what you're doing. You nearly brained me!'

Good, Julian thought; then, *For pity's sake, that's my brother Desmond, last thing I want to do is drop a heavy ladder on him.* There was no time to consider the paradox, however; the flames were visible now, surging up at him like a burning oil-slick on a surfer's dream of a wave. 'Help!' he squealed, backing away from the fiery curtain, while at the back of his mind he thought, *Nothing like this ever happened when it was us and the wolf; sure he kept blowing down the house, but it never felt dangerous, just extremely annoying.* He backed away but the fire was quicker than he was, had more time and space to manoeuvre. Then, as he drew near to the edge, he put down a trotter and realised that he was standing in thin air, like the unhappy cat in a Tom & Jerry cartoon.

'Aaaagh!' he screamed, as the past life slideshow started up in front of his eyes. Scrolled through quickly, his life seemed to have been about as interesting as a race down a window-pane by two docile flies. Then the ground reared up and hit him.

'There he is!' Desmond was shouting. 'Quick, grab the bugger before he gets . . .'

Julian squirmed. He'd landed on his back, cushioned somewhat against the fall by a broken-down straw bale, and he thrashed his legs in the air like an overturned woodlouse until, after what seemed like a very long time, he contrived to flip himself over right way up, find his feet and make a run for the door. It was a close-run thing, at that; he had to swerve violently to avoid Eugene's outstretched trotters, and a pitch-fork hurled by Desmond nearly kebabed him before he bounded out into the sunlight, leaving the smoke and the heat and the shouting behind him.

Odd thing was, while he was making his escape under such difficult circumstances his attention was elsewhere. He steered his narrow course between fire and assault on a com-bination of instinct and extremely good luck, while his brain was entirely preoccupied with a topic far more engrossing and fascinating than mere survival.

He cleared the farmyard and trotted up to the top of a low hill, from which there was a fine panoramic view of the valley, the farm, the huge column of black smoke reaching up into the clouds. He lay down in the shade of a young oak tree and tried to figure it all out.

It had been in that brief moment, no more than the slightest paring from Father Time's toenail, when he'd been falling and (as advertised, and nicely on time) his past life had flashed in front of his eyes in a subliminal blur.

He hadn't remembered any of it.

Oh, the memories were all exceptionally clear and strong: falling off his first ever tricycle, lying awake on Christmas Eve waiting for Santa, fishing off the end of the pier with his Uncle Joe, the first time he'd ever set eyes on Tracy – splendid memories all of them, utterly convincing, a selection you'd be ever so pleased with if you'd bought them by mail order; but not his. Somebody else's perhaps, but not his.

In particular, the flashback had been markedly reticent on such subjects as wolves, houses and sudden, destructive gusts of doggy-breath. As far as his memory was concerned, none of that had ever happened. Except that it had.

Had it?

Below in the valley, the fire had spread from the barn to the cowsheds and, with a cluck-cluck here and a quack-quack-*aaagh!* there, Old Macdonald's life work was going up in flames. Viewed from a distance it was rather a grand spectacle, though of course most of the piquant detail was lost. No sign of Eugene and Desmond, which implied that either they'd been consumed in the inferno or else they were showing signs of hitherto unexpected good sense and keeping well out of the way. Under other circumstances his heart would have bled for Old Macdonald; except that he knew for a fact that the old swindler was up to his ears in entirely justified aggravation from the Revenue, and the whole place was heavily overinsured. Julian salved his sense of universal guilt by picturing Old Mac wandering round the burnt-out shell of his property with a big silly grin and a claim form, scribbling down *here a cluck, there a cluck, everywhere a cluck-cluck*, while the figures in the right-hand column soared exponentially.

My name is Julian. I am a little pig. All my life I've been terrorised by a big bad wolf, who used to huff and puff and blow our houses down; first the house of straw, then the house of sticks –

Put like that, of course, the whole thing sounded absurd. First: who'd be thick enough to try building houses out of straw or sticks? Second: there are many ways of demolishing buildings, especially buildings made out of one hundred per cent organic and biodegradable materials sourced from sustainable natural materials, but simply blowing on them isn't one of them. Surely, therefore, those memories couldn't possibly be true. Could they?

Well, of course not; so it was just as well that he had a second layer to the onion of his memory, a recollection of buildings massively fortified and defended, blockhouses that ought to have been able to withstand direct hits from nuclear warheads; except that that was absurd as well, since pigs, even pigs as clever and resourceful as he was, can't do that sort of work. It'd take an army of skilled craftsmen with an open cheque from the UN two years to put together some of the structures he seemed to remember throwing together in an afternoon – only to see them going down like cardhouses at one mild puff from the Wolf. Impossible. And what's impossible can't be true. Therefore . . .

But I remember. I was there. It happened.

All of it.

Both versions.

I am not a number. I am a free pig.

Julian frowned and rubbed his shoulder against the trunk of the oak tree. That last bit wasn't him either; it had seeped through from those damned synthetic memories that had somehow got into his head while he was falling – hardly surprising, seeing how vivid and evocative they were, like a hologram show inside his mind, but completely alien. He took a deep breath and allowed himself to examine them, as objectively as he could. They were fine memories, to be sure; and through them ran a convincingly logical thread; a bad case of sibling rivalry between himself, the puny but brainy younger piglet, and his two big thick brothers. He distinctly recalled, as if it was yesterday, that first tree-house their Dad built for them in the low branches of the old, droopy crab-apple tree; how Des and Gene hadn't let him go with them to play in it, how he'd gone off on his own and built another, better tree-house in the tall sycamore, how Des and Gene had almost died of jealousy and had pulled it down and smashed it; how he'd built another one after that, which they'd also wrecked. The pattern was perfect, the way his patient perseverance had only served to infuriate them further, until one day –

No, it hadn't been like that. The hell with what's logical and what's possible. We're three little pigs who built houses out of stupid stuff and had them all trashed by a wolf. The wolf blew on them and they fell down. The wolf was not my brothers. I know. I was there.

– Picture of himself standing blubbering in front of his father, telling him what they'd done; and Des and Gene, red in the face and looking away. He could hear Gene's voice in his head as clear as anything; *wasn't us, it was the big bad wolf.*

And a little voice said in the back of his mind that the past doesn't matter anyway, who can say for certain what happened in the past, because the past doesn't exist any more, it's only there to explain the present, and if this version explains the present better than any other version, then why the hell shouldn't it be the past? So much easier. So much more convenient for all concerned.

Away in the distance, there was a queue of backed-up fire engines waiting at the farm gate, which was chained and padlocked; and there was Old Macdonald himself, furtively creeping round the back of the cider house with a can of petrol. In his past, no doubt, facts were quietly stabbing each other in the back, pushing each other out of twelfth-storey windows, sorting out an expedient explanation of the present that would result in the highest possible insurance payout. Here a barn full of valuable antique furniture, there a barn full of valuable antique furniture. So much more convenient.

Julian grunted. Then he stood up and went into the wood to gather sticks.

*

'Completely,' the Brother Grimm confirmed into his mobile phone, 'and utterly. In fact, I reckon it's getting near the point where it's beyond salvaging . . . Yes, possibly, but would it be worth it? Surely it'd be simpler to start over again from . . . Okay, sure, you're the boss. We'll see what we can do. Yes, goodbye.'

He closed the phone with a snap and slid it back in his inside pocket. 'They want us to go ahead,' he said. 'Bloody stupid idea if you ask me, but . . . why are you looking at me like that?'

His brother shook his head. 'I'm not,' he replied. 'What makes you think . . . ?'

'Oh, come off it, you're my brother, I know when there's something you're not telling me. Spit it out.'

'Well . . .' Grimm #2 spread his hands in a gesture of contrition. 'I just thought you'd have worked it out for yourself by now, that's all. Think about it, will you? We've got orders to take advantage of the present systems breakdown to seize control of the kingdom, right?'

His brother nodded sadly. 'Completely unrealistic,' he said. 'Who do they think we are, the A-Team?'

'Actually,' said Grimm #2, 'it's not. It'll be relatively straight-forward, once we've re-established the Mirrors network and altered all the access codes so we're the only ones who can operate the system.'

Grimm #1 stared at him. 'You knew all along,' he said accusingly.

'Of course. And I didn't tell you for the same reason that I haven't recently reminded you of the fact that you have a nose. I thought you'd realised. For pity's sake, you don't think those three Realside kids hacked into the system all by themselves, did you?'

Grimm #1's jaw slumped. 'You mean to say we helped them?'

'Naturally,' Grimm #2 replied. 'Obvious thing to do, use an innocent third party to bust our way in. If it works, we're home and dry. If it doesn't, we can claim we knew nothing about it and it was just an irresponsible act by a bunch of antisocial delinquent nerds, nothing to do with us at all. Standard operating procedure for subverting a friendly government. Don't you *ever* read the tactical planning memos?'

'No,' Grimm #1 said, 'you do. Look, is this all one of your jokes? I can't believe we really do things like that. I thought it was all media paranoia and stuff.'

'Ah.' Grimm #2 grinned. 'That's what they *want* you to believe. But it isn't true. It's just –' He hesitated for a moment and grinned as widely as the Grand Canyon. 'Just a fairytale,' he said.

'Fairytale?'

'Yeah, why not?' Grimm #2 sat down on a tree-stump and lit a cigarette. 'That's what fairystories are for, after all. Scare stories. Bogeymen. Give people something imaginary to be afraid of and they won't worry about the real story, the thing we're actually trying to cover up.' He grimaced. 'Works, doesn't it? You're so accustomed to hearing alarmist rumours about dirty tricks and cover-ups, you assume it's just paranoia and bad craziness. And so it is, ninety-five per cent of the time. That ninety-five per cent's a smokescreen so that nobody'll believe we actually do the other five per cent.'

'So those kids –' Grimm #1 shuddered. 'We *sent* them here?'

His brother laughed. 'Good Lord no, that'd be really irresponsible. No, they came of their own choice. We didn't suggest the idea to them, either. Absolutely no way the parents'll be able to sue if anything goes wrong.'

Grimm #1 shook his head doubtfully. 'That's not right,' he said. 'We shouldn't do things like that. It's—'

'Expedient. And efficient. And all's fair in love and narrative. What'd you rather we did, send in the marines? And a lot of people'd have got hurt, our boys included. No, the hell with that.'

Grimm #1 scowled. 'So why not just leave them the hell alone? What harm were they doing us?'

'None of our business,' Grimm #2 replied sternly. 'Look, if you want a nice, easy answer, they're *different*, see? When you've said that, you've explained everything. It's the basis of all our fundamental policy. Different's a threat, and so it's got to go. Jeez, next off you'll be asking why there's a United Nations.'

Grimm #1 thought about it and came to the conclusion that he didn't want to think about it. 'Anyway,' he said, 'I take it you know how to get the system back on line again.'

'More or less,' his brother replied. 'Even brought our own mirror,' he added, opening his briefcase and reaching inside. 'Look,' he said, holding up a small looking-glass with a grey plastic frame and a serial number stencilled on the back. 'Latest model, state of the art. Million times better than anything they've . . .'

It was, considered with hindsight, a freak accident, the sort of thing that could have happened to anybody. The handle slipped through his fingers, did a salmon-up-a-waterfall impression and hit a stone. Crash, tinkle.

'Neat trick,' growled Grimm #1. 'That's supposed to be seven years' bad luck, isn't it?'

Grimm #2 stared blankly at the shiny white shards. 'Supposed to be doesn't enter into it,' he whimpered. 'And that's seven years *minimum*. How the hell do you think the superstition came about in the first place?'

'Ah well,' said Grimm #1, 'no use crying over bust mirrors. We'll just have to find another one, that's all. Come on, we've got work to do, and the sooner we make a start, the sooner we'll be finished and we can go home.'

'You think that's all there is to it? We get here and the first thing we do is crash their mirror?' Grimm #2 laughed wildly. 'You think that was just an *accident*?'

'It's really got to you, hasn't it? Look, I'm supposed to be the one with the grave misgivings about this. Are you just going to stand there watching the stalagmites grow, or are you coming?'

Grimm #2 shook his head. 'What the hell,' he said. 'Yeah, let's go and find a mirror. Doesn't even have to be glass. A pool of water'll do.'

'True, but the response time's lousy,' Grimm #1 looked around; and, by sheer coincidence, caught sight of a quaint little cottage nestling among the trees. 'Let's try that house over there,' he suggested. 'Bound to find one there, I reckon.'

'What if they don't want to part with it?'

'They will, you'll see. Chances are it's only some old biddy we can put the frighteners on. It'll be easy as shelling peas.'

Grimm #2 nodded uneasily. He wasn't sure he'd liked the rather cheerful note that had entered his brother's voice when he'd started talking about frightening old biddies. There had been this slightly unpleasant side to his brother's nature ever since they'd been kids. It wasn't a nice thing to have to admit about his own flesh and blood, but there it was. For all his earlier pontificating about dirty tricks and doing the right thing, Grimm #1 rather enjoyed watching things break. His idea of shelling peas probably involved a three-hour barrage from a battery of twelve-inch naval guns.

'All right,' he said, 'but let's not get carried away.'

'Agreed,' Grimm #1 replied with a grin. 'If everything goes to plan, it won't be *us* getting carried away, you have my word on that.'

'Do I? Oh good. That makes me feel so much better.'

Grimm #1 shook his head, muttered something under his breath about half-hearted prima donnas and set off for the quaint little cottage.

'At least try asking nicely first,' Grimm #2 puffed as he struggled to keep up. 'Can't do any harm, and . . .'

'All right,' his brother grunted, 'if it'll keep you happy. Right, door's locked. I expect you want me to knock first.'

'I'd have thought it'd be the polite thing to do.'

Grimm #1 reached out and tapped the door gently with the knuckle of his index finger. 'Satisfied?'

'Well . . .'

'I knocked first, like you said, and no reply. So—'

He raised his left foot and kicked the door hard. It snapped open, swung back and slammed into the wall behind. Something yowled and scuttled away. 'Cat,' Grimm #1 explained. 'And where there's a cat, there's always an old biddy. Damn,' he added, 'I knew I should have brought my brass knuckles.'

'You know,' muttered Grimm #2 as they walked in and looked around, 'there's something odd about this place. Reminds me of something, but I just can't seem to – And what's that funny smell?'

Grimm #2 sniffed. 'Search me,' he replied. 'Boiled cabbage, probably. Come on, let's see what we can find. You look down here, I'll try upstairs.'

He clumped up the rickety wooden staircase and found himself in a dark, musty room with a low ceiling, most of which was taken up with an enormous four-poster bed. He was heading for the window to open the curtains and let some light in when a movement at the periphery of his vision stopped him in his tracks.

There was someone in the bed.

Burglars take these things in their stride; but Grimm #2 wasn't a burglar. He swivelled round, lost his balance, slipped and fell backwards into a coalscuttle.

'Who's there?'

Old biddy voice, coming from somewhere in the heavy-duty darkness behind the drapes of the four-poster. Damn, thought Grimm #2, now what? The obvious thing to do was beat as hasty and unobtrusive a retreat as possible; but with his bum wedged in a coalscuttle he was in no position to demonstrate his precision-honed Special Forces running-away techniques. A pity. All that training wasted.

'It's okay,' he said. 'Nothing to worry about.'

Then he caught sight of the eyes.

'Help,' said the old biddy. 'Help help.'

That's what she said; but anything less frightened-sounding would be hard to imagine. To judge from her tone of voice, she was marginally less terrified than a full-grown tiger in a cage full of lemmings. And the eyes . . .

'Sorry,' he said. 'Didn't mean to frighten you. I didn't think anybody was at home. I just wanted to, um, ask the way.'

'Where to?'

To his dismay, Grimm #2 discovered that his brain wasn't working. 'New York,' he said. 'I think I may be . . .'

'Turn left as you go out the front door, first right then second left off the main forest road till you come to a derelict water-mill, turn left past the Cat & Fiddle and carry on down about six thousand miles and you can't miss it.'

'Ah. Thanks.' Grimm #2 started to back away, still staring at the eyes. 'Much obliged.'

'Don't mention it.'

Something buried deep in his mind, down among the silt and potsherds of childhood, told him not to say it; but he say it anyway. 'Nothing personal,' he said, 'but what big eyes you've got.'

'All the better to see you with, my dear.'

Fair enough, Grimm #2 said to himself. Best leave it at that and go, now. But he didn't.

'What big ears you've got,' he mumbled, though he couldn't see any ears in the gloom, only the two red eyes. For all he knew, she could have ears like a Ferengi or two pinholes drilled flush with the side of the head.

'All the better to hear you with, my dear.'

'Quite. And, um, what big hands you've got.'

A dry, rasping chuckle came from behind the bed curtains. 'All the better to hold you with, my dear.'

Thanks, but you're not my type. 'And, um, don't take this the wrong way, but what big teeth you've . . . Oh shit.'

The curtains billowed up like a storm-tossed sail or a cheap umbrella blowing inside out ten minutes after you've bought it, and there was something huge and dark and rank very close to him. He could feel its breath on his face; could smell it too, like the inside of a badly neglected fridge. 'All the better to eat you with, sucker,' said the voice. 'Prepare to—'

'Help!' But as Grimm #2 cowered back against the door, his arms in front of his face, he still couldn't help noticing that the thing squatting in front of him, poised to spring, wasn't a little old lady any more. Not even a big, nasty, savage little old lady with coal-red eyes and teeth like a vampire Ken Dodd. She'd changed.

Changed into a wolf.

'Unless,' the werewolf went on, 'you feel like negotiating.'

'Um,' Grimm #2 replied; and in the circumstances, neither Oscar Wilde nor Noël Coward could have done much better. 'Sure,' he added. 'What had you in mind?'

'Depends,' said the werewolf, 'on what you've got to offer.'

Offhand, Grimm #2 couldn't think of anything to say, except possibly *Well, that explains a lot about the story of Little Red Riding Hood*. He didn't say that, however, for obvious reasons.

'Well?'

'I've got two tickets for the Splitting Heads gig on Wednesday night,' he ventured. 'You could take a friend.'

'Thanks,' snarled the werewolf, 'but no thanks. I was thinking of something rather more – traditional, let's say.'

'Traditional.'

'That's right. Your daughter and half your kingdom, for instance. Or a monthly tribute of oven-ready virgins, with side-salad and something from the trolley to follow?'

Grimm #2 thought for a moment. He didn't have a daughter or a kingdom, and he doubted whether a goldfish and the kitchen and spare bedroom of his flat would be sufficiently tempting. As for monthly virgins, that was a non-starter. Even if he could get the girls from the office to co-operate, he had a feeling that some of the criteria were a bit too stringently drawn. 'How about money?' he suggested.

The werewolf frowned. 'You mean the chocolate stuff with the gold foil wrapping?' She shook her head. 'Gives me wind.

Come on, you're the one in the hot seat. You think of something.'

Grimm #2 thought hard. He thought until he imagined he could feel his eyes getting squeezed out of his head. But nothing came, and the old lady was slowly but surely edging closer. Then inspiration struck –

'I know,' he said. 'What about my brother?'

The werewolf hesitated for a moment. 'I don't know,' she said. 'Why him and not you?'

'Taste,' Grimm #2 answered frantically. 'Flavour. Not to mention being high in polyunsaturates and free of artificial colourings. He doesn't contain nuts, either.'

The werewolf looked at him contemptuously. 'That'd go for you too, if you ask me,' she said. 'Where I come from, we have a saying: *a man in the fridge is worth two in the bush.* Besides,' she added horribly, 'I've taken a liking to you. Now then—'

'All right!' Grimm #2 screeched. 'What about the secret of absolute power? Any use to you?'

'Might be,' the werewolf conceded. 'What had you in mind?'

'The Mirrors network,' Grimm #2 panted, trying to draw breath through his nose like someone trying to suck up the last half-inch of a thick milkshake through a bent straw. 'The operating system that runs this lousy place. You know, as in com—'

The werewolf looked at him oddly. 'What do you mean, operating system? If by this place you mean the kingdom, it's run by the wicked queen. Everybody knows that.' She shook her grizzled head. 'I should know better at my age than to waste time listening to chatty food,' she said. 'Now, are you going to hold still or do I have to tenderise you a bit first?'

'It's the wicked queen's magic mirror,' Grimm #2 said quickly, and the words tumbled out of his mouth like spoons from a kleptomaniac's sleeves. 'It's what she runs the country with. I can, um, give it to you.'

'You don't say.'

'Or at least, I could give you the power to work it. If you've got a mirror handy, that is.'

The werewolf sniggered messily. 'Odd you should mention that,' she said. 'What with one thing and another, mirrors aren't something I have much truck with, if you take my meaning.'

Grimm #2 tried to smile. 'Oh, it's not so bad,' he said. 'A smart suit with shoulder pads, a bit of eyeshadow—'

'They don't work too good when I'm around,' the werewolf explained irritably. 'Goes with the job, I'm told. Like, there's no point in me polishing the silver till you can see your face in it, because I can't.'

'Hm?' Grimm #2's brow furrowed in bewilderment, then relaxed. 'Oh I *see*,' he said. 'Because you're a . . .'

'That's right, dear.'

'So I suppose you're not too keen on garlic, either. Or silver bul—'

'Boy, what a loss *you* were to the diplomatic service. Yes, that's right. Though what all that's got to do with you getting eaten . . .'

(Behind her, the door opened.)

'Never mind all that now,' said Grimm #2, holding up a hand in mild reproof. 'You've just given me an idea. How'd you like to work for the government?'

The werewolf glowered at him. 'Wash your mouth out with soap,' she replied sternly. 'I may be an evil old lycanthropic witch, but I'm not *that* far gone. Now hold still while I—'

She got no further than that, mostly on account of Grimm #1 creeping through the open door, sneaking up behind her and nutting her with a three-legged stool.

'Thanks,' his brother muttered. 'I just hope to God you haven't killed her, is all.'

Grimm #1 scowled at him, as if he'd just advised a high-class gift horse to brush and floss thoroughly after every meal. 'Oh, I'm terribly sorry,' he said. 'I'd somehow got it into my muddled old brain that you might actually *like* to be rescued.'

As she lay on the floor, looking for all the world as if someone ought to come and paint a thick white line all round her, the werewolf was changing back into human form. On balance, Grimm #2 muttered to himself, I preferred the wolf version.

'Or given her amnesia,' he went on, 'which'd be almost as bad. Oh well, only one way to find out. While I'm tying her up, nip downstairs and get a bucket of cold water.'

'All right,' said Grimm #1. 'Just as soon as you explain to me why, after I've been to all the trouble of knocking the old bat out, you immediately want to bring her round again. What is it? Compunction? Remorse? Missed it the first time and want a replay?'

Grimm #2, who had been checking the old biddy's pulse, looked up and grinned. 'Because she might just be the answer to all our prayers, that's why,' he replied.

Grimm #1 leaned over and took a good look. 'What on earth for?' he said. 'I can just about imagine a keen gardener having a use for her if he was having trouble with crows on his seed beds, but we both hate gardening. Or were you planning to set up a bespoke nightmare service for people who're allergic to cheese?'

Grimm #2 stroked his chin. 'Actually,' he said, 'that's not a bad idea. Remind me of that when this is all over. Meanwhile, though, think about werewolves.'

'Werewolves?'

'And witches and the undead generally, but werewolves in particular. See what I'm driving at yet?'

'Can't say I – oh *wow*!' Grimm #1's face lit up like a fire in a match factory. 'As in not making a reflection in mirrors?'

Grimm #2 grinned like a dog. 'Got there at last,' he said. 'Well, don't just stand there, go fetch the water.'

Grimm #1 hurried off down the stairs, while Grimm #2

played DIY Egyptian Mummies with a dressing-gown cord and three balls of wool he found in the old biddy's knitting basket. By the time his brother returned with the water, she looked like a ball of string with a head sticking out of one end.

'Hold it,' Grimm #2 said, as his brother lifted the bucket over her head. 'Not so fast. Put that bucket down carefully and let me try something.'

Once the ripples on the surface of the bucket had died away, Grimm #2 bent over it and muttered a string of what sounded suspiciously like gibberish. It seemed to have the desired effect, however, for not long afterwards several lines of glowing green text materialised just under the surface.

'Well?' asked Grimm #1.

'Message from HQ,' Grimm #2 replied. 'Asking us why a routine patrol exercise is taking such a long time, and why we haven't acknowledged receipt of the latest written orders.'

'Fair question,' Grimm #1 conceded.

Grimm #2 shrugged his shoulders. 'You *would* say that. We'd better get a move on, before they get really difficult.'

Grimm #1 nodded, and let fly with the water. There was a splash, a loud curse and a spluttering noise; then –

'Oh balls,' Grimm #2 muttered. 'That's awkward.'

'Not nearly as awkward as it'd be if she wasn't tied up,' Grimm #1 replied, taking several steps backwards. 'You sure those knots'll hold?'

'Here's hoping. Any idea how we turn her back?'

On the floor before them lay a huge grey she-wolf.

CHAPTER EIGHT

'I don't care about the marketing possibilities,' snapped the Baron irritably. 'I think it looks ridiculous, and I want it out of here now.'

Igor sighed. Ever since it had made its unscheduled and unexpected appearance, he'd become curiously fond of the little wooden puppet, with its perky smile and quaint features; in addition to which, there was no question but that in some highly unorthodox but nevertheless effective way, the thing was alive. Far too alive to be lightly thrown on the fire or buried in the compost heap. 'Can I have it, then?' he asked. 'It's not for me, you understand, it's for my sister's kid. She'd love to have something that actually came from the castle.'

'So long as you get the stupid thing out of my sight and keep it there,' the Baron replied. 'I'm sick to the teeth of its horrible simpering expression. Its eyes seem to follow me all round the room.'

Igor knew how the Baron felt; there was something strange about the thing, sure enough. Not creepy; it was too naus-eatingly cute for that. The worst it could do would be to adore you to death. Nevertheless, there was clearly more to it than met the eye. The fact that it was apparently alive, for a start.

'Thanks,' Igor said, scooping it up and stuffing it inside his jacket before the Baron changed his mind. 'My nephew'll be ever so pleased.'

'Pleasure. I'll stop it out of your wages.'

What with tidying up the mess left behind by the experiment and keeping well out of the Baron's way, it was late evening by the time Igor returned to his cramped, musty little cottage next door to the formaldehyde store, and he wasn't in the mood to examine his new acquisition closely. Accordingly he dumped it on the table, crammed a handful of stale cheese rind into his mouth and fell into bed. Not long afterwards, a snore you could have cracked rocks with shook the rafters, and the puppet decided it was safe to take a look round.

If the first day was anything to go by, he decided, Life was a bit like a frog sandwich; some parts of it were better than others. The not being an inanimate section of log, for example, was quite invigorating; likewise the bewildering flood of sensory information and the countless new experiences. The sense of being absolutely surplus to requirements wasn't so good, and the puppet wondered if there was anything it could do about that. It had an idea that being loved might help, though where the idea came from . . .

Help! Help! Let me out!

. . . It wasn't sure. Either it was an exceptionally quick learner, or else it'd known a lot of useful stuff before it came to life. Which was impossible, surely.

'Hello, world,' it said, noticing as it did so that its voice was high and squeaky, not at all as it had imagined it would be.

Please, PLEASE listen to me. I'm a human being, and I'm stuck in this horrid wooden Disney thing. Can anybody hear me?

The puppet stood very still. 'Hello?' it said.

Hello?

'Hello.'

Oh, will you please stop repeating every word I say? Listen, you've got to help me. I can't stay here, my mum'll be worried sick. I've got homework to do, and there's a maths test on Friday. Please?

'Hello?'

Oh no, don't do this to me. Look, if you help me I promise I'll be your friend.

'He— you will?'

Yes. Promise. Cross my heart.

'Gosh. That sounds nice. What's a friend?'

I really don't have time for – no, wait, don't go all droopy on me. A friend is someone who loves you. Very much.

'Ah,' said the puppet. 'I think I'd like one of those.'

I know you would. Now then, this is what I want you to do. Over there by the window there's a—

'What's a window?'

You're doing this on purpose, aren't you? Well ha ha, very funny. I hope you get woodworm.

'Oh.' The puppet slumped against a hairbrush, its joints all floppy. 'Does this mean you aren't going to be my friend after all?'

No, no, I really really *want to be your friend, but you've got to do exactly what I tell you. Are you listening?*

The puppet's head lifted and dropped. 'Hello,' it said.

Right then. Now, I want you to stand up – can you manage that all right, because I'm not sure I can talk you through it if you can't.

'Easy.' The puppet stood up. 'Look, no strings,' it announced proudly. 'What's a string?' it added.

Oh, I see what's happening. Somehow you're getting a few thoughts and turns of phrase from my mind, but your excuse for a brain can't understand them. Well, never mind that for now. Turn your head left – sorry, forgot. Just turn your head until I say Stop. Right, are you ready? Fine. Now, start turning.

The puppet's head started to turn, like the turret of a dear little wooden tank. 'Am I doing this right?' it asked nervously.

Carry on, you're doing just fine, it's – hey, stop!

'Here?'

No, back a bit, you've gone too far. No, that's too far the other way. Slowly now – and there, we've done it.

'Oh, hooray! This is tremendously exciting, you know. Can we do it again?'

No, certainly not. You have no idea how dizzy it makes me feel when you turn that thing. Not that I'm all that fussed, mind. After all, this is your head I'm stuck in, and if I get travelsick and throw up, I'm not going to be the one with a filthy smell between his ears. Right, you see that white shiny thing, there by the empty milk bottle?

'I think so. Bearing in mind that I don't know what an empty milk bottle looks like.'

Don't worry about it. You can see the big flat shiny thing?

'I suppose so. What does it look like?'

Oh for – there, that's it. No, back just a – stop right there. Don't move till I tell you.

'Of course not, Friend. Anything you say.'

Look at the shiny thing. That's what we call a mirror. Now, can you see your reflection?

'How should I know? All I can see is this horrible dangly thing with a funny look on its face and a very big nose.'

Don't worry, just hold it. Now, repeat after me.

'You sure? I really don't like the look of—'

Oh, grow up. That's you, you idiot.

'Me?' The puppet quivered slightly. 'Gosh. Hey, I look horrible. Is my face really that disgustingly soppy?'

Repeat after me.

The puppet listened for a while; then it cleared its wooden throat and said, 'Mirror.'

At first, nothing happened; there was only the puppet's reflection, grinning inhumanly right deep down into the silver backing. Then –

You've done it, we're in! Now, keep doing exactly what I tell you to, okay?

The face in the mirror wasn't a cute wooden puppet any more. It was a stern, humourless, rocklike expression, more than a little reminiscent of a bust of Mr Spock done by the Mount Rushmore team. It stared out of the mirror for a long three seconds, then said, 'Running DOS.'

Yippee! Now then—

'YIPPEE! Now, then.'

The face in the mirror raised a sardonic eyebrow 'Bad command or file name,' it said.

No, not that, you idiot. And don't say that. Don't say that, either. God, you're almost as stupid as my Amiga. All right, start again. Tell it –

The puppet listened, then carefully enunciated, 'C colon backslash reality. Excuse me, but what are you doing?'

Huh? Oh, I'm trying to bypass Mirrors and find a way of linking up with my PC back home, assuming my mum hasn't pulled out the plug or switched the modem off. Before I do that, though, I need to rig up some kind of makeshift IP protocol. And before you ask, you don't want to know. Really you don't. Ready?

'Oh yes. This is *fun*.'

You really think so? Jeez. Get a life, will you!

The puppet looked confused. 'I thought I already had one,' it replied.

That's what all the nerds say. Now, after me. Zed exclamation mark arrow equals backslash –

Seen from a distance, the cottage didn't seem in the least ominous or threatening – which was odd, Fang couldn't help thinking. There seemed to be a rule in these parts that if a place was trouble, it had to be marked as such so clearly that the tell-tale signs would be visible from orbit. This was so much an accepted way of life that the estate agents' particulars tended to read something like *highly desirable and sinister isolated hovel, set under looming lead-grey clouds riven by forked lightning, storm-gnarled dead trees at front & rear, creaking doors & floorboards, twisted chimneys, own ravens, would suit first-time wicked stepmother/DIY enthusiast, viewing essential . . .* This place, on the other hand, broadcast cosiness and home-baked muffins; which, in a sinister-plot-twist area, was a clear breach of the planning regulations.

The door was slightly ajar, and as the handsome prince crawled up and put his ear to the crack, he could hear voices –

'. . . Absolutely fucking *brilliant*, like having an unbreakable password. We could do what the hell we want and nobody'd be able to do anything about it.'

Another bit of odd, he reflected; my, Granny, what a deep voice you've got. All the better to bullshit you with, my dear. Still; you never knew with these witches.

'All right,' he said, 'I'm going in. It's probably going to be dangerous, so –' He took a deep breath. Nobility and generosity of spirit weren't exactly his cup of tea, and he didn't feel confident with them. 'So you just get lost. Piss off. Go do whatever it is you little buggers do. And, um, thanks for your help.'

'Huh?'

'You heard.'

The elf grinned so widely that its face should have split. 'Am I really hearing this? Do my pointy ears deceive me? You're really letting me *go?*'

'Yes. Now scram, before I change my mind.'

'Certainly not. Wouldn't miss this for all the mushrooms in Thailand. Besides, you'll probably need me to save you.'

'In your dreams. Look, I won't tell you again.'

'It's the handsome prince outfit,' the elf commented sagely. 'It's getting to you. You're starting to be nice.'

'Say that again and I'll splat you. All right, it's up to you. Follow me.'

He pushed the door open and ducked under the lintel. It was pitch dark inside, and he hadn't gone three paces when he felt something brush against his leg and there was an ear-splitting crash, as of splintering china. Tea-set, probably.

He swore under his breath. Still, nothing he could do about it now, except possibly run away. 'Hello?' he called out. 'Anybody home?'

Overhead, feet clumped on the ceiling, answering his question. The springs of a bed groaned, and a wardrobe door slammed. Two of them, he guessed. At least. He gritted his embarrassingly white toothpaste-ad teeth and climbed the stairs.

'Hello?'

In the upstairs room there was a little light; a pale smear, seeping through a crack in the heavy brocade curtains. There was somebody or something in the bed –

Looked like a wolf.

Correction; it looked like a wolf in the same way a child's drawing of a tree looks like a tree. Someone *dressed* as a wolf? But why?

Be that as it may; if whoever it was wanted to be taken for a wolf, it'd be diplomatic to humour them, at least to begin with. 'Hello,' he repeated. 'Are you a wolf?'

'Woof.'

'Gosh.' Dammit, Fang muttered to himself, this is degrading as well as silly. *I'm* a wolf, *this* is a human. Except – well, enough said. 'What small eyes you've got!'

'What? Oh shit. I mean, yes, all the, um, worse for seeing you with.'

'Really? And what little ears you've got!'

'All the worse for hearing you with.'

'*Psst!*'

The figure in the bed started, then leaned its head sideways. Right, Fang said to himself, the other one's hiding under the bed.

'*What?*'

'Say "*my dear*".'

'*What? Oh, right.*' The figure sat up again. 'All the worse for hearing you with, *my dear.*'

Fang took a step closer. 'Come to think of it,' he said.

'What small teeth you've got. And other things too, but there's no need to be gratuitously insulting.' He reached forward and grabbed a handful of curtain, flooding the room with light; quite possibly, the first decent illumination it had ever had. For a split second the whole room seemed to blur, as if the deep shadows in the corners were being panicked into deciding what was in them. 'Wolf my arse,' Fang sneered. 'You're just a human with a wolfskin rug tucked round you. What've you done with the witch?'

As he spoke, he sidestepped; with the result that, when Grimm #1's head poked out from under the bed, he was ideally placed to slam his boot into it. Which he did.

'All right,' he growled, grabbing Grimm #2 by the throat and squeezing, 'that'll do. I'm arresting you on charges of witchnapping and impersonating a Wolfpack officer. You are not obliged to say anything, but anything you do say may be taken down and retold in very simple words for the under-fives. Right, what's going on? Who are you, and what's with the wolf imitations?'

'None of your business,' Grimm #2 replied. 'Does the expression *diplomatic immunity* mean anything to you?'

Fang's brow furrowed. 'Yes,' he replied. 'It's a coded message for *make sure nobody ever finds the bodies*. Are you sure you wouldn't rather co-operate?'

Grimm #2 wilted. 'It's all just a silly misunderstanding,' he said. 'My brother and I were out walking in the woods and we lost our way and it was getting dark, so we knocked at the door but there was no one here, so we—'

Fang shook his head. 'Wrong cottage,' he growled. 'The Three Bears are over in the south plantation. This is Little Red Riding Hood's granny's place. As you well know,' he added. 'So explain about the wolf's disguise, before I get irritable.'

Grimm #2 shrugged. 'You call at the werewolf's house, you expect to see a werewolf. What's to know about that?'

'Were—' Fang blinked twice, then made a faint choking

sound. 'Oh, one of *those*. God almighty, I should have guessed.' He scowled, and spat.

'You don't like werewolves?'

'Hah! Wolves who dress up in humans' clothes? Disgusting, I call it . . .' He tailed off, and blushed. 'Anyway,' he went on, 'that still doesn't explain who you are and what you're doing here.'

'Ah.' Grimm #2 grinned feebly. 'Good question. The truth is, we were just looking for a mirror.'

'A mirror?'

'That's right.'

Fang raised an eyebrow. 'Not wishing to be personal,' he said, 'but with the wolfskin rug and the mob cap and the flowery eiderdown, I think a mirror's the last thing you need. Just take it from me, you don't want to see it.'

Grimm #2 blinked twice in rapid succession. 'Maybe you're right,' he said quickly. 'Oh well, blow that, then. I think we'll be going now.'

Fang looked at him narrowly. 'You're *sure* it was just a mirror you were after?' he said.

Grimm #2 nodded. 'Oh,' he added, 'and there's a werewolf in that wardrobe over there. We'll take that one with us as well, I think. I mean, waste not want not, and if we ever happened to find ourselves in a situation where a werewolf might be useful . . .'

Fang held up a hand. 'Oh no you don't,' he said. 'If by werewolf you mean witch, you can't have her. She stays.'

'That's not fair,' Grimm #2 objected. 'I mean, we found her first. And we went to all the trouble of knocking her out—'

'Just a moment. What do you want her for?'

Grimm #2 was about to reply; then he stopped, and smiled. 'Come to that,' he said, 'what do *you* want her for? Don't mind me,' he added. 'I'm terribly broad-minded.'

'I want her to turn me back to my proper shape, if you must know,' Fang replied awkwardly. 'You see, I'm not really a handsome prince.'

'Get away. You certainly had me fooled.'

'I don't want to fool anybody,' Fang snapped. 'And I most certainly don't want to be a handsome prince for a moment longer than I have to. Which is why I really *need* that witch.'

'Fair enough,' Grimm #2 said. 'If you don't mind my asking, what . . . ?'

'A wolf.'

Grimm #2 shrank back a centimetre or so. 'A wolf?'

'Yes, a wolf. A big, bad wolf. You got a problem with that?'

'Me? Good God, no.' Grimm #2 kept perfectly still and smiled broadly. 'Nothing but the greatest respect for big, bad wolves. Fine body of, um, predators. On second thoughts, you keep her. Your need is greater, and all that stuff. And now we'll be—'

'Stay where you are!' Fang growled. 'Nobody's going anywhere until we've got this sorted out. You haven't told me what *you* want the witch for.'

'Haven't I? Oh gosh, how remiss of me. Well, it's like this. My brother and I, we . . . we work for this major pharmaceuticals company, you see, in their research and development department, and we've got this amazing new drug we need to test.'

'Drug?'

'Medicine, I should have said. Anyway, we want to test it, obviously, and the government won't let us test it on humans and the anti-vivisectionists won't let us test it on animals, so we thought . . .'

Fang bared his teeth. It wasn't quite the gesture it should have been; the only threat they posed was of being blinded by the sparkling sunlight reflecting off them. Nevertheless, Grimm #2 did a very lifelike impression of a live slug in a salt cellar.

'You're lying.'

'Yes, in a sense I am, rather. Sorry. Would you like to hear the truth now?'

'Grrr!'

'I'll take that as a Yes. The truth is –' He hesitated. 'You may have trouble assimilating this,' he said. 'It may sound a bit, you know, weird. You won't mind that, will you?'

'Get on with it, before I mistake you for a long pink dog-chew.'

'Right.' He took a deep breath. 'The truth is, we're agents of a foreign power – foreign as in from a whole different dimension or reality or whatever – and we're here to subvert your entire civilisation and culture by gaining control of the Mirrors network. Does that make any sense to you?'

Fang pursed his lips. 'You're trying to tell me you're a little green man, right? Or a bug-eyed monster?'

'Not in so many words,' Grimm #2 replied. 'Although if you prefer to think of it in those terms, I expect it's an entirely valid viewpoint with a lot to recommend it.'

'All right,' Fang said. 'You're not green or bug-eyed, but you're still aliens?'

'*Good* word. I like it. Aliens. Yes, we're aliens.'

'And you're here to kidnap a witch and take over the world?'

'Yes, I suppose you could—'

'You're here to take over the world, and you're frightened of *me*.' Fang clicked his tongue. 'You know, somehow I don't see myself losing a lot of sleep over any threat you lot might possibly pose. I've seen craneflies more dangerous-looking than you two. No, I still don't believe you. I think you're just ordinary burglars, and round here we have a traditional way of dealing with burglars that makes Islamic law look like an exercise program. Now—'

'Hey!'

Fang glanced down. The elf was tugging at his trouser leg. 'Well?'

The elf looked down at its miniature shoes. 'Sorry to bother you,' it said, 'but we'd appear to have more company.'

'What? What kind of –?'

A figure appeared in the doorway. It was dark, stocky, menacing . . .

Short . . .

'Howdy,' it said.

The queen sat down, pulled out a small flat tin box from somewhere inside her gown, and opened it. Inside was a complicated-looking brass machine, quite unlike anything Sis had ever seen before, and next best thing to impossible to describe. However; imagine that a slide-rule fell in love with a sextant, and they had a daughter who eloped with a pair of kitchen scales, and their daughter married the illegitimate grandson of a stirrup-pump . . .

'Got it,' the queen exclaimed, after a few minutes of fiddling with the thing. 'Unless – confound it, which way's north?'

Sis shrugged her shoulders. 'I don't know,' she said. 'Can't you work it out by looking at the sun?'

The queen shook her head. 'Not here,' she said. 'Obviously you haven't noticed, typically enough, but we don't have your boring old sequential days and nights here. That sort of thing's all governed by—'

'Don't tell me,' Sis groaned. 'Narrative patterns.'

'Oh, so you do listen sometimes, then. That's right. Also the seasons, phases of the moon, tides, all that sort of thing. And before you get all scornful and snotty about it, remember who it was who thought feet and inches were a perfectly practicable way of making sense of the world. Wasn't us.'

'Before my time,' Sis replied smugly. 'So? What've you found out?'

The queen twiddled a few more dials, slid the sliding thing up and down the scale a few times, counted to seven on her fingers and grinned. 'Your brother,' she said. 'What did you say his name was?'

'Carl,' Sis replied, after a moment's panic when she couldn't quite remember. 'His name's Carl – you know, it's the strangest thing, I can only just remember him. I think. It's almost –' She stopped and turned pale, with a very slight greenish tinge. 'It's almost as if he wasn't a real person, just someone out of a story.'

'*Yes!*' The queen thumped her fist in the air. 'Brilliant! Oh, I'm so relieved to hear you say that.'

Sis stared at her. 'You are? Why?'

'Because,' the queen replied, fiddling wildly with the funny brass thing, 'it means he's still alive and still here, *and* he's trying to sort things out; which is good,' she added, 'because he caused all these problems in the first place, so he's probably best qualified to get them fixed again. Not,' she added, 'that the competition's exactly fierce. Just out of interest, *why*?'

'Why what?'

'Why in hell's name did he bother? What on earth possessed him to go clowning around with the operating system of a dimension he knew nothing about, without any provocation whatsoever?'

Sis shook her head. 'It's one of those nerd things, I suppose. You know – because it's there, and all that. The same reason why they hack into the Pentagon computers and make people think there's going to be a nuclear war.'

The queen considered this. 'You mean good-natured fun? Anything's possible with your lot, given that you're all completely random, with no narrative patterns to make sense of anything you do. Must be a really horrid way to live, though.'

'Never mind all that,' Sis interrupted. 'What makes you think he's all right? And where the hell is he?'

'Look.' The queen pointed at one of the dials on the Thing. 'See? It's reading 3945321.87.'

'How absolutely fantastic. Ring all the church bells and declare a national holiday.'

'Don't be sarcastic, you aren't very good at it. No, the point is, that's near as dammit four. *Four* consecutive versions of reality. What do you call that, then?'

Sis thought for a moment. 'Dolby?' she hazarded. 'I don't know. It sounds *awful*.'

'Oh it is, certainly. But the last time I checked, there were only three. Someone's set off *another* one, and that's the point. There's the real one, the post cock-up variant, the post cock-up variant modified by someone else who's trying to run me out of town, and now this one too. Which means,' she explained, as Sis made a very quiet whimpering noise, 'there's now someone else who's got into the system and is fooling around with it. Someone else who has at least a tiny fragment of an idea how the thing works. Go figure.'

'You think it's Carl?'

The queen nodded enthusiastically, her head moving like a tennis ball on a string. 'I'm sure it is, because you're having trouble remembering him. You have this strange feeling he's someone in a story. Which means, God help us all, he's become part of the system somewhere.'

'Which means he's still alive—'

'Which means,' the queen said, 'he's alive and operational, and he's using that perverted little brain of his to get into Mirrors. Well,' she concluded, 'maybe it's not exactly optimal, the entire future of this dimension resting in the hands of a recklessly irresponsible adolescent with an anorak and acne—'

'How did you know that?'

'Call it intuition. Are you *sure* it was just a whim on his part? He didn't get any encouragement from outside before he started all this?'

Sis ransacked her memory, what was left of it after the mice of transdimensional entropic shift had nibbled it threadbare. 'Well, he kept getting letters from somewhere official, because they had those printed things in the top right-hand corner instead of stamps. And I think he got lots of messages from them through the Internet as well.'

'Quite possibly,' the queen said thoughtfully. 'Once they'd got him hooked, they'd have wanted to keep it all as quiet as possible, and they've probably gone back into his system and erased them all now. It's like that old saying about the e-mail of the specious being deadlier than their mail. And no prizes for guessing,' she added darkly, 'who *they* are.'

'Really? Who did you have in mind, then? You think it's all the CIA, or is this just another of those the-Milk-Marketing-Board-murdered-Elvis theories?'

'Really?' The queen looked shocked. 'I never knew that.'

'Oh, for pity's sake—'

'And anyway,' the queen went on, 'that can't be true, because if you'd read last week's edition of the *Dependent On Sunday*, you'd know that it's been incontrovertibly proved that Elvis is the face on the Turin Shroud.' She hesitated, and frowned. 'Now how in hell's name do I know that?' she asked. 'Dear God, it must be something that's leaked through from your dimension.'

Sis's eyes lit up. 'Carl!' she said.

'It's possible,' the queen replied. 'Though I'd have thought he was a bit young to have heard of Elvis.'

'I think they did him in History at school,' Sis replied. 'Look, is there any way of proving all this, or is it just a theory?'

The queen looked round. 'There's always that confounded unicorn,' she said. 'Go and see if it's still there while I check these settings.'

Not long afterwards, Sis returned. The unicorn was with her.

'Ah,' said the queen, looking up. 'You decided to let him go, then?'

The unicorn growled. 'Let him go, my arse,' it said. 'No, this fleet of helicopter gunships flew over and pulled him out. After they'd bombed the whole glade flat and sprinkled napalm all over everything, of course. You ever been strafed from the air by Santa's little helpers? Not recommended. It's not so much the cluster-bombs that get to you, it's the fact that they're all tastefully wrapped in coloured paper and tied up with silver ribbon.'

Sis and the queen exchanged glances. 'That sounds like Carl,' Sis whispered. 'He loves watching action videos.'

'You amaze me,' the queen replied, grinning. 'Also of interest is the fact that while all this was going on about a hundred yards away, we didn't see or hear a thing. I think we can safely say your brother's on the case.'

Sis took a deep breath and let it go again. 'Wonderful,' she said. 'How very reassuring.'

Julian stopped what he was doing, stared up at the sky and pulled a face. It was hot, he was sweating (appropriately enough) like a pig, and by his calculations it had now been midday for four and a half hours.

Shouldn't be like this, he said to himself, as he stooped down to pick up another bundle of sticks. *Midday should be at twelve o'clock precisely, not for as long as it takes.* He didn't know where any of these strange thoughts came from; why midday should be twelve o'clock, for example. All he knew was that he had them, and they made his head ache.

Still, it was coming along nicely. Once he'd decided to build his new fortified sty out of sticks (*why sticks? Dunno. Seemed like a good idea . . .*), he'd taken the time to sit down with a pointed twig and a flat patch of mud and sketch it all out in detail. A nearby blackcurrant bush had provided the makings of an ersatz abacus, and he'd calculated the various factors – co-efficients of stress against tensile strengths of various woods (elm 68 Newtons per square millimetre, ash 116, oak 97, Scots pine 89, making ash the obvious choice) – before drawing up a final 1/100th scale blueprint with material specs, quantities and a first draft of a schedule of works. Then it had been a long, hard slog in the woods cutting the sticks and bundling them up into sheaves, all to a standard size and weight to allow completely modular construction; and now he was on the longest and hardest stage of the job, actually fitting it all together.

He'd started off with the south-west African *kraal* house as his basic design concept, with heavy influence from clinker-built ships, the Eskimo igloo and the classical Roman arch. A high-stacked D-section dome constructed out of overlapping bundles of sticks tied and pinned in an upwards spiral keyed off with a single massive osier knot at the top would, he calculated, give the optimum level of structural integrity (by virtue of the counterbalancing of forces under external compression) without sacrificing the unique insulating properties of thatch. All in all, it was a very impressive piece of work; and although he still couldn't quite see what had possessed him to build a house out of sticks when he could have strolled down to the nearest builders' merchants and ordered a big load of breezeblocks, at least he had the satisfaction of knowing that as stick-built realty went, this was the state of the art.

Nevertheless . . .

He put the bundle down again and turned to face the forest; what there was left of it now that he'd cut and slashed a substantial hole. Was he imagining things, or had something flitted stealthily past just inside the curtain of leaves and brushwood? Eugene and Desmond? He hoped not. It wasn't likely, either. His brothers had the same aptitude for stealthy flitting as a dinosaur has for brain surgery. If Gene and Des were headed this way, he'd have heard the crashing sounds hours ago.

There it was again; a flicker of movement, the flash of sunlight on some dark metal, the faintest *snap!* as a foot landed on a wisp of twig. Definitely someone there; and Julian, who had come to regard paranoia as his only true friend in all the world, abandoned his bundle of sticks and ran for home.

It's not perfect, he told himself as he rolled the door-stone into place behind him (note the cunningly contrived system of balances and counterweights that makes it possible for a three-ton boulder to be effortlessly manipulated from within the house). *But it'll probably do.* He peeked out through the tiny loophole in the front elevation and saw a shadowy figure looming in a gap in the trees. Right now he wanted nothing at all to do with shadowy figures, not even if they came surrounded by beautiful young sows bearing golden platters of swill to tell him he'd just won the lottery. He growled and turned up the propane burner under the big cauldron of molten lead that was simmering cheerfully away on the ledge of his lookout post.

He'd just finished adjusting the regulator of the propane bottle and was testing the tension in the ropes of the giant siege catapult when the shadowy figure stepped out of the forest into the clearing. Not an encouraging sight for a nervous pig; whoever he was, he felt the need to dress from head to toe in shiny black armour, wear a helmet with a mask visor and a huge neckpiece and carry a whacking great two-handed sword. Either the Jehovah's Witnesses in this neighbourhood had abandoned the Mr-Nice-Guy tactic, or here came trouble.

Six more followed him, which made Julian feel a whole lot worse. They didn't seem to be in any great hurry, and they weren't being particularly furtive about their movements; maybe what he'd taken for stealthy flitting was just the natural demeanour of heavily armed men trying to move through dense undergrowth without tripping over and being unable to get up again. Quite possibly; and maybe the swords were just for clearing a path through the briars. But that still didn't explain what they wanted.

'You in the tinfoil,' he shouted. 'This is private property. Clear off, or I'll set the dragon on you.'

The nearest intruder looked up and pushed back his visor. 'Hello?' he called. 'Oh, there you are, I didn't see you in all that firewood. What are you, a charcoal-burner or something?'

So that was it, Julian muttered to himself; they're planning on burning me out. Little do they know that every single twig in this lot has been treated with the latest in asbestos-free fire-retardant. 'You deaf or something?' he bellowed. 'I'll count to ten and then I'll turn Sparky loose. One. Two.'

They didn't seem particularly worried, which was a pity, since the nearest thing he had to a dragon was a small beetle that had crawled down the back of his neck a couple of hours

ago and was apparently building a house of its own somewhere between his shoulder-blades. He got as far as nine,
then stopped.

'I'm warning you,' he said. 'I don't want to do this.'

'Oh,' the intruder replied. He sounded disappointed. 'Pity.
I've always wanted to see a dragon.'

Julian winced. 'You reckon?' he replied; and the sneer he'd
intended to accompany the words somehow got turned into
a sad little simper.

'Oh yes,' the intruder replied, planting his sword in the
ground and leaning on it. 'Dragons are a traditional symbol
of hope and spiritual rebirth. Have you really got one we can
look at?'

Some pigs, Julian reflected bitterly, have it easy. Nice quiet
life, regular meals, no predators, nothing to worry about except
the prospect of ending up between two slices of bread. Try to
make something of yourself, and the world's suddenly your
enemy. 'No,' he admitted, 'I was just trying to get rid of you
without having to resort to overwhelming force. Now bugger
off before I lose my temper.'

'You sound a bit hostile,' said the intruder, 'if you'll pardon me for saying so. My guess is that this comes from not
being at peace with the Elements. Have you ever considered
a properly structured course of meditation?'

Oink, thought Julian. 'Go away. This is your last warning.
After that, on your own heads be it.'

Maybe the phrase wasn't familiar to the intruders; they
made a big performance out of looking up, taking off their
helmets and inspecting them, patting the tops of their heads
and so on. Julian could only take so much of that; in a sudden
spurt of rage he grabbed a handy billhook and slashed through
the rope that restrained the arm of the catapult.

It was a *big* catapult; frame made out of the trunks of four
mature oak trees, with wrought-iron fittings and the finest
horsehair ropes to provide the torsion. In theory it could have
shot a six-hundredweight rock over two hundred yards. Since

there was no way Julian could pighandle a rock that size up on to the lookout point all on his own, however, he'd decided to use a little initiative and an alternative projectile. To be precise, three hundred kilos of well-rotted horse manure, all neatly packed in 25-kilo sacks and piled up in the throwing arm of the catapult.

Unfortunately, he hadn't quite thought it through.

Later, he worked it out as a simple matter of relative sectional density, surface area and wind resistance; a set of equations so simple that any six-week-old piglet could have done them in its head. In the rush and bother of building the house, however, Julian simply hadn't had the time or the patience. Accordingly, as soon as he cut the rope, the catapult's payload rose straight up in the air until, after a stern word and a shake of the finger from gravity, it came down again, giving it plenty of that old thirty-two-feet-per-second-per-second and landing directly –

On their own heads be it, he'd said. If only.

'There's a passage in the scriptures,' one of the intruders said, once the last sack had landed and split wide, and the last tottering remains of the house of sticks had fallen in (Julian had known about that particular weak spot from the outset, but he hadn't been expecting an attack from directly overhead) 'about the man who spits at heaven. Later on, perhaps, when you're more in the mood—'

'A bath wouldn't hurt, either,' added a colleague. 'Being one with the basics of nature is all very well, but wearing 'em's a different matter entirely.'

Sitting among the ruins of his house, the tattered remnants of a dung-sack festooned around his neck like a Jacobean collar, Julian groaned. 'All right, then,' he said, 'I quit. You win. I've had enough. Ham and eggs, bacon sandwich, gammon Hawaii, sweet and sour pork balls; you name it, I'm your pig. Just get it over with, will you?'

There was a brief silence; then the first intruder cleared his throat. 'Actually,' he said, 'we're vegetarians. All we wanted to know was, are we on the right road for the Hundred Acre Wood?'

Julian nodded. 'Follow your nose as far as the next clearing but one and wait for a dramatic plot reversal,' he sighed. 'There's usually one along every ten minutes or so.'

'Many thanks,' the intruder said. 'If it's any consolation, the river of predestination has many bends but few bridges.'

'I'll bear that in mind,' Julian assured him. 'And now, if you don't mind—'

'Carry on,' replied the intruder. 'Be seeing you. Strive to be at peace.'

'Same to you with knobs on. Look,' he added irritably, 'it's probably none of my business, and really I can't be bothered with anything much right now, but who *are* you guys? My brothers didn't send you here, by any chance?'

The intruder regarded him inquisitively. 'Your brothers?'

'Eugene and Desmond.'

'And they'd be, um, pigs? Like you?'

'That's right. Unless my mum had a really adventurous time before she met my dad, all my brothers are pigs.'

'And the sages teach us that all pigs are our brothers,' the intruder replied politely. 'But no, can't say they did. In fact, I don't think I've ever met a talking pig before. Actually, we're samurai.'

'Samurai.' Julian thought hard. 'That's a kind of Italian sausage.'

The intruder conferred briefly with his colleagues. 'Not really,' he said, 'except insofar as all things are, at the most fundamental level, one and the same. Mostly, though, we're warrior-philosophers, and we're off to kill a wicked queen.'

'Really?' Julian, who'd never cared much for politics, backed away a little. 'Gosh,' he added.

'It's our calling,' explained the first intruder. 'To defend the weak against the strong, the oppressed against the oppressor, the humble and meek against the overbearing – sorry, am I boring you?'

'No, no,' Julian assured him. 'I was just, er, counting you. I make it seven.'

'Congratulations. Well done.'

Julian frowned hopelessly. 'Yes, but *seven*,' he said. 'Seven *samurai*. Seven samurai defending the weak and oppressed and all that. No offence, lads, but are you sure you aren't dwarves?'

The intruders looked at each other. 'I don't think so,' said one of them. 'We'd have noticed something like that.'

Julian shrugged. 'Oh well, never mind, it was just a thought. Best of luck with the, um, wicked queen.'

The intruders bowed politely and strolled away back into the forest, leaving Julian alone with his scattered bundles of sticks and his aromatic artillery. Seven, he thought. Seven samurai. Seven dwarves. The Secret Seven. The Secret Magnificent Seven Dwarf Samurai Against Thebes.

Whatever.

He pulled the sack off his neck, brushed himself down and went off to look for some bricks.

CHAPTER NINE

'**M**y God,' muttered Grimm #2. 'It's a gnome.'

Dumpy growled like a hungry tiger who's just received a tax demand. 'You just say something, friend?' he hissed. 'Or was that just my imagination?'

'It's all right,' Fang said, standing in front of Grimm #2. 'I'll deal with this.' He leaned forward, until he and the dwarf were almost touching noses. 'You,' he said. 'No trouble, understood. You want trouble, go pick on someone your own size.'

'He jes' done called me a—'

'Yes,' Fang interrupted quickly, 'I know. But he's thick as a brick and foreign. Make allowances.'

Dumpy stared back. 'Do that all the time,' he replied. 'Especially when they're running, otherwise you miss 'em behind. *Nobody* calls me a gnome and gets away with it, understood?'

Fang straightened his back and turned to stare at Grimm #2. 'You,' he snapped. 'Did you just call this gentleman a gnome?'

'Ye— no,' Grimm #2 said, 'certainly not. Wouldn't dream of doing such a thing.'

'See?' Fang said. 'And you there, in the doorway, the other short gentleman. Did you hear anybody call anybody a gnome?'

Rumpelstiltskin shook his head. 'I wasn't listening,' he said diplomatically. 'In fact, I'm morally certain I wasn't even here at the time. I was probably somewhere else entirely. Look, can we shelve the posturing just for now and get on with the business in hand? I hate to break up a good confrontation, but we're on a schedule.'

Fang growled a bit more. Wolfpack didn't hold with dwarves, and a Wolfpack officer is afraid of no one; even if they're four foot nothing and mostly made up of nose, beard and shoes –

(*Huh?* demanded Fang's logic centres.

You know, replied the provisional wing of his memory. *Dwarves. Little punk tough guys who're always starting fights and throwing their weight around. At least, we think they're always starting fights. We seem to remember it that way.*)

'All right,' Fang said. 'Say what you want and then get out.'

Dumpy made an aggressive noise at the back of his throat; but before he could turn it into words, Rumpelstiltskin interrupted. Born diplomat, that little guy. That would explain, Fang rationalised, why I don't like him.

'Dead simple,' Rumpelstiltskin said smoothly. 'We were looking for the witch, that's all.'

'You too?' Grimm #2 broke in. 'My God, she's popular today. Sorry, but you'll have to join the queue, because we saw her first.'

'Since when've folk been standing in line for witches?' Dumpy said, frowning. 'Always thought the trick was stayin' out of their way, not findin' them. 'Cept when there's a new witch in town, of course, an' everybody's tryin' to find out if she's good. Like they say, a new broomstick sweeps clean.'

'Fair enough. So what do you want her for, then?'

Dumpy muttered something and looked away. 'We're stuck,' said a voice from Rumpelstiltskin's hat. 'He's supposed to be rounding up seven dwarves, but we've only been able to find four.'

Fang blinked. '*Four* dwarves?' he queried. 'You can't have looked properly.'

'You reckon?'

'But dwarves always come in sevens,' Fang replied. 'Like cans of beer always come in sixes. It's . . . it's . . .'

'It's in the story,' Tom Thumb finished the sentence for him. 'I know. But suddenly they don't any more. And I for one'd like to know why.'

While this conversation had been taking place, Fang's elf had been sitting on the mantelpiece behind a framed hand-stitched sampler, swinging her legs in the air and chewing on a hunk of ancient grey-streaked chocolate that had turned up among the fluff and broken rubber bands in Fang's handsome-prince issue embroidered waistcoat. Now, how-ever, she was sitting in rapt attention with a look on her face that could only have had one of two possible explanations, either chronic indigestion or a bad case of love, and as far as he knew the elf had a digestion like a cement mixer. True, it should have been the handsome prince and some generic industry-standard princess getting the treatment rather than a very small, hat-dwelling person and a maladjusted elf. Now sure enough, Fang was greatly relieved at not being in the frame; but he was puzzled as well; the same level of curiosity as a man might exhibit if he'd just walked blindfold across a minefield and not been blown up.

'You were saying,' he said. 'About the witch. What's she got to do with an apparent national dwarf shortage?'

'We were hoping she'd agree to shrink some people for us,' Rumpelstiltskin admitted sheepishly. 'And turning the mole into something wouldn't go amiss, either.' He stopped and looked round. 'Hell's buttons, where's the blasted animal gone off to now?'

'Here,' replied a small, muffled voice under the bed. 'Hey, there's beetles living under here.' [Crunch, crunch] 'I

180 • Tom Holt

wouldn't mind sticking around for a bit, unless other people have got things they want to do elsewhere. Last thing I'd want to do is' [crunch] 'hold anybody up.'

'Mole?' Fang queried. Rumpelstiltskin pulled a sour face. 'Don't ask.'

'What? Oh, right. Good idea at the time?'

'Desperation, more like. That's why we thought we'd try the witch, see if she could help us out with a little down-sizing.'

'Sorry, guys,' Grimm #2 said. 'She's spoken for. If you're patient, there's bound to be another one along in a moment. Narrative pat—'

He shut up quickly, aware that he'd almost made a potentially disastrous mistake. The theory was that if ever the inhabitants of this peculiar pocket universe found out that they were just characters in stories, the dramatic illusion would melt down like a fusion explosion and that'd be the end of it. Even a few of them knowing would seriously bend things . . .

Grimm #2 caught his breath. Maybe they already had. Which would explain – oh, all sorts of things. His fingers itched for his ambience meter, tucked inside his jacket, but he didn't dare reach for it in present company. Nobody likes to fade away and never to have existed in the first place, which was what might happen if he gave the game away to one of the natives.

On the mantelpiece, the elf was ostentatiously looking the other way while pulling handfuls of dead leaf out of an old, dusty flower arrangement. Tom Thumb was doing more or less the same thing except that, since there were no flower arrangements inside the brim of Rumpelstiltskin's hat, he had to be content with ripping out fistfuls of felt. Fang and Rumpelstiltskin, having noticed their respective colleagues and resisted the temptation to throw up, met each other's eye.

'I know,' said Rumpelstiltskin. 'Let's toss a coin for her. Heads wins.'

Fang shook his head. 'Nice try,' he muttered; he knew, of course, that the wicked queen's coinage had her bust on both sides, ostensibly because it was a nice bust and beauty is truth, truth beauty; really, so the local tradition went, to save her having to choose which of her two faces to put on the money.

That, of course, was when she was still wicked. Now, Fang realised, instead of regarding her with the proper degree of loathing he'd have felt this time last week, the very thought of her was enough to make him want to run out into the street waving a little flag on a stick.

'All right,' Rumpelstiltskin conceded, 'some other kind of game.'

'Five card stud,' Dumpy said enthusiastically. The others had the good sense to refuse. Compared to playing poker with a dwarf, playing heads and tails with a double-sided coin was positively fraught with uncertainty.

'Hide and seek,' Fang suggested, aware that in spite of everything he still had a better sense of smell than anything that was entitled from birth to walk on two legs.

'I spy?' Tom Thumb chimed in, not taking his eyes off the elf. 'Um, what do you, er . . . ?' he asked her.

'Wonderful idea,' she croaked back. 'That was a really intelligent suggestion.'

Thumb blushed, until he looked like a stray tomato in Carmen Miranda's hat. 'Oh, I expect if I hadn't suggested it, you'd have thought of it straight away.'

'It's very kind of you to say so.'

'You too.'

Fang could feel the moment drifting away from him, like a dropped spanner in a space shuttle. 'Not I Spy,' he said firmly. 'Hey, what about charades?'

'Charades?' repeated a general chorus.

'Yeah, why not? Oh come on, try to think positive. The sooner we get this done, the better. Before,' he added ruefully, 'those two start chewing each other's faces off.'

'Don't know what you mean,' the elf snarled at him. 'Some people will insist on jumping to conclusions.'

'I hate that,' Thumb added.

'Oh, do you? Me too. If there's one thing I can't stand, it's people jumping to conclusions.'

'Really?'

'Oh yes.'

'Gosh!'

Just then there was a groan from under the bed; not, as Fang logically assumed, the sound of someone reacting quite naturally to the show Thumb and the elf were putting on, just Grimm #1 making waking-up oh-my-head-hurts noises.

'Dear God,' he mumbled. 'I really and truly hope that there was this amazingly good party last night and that's why my head hurts. It'd be dreadful to be in this much pain without having done something to deserve it.'

'You did,' Fang growled, 'but it wasn't a party. Come out from under there. We're about to play charades.'

'Charades.'

'Yes.'

'That settles it,' Grimm #1 said. 'Must've been one hell of a party, because I'm still hallucinating. Oh Christ, I didn't marry anybody, did I?'

'Oh for pity's sake,' his brother snapped. 'You aren't hallucinating. We really are about to . . . '

'Yes I bloody well am hallucinating,' Grimm #1 interrupted. 'At least, I sincerely hope I am. For instance, if I didn't know better I'd think the room was full of little *short* people. It'll be pink elephants next.'

Grimm #2 replied loudly, to cover the inevitable groundswell of muttering from Dumpy and Co. 'Shut up,' he advised. 'They're dwarves, and they're after our witch. That's why we're about to play charades.'

Grimm #1 cradled his head between his hands. '*Bad* party,' he said. 'It's a tragedy I can't remember it. Never could see the point in having a party so good you've got to rely on your friends to tell you next day just how good it was.'

'Are you two ready?' Fang growled.

'No. You go first. I'm still trying to remember who I am and where I might have left my head.'

Fang thought for a moment; then he was suddenly inspired. 'Ready or not,' he said, 'here we go.'

He dropped on to all fours, growled and stalked up and down the room, wagging an imaginary tail. From time to time he paused, sniffed and pawed at the ground. Finally he sat up on his haunches and howled a blood-chilling serenade to a virtual moon.

There was a long silence.

'Is that it?' asked Grimm #1.

'Yes.'

'Oh.'

Dumpy and Rumpelstiltskin conferred in loud whispers. 'We think it's *101 Dalmatians*,' he said.

Fang looked offended. 'Wrong.'

The Grimms similarly compared notes. 'What about "How Much Is That Doggie In The Window?"'

'Wrong again.'

'"Daddy Wouldn't Buy Me A Bow-Wow"?'

'You're starting to annoy me. And no.'

Dumpy leaned over and muttered something in his colleague's ear. 'We think it may be "A Four-Legged Friend".'

'You do, do you? Well, you're wrong.'

'Oh.' Both teams conferred again. 'You sure it wasn't *101 Dalmatians*? Rumpelstiltskin queried. 'Because if it wasn't, it should have been.'

'You don't know, do you? Come on, admit it.'

'Give us a bit more time,' Grimm #2 replied. 'I know, what about "Rudolph The Red-Nosed Reindeer"?'

'You're only making things harder for yourself,' Fang said coldly. 'Pack it in, I'll take my witch and get out of here. Come on, you know it makes sense.'

'One more guess,' Rumpelstiltskin said. 'I reckon it must be *Cat On A Hot Tin Roof.*'

'Well, it wasn't. It was "Leader Of The Pack". As you'd have guessed,' Fang added savagely, 'if you knew *anything* about wolves.'

Dumpy stood up. 'Now you just hold your hosses there, stranger,' he said, ''cos I ain't happy with that. Reckon as how you're cheatin'. 'Cos that weren't nothin' like any wolf *I* ever seen.'

'Oh really? And what the hell would you know about wolves?'

'Enough to know they don't act anythin' like *that*,' Dumpy replied scornfully. 'Wolves is kinda graceful and purty, y'know? They don't stomp around the joint like flat-footed steers. Nor they don't waggle their butts in the air, neither.'

'I agree with him,' Grimm #2 added. 'It's just conceivable that that could have been a very elderly, constipated wolf with terminal piles and thorns in all four paws, but you should have specified that before you started. Next time you're passing a zoo, nip in and take a look at the real thing, you'll see what I mean.'

Fang felt more or less as if he'd looked in a mirror and seen Winnie the Pooh. 'But that's crazy,' he protested, 'I know more about wolves than any man living—' Then he clamped his mouth tight shut, while his words echoed round inside his head. *I see. So you reckon you're one of* them *now, do you? And maybe you're right.* 'The hell with this,' he said, with a slight edge of panic in his voice. 'I *need* that witch. Dammit, you're welcome to her just as soon as she's turned me ba— done a little job for me. All we've got to do is take turns. In fact, if we'd agreed on that in the first place, we'd all be through by now.'

That did seem to be a fairly convincing argument. 'All right,' said Rumpelstiltskin. 'You go first, then us, and then you two can have her to keep. Agreed?'

The dwarves grumbled a bit, but eventually agreed. 'Jes'

so long as you don't break her,' Dumpy put in. 'I hear as how they're darned inflammable.'

Grimm #2 nodded towards the wardrobe, whereupon Fang bounded over and ripped the door open –

'All right,' he said, 'quit fooling around. Where is she really?'

'In the—'

But when they looked there, the cupboard was bare. So to speak.

'Psst!' said a bush.

Sis had thought she was way past being surprised by anything she saw or heard; just shows how wrong you can be. She jumped about two feet in the air, but the wicked queen just kept on walking.

'Not now, Beast,' she said. 'We're busy.'

'But you've got to help me,' whined the bush. 'This time she's going to catch me, I know it. Look, you're supposed to be the law around here—'

'That,' the queen replied severely, 'is a moot point. Moot, in fact, as all buggery. And even if I was, I wouldn't help you. Go on, clear on out of it. Scram.'

'But I'm desperate!'

'So I'd heard,' the queen said. 'And that remark is less than flattering, if I may say so. Go away.'

The bush shook, and out from behind it stepped the ugliest, most revolting-looking creature Sis had ever seen outside of a televised Parliamentary debate. 'He's from *Beauty and the Beast*, right?' she whispered.

'You've got it. And I'll bet you'll never guess which one he is.'

'I'm sure he's very nice when you get to know him,' Sis replied defiantly. 'It's in the eye of the beholder, you know.'

'What is?'

'Well, beauty, of course.'

'What, that old thing? I thought you were talking about a bit of grit or a fly or something.'

Wheezing and panting like a ninety-year-old chain-smoker, the Beast waddled up to them, sighed and flumped down on the stump of a tree. 'Thank you,' he gasped. 'It's so nice finally to meet somebody who cares.'

The queen snorted. 'You make me sick, you hypocritical bastard,' she said. 'Though I reckon that on you, vomit'd be a fashion statement. Get on with it; then we can ignore you and be on our way.'

'It's Her,' the Beast muttered, his voice shaky. 'She can't be far behind me.'

The queen nodded. 'How'd you get out this time?' she asked.

'Ah,' replied the Beast, and some of the more mobile components of its face moved together in a vague approximation of a grin. 'I dug a tunnel and got out through the drainage system.'

'Thereby going into the record books as the first person ever to lower the tone of a sewer.' She sniffed tentatively. 'Well,' she conceded. 'It saves you having to have your bath this year. Why *do* you keep bothering to run away, though? She always catches you in the end.'

'Not this time,' replied the Beast with grim determination. 'Whatever happens, I'm not going back. I'd rather she killed me first.'

'Who's *she?*' Sis interrupted. 'Not Beauty, surely?'

At the word *Beauty*, the Beast shivered uncontrollably. 'Not so loud,' he whispered. 'You never know who might be listening. All the dear little birds and cuddly little animals in the forest are her friends. They'd grass me up to her so fast my feet wouldn't touch.' He calmed himself down by breathing in deeply. 'You don't believe me,' he said, hurt. 'You think I'm exaggerating. Well, you try being her prisoner for six months in that horrible castle, see how you like it.'

''Scuse me?' Sis interrupted. 'Shouldn't that be the other way . . . ?' She checked herself and remembered. 'Sorry,' she went on, 'mixing you up with someone else.'

The Beast stifled a sob. 'Sometimes I think I'll never get away,' he groaned. 'A couple of weeks ago this nice dragon came by, saw me locked up in the highest tower of the castle and tried to rescue me. She killed it, of course. She always does. Half of the furniture in the Great Hall's got dragonskin loose covers now.'

'All right,' the queen admitted grudgingly, 'so she's a tough cookie. And maybe,' she added, a trifle less roughly, 'just maybe she's more than you deserve. I don't see why you expect us to get involved. Like I said just now, my official status is a bit blurred right now.'

'I think we should help,' Sis said firmly. 'After all,' she added, 'if all this stuff you've been telling me about narrative patterns is actually true—'

'We could boost ourselves into a better storyline,' the queen said, 'one we could use to get where we want to be. Not bad, girl, you're learning. All right,' she said, turning to face the Beast, 'what's she up to now? When you last saw her, I mean.'

'That's just it,' the Beast said. 'She's gone crazy. Well, she was never exactly what you'd call a stable personality to start with. She's got mood swings that's make a pendulum dizzy. But ever since she got that message from her accountant—'

The wicked queen froze. 'Did you say accountant?'

'That's right. Apparently he's a little man who does sums.'

'I know what an accountant is,' the wicked queen said, with feeling. 'This wouldn't be a little gnomelike twerp—'

'Leprechaun, actually.'

'That's right. Lives in the middle of a swamp.'

'For some reason best known to himself. Yes, that's him. Anyway, he sent her a message offering to sell her something. No idea what it was, but it must have been quite valuable, 'cos she hired Jack and Jill to go fetch it, and they're *expensive*. Anyway, ever since then, she's been sitting in front of her mirror talking to it. And doing this weird wicked-queen laughing – oh, sorry, no offence.'

'None taken,' the queen replied. 'I used to pride myself on my evil laughter.' Something she'd just said made her suddenly thoughtful. 'Hellfire, yes,' she added quietly. 'Didn't I just. I'd forgotten all about that until you mentioned it just now.'

'Anyway,' the Beast went on, 'it's downright scary listening to her. It was bad enough when she used to talk to the furniture and the crockery. At least they didn't talk back.'

'Had more sense, probably,' the queen said. 'But the mirror does?'

The Beast nodded, and several of the floppier extremities on his face wobbled revoltingly. 'They chat away for hours up there,' he said, shivering a little. 'And there's lots of that spooky laughter. Not all of it's her, either.'

'Really?' The queen stood up. 'We'd better go and look into this,' she said. 'Do you know a narrative thread that'll take us there without being seen?'

The Beast thought for a moment. 'There's an unresolved plot strand that comes up slap bang in the middle of the deserted east wing of the castle,' he said. 'Will that do?'

'It'll have to, I suppose,' the queen replied dubiously. 'But I know those UPSs. You can always tell them by the way they have these big neon signs saying TRAP THIS WAY!!! just above the entrances. Still, there's no bucking the story. Just a minute,' she added. 'What the hell would you know about narrative threads and unresolved plot strands? You're just a civilian.'

The Beast shrugged helplessly. 'Search me,' he said. 'I just do, that's all. Feels like I've known it all my life, except . . .'

The queen nodded sympathetically. 'You don't have to explain to me,' she said. 'Let's just say there's a lot of it about. You feel as if you can't remember a time when you didn't know about whatever it is you now suddenly realise you know. Which,' she said with a sour grin, 'is fairly close to the truth, I reckon. Lead the way, then, and let's get this horrid chore over and done with.'

'Thank you,' said the Beast, rearranging the mess on his face into something smile-shaped and horrible. 'You've no idea how much this means to . . .'

'Shut up.'

'Yes, of course, I'm sorry. I should have thought before I opened my mouth. Sometimes I know I can be dreadfully inconsiderate and I'm trying not to, but sometimes it can be a bit . . .'

The queen sighed. 'Now can you see why I hate him so much?'

'Yes.'

'*Slowly,*' observed Mr Hiroshige, '*the falling snowflake*—'

'Sorry, I missed that,' said young Mr Akira, catching up. 'Could you start again, please?'

If the senior samurai was put out by the interruption, he didn't show it. 'Of course,' he replied; then he cleared his throat and declaimed:

> '*Slowly, the falling snowflake*
> *Mingles with the cherry-blossom, falling;*
> *Where the hell are we?*'

Young Mr Akira, who was learning to appreciate the essentially transitory nature of all material objects by carrying everybody else's equipment, scratched his head and looked round for a landmark. 'Sorry,' he said, 'I haven't got a clue. And besides,' he went on, 'didn't you say just now that all roads are in essence the same road, and that to travel is by its very nature to arrive at all destinations simultaneously?'

'Yes,' agreed Mr Hiroshige, 'but that was before my feet started to hurt. I think we should have turned left back there by the old abandoned mill.'

'We could ask somebody, I suppose,' suggested a small samurai at the rear of the column. 'Although since all directions are simply facets of the same universal jewel, we might do just as well if we sit down here for a cup of tea and a smoke.'

Mr Hiroshige sighed. 'Good idea,' he said. 'It so happens I have a flask in my kitbag.'

(And, since all kitbags are one universal kitbag and young Mr Akira was carrying it, he knelt down and started undoing straps and peeling back Velcro until he found it. It held just enough for six cups.)

'This is getting boring,' said Mr Nikko, taking off his left boot and evicting something small and energetic from it. 'Surely it can't be all that difficult to find a wicked queen in her own forest.'

'Ah,' said young Mr Akira, pouring tea, 'but since all people are merely segments of the great orange of mankind, doesn't it follow that to find any one person is to find all humanity, looked at from a perspective uncluttered by the foliage of sensory perception?'

'No,' answered Mr Miroku. 'I don't suppose there's anything to eat, is there? Some of us didn't have any breakfast.'

Young Mr Akira looked up. 'There's sandwiches,' he said. 'There's raw fish and seaweed, fungus and beancurd, mixed raw fish or mixed seaweed.'

'Oh. No sashimi?'

Young Mr Akira looked in the packet. 'No,' he replied. 'Sorry.'

'Sorry,' Mr Miroku mimicked. 'I don't think that's quite good enough. When I was your age, if I'd forgotten the sashimi sandwiches, I'd have been expected to disembowel myself on the spot, and no excuses.'

Mr Akira's eyes opened wide. 'Gosh,' he said. 'And did you, ever?'

'It's all right,' Mr Hiroshige said quickly, before Mr Miroku had a chance to reply, 'he's just a bit young still. And stupid too, of course. But young he'll grow out of.'

They sat for a while in silence (unless you count the sound of sandwiches being eaten. There were six rounds of sandwiches). Finally, young Mr Akira cleared his throat. 'I heard a good joke the other day,' he said. 'How many fifth-level wizards does it take to change a light bulb?'

The samurai considered this for a moment. Two of them took off their steel gauntlets and counted on their fingers.

'One,' said Mr Nikko.

'No, that's not right,' young Mr Akira said. 'You're not doing it properly.'

'Oh. How should it be done, then?'

'Well,' Mr Akira replied, 'I say how many fifth-level wizards does it take to change a light bulb, and you say, I don't know, how many fifth-level wizards *does* it take to change a light bulb, and then *I* say it depends on what he wants to change it into. Get it?'

The silence that followed was so stony, you could have built bridges out of it.

'Oh I see,' said Mr Hiroshige at last. 'You mean how many wizards does it take to change a light bulb *into something else.* You know, that question was rather ambiguous. You didn't make it clear whether you meant change as in turning things into things or change in the sense of replace or renew. Now if you'd said *how many wizards does it take to* transform *a light bulb . . .*'

'Better still,' said Mr Nikko, 'what about, *If a collection of fifth-level wizards wanted to turn a light bulb into something, for instance a thousand paper cranes, how many of them would it take?* Then there'd be no risk of being misunderstood.'

'Although on a more fundamental level,' argued Mr Hiroshige, 'the light bulb and the paper cranes are all part of the same great nexus of concrete existence, so where's the point? In fact, wouldn't you say it was *presumptuous* to change it into something else? You'd be usurping the prerogative of the continuum. Whereas if you meditated long enough and in the proper manner, you'd pretty soon be able to see the light bulb as whatever it is you wanted it to be, which is surely every bit as good as far as you're concerned.'

Mr Wakisashi, the smallest of the samurai, nodded eagerly.

'It's a pity we haven't got a light bulb,' he said. 'Otherwise we could experiment.'

'You'd need two, though, surely,' said Mr Nikko. 'One to be the broken one and one to be the one you replace the broken one with –' He stopped to count on his fingers. 'And a cauliflower,' he added, 'to be the thing the light bulb eventually gets changed into.'

Mr Akira looked glum. 'If I'd known it was this complicated,' he said, 'I'd never have started it in the first place. It was only meant as a joke.'

'Raises an interesting point, though,' said Mr Wakisashi, who was one of those silent, mystic types who don't say a word for years and then suddenly burst out with a whole lot of gibberish. 'We could meditate until the next person we see *is* the wicked queen. And then, of course, we kill her.'

Mr Miroku looked down at the crusts of his sandwich. 'I've tried meditating that into sashimi,' he said, 'but all I seem to get is tomato and onion quiche. And of the two, I definitely prefer the mixed raw fish sandwich.'

After that, the debate hotted up a little, and the samurai were so engrossed in it that they almost didn't notice the witch as she ran past. If it hadn't been for young Mr Akira calling out 'Coo! A witch,' she'd have got clean away.

As it was, Mr Miroku was the first to spin round, flip a five-sided throwing star out of the top of his boot, hurl it through the air and pin the witch to a tree by her ear. '. . . *Substantially* the same as the raw fish sarny,' he continued, 'except for the sensory perception, or should I say *de*ception, that it's a plate of sashimi. Whereas looked at from a totally different perspective . . .'

'Eeeek,' growled the witch; and then, 'Woof!' as the shock and associated adrenaline rush kicked in and triggered the transformation protocols in her DNA –

(which, given that in this dimension all living creatures are constructs of the stories they inhabit, stands for Does Not Apply . . .)

– and turned her into a wolf.

'Stone me,' breathed Mr Hiroshige. 'Now if that isn't a case in point, I don't know what is. Pretty nifty meditation there, somebody.'

'Wasn't me,' muttered Mr Nikko. 'Wish it had been, but I didn't even see her till you chucked the star.'

'Wasn't me either,' said Mr Miroku. 'Anybody?'

One by one the other samurai disclaimed responsibility, until only young Mr Akira was left. 'So it must have been you,' said Mr Hiroshige, with a slight tone of awe in his voice. 'Well, well, well. You must be a natural.'

Mr Akira looked stunned, shocked, guilty and pleased, all at once. 'Well it's true,' he said, 'I did think to myself as she was running by, dear God, what an evil-looking bitch. And bitches are dogs, and dogs are sort of wolves. In a sense.'

'Did it without even knowing he was doing it,' said Mr Nikko respectfully. 'That's quite remarkable. And also,' he added, 'potentially awkward. Just as well the kid's got a nice sunny disposition.'

The other samurai suddenly noticed that young Mr Akira had been carrying all the luggage, and that didn't strike them as a particularly fair division of labour. Mr Miroku realised that young Mr Akira hadn't had anything to eat and politely offered him the ruins of a raw fish sandwich, while Mr Wakisashi wondered aloud whether this highly developed innate ability of his might be harnessed into, for example, predicting the results of greyhound races.

'Talking of greyhounds,' said Mr Akira, 'what about the witch? Or the wolf, or whatever. Are we just going to leave her there?' He hesitated. He'd thought of a joke; and although his last effort hadn't been greeted with the acclaim he'd hoped for, there was a chance that his sudden new access of popularity might change all that. He decided to risk it. 'After all,' he said, 'I've heard of keeping your ear to the *ground*, but this is ridiculous.'

The samurai exchanged furtive glances. Mr Nikko mimed

helpless laughter, and once the others had worked out that he wasn't having a stroke, they took the hint. Mr Akira blushed. Meanwhile, the witch had started making whimpering noises.

'Perhaps we ought to let her go,' Mr Akira suggested.

'Possibly,' said Mr Hiroshige, thoughtfully. 'I mean, that's an excellent suggestion and one to which we should give serious attention.'

'Absolutely,' added Mr Miroku. 'But if I could just pick you up on a small detail of interpretation, I think that what our colleague here was really saying was, we should let her go *after* we've found out if she can be useful to us.' He turned to face Mr Akira and smiled ingratiatingly. 'That was what you were getting at, wasn't it?'

'Was it?' Mr Akira thought about it for a moment. 'Yes, I suppose it was,' he said.

'I thought so,' Mr Miroku replied. 'Just thought I'd check, though, just in case I'd missed the point.'

'All right,' said Mr Akira. 'So what do we want to do with her?'

The other samurai looked at each other. 'Archery practice?' suggested Mr Wakisashi hopefully.

'We could ask her where the wicked queen is,' Mr Nikko said. 'After all, it's about the right place in the narrative for somebody to tell us something. What do you think?' he asked Mr Akira. 'I really would value your input at this stage.'

Mr Akira shrugged. 'Sounds good to me,' he said. 'Who's going to ask her, then?'

'I think you should,' said Mr Nikko.

'You'd do it awfully well,' agreed Mr Hiroshige.

'You really think so?' Mr Akira enquired. 'Gosh.'

'Oh definitely,' Mr Wakisashi said, with a smile so warm you could have toasted muffins over it. 'No question about that. You've got the knack, if you don't mind me saying so.'

'Innate gift,' confirmed Mr Suzuki, his head bobbing up and down like something in the window of an elderly Cortina. 'Born with it. Something you've either got or you haven't, and he has.'

'All right,' Mr Akira said, 'I'll give it a shot if you like. Hey, you.'

'Wonderfully authoritative tone,' Mr Nikko muttered under his breath.

'Authoritative without being unfeeling,' Mr Hiroshige amended. 'I mean, it's not as if he's some kind of neo-fascist security chief. Here's someone who really knows how to communicate, don't you think?'

The witch tried to move her head, then winced. 'You talking to me?' she gasped.

'Yes.'

('Good answer. *Good* answer.'

'Always said he's got a marvellous way with words.')

'Oh,' said the witch. 'All right then. If you want the wicked queen, you'll find her up at the—'

She got no further; because at that precise moment (and it couldn't have been more precise if they'd had all the scientists in NASA doing the calibrations) a tall, fair-haired, extremely handsome young man jumped out of the bushes just behind her with a mop-handle in one hand and a dustbin lid in the other and yelled, 'Gerroutavit, yer ugly bastards!'

Immediately, six of the seven samurai drew their swords. The handsome prince took one step backwards, with the air of a man reassessing the situation, and raised the dustbin lid.

'Hands off,' he said. 'She's my witch. Go find your own.'

'Excuse me,' said Mr Hiroshige, his sword-tip held unwavering in a perfect exhibition of the classical guard. 'Why are you waving a mop and a dustbin lid?'

It was at times like this, Fang reflected wretchedly, that being a handsome prince really irritated him. It was bad enough being outnumbered seven to one by heavily armed professional warriors when all he had to defend himself with was the mop he'd grabbed from the witch's cupboard under the stairs and the lid off her dustbin. The bemused and blank expressions on his assailants' faces, and the embarrassment they caused him, served to twist the knife in the wound by some forty-five degrees.

'Aha,' he replied. 'Stick around long enough, my friend, and you might just find out.'

'I know,' suggested young Mr Akira, who had tried to draw his sword too, but had succeeded only in cutting through his own sash. 'It's another of those philosophy things, isn't it? It's to show that, in the hands of the true master of the Way, a mop-handle is every bit as effective as a twenty-six-inch razor-sharp *katana* and a pouch full of poison-smeared throwing stars.' He rubbed his chin. 'The dustbin lid's a bit too deep for me, but I'm sure there's a perfectly good . . .'

'Balls,' Mr Nikko interrupted. 'He's just an idiot, that's all. Come on, you guys, let's *slice* the sucker!'

Before Fang could say a word, Mr Nikko chopped off the first six inches of the mop-handle and was swinging the sword back over his shoulder for a full-welly headsplitting slash when he caught sight of something that made him check his swing and gradually lower the sword.

'That's right,' Dumpy said approvingly, as he ducked under the branches of a small gorse bush and strode into the clearing. 'Nice and easy, keep the sword where I can see it. Same goes for the rest of you,' he added sternly.

'Dwarves!' breathed Mr Hiroshige under his breath. 'We've been ambushed by dwarves.'

The rest of the rescue party was out in the open now; besides Fang and Dumpy there were Rumpelstiltskin and Tom Thumb, the Brothers Grimm and the elf. Making a total of –

'Seven,' muttered Mr Wakisashi, who'd been counting. 'Well, I guess we walked straight into that. I suppose a straight-forward surrender would be out of the question?'

'That's right,' added Mr Akira, who'd at last managed to get his sword free of the scabbard and was twirling it with enthusiasm, though not much else. 'Throw down your weapons immediately and we might just—'

'Not them,' Mr Hiroshige hissed. 'Us. And for pity's sake

stop playing with that thing, before you put someone's eye out.'

Mr Akira's jaw dropped. 'But that's silly,' he protested. 'There's just as many of us as there are of them, and they're only little—'

'The word you're looking for,' Mr Nikko interrupted quietly, 'is *dwarves*. Now put it down before you get us all killed.'

Mr Akira shook his head. 'I still don't understand,' he said stubbornly. 'They're little short people, and we're samurai. We've got swords and they're unarmed. We could take them out like *that*.'

'Yes, but –' Mr Nikko hesitated. Inside his brain, the hard disk was crinkling furiously, trying to access some deeply buried path where the explanation – the perfectly simple and logical, patently and painfully obvious explanation – lay buried. He *knew* that there was a perfectly good reason why big, strong trained fighting men ought to be terrified of little cute people with long white beards and brightly coloured jackets with big round brass buttons. He could remember distinctly –

He could remember remembering –

He could remember having remembered –

'Yes,' he said slowly. 'We could, couldn't we?'

'Of course,' Mr Akira was saying, 'that's always supposing that we wanted to. And that's a big supposing, because after all, they've done us no harm, can't actually see how they could possibly ever do us harm, what with them being so small and weedy, so the chances of our ever *wanting* to take them out just like that are pretty damn small. All I'm saying is, in the unlikely event . . .'

He realised that nobody was listening. Instead his six colleagues were advancing on the seven newcomers, brandishing their swords and uttering strange guttural cries, while the newcomers – call them the seven dwarves, it's easier – were backing away with that worried, sheepish look of people whose bluff has just been definitively called. He had the feeling that somehow, this shouldn't be happening. It was a strong feeling, bordering on a conviction. Unfortunately, he hadn't a clue how to stop it.

'Here, you,' he snapped at the witch, who was grinning like a thirsty dog. 'Do something.'

'What d'you mean, something?' she replied.

'Stop them, before they do something they'll regret later.'

The witch's eyes sparkled. 'Not a lot I can do with this thing pinning my ear to this tree,' she replied, reasonably enough. 'Now if you were to pull it out—'

'All right, all right,' Mr Akira sighed, as Mr Hiroshige lashed out with his sword and neatly snipped off the little bobble on Dumpy's sky-blue hat. 'Keep still, and we'll have you out of there in a—'

As soon as he'd prised the throwing star out of the wood, the witch sidestepped, sneaked past his flailing hands, slipped back into her human form with the practised ease of a model changing clothes behind a catwalk, grabbed the mop-handle out of Fang's grasp, jumped on it and shot up in the air like a firework. Whatever he may have thought of the lost opportunity to get back to his real shape, Fang reacted well; he tripped the samurai with his heel, clobbering him with the dustbin lid as he went down, then snatched the sword away from him and, just before overbalancing and falling flat on his face, took an almighty swipe at Mr Hiroshige's head. He didn't actually connect, but Mr Hiroshige did a first-class impression of the Apollo 11 moonshot launch and collided with Mr Nikko, knocking him over. Mr Nikko knocked over Rumpelstiltskin, who tripped up Mr Miroku, who landed quite heavily on Tom Thumb, who squeaked so loudly and shrilly that Mr Suzuki, under the impression that he was under attack from behind, spun round and collided with Mr Wakisashi, who staggered backwards and trod on Dumpy's foot, causing him to jump up and down, lose his footing on a patch of damp moss and lurch into Mr Akira, inadvertently head-butting him in the solar plexus and bringing him down on Grimm #2, who grabbed at his brother to keep himself from going under and pulled him over as well. The net result was something like a cross between the Last Judgement and a Charlie Chaplin movie.

'Hell,' Fang growled, as he removed Mr Nikko's foot from his ear. 'She got away.'

Mr Nikko tried to kick him with his other foot. 'Idiot,' he wailed. 'Fine handsome prince you turned out to be. Didn't anybody tell you you're supposed to rescue the main chick, not the witch?'

'But I'm not a handsome prince, I'm a big bad wolf,' Fang almost sobbed. 'I'm just—'

'Filling in between engagements? Well, I suppose it beats working in a hamburger bar.' Mr Nikko got up slowly and painfully and retrieved his helmet, which had come off. One of the sticking-out horn things had got itself bent double, and when he tried to straighten it, it snapped off. 'And besides,' he added, 'you can't be the big bad wolf. She was.'

Fang stared at him. 'Who?'

'The witch,' Mr Nikko said wearily. 'She was one of those werethingies. Didn't you see?' He dropped the helmet and kicked it into the bushes. 'He meditated her,' he added, jerking a thumb at young Mr Akira, who was trying to sort out whose leg was which with the Brothers Grimm. 'Here, that's a thought. Can you meditate her back?' he asked his junior colleague. 'Preferably with prejudice. Hideously agonising cramps in the head and stomach for choice, but a forced landing in a clump of nettles would probably do at a pinch.'

Young Mr Akira pressed together the tips of his fingers and closed his eyes. 'Any luck?' he asked.

'Not so far. Come on, you can do better than that.'

'I – I don't think I can do it on purpose,' Mr Akira said uncertainly. 'It's like when you go to the doctor and he gives you the little bottle to fill—'

Fang sagged at the knees and sat down on the ground. 'Damn,' he said. 'This is starting to annoy me. Why is it, as soon as I want a witch, they're suddenly as rare as true facts in a newspaper. Normally you can't stub out a fag-end in this godforsaken forest without setting fire to at least one.'

'Just a minute.'

Fang looked round, then down at ankle level. 'Well?' he said.

'Couldn't help overhearing,' said Tom Thumb. 'Did you just say you're really the Big Bad Wolf?'

Fang nodded sadly. 'Used to be,' he replied. 'It's a long story. But, basically, yes.'

'The same big bad wolf that used to blow down the three little pigs' houses?'

It took a moment's hard thought, but Fang located the memory file. 'That's right,' he said. 'Back in – hell, I was just about to say the good old days, but it can't have been all that long ago, surely. Yes, that's me. Why do you ask?'

Tom Thumb shrugged his microscopic shoulders. 'Oh, no reason,' he replied. 'Would you mind waiting there just two seconds? Be right back.'

He wandered away, ducking under a dandelion and using a convenient floating leaf to cross a small puddle. While he was conferring with his colleagues, Fang looked round for his elf.

'You and the small fry,' he said, indicating Thumb with a jerk of the head. 'Just now, you seemed quite—'

'Mind your own business, you overgrown terrier.'

'Please yourself,' Fang replied, hurt. 'I was just asking, trying to take an interest. Good industrial relations, that's all.'

'Bullshit,' the elf replied. 'You were going to make fun, weren't you? Just because, after all these years, I may just possibly have found someone I can really relate to, you know, kind of respect and look up to—'

'Look *up* to? Hellfire, elf, he's even shorter than you are.'

The elf scowled. 'There you go,' she said sourly. 'And anyway, that's only true in the strictly empirical sense. Looked at through the greater perspective of the Way—'

'Don't you start,' Fang muttered. 'Hey, look, your boyfriend and his chums are all coming this way. Wonder what they want.'

The elf pursed her lips. 'Given that they've borrowed a couple of swords, three bows and a big spear from the samurai and are spreading out in a classic encircling formation,' she replied, 'I really haven't the faintest idea. However,' she added, just before Dumpy gave the order to charge, 'if I were you, at this point I might well consider –'

There was a brief struggle; at the end of which Dumpy pulled a rope tight around Fang's neck, tugged on it, and cried 'Gotcha!' while his six companions clustered ghoulishly round, like commentators on election night.

'– Running away.'

In all the excitement, Dumpy quite failed to notice that he was a dwarf short – rephrase: that he'd mislaid one of his companions. The missing person in question was Rumpelstiltskin, who had missed his footing in a clump of briars and fallen head first down a hole.

If he'd known as he fell that a few minutes previously a huge white rabbit had scurried down the same hole, repeatedly checking an old-fashioned fob watch and exclaiming 'I'm late! Oh, my ears and whiskers!' as it did so, it probably wouldn't have meant very much to him. It wouldn't have made the tunnel any less dark or steep, or the bump on the head he suffered when eventually he finished sliding any less painful. Even if he'd understood the significance of the white rabbit, it'd probably only have depressed and worried him. The fact is, there are times when it's far better not to know.

The same goes for the fact that while he was lying in the darkness unconscious and bleeding from a shallow scalp wound, a rat, a toad and a badger, all armed with cudgels, pistols and cutlasses, stepped over him under the impression that he was a tree root, passed on round a bend in the tunnel and were never seen or heard of again.

CHAPTER TEN

'**S**queak.'

The other two mice ignored her. It had been a mistake bringing her in the first place, of course, but there was nothing to be done about it now.

'Squeak.'

(Roughly translated: I think this is probably the larder. There's a strong smell of cheese. Follow me.)

The largest of the three blind mice twitched its nose. 'Squeak,' it said.

'Squeak,' replied the third mouse irritably. '*Squeak*.'

(Simultaneous translation: (a) That doesn't smell like Camembert to me. That's that industrial grade cheddar they put on cheeseburgers. (b) Oh put a sock in it, will you? Cheese is cheese. And besides, what d'you expect them to do, put the brand name on the labels in braille?)

In the big four-poster bed at the opposite end of the room, Snow White slept fitfully, her dreams strangely troubled by an image of a little wooden puppet with a perky expression, an Alpine hat and a very long nose, which grinned out at her every time she looked in the mirror. She grunted and turned over; there it was again, dammit, smirking at her out of the polished brass doorknob, wanting to be her friend . . .

'Squeak,' whispered the first mouse, and he wasn't exaggerating. The other two mice froze in their tracks until the sleeper in the bed stopped thrashing about and started to snore again, making a sound like a bandsaw grating on a concealed nail. No great risk of her hearing them over that racket.

'Squeak?'

'Squeak,' replied the first mouse, suiting the action to the word. Immediately the other two followed, and with exquisite caution they tiptoed along the mantelpiece, down the tie-back on to the curtain, and dropped the last inch to the floor.

'Snff.'

'Squeak!'

'Snff snff. Squeak.'

The third mouse had a point, although she could have expressed her concerns in a rather less vulgar manner. They didn't know what they were looking for; it was all very well to home in on a strong cheese smell and follow it to its logical conclusion, but in this case there were other elements that had to be factored into the equation. For example: a sleeping human, and a powerful scent that the mice weren't to know was something as innocuous as Mr Hiroshige's armour polish. The whole enterprise was, to quote the large mouse, completely *squeak* from the word Go.

Nevertheless, mouse's reach must exceed mouse's grasp, or what's a whisker for? The first mouse took a deep breath, fed the spatio-temporal co-ordinates of the cheese smell into his superb natural navigation computer, and scuttled across the floor . . .

'Squeak!' he cursed, sitting up and rubbing his nose. Without further data it wasn't possible to say what exactly he had just scuttled full-tilt into; but it was big and made of wood, and it was standing in the middle of the floor.

'Tick,' it said.

The first mouse ran a quick analysis. Large, made of wood and given to saying 'Tick' ruled out the vast majority of known predators, which was a good sign. On the other paw, there wasn't anything about it that implied the presence of cheese. Yet it was directly in line with the source of the cheese smell. Decision time. Round, over, up or under?

'Squeak?'

'Squeak. Squeak squeak.'

The first mouse's whiskers bristled. *Squeak*, it muttered to itself, and that was fair enough; this was a cheese heist, after all, not a parish council meeting, and the concept of one mouse, one vote was as out of place in this context as a battleship in a milking parlour. That aside, up was indeed as good a choice as any, given that none of them had a clue where they were.

The mice ran up the clock.

At 1:01 precisely (the clock was a minute slow) the whole structure began to vibrate alarmingly and a terrible noise shattered the silence. '*Squeeeeeak!*' wailed the mouse who ought to have been left behind; then she turned tail (what was left of it after the last time) and ran back down again, hotly pursued by her two colleagues.

It wasn't, unfortunately, a straight-sided clock. Instead, it had a sort of concave knee arrangement which could have been purpose-made to trip up a speeding mouse and catapult it through the air at an angle of forty-five degrees. There would, of course, be no saying where such a mouse would land; a lot would depend on how fast the mouse was going, whether he made an effort to stop in the final heart-crimping fraction of a second before his paws lost traction on the polished walnut, the effect of wind resistance and drag on the ultimate escape velocity, and so forth. One thing, though, is tolerably certain: the chances of said mouse landing in a nearby bucket of water would be effectively *squeak—*

Splosh.

Followed in quick succession by splosh, splosh.

Maybe it served them right; certainly, successive generations of moralising mice thought so, which is where the
expression *away from the farmer's wife into the bucket* is reputed
to come from. All in all, a pretty sorry state of affairs. But it
wasn't until the bucket burped, rippled and said 'Running
DOS' that the mice realised the full extent of the problem. Of
course, the mice weren't to know that this was the most valuable and significant bucket of water in the whole domain,
sold to its present owner by an opportunistic leprechaun
accountant for rather more money than the domain's economy actually contained at any given time.

'Squeak?' spluttered the big mouse, frantically pawing water.

The first mouse replied to the effect that he didn't know,
but whatever the hell DOS was he didn't plan on hanging
around long enough to find out. One desperate push with the
hind paws, and the first mouse was scrabbling against the
sheer side of the bucket, failing to find a pawhold of any kind.
No prizes for guessing what he said.

'Bad command or file—'

'Squeak!'

'Running Help,' said the bucket calmly. 'Please wait.'

It couldn't have said anything more aggravating if it had
tried. 'Squeak!' said the big mouse with admirable restraint.
'Squeak squeak *glug*—'

'Running SQUEAK. Please wait.'

The mouse who should have stayed at home tried to say
'?', but since her head was an inch underwater, all that came
up was a small cluster of bubbles. Fortunately, Bubbles 3.1.1.
For Mirrors was included in the accessories menu. 'Glublub-
lububub,' the bucket enunciated; then a small hole appeared
in its side and the water started to stream out on to the floor.

When the bucket was completely empty, the three blind
mice huddled in the bottom and tried to ride out the after-
math of the shock and panic. They shivered, and their teeth

clicked together. That in itself would have constituted a valid command, if it wasn't for the fact that, with its wet drive completely splashed, the bucket was useless. Inert. Just a bundle of beechwood palings wrapped round with a couple of iron hoops.

'Squeak?'

'You can say that again,' muttered the mouse who shouldn't have come, spitting out a bit more of the water she'd in-advertently inhaled. 'I really thought we'd had it that time; I mean, my past life flashed in front of my ears, there was this absolutely heavenly smell of Limburger cheese, and I—'

She stopped, listening to the echo of her words. There was a moment of utter silence.

'*Squeak?*'

'Apparently,' she replied, in a voice on the edge of hysteria. 'At least, I think I am. But I can't actually hear myself talking, and as far as I know I'm still *thinking* in Newsqueak, even if you're right and what's coming out is in Big. Do you think it's something to do with the water in that crazy bucket? Only, you see, I did swallow some, and . . .'

'Squeak?'

'What're you asking me for? Just because I can suddenly talk this godawful crackjaw language doesn't mean I can— Oooo.'

'Squeak?'

'No, it's just that I thought of something. In fact,' the mouse added, horrified, 'I just thought of a whole lot of things. A *whole* lot.' She shuddered. 'For example,' she said, 'did you know that the whole of this domain is run by a highly complex and intricate operating system that apparently was stored in the water in that bucket, which also happened to be the only surviving copy?'

'Squeak!'

'I don't *know* how I know,' the mouse wailed, 'I just *do*. No, hang on, it's coming through. I know because I drank some of the water, which means that I'm now a zipped database, whatever in Cheese that's – Oh hell.'

'Squ—'

'I'm *it*,' the mouse whimpered. 'The operating system, I mean. It's all inside *me*. Just a minute, though,' she added, wrinkling her nose and twitching her whiskers. 'Just a cotton-picking minute, let's try this. All right.' She cleared her throat. 'Let there be cheese.'

There was a dull thud.

'Squeak!'

'Because I didn't specify which kind,' the mouse explained crossly. 'Obviously Gouda is the default cheese. Next time I'll make sure I specify cheddar. Satisfied?'

'Squeak.'

'So I should think,' the mouse retorted with her mouth full. 'Hey, this stuff isn't half bad, for a default setting. Try some.'

The other two mice didn't need a second invitation. While they were busy gorging themselves, however, the mouse who shouldn't have come sat perfectly still and quiet. Then she opened her eyes.

'Look,' she said. 'I can see.'

'Squeak.'

'Squeak squeak.'

She shrugged her sleekly furred shoulders. 'I agree,' she said. 'Not what it's cracked up to be at all, this vision stuff. Still, it'll come in useful, I'm sure. Now shut up for a minute while I access the settings.'

More silence. If talking to yourself is the first sign of madness, then listening to yourself must be ten times worse; the first sign, quite probably, of a burgeoning desire to go into politics. 'Coo,' she muttered after a while. 'You wouldn't believe the things I can do if I want to. For example, if I want to stop being a mouse and change myself into, let's say for the sake of argument a beautiful princess, all I have to do is—'

'*SQUEEEEEAK!*'

The warning came too late. By the time the mouse who shouldn't have come realised the possible risks she'd already issued the command, or at least formulated the wish. Before she could think CANCEL she was already five feet two inches high and standing on her back paws, half in and half out of an old bucket. She looked down –

And there are certain things about being a fairytale princess that just come with the territory, whether you like them or not. They aren't pleasant, or helpful, let alone politically correct. They're all to do with that dreadfully outmoded and patronising view of female psychology that was prevalent back along when fairytales first crystallised, an inherent part of which is that fatuous old scuttlebut about women being terrified of mice –

'Eeeek!'

Even as she leapt out of the bucket and scrambled up on to the nearest available chair, a section of her brain was shouting, *No, this is silly; dammit, I'm a mouse too.* But the quiet, calm voice of reason was shouted down by the clamour of a million preconceptions, all of them insisting that mice were horrid dirty creatures that ran up your skirts and bit you where you really didn't want to be bitten.

It was at that moment that Snow White woke up.

Possibly it was wave-echoes in the operating matrix, or a freak flash of telepathy, or the effects of the last-thing-at-night cheese sandwich whose pervasive smell had brought the three blind mice here in the first place. Whatever the cause, its effect was that Snow White awoke out of an entirely appropriate dream and demanded, 'Who's been standing in *my* bucket?' Then she noticed the ex-mouse.

'What the—?' she began.

'M-m-mouse,' the ex-mouse gibbered, pointing at the bucket.

'Eeeek!'

Fortunately there was another chair just beside the bed. With a single chamois-like leap, Snow White hopped on to it, gathered her nightdress tightly around her and whispered, 'Are you sure?'

'C-c-course I'm sure. I *am* one.'

'Eeeek?'

'Long story. Look, can you call someone? A big strong man, for instance?'

'I –' Snow White began; then she swore. 'Useless bunch of pillocks,' she went on, 'I sent them out to do something for me and they aren't back yet. Look, who *are* you?'

Then the significance of the empty bucket hit her.

Thanks to her newly augmented mental powers, the ex-mouse-who-shouldn't-have-come didn't need to be told. She knew. 'I'm most dreadfully sorry,' she said. 'It was an accident, honest.'

'You stupid cow!' Snow White screeched. 'Have you any idea what you've done?'

The ex-mouse nodded. 'Oh yes,' she said. 'But you see, it's all right, because I drank some of the water, which makes me a sort of honorary mirror. I can make it all work, you see, and—'

'You can *what?*'

'I can make it work,' the ex-mouse repeated. 'That's how come I can see. And why I'm a girl instead of a mouse. In fact,' she added, with a strange edge to her voice, 'I think I can do anything I like.'

'Oh.' A substantial degree of her former belligerence faded out of Snow White's voice. 'Then why don't you get rid of the mice?' she added, reasonably enough.

'They're my brothers.'

Snow White considered this. 'So?' she said.

The ex-mouse hadn't thought of it in those terms before. It was a seductive argument for the only girl in a family of a hundred and six. A whole string of memory-related convincing arguments, some of them dating back to her very earliest recollections, added their weight to the proposition. 'Well . . .' she said hesitantly.

'Not permanently, necessarily,' Snow White continued. 'You could always bring them back later.'

'That's true.'

'Much later, if you decided you wanted to.'

'Hmmm.'

'And it'd teach them a lesson, wouldn't it?'

'It'd do them good to be taught a lesson,' the ex-mouse agreed. 'Sorry, we haven't been introduced. My name's Souris, but you can call me Sris for short.'

'Snow White,' Snow White replied. 'Go on, then. I dare you.'

Souris grinned. 'All right, then. Boo!'

At once, the two mice in the bottom of the bucket vanished. Where they went to, only a highly trained folklore engineer could say. Possibly they found themselves pulling thorns out of the paws of lions, or drawing a pumpkin coach, or hiding under the bed until Mr Aesop had stopped prowling around and gone off with Uncle Remus for a swift half. The practical effect was that, with the threat they posed safely removed, Snow White was able to jump off her chair, snatch up the three-foot long *daïsho* that Mr Nikko had left lying about in the potting shed and take a savage swipe at Souris, whose instincts as a persecuted domestic pest only just saved her from spectacular decapitation.

'Come back!' Snow White screeched, as the ex-mouse bolted through the door and pattered down the stairs. It was, in context, a foolishly optimistic thing to say. The front door of Avenging Dragon Cottage slammed shut behind her, and the darkness covered her tracks.

'Come back!' Snow White repeated, livid with frustrated rage. 'Are you a girl or a mouse?'

Apparently the concept of dual nationality wasn't one she was familiar with.

'This time,' said the Baron, 'try to get it right.'

Igor nodded, and turned the crank that jump-started the

big transverse flywheel. It hiccuped a couple of times, then started to spin.

'Quite apart from everything else,' the Baron went on, 'we haven't got enough components in stock to go around wasting them. You got any idea how hard it is to get quality ankles these days?'

There was a crackle and a hiss, and the first fat blue spark flolloped across the points of the auxiliary generator. In the relay fuse bank, something blew. Igor hurried across, found the soot-blackened slide, hauled it out and slammed home a new one.

'Not to mention skin,' the Baron went on gloomily. 'Fifty kroner a square metre I had to pay for that last batch, and I've seen better stuff on a sausage. Some of these body-snatchers, they're no better than common thieves. All right, take it up to quarter power and for God's sake keep an eye on the amps.'

'Sure thing, boss.'

'And put a cloth or something over *that*, will you?' the Baron added, jerking a thumb in the direction of the cute little wooden puppet propped up on the workbench. 'Heaven alone knows what possessed you to bring it in here.'

'I like the little fellow, boss,' Igor replied. 'He's like a sort of mascot.'

Before the Baron could tell Igor what he thought of that, another bank of fuses blew, and he jumped down from the quarterdeck to replace them. Igor frowned; he could have sworn he'd seen the puppet move, out of the corner of his eye. But that was impossible; after all, the little fellow had given his word he'd stay perfectly still and quiet.

'All right,' the Baron said, wiping sweat out of his eyes with his sleeve, 'now we're getting somewhere. Up the feed by fifteen per cent; and gently, for crying out loud. This is a scientific experiment, not a barbecue.'

Igor didn't say anything; not his place. Instead, he eased back the lever, carefully watching the needle climb. Smooth as silk, if he said so himself.

'Now then,' said the Baron, 'I think this may be where we went wrong the last time. Instead of routing the main feed through the collimator matrix, I'm going to backfeed via the auxiliaries and then bring it up to three-quarter capacity almost immediately. You got that?'

'Sure thing, boss,' Igor replied dutifully. Half the time, he felt sure, the Baron was making it up as he went along. Chances were, if you really pressed him, he'd have to admit he wouldn't know a collimator matrix from half a kilo of bratwurst. Ah well, Igor smiled to himself, just as well one of us knows about these things.

The low hum of the generator became a growl, and there was a faint shrill edge to it, the first querulous complaint of stressed metal. Igor's steady hand feathered the damper toggles, compensating for the surge effects while maintaining a constant supply to the main feed. There was a very slight smell of singed flesh, but that was only to be expected.

'On my mark,' the Baron said, his voice raised above the growing roar of the generator. 'Up to eighty per cent and hold it steady. And . . . *mark!*'

Igor shook his head. Melodrama, he thought. Ah well. After all, it's his train set. He slid the lever forward, wondering as he did so how Katchen's sister's husband had got on at the chiropodist's. There was a loud hiss as a whiff of evaporated coolant escaped from the manifold; he shut down the conduit and transferred smoothly to the backup. No worries.

'More power! Igor, more power! Ninety per cent!'

'Sure thing, boss.' Once, just once, it'd be nice if he said *please*. He nudged the throttle up another two per cent; okay, so he was the boss, but there's unquestioning obedience and there's blowing the gaskets. On the table, a finger quivered.

'More *power!*'

Igor allowed him another one per cent, noted that two fingers were at it now, and let his mind drift back to what he was going to get little Helga for her birthday. Silly kid had set her heart on a porcelain doll, but there was no way he could afford that on a lab technician's wages. A thought struck him, and he glanced over his shoulder at his little wooden pal, sitting propped up against the Bunsen burners. A lick of paint, some crepe hair, the missus could make a little dress out of offcuts from the curtains she was making for the dowager duchess . . . True, he'd half decided on giving it to his nephew Piotr, but Piotr was nearly nine and he'd far rather have something *useful*, like a carpentry set or a Kalashnikov rifle, something that'd be handy for when he came to decide which of the two trades traditionally practised by young men in this part of the mountains he was eventually going to follow.

'More *POWER!*'

'You got it, boss.' He slid the lever forward to ninety-seven per cent, and then jumped sideways as the static feedback bit him. Nasty, dangerous contraption it was; still, it was this or go back to working in the slate quarries, and what kind of a life was that?

'It's working!' The Baron was pointing at the Thing on the table, while sheets and snakes of blue fire shimmered and ebbed and surged; just, Igor thought, like when you light the brandy on the Christmas pud. 'I've done it, Igor! I've created a life!' He raised his head in triumph, caught sight of the little wooden puppet, frowned, and added, 'A *proper* one.'

Create a life? You'd be better off getting one. 'Well done, boss!' Igor replied. 'Will you be wanting the rest of the power now?'

'What? Oh Christ, yes. Everything you've got, quickly.'

Gingerly, Igor prodded the lever home and jumped back quickly; and at once the shape on the table sat up with a click, pulling the electrodes out of its skin. Well, well, Igor thought, so he's actually done it after all, he's created a life. Big deal. Me and Mrs Igor have created seven, and our way was more fun and didn't cost us a fortune in electricity bills. That reminded him: better shut down the power. Even at off-peak rates (you've never wondered why the Baron always insisted on conducting his experiments at dead of night? Now you know) all this was costing the boss a fortune; enough to reduce the chances of a staff Christmas bonus to virtually nil.

The Thing on the table groaned, as well it might. Its eyes closed, then opened again. It yawned, and took a deep breath. *Hope the glue holds*, Igor muttered to himself, absently swatting at a passing fly. *I told him epoxy resin'd be better, but he wouldn't listen.* But there was no tearing sound or hiss of escaping air, so that was all right.

'My creation!' the Baron crooned, holding out his arms towards the Thing. 'My Adam! My life's work . . .'

The fly, having circled the Thing's head, landed on its nose. 'Ha-a-a-,' it said, and then '*SHOOO!*' There was a noise like a sheet being torn in half, and the Thing flopped back down on to the table with a bump and lay perfectly still. The Baron stared at it.

'Bugger,' he said.

Once again, Igor got a curiously itchy feeling in the back of his neck that prompted him to turn round and look at the little wooden puppet. It winked at him.

Igor smothered a grin. *Wonder how he does it*, he muttered to himself, as the Baron fussed round with glue, brown paper and string. *Bloody glad he's on my side*, he added. *At least I hope he's on my side.*

'All right,' the Baron said wearily. 'Let's try again.'

Somehow, the second go lacked the feeling of awe and wonder there had been the first time around. Understandable, in a way; thousands watched in awe as Louis Bleriot flew the Channel for the first time, whereas now thousands sit around in airport terminals snarling about delays in air traffic control. Oh sure enough, there were crackles and hisses and lots of flashy blue fire; but it was playing to a sleepy Wednesday afternoon matinee rather than a first night. So, when the repaired Thing sat up this time, the Baron just grunted and started checking its seams for stress damage.

'Hello,' it said.

That got the Baron's attention sure enough. 'Hell's teeth, it can talk,' he said. 'It's not supposed to be able to do that. I formatted its brain. Damn thing should be clean as a whistle.'

'Hello.'

The Baron shook his head sadly and reached for a screwdriver. Before he could make contact, however, the Thing's hand shot out and grabbed him by the wrist, making him squeal with pain.

'Hello,' it said.

Igor jumped up to go to the Baron's assistance, but somehow the lab stool he was sitting on managed to topple, dumping him painfully on his backside. Once again, he felt the urge to look round at his little wooden pal.

Its eyes were shut. Lights out. Nobody at home.

And the Thing turned its head and winked at him.

'Hi,' it said, 'my name is Carl. Mind if I use your mirror?'

CHAPTER ELEVEN

Somewhere in the darkness, a rat scuttled.

'Ah,' said the Beast, relieved. 'I was just starting to think I was lost.'

Sis shuddered. It was *dark* down here; not Hollywood-dark, which is an environment where people are deemed not to be able to see even though the heat from the rows of sodium lamps behind the camera is enough to peel the skin off your nose, but dark as three feet down a long bag. Add the scuttling of offstage rats, and the result was something she didn't much care for. 'Are we nearly there yet?' she quavered.

'We should be,' replied the Beast. 'That rat's the first hint of the big cellar full of rats bit that comes up just before we stumble through into the castle. Follow me.'

'Big cellar full of rats?' Sis echoed. 'You are joking, aren't you? Because if you think I'm going anywhere near a cellar full of rats . . .'

'Nothing to be afraid of,' the wicked queen interrupted briskly. 'They're just doing their job, same as the rest of us. Just think of them as – oh, I don't know, what about decor?

Or atmosphere. Like rafia-covered Chianti bottles in an Italian restaurant. They're there to tell you where you are and when the adventure's likely to begin.'

'I see. Wouldn't a simple signpost do just as well?"

'Wouldn't be able to see a signpost in the dark. But every-body can understand the significance of a carpet-of-squirming-rodents noise. It's a convention, like the stylised pictures of men and women on lavatory doors.'

'I don't like rats,' Sis replied sullenly.

'Good. You aren't meant to. A secret gateway that leads directly into the very heart of the castle isn't meant to be *fun*. It's all about brooding menace and all your secret phobias suddenly brought to the – Hello, what's this?'

'You tell me.'

'I'm not sure. But it feels oddly like carpet.'

'*Carpet?*'

'Carpet,' the queen confirmed. 'Quite definitely. Hey you, Beast, what's all this in aid of?'

'Don't look at me,' the Beast replied. 'Not that you would if you had any sense and the lights were on, but . . .'

'Don't drift off-topic. Why's this tunnel carpeted, like something out of *The Hobbit*? Have we come the wrong way?'

Because of its unique collection of hideous physical deformities, you could *hear* the Beast shrug its shoulders. 'No hobbits in these parts,' it said. 'Used to be one or two who had weekend tunnels down here; you know, caved-in old mineshafts they buy up and have all done out in stripped pine and Habitat –'

'You mean Hobbitat, surely,' Sis muttered.

'– But they soon got fed up and moved away. Said the TV reception was hell and they couldn't find anybody that delivered pizzas. Nobody here these days but us storybook types.'

The queen knelt down and groped with her fingertips. 'Not just carpet,' she said. 'Thick, deep, good quality carpet. Might even be Axemonster.'

'Shouldn't that be Axminster?'

'You don't want to know. Well, if this is what passes for all your secret phobias suddenly made real in this neck of the woods, I can't say I'm impressed. Unless it's all sort of post-modern secret phobias stuff; you know, the carpet clashes unbearably with the wallpaper, and the curtains don't go with the loose covers . . .'

'I don't think so,' the Beast said. 'Not even with the subdued lighting effects. It wasn't a bit like this when I was last here. Or at least,' it added, 'I can't quite recall—'

'Enough said,' sighed the queen wearily. 'It's just another cock-up in the system. Instead of thickly carpeted *with* rats, it's thickly carpeted *by* rats. Any minute now—'

'Halt! Who goes there?'

('Told you,' muttered the queen.)

Suddenly the tunnel was filled with blinding light. Up ahead they could see a figure, clearly identifiable by the shape of its ears as rat, despite the fact that the savage back-lighting reduced it to a silhouette. 'Beast?' it said. 'Is that you?'

'Oh, so *he* knows *you*, then,' breathed Sis, with an edge to her voice you could have shaved with.

'At least you don't sound quite so frightened any more,' the Beast replied.

'What's there to be frightened of?' Sis said. 'That's not a rat. That's just Mickey Mouse's disreputable younger brother. I'm only afraid of *real* rats, not unemployed actors in costume.'

'Excuse me,' said the wicked queen firmly, 'but are we going the right way for Beauty's castle?'

The rat nodded. 'Follow your nose up the tunnel,' it said. 'You can't miss it. Only, would you mind awfully wiping your feet before you go any further? In fact, if you could just wait there, I'll put down some newspaper.'

It bustled away, leaving the queen to admit that an obsessively houseproud rat made quite a good secret phobia. When it came back and had finished putting down pages from last week's colour supplements, it gave the queen a long, hard look.

'Don't I know you from somewhere?' it said.

The queen shrugged. 'Possibly,' she replied. 'I used to be something of a public figure around here. Why do you ask?'

'No reason. Well, carry on. And please – don't touch anything, will you? I've just done a thorough spring clean, and—'

The queen did a double-take. 'Spring cleaning?' she demanded.

'That's right.'

'As in "Hang spring cleaning!" and everything that implies?'

The rat twitched its whiskers. 'Don't know what you're getting at,' it said. 'And now, if you'll excuse me.'

The queen nodded, and they carried on up the newspapered passageway, past what seemed like miles of sofas, coffee-tables, Parker Knoll reclining chairs, embroidered footstools and the like. 'Now I know where we are,' the queen whispered, as soon as they were out of earshot. 'This confounded tunnel's mutated into *Wind In The Willows*. Which means that where we're headed for is going to turn out to be Toad Hall.'

'Oh. Is that bad?'

'I'm not sure,' the queen confessed. 'You see, it won't be your actual Toad Hall, because of all these horrid random mutations. It'll have turned into something ostensibly similar but effectively different, just like everything else has round here. And without knowing what that is, I haven't a clue whether it'll be good for us or not. See what I'm getting at?'

'I think so,' Sis muttered. 'Look, I don't know if this is at all important, but when Carl was a kid, he really used to like *Wind In The Willows*. Well, the cartoon version, anyhow, he never was a great one for books. Not unless they're the right height for propping up a wobbly computer workstation.'

The tunnel had come to an abrupt end. 'Which means,' the wicked queen said, as she groped in the darkness, 'that somewhere here there's got to be a trapdoor or something of the like. It's one of the immutable laws of physics in these parts: mysterious tunnels always come out somewhere important. Causes a hell of a lot of problems for big rabbits, I can tell you.'

'Here,' grunted the Beast. 'I think this may be what you're . . .'

The rest of his sentence was cut off as he tumbled sideways into a sudden wash of bright light. The queen scrambled after him, but before Sis could follow, the door slammed shut.

Odd, Sis reflected as she screamed and hammered with her fists against the unyielding panel, that we should have been talking about secret phobias only a moment ago. What you might call a curious coincidence. A trifle bizarre, you might say.

Another thing you might say (and Sis did) was '*HEEEEEEELP!*' It didn't seem to do any good, though. It rarely does.

Now then. Calm down. In the immortal words of Lance-Corporal Jones: don't panic. All you have to do is go back down the tunnel till you meet the nice rats –

(Nice rats. Just listen to yourself. You've been here way too long . . .)

– And ask them if you can borrow a screwdriver or a big hammer or a couple of sticks of dynamite, and then you can be through here and out the other side in no time at all. This sort of thing happens all the time. People are buried alive every day of the week, and . . .

'*HEEEEEEELP!*' she repeated hopefully. As a problem-solving technique its main virtue was consistency; it didn't work but at least it kept on not working, so at least you knew where you stood. Looked like it came down to a choice between staying here and losing weight the sure-fire way, or the nice rats.

Query: down a long, dark tunnel with no visible vegetation

or animal life, what do the nice rats find to eat?

Maybe not the nice rats.

'Ah'm.'

In any list of things not to do in a five-foot high tunnel, suddenly jumping six feet in the air must come pretty close to the top. 'Ouch!' Sis remarked twice; once when her head bumped against the roof, the second time when she sat down hard on what felt suspiciously like a bone.

'Sorry. Did I startle you?'

Sis had been intending to say *EEEEEEK!* or something along those lines; but the voice sounded so soft, quiet, gentle and terrified that instead she sat up, rubbed her head and said, 'Yes.'

'Oh. I hope you didn't hurt yourself.'

'What?' Oh, no, not really. Who are you?'

The voice didn't say anything for a moment. Then it said, 'I'd rather not say.'

'Huh?'

'Well – only if you promise not to laugh.'

'What?'

'People do, you see. Or else they assume I'm taking the mickey. You won't laugh, will you?'

'I don't know,' Sis replied. 'Depends on whether it's funny or not.'

'All right. My name's Rumpelstiltskin.'

'Really? Fair enough.'

'You're not laughing,' Rumpelstiltskin said.

'Why should I? Listen, compared with some of the stuff I've been subjected to since I got stuck in this beastly continuum or whatever it is, your name's about as funny as the second season of *George & Mildred*. Do you know a way out of here?'

'Well, I can recommend the way I've just come, if you don't mind spartan but functional. Nice straight tunnel, nothing fancy, no frills.'

'Really?' Sis replied. 'What about the rats?'

'Rats?'

'You didn't come across a whole load of rats, then?'

Rumpelstiltskin shivered. 'Certainly not.'

'Rats in pinnies with carpet sweepers and feather dusters who put down newspaper for you to walk on?'

'Don't be silly,' Rumpelstiltskin replied. 'Rats don't do that. You're thinking of the Beatrix Potter mice, and they live over the other side of the forest, just across from the sewage farm.'

'No rats,' Sis repeated. 'Oh well. I've stopped being surprised by things like that now. After you, Mr Rumpelstiltskin. And if you've been lying to me and there *are* rats, I'll kill you. Got that?'

They turned a corner and hey presto, there the rats weren't. Instead, there was a door.

'That's odd,' Rumpelstiltskin said, rubbing his battered nose. 'There wasn't a door here just now.'

'I know,' Sis replied. 'There were rats. In frilly aprons. Well, aren't you going to open it?'

'I don't know,' Rumpelstiltskin said thoughtfully. 'You hear all sorts of things about unexplained doors and stuff in this neighbourhood. There's supposed to be one in the back of a wardrobe somewhere that's an absolute menace. You can get into a lot of trouble going through doors.'

'You can get into a lot more not going through them,' Sis pointed out. 'If you don't believe me, I can arrange a demonstration.'

'Please try not to be so aggressive,' the dwarf replied. 'Really, it never helps in the long run. I'll open this door if you insist, but don't blame me if you don't like what's on the other side of it.'

'Oh, get out of the way and let me do it,' said Sis impatiently. 'So long as it's not the rats again, I don't mind what it . . .'

Mistake.

'Oh *marvellous*,' moaned the wicked queen. 'That just about wraps it up as far as I'm concerned. Now what do we do?'

The Beast shrugged its asymmetrical shoulders. 'Depends,' he said. 'If she had any luggage, we could sell it.'

The wicked queen tried the panel again, but it wouldn't budge. 'Nothing for it,' she sighed. 'We'll have to get out of the castle, go round to the entrance of the tunnel and go back in to look for her. What a nuisance.'

The Beast clicked its tongue. 'Actually,' it said, 'that might not be possible. You see, I have an idea the tunnel isn't there any more.'

'Oh? What makes you say that?'

By way of reply, the Beast banged its fist against the panel. 'Solid,' he pointed out. 'Therefore, no tunnel. Not in this version of the story, anyway.'

The queen closed her eyes and counted to ten. 'I've had about enough of this,' she said. 'This domain was never exactly what you'd call stable at the best of times, but at least you used to be able to walk through a door without it turning into a wall the moment your back's turned. It's intolerable. Think of going to the lavatory, for instance.'

'Odd you should mention that,' mumbled the Beast, shuffling its feet uncomfortably. 'Would you excuse me for just a moment? Only—'

'Stay right where you are,' the queen snapped. 'You'll just have to wait.'

'Sorry, I don't think that's going to be possible. I'll be right back, I promise.'

He scampered off down one of the three dark, gloomy corridors that converged opposite the panelled wall they'd emerged through. For a while the queen kept herself amused by poking and prodding at the corners and edges of the panelling; nothing happened. As she did so, it occurred to her that she'd never before met anybody in the domain who'd had to interrupt the adventure to sneak off and have a pee. That sort of thing doesn't happen in narrative, ever; it's in the Rules. Why, then, should the Beast be taken short at what was obviously a crucial moment in the story? Good question.

He was gone an awfully long time.

Eventually she got tired of waiting and set off to find him. That was easier said than done; the corridors wound on and on, the way that only corridors in an interior that has no exterior can do. At last, just as she was cursing herself for not marking her way with bits of torn-up paper or a thread or something, she came across a rather disagreeable sight.

On the floor there was a small puddle; but that wasn't the bad part. What the queen really didn't like the look of were the chunks of plaster gouged out of the wall, the splashes of blood, the stray bits of Beast fur scattered in all directions, the scorch-marks and the words chalked on the wall just above the puddle. They read:

HE SHOULD HAVE GONE BEFORE HE CAME OUT

Well. These things happen.

She walked carefully round the puddle and carried on up the corridor. As well as having a missing girl to find and a Beast to avenge, she was by now hopelessly lost in a building that could be a castle, Toad Hall or pretty well anything that has long winding corridors with no doors in them and no lighting apart from the occasional flickering torch set in a sconce high up on the wall. You could have played Doom in there for hours, assuming you survived that long.

Arguably, the wicked queen muttered to herself, that's precisely what I am doing. What fun.

She wandered around for another ten minutes or so, but all she found were more corridors. They were, she noticed, all carefully swept and dusted and free of cobwebs; and that set her thinking. Housework – castlework, even – doesn't do itself. Therefore –

No sooner had she formulated the thought than she heard in the distance the sound of somebody humming, off-key. She ducked behind a pillar and waited.

Not long afterwards, someone came. It was a cosy-looking

middle-aged woman in an apron, wheeling one of those big housekeeping trolleys you see in hotels. Every fifteen yards or so she'd stop, unload a broom or a dustpan and brush or a long-handled feather duster, clean up, put new torches in the sconces, polish the noses of the gargoyles and move on. The tune she was humming was almost but not quite recognisable; it was probably a theme song or an advertising jingle, and she hummed the same bit over and over again.

'Excuse me,' said the queen, stepping out from behind her pillar.

'Gaw!' The woman started, then clicked her tongue. 'Gave me a fright, you did, jumping out like that.'

'I'm sorry,' the queen replied. 'The fact is, I'm lost.'

The woman smiled sympathetically. 'Confusing, isn't it, till you're used to it? Where was it you was wanting to go to?'

'Actually,' the queen said, selecting a silly-me sheepish grin from her repertoire of facial expressions, 'I'm not even sure where this is. You see, I was in this secret passage—'

'Oh, one of them,' the nice woman said, with a knowing smile. 'Ever such a lot of them, aren't there? And you come up out of it and you haven't a clue where you are, right?'

The wicked queen nodded. 'That's it,' she said. 'You see, I thought this was Beauty's castle, but then it seemed as if it had turned into Toad Hall, and now – well, I'm completely foxed. I mean, it could be *anywhere*.'

The nice woman laughed. 'Funny you should say that,' she said. 'Oh well, best of luck. Some of 'em do get out eventually, so they say.'

The wicked queen's happy smile faded abruptly. 'Well, couldn't you, um, point me in the right direction for the way out? If it's no trouble, that is.'

'Sorry, love.' The nice woman looked genuinely sorry. 'But I'm just the housekeeper. And that's a job and a half, I can tell you. All of this to keep clean and tidy, and never a word of thanks. I reckon they think it all cleans itself, you know.' She loaded her tackle back on to the trolley and prepared to move on. The wicked queen grabbed a trolley handle.

'Please don't do that,' the housekeeper said.

'Look, I really don't want to cause trouble, but—'

'Funny way you got of showing it,' the housekeeper said, making the wicked queen feel rather wretched; after all, the poor woman was only doing her job, and it looked as if it was a fairly horrid job and in all probability she only got paid a pittance for it. 'Now you take your hands off my trolley. You'll get me in trouble, you will. I'm behind with my rounds as it is.'

The wicked queen shook her head. 'I don't think you quite understand,' she said. 'I really have got to find a way out of here, and you obviously know your way around. Couldn't you just see your way to—?'

The housekeeper tried to move the trolley forward, but the wicked queen jammed her foot against one of the wheels, making it veer off into the wall. 'Please,' she said. 'I honestly don't want any unpleasantness, but . . .'

She broke off, mainly because the eight-inch dagger the housekeeper was pressing against her jugular vein made talking somewhat uncomfortable. 'Mind you hold still, dear,' the housekeeper said, in a horribly matter-of-fact tone. 'I've got enough to do without mopping up blood all over the place. It can be a real pain, getting blood off these tiles.'

'Anything you say,' the queen croaked. 'The last thing I'd want to do is make extra work for you.'

'Should've thought of that earlier, shouldn't you?' the housekeeper replied reproachfully. 'Now where did I put those dratted handcuffs? There's so much stuff on this trolley, you don't know where to start looking. Ah, here we are. Now, you just hold your hands out where I can get at them, that's the ticket.'

The ratchets of the handcuffs clicked into place around the queen's left wrist; then the housekeeper passed the central links under the handle of the trolley and fastened the right cuff as well. 'That ought to do it,' the housekeeper said. 'Now you'll just have to wait there till I finish off my rounds, I'm afraid. I haven't got too much more to do, just this wing and the east wing and the main hall and the old guard tower and the refectory and the dortoirs and the garderobe and the north dungeons and the inner keep and the solar and the bailey. Pity you can't give me a hand,' she added wistfully. 'Could be through it all like a dose of salts with another pair of hands.' She stopped, thought for a moment, looked at the large knife and the queen's wrists, then shook her head. 'In a manner of speaking,' she added.

'I don't mind helping, really,' the queen replied, with perhaps just a touch too much eagerness in her voice.

The housekeeper shook her head sadly. 'Sorry, love, but you know how it is,' she replied. 'Not that I'm saying I don't trust you or anything like that, you understand.'

The wicked queen muttered something uncouth under her breath as the housekeeper carried on with her dusting and her rather unbearable humming. After a while the house-keeper relented and let her push the trolley, but apart from that it looked very much as if negotiations had reached stalemate. If she tried to say anything, the housekeeper simply hummed a bit louder, or accidentally clouted her across the face with a feather duster. Tactically speaking, it was a mess.

But the queen did have one advantage. Sooner or later, she figured, they'd come to the place where the Beast had had his nasty experience, and that was going to take some clearing up. The housekeeper was going to need the mop and bucket, the broom, the dustpan and brush, the floorcloth and (assuming she was going to do a proper job, which, to do her credit, seemed likely) the tin of floor wax and the electric polisher. To make the electric polisher work, she'd need a power source; and although there hadn't been any signs of electrical sockets in the walls when she'd been this way earlier, that was probably because she hadn't been looking for them. The combination of electrical appliance, power source and puddle of nameless liquid suggested various avenues for exploration by a keen strategic mind, although it was pointless trying to formulate a detailed plan of action until she could get another look at the actual terrain.

'Dah dah dee dah *dah*,' the housekeeper warbled; then she broke off in the middle of a mangled bar and tutted loudly, her hands on her hips. 'Oh for crying out loud,' she complained, and the queen smiled. *Ah*, she said to herself. *We're here.*

'Some people,' the housekeeper was saying, and her back was turned. Very carefully, so as to prevent the links of the handcuffs clinking against the trolley handle, the queen reached out for the polisher flex –

'And you leave that flex alone,' the housekeeper said, without turning her head. 'Don't think I don't know what you're up to, 'cos I do.'

Baffled, the wicked queen slumped forward; and the trolley moved. The housekeeper had forgotten to apply the brake.

Quickly, the wicked queen made a mental assessment of the odds. They weren't good; she stood about as much chance as an egg in a game of squash. But they were still better than nothing. She took a deep breath, threw her weight against the trolley and pushed for all she was worth.

'Hey!' shouted the housekeeper, dropping her mop and making a grab for the rail. 'You stop that, or I'll—'

Supermarket trolley syndrome. Honestly, the wicked queen didn't mean to do it, but the navigational matrix of any heavily laden independent wheel carriage when savagely nudged is at best erratic, usually uncontrollable – or, to put it another way, any sudden movement and they home in on people's ankles like sharks in bloodied water. 'Yow!' the housekeeper shrieked, as the trolley cannoned into her Achilles tendon; then she fell over.

Occupational hazard, the wicked queen rationalised as she shoved against the dead weight of the trolley. *A job like hers, on her feet all day, stands to reason the poor soul's got bad ankles.* She felt awful about it, up to a point; the point being the sharp one on the end of that very big knife she'd had digging in her throat not so very long ago. When she considered that, she didn't feel quite so bad after all.

She still had the minor problem of being chained to a very heavy trolley, which she was having to push along at one hell of a lick just to keep the momentum going. She'd reached the stage by now where the thing was moving quite well, but she couldn't help feeling that any attempt to steer it, for example round a corner, was going to be fraught with unpleasant difficulties. Stopping it in anything less than a hundred yards of clear, uncluttered straight was more or less out of the question, unless a messy and spectacular crash counted as a stop for the purposes of the exercise. All in all, it was an unhappy state of affairs, and she couldn't help feeling that she was now so thoroughly settled into the shit that she could quite legitimately apply for citizenship and a work permit.

So preoccupied was she with this train of thought that she didn't notice the door until it was too late.

The results were quite spectacular. The trolley hit the door, crumpled up like the sacrificial front end of a Volvo, and came to a juddering halt. The door, having auditioned unsuccessfully for the part of immovable object, got out of the way in a jumble of flying splinters, just in time to let the remains of the trolley come skidding through on its side. At some point in all this, the struts that supported the handle must have come under a sufficient degree of torque to pull the heads of the retaining rivets clean through seventy-five thousandths of an inch of steel tubing, leaving the handle (and, incidentally, the wicked queen) conveniently behind.

Fortuitous, you might say.

The queen stood up and checked herself for damage. There was something wrong with her left knee and her ribs ached; but the chain linking the handcuffs had broken and she no longer had the housekeeper's humming to contend with, so on balance she was in better shape than she had been. After a quick glance back through what was left of the door (about enough to provide sticks for two dozen ice lollies), she set off at an express limp in the opposite direction.

Fairly soon she found herself standing in what could only be the great hall of the castle. There was a wide oak table, marginally shorter than the M1 but much more highly polished, and beyond that a raised dais with another long oak table running from side to side; in the corners of the hall behind that were the wells of two spiral stone staircases, which presumably led to the minstrels' gallery. There was also, improbably, a bell-rope dangling from inside a cupola in the centre of the roof, quantities of big free-standing wrought-iron lamp-stands, some life-sized stone statues of saints and crusaders, any number of chairs, footstools and other easy-to-trip-over furniture, floor-to-ceiling tapestries on the walls – lots of clutter and excitingly varied levels, in other words.

Which could only mean one thing.

As soon as she'd made the connection in her mind, the queen started to back away in the direction she'd just come from; but she'd left it too late. Out of the archway leading to the tunnel erupted two male figures, both dressed in white shirts and tight trousers. They were swordfighting.

Because this was, of course, the swordfighting area of the castle. Build a great hall to these dimensions and furnish it in this manner, and you can't complain if you find it constantly infested with clashing blades, smashed chairs, decapitated statues, overturned tables, chandeliers that'll never hang straight again after having been swung on. Fly-papers attract flies, great halls attract swordfights. If you can't stand the heat, stay in the kitchen.

The queen's first instinct was to hide under a side-table, but she resisted it; fortunately for her, since it was one of the first casualties of the duel. Swordfighter A turned it over and ducked behind it, swordfighter B ran it through, almost but not quite kebabing his opponent, and while he was struggling to pull his sword out again, swordfighter A aimed a doozy of a backhand slash at his head, missing him by inches and slicing off one of the table's legs. By the time they'd finished picking on it and had moved on to beating the bejabers out of a rather fine elm-backed settle, it'd have had trouble getting a job as a drinks mat. The duellists, needless to say, didn't seem to give a damn what they smashed up, thereby illustrating the old adage that good fencers make bad neighbours.

The wicked queen cleared her throat. 'Excuse me,' she said.

The duellists froze in mid-stroke, turned and looked at her. They were more or less identical; same clothes, same hair-style, same pencil moustache on the upper lip. Briefly the queen wondered which one was the hero and which was the villain; nothing to choose between them. For all she knew, they took turns.

'Well?' said A.

'Sorry to butt in when you're obviously busy,' the wicked queen said sweetly, 'but I was wondering, could you very sweetly point me in the direction of the way out of this castle? I'd appreciate that ever so much.'

By the looks of it, the duellists weren't sure what to make of the interruption, though to judge by the somewhat hostile glint in their eyes, mincemeat was probably top of their list of preferences.

'And about time too,' said A, irritably. 'We couldn't wait any longer so we started without you.'

'Ah,' said the queen. 'Gosh.'

The duellists glowered at her. B tapped his foot on the flagstones.

'Well?' he said.

'I'm sorry?'

'Get on with it, girl. Now you're here you might as well.'

The queen converted her bewildered gawp into a charming smile. 'I think I may not be quite up to speed here,' she said. 'What exactly is it you want me to do?'

A's face creased into an Oh-for-pity's-sake expression. 'Scream, of course,' he said. 'Then, when he's knocked the sword out of my hand and he's getting ready to stab me, you bash him over the head with a candlestick.'

The famous imaginary light bulb so popular with cartoonists lit up in the queen's brain with an almost audible snap. 'How dreadfully slow of me,' she said. 'All right, then, here goes.' She closed her eyes and took a deep breath. '*EEEEEEEEE!*' she said.

The duellists looked at each other.

'I know,' said B with a wry smile. 'But she's all I could get at short notice.'

'Oh,' A replied. 'What happened to the usual girl?'

'It's her mother's birthday. Ready?'

'Ready.'

Immediately, the fight resumed. This time, the casualties included an alabaster figure of St Cecilia (no great loss), half a dozen specialist matchwood chairs (guaranteed to shatter at the slightest touch or your money back) and, needless to say, the bell-rope (with A halfway up it). The wicked queen, who had been following the moves carefully, recognised her cue, selected the likeliest-looking candlestick, sneaked up behind the duellists while they were locked in one of those mechanical-advantage arm-wrestles and did her stuff. There was a deep, clunking noise. The swordfighter she'd just clobbered turned round.

'Not me, you fool,' he said. 'Him.' Then he fell over.

The queen took a step back, while the remaining swordfighter closed his eyes and made a face. 'You clown,' he sighed. 'You realise what you've just done? You've nutted the hero.'

'Oh.'

'That's all you've got to say for yourself, is it?' said the swordfighter angrily. 'All these years we've been working together on this, all the hours we've put in, the strains on our marriages, the quality time we haven't had with our kids, and all you can say is, Oh. Well,' he went on, stooping down and picking up his opponent's sword, 'there's nothing else for it. Here, catch.'

The queen just managed to grab the sword before it impaled her. 'Excuse me?' she said.

'You bashed him, you take his place,' the swordfighter replied. 'Only reasonable. And remember,' he added, as he aimed a swipe at her that would have done to her head what your butter-knife does to your breakfast hard-boiled egg if she hadn't managed to duck at precisely the last possible moment, 'you've got to win. Okay?'

'But I . . .'

The swordfighter wasn't listening, and fairly soon the wicked queen was far too busy to talk, unless you count largely involuntary remarks such as 'Eeek!' as talking. Even while she was dodging the blows, however, a select committee of her mind was pointing out that this sort of thing was exactly what she ought to have been expecting, given the foul-ups in the narrative patterns and the hopeless tangle the various alternative versions had got into by now. In fact, the committee reported, a simple role reversal was about the mildest form of nuisance possible at this juncture; think how much worse it could have been if this was one of those junctures where the current narrative was gatecrashed by bits of another story . . .

It was while the committee was considering its findings and filing its expenses claim that the big doors at the far end of the hall suddenly burst open. The swordfighter, who had just knocked the sword out of the wicked queen's hand and was preparing to run her through, hesitated, looked round, muttered, 'Oh for God's sake!' and let his sword-arm drop to his side.

In the doorway stood seven samurai.

'Now what?' Grimm #1 asked.

They were standing under a tree, over a low branch of

which they'd slung a rope. One end of the rope was tied round the trunk of the tree, and the other had been worked into the noose around Fang's neck.

'Guess,' replied Dumpy grimly. 'Now, when I say *pull*—'

'Something's not quite right,' interrupted Tom Thumb. 'We're missing an important point here, I'm convinced of it.'

Dumpy waved his hands in a dismissive gesture. 'Sure, he should be on a horse,' he replied. 'But we ain't got no horse, so we'll just have to make do. And *one*, and *two*, and . . .'

Fang, meanwhile, had caught the elf's eye, and she'd tip-toed over to the tree, shinned up it and settled herself in a low branch next to Fang's ear.

'Gggugg,' Fang muttered. 'Ggg. Gg.'

The elf shook her head. 'Relax,' she replied, 'it's going to be all right. You know as well as I do what happens now. Just when they're about to do the business, an arrow comes whistling out from the nearby trees and cuts the rope, you roll away and escape in the confusion. It's a stone-cold certainty. You could bet your life on it.'

'Ggg!'

'Hang on,' said Tom Thumb, as Dumpy and the Brothers Grimm took up the strain, 'I've figured out what's wrong. No,' he added loudly, '*stop!*'

'But you just said hang . . .'

'Figure of speech. Look, you're going about this entirely the wrong way. That's now how you waste big bad wolves. They've got to drop down chimneys into big tubs of boiling water.'

Dumpy scowled at him. 'Quit horsin' around, partner,' he grunted. 'That ain't no way to run a lynchin'.'

'But that's the proper way of doing it,' Thumb objected. 'Everybody knows that, surely. I learnt that at my mother's knee . . .'

'Ain't never heard such foolishness,' Dumpy growled. 'Look, are we lynchin' this sucker or ain't we?'

('Any minute now,' the elf whispered confidently. 'Pfft.

Whizz. Snick. Job done. Any ideas where we're going to have lunch afterwards?')

'All I'm saying is,' Thumb said, 'we'd better get this right because we only get one shot at it. I mean, if we do it the wrong way and the clients throw a wobbly and refuse to pay up, we can't very well bring the wolf back to life and have another go.'

Dumpy thought it over for a moment. 'Guess you may be right, at that,' he conceded. 'Only question is, where the Sam Hill we gonna find a big tub o' boilin' water and a chimney out here in the backwoods?' He looked round and –

'Just a second,' Grimm #2 objected. 'That cottage wasn't there a minute ago, surely.'

Dumpy grinned. 'You figure it just done sprung up like a mushroom, son? Maybe that kind o' thing happens where you're from, but not hereabouts.'

'Of course it doesn't,' Grimm #2 replied, or he would have done if he hadn't suddenly thought of Milton Keynes. 'Of course it doesn't happen *often* where we come from,' he said. 'And it shouldn't happen here, either. Something funny's going on here if you ask me.'

'Well I didn't, so get the sucker down and let's mosey on over and have a look-around. We'll be needin' a long ladder, I guess.'

'Now that's odd,' said the elf, as the Brothers Grimm slackened the noose round Fang's neck. 'By rights, there should have been an arrow, but there wasn't. Something's gone wrong. Most disappointing.'

Fortunately, Fang was in no fit state to reply, so he had to keep his views on the elf's choice of the word *disappointing* to himself. He spent the time taken in reaching the cottage in compiling a shortlist of disappointments he'd have liked to share with the elf, up to and including total immersion in boiling groundnut oil.

'This is weird,' muttered Grimm #1, examining the door of the cottage. 'Didn't we just come from here?'

'All these cottages look the same to me,' his brother replied. 'Back home, of course, it'd have two Porsches and a Volvo parked outside, and the kitchen would be all Delft blue and yellow with a split-level grill and lots of pine.'

'Talking of kitchens,' said Grimm #1, 'keep an eye out for something to eat. I'm starving. Is it my imagination, or don't these creeps eat food?'

'Only when it helps the story along. Haven't you got the hang of how things work here yet?'

'Huh. Well, what *I* think this story desperately needs right now is a deep-pan Seafood Special with extra anchovies. It's what Shakespeare would have done. And Ernest Hemingway.'

Inside the cottage it was dark and gloomy, and there was an offputting smell of damp. It didn't feel lived in at all.

'Okay,' Dumpy sang out, 'let's make a move. You two, go find a big pot and fill it with water. Thumb, light a fire. Rumpelstiltskin, you're with me . . .' He stopped dead and looked round. 'Hey,' he said. 'Anybody seen Rumpelstiltskin?'

There was a moment of thoughtful silence while everybody realised that they hadn't. Dumpy sighed, then shrugged. 'Makes no never-mind,' he said. 'He weren't no good nohow. Right, I'll go find a ladder. Thumb, guard the prisoner.'

'Oh yes?' demanded Tom Thumb, as Dumpy disappeared through the door. 'And how exactly am I supposed to . . . ?'

The door shut, leaving Thumb alone with Fang and the elf. There was a moment of awkward silence.

'Don't make it hard on yourself,' Thumb said, trying to raise a snarl but getting a whimper instead. 'You just sit still and everything's going to be just fine.'

'Except that I'll be chucked down a chimney into a tub of boiling water,' Fang replied. 'Apart from that, though, I'll have absolutely nothing to worry about. Elf, get these damn ropes undone quick.'

'I . . .' The elf hesitated. 'Look, I hate to be a wet blanket, but . . .'

'That's just fine,' Fang snapped. 'You don't like being a wet blanket, I don't like dying horribly painful deaths. We can avoid both if you'll just get the fucking ropes.'

'Yes, but . . .'

'But?'

The elf came up close to Fang's ear. 'If I untie you and you escape,' she whispered, nodding her head in Tom Thumb's direction, '*he'll* get in trouble. I mean, he's supposed to stop you escaping, and that dwarf's got a foul temper.'

'I see,' said Fang. 'I'm supposed to go plummeting to my doom just so your boyfriend there doesn't get yelled at. I'm so grateful to you for explaining it so clearly.'

The elf pulled a face. 'Don't be like that,' she said. 'Really, you're putting me in a really difficult position here, you know?'

'*I'm* putting *you* . . .'

The elf sighed. 'Look,' she said, 'we only just met and, to be really up-front about this, when you're my size you don't get so many offers that you can afford to go pissing guys off before you've even been to see a film together. Don't you think it's cute the way his hair curls round his ears? I think that's just so adorable . . .'

'Elf . . .'

'Look,' the elf replied wretchedly, 'I said I'm sorry. But that dwarf person *trusted* him, and he's trusting me, and if you haven't got trust, what kind of relationship are you going to have anyway? And stop looking at me like that,' she added angrily. 'The last thing I need at what may well be an important stage in my personal development is a whole load of heavy guilt.'

'Elf,' said Fang, with terrifying solemnity, 'when I first met you, as far as you were concerned, love means never having to say *Aaaargh!* Where in hell's name has all this deep and meaningful crap come from?'

The elf didn't reply; instead, she slumped on to the floor and started to cry.

'Elf?'

'Snff.'

'Elf? Elf, you get your bum over here and untie these ropes, or you'll be very sorry.'

'Snff snff.'

A stray bundle of memory slipped in through the cat-flap of Fang's mind. 'Unless you untie these ropes *now*,' he threatened, 'I'll say I don't believe in fairies.'

The elf frowned. 'Neither do I,' she replied. 'What's that got to do with anything?'

'Oh. I thought that if someone said that, somewhere a fairy turns its toes up and snuffs it.'

'Quite possibly. But I'm a elf, not a fairy. And anybody who goes around saying he doesn't believe in elves gets petrol through his letterbox. Understood?'

Fang was about to take the argument further when the front door flew open and a round pink shape whizzed in and cowered behind a sofa.

'Don't let them know I'm here,' he said. 'I think I got rid of them this time, but I'm not taking any risks.'

Fang stared for a moment, speechless. Then he started to laugh.

'He's a pig,' he said, in reply to the elf's request for further and better particulars. 'In fact, I reckon he's one of the three little pigs who used to live on my patch. Now what on earth . . .' He leaned forward and had a closer look. 'Hello, it's Julian, isn't it?'

'Who the devil are you? No, don't tell me, I don't want to know. Just don't let my brothers know I'm here, all right?'

'Sure,' Fang replied. 'After you, are they? That's odd. You people always struck me as being just one happy family.'

'I don't know what's got into them,' Julian said sadly. 'Behaving like utter swine, both of them.'

Fang shrugged, as far as he was able with a quarter of a mile of rope tied round him. 'I won't say a thing, promise. And in return you could do a small favour for me.'

'Such as?'

'Undoing these ropes'd be favourite. Come on, before I die of old age.'

The pig did as he was told. For some reason, Thumb (who could easily have fitted inside Julian's ear) made no effort to stop him. The elf, who'd been anticipating having to race to Thumb's rescue and defend him with, if necessary, all reasonable force (she'd been looking forward to that) sat open-mouthed.

'You're not just going to cower there while the prisoner escapes, are you?' she said at last.

Thumb shrugged. 'Why not? No skin off my nose.'

'But . . .'

The elf's first reaction was to mention such concepts as duty, loyalty, my comrades right or wrong; but there was something in Thumb's manner that suggested that he wasn't likely to respond well to that sort of argument. 'That dwarf'll flatten you if you don't,' she therefore said.

'So? And the pig'll flatten me if I do. Besides, Dumpy'll have to catch me first. He may be big but I'm small, if you get my meaning. There may be nowhere on Earth a dwarf won't dare to go, but there's ever so many places he won't *fit*.'

'But . . .' The elf hesitated. Somehow, she'd assumed that, just because he looked fairly like the dream man she'd imagined for herself over the years, the interior specifications would match the externals. The idea that he might turn out to be a coward (defined in her world view as someone who doesn't joyfully embrace a potentially lethal fight with a much larger, stronger opponent without a better reason than not letting down a colleague he couldn't actually stand) came as a bitter disappointment. 'Oh, go on, then,' she snarled. 'Get out of my sight before I tread on you.'

'Hey!' Thumb stared at her in pained surprise. 'What's all that about, then? I thought we were, well, you know . . .'

'Did you? Then you were wrong.' She reached down and grabbed his ear, so that he had to stand on tiptoe to avoid becoming a permanent Van Gogh lookalike. 'I really thought you were something special, you know? Someone I could rely on. Someone I could look up to.' She stifled a sob and twisted his ear another thirty degrees. 'Just goes to show how wrong I was, doesn't it?' she said, and let him go. He fell to the ground with a bump. 'Come on,' she said to Fang, who was free of his ropes at last, 'let's be getting out of here. You wouldn't happen to have such a thing as a white feather about you anywhere, would you? It so happens I need one.'

Before they could get to the front door, however, there was a tinkle of broken glass and a rock sailed in through the window. Fang reached for the doorhandle and wrenched it open, then jumped back with a yelp of terror as an arrow shot through his hair and embedded itself in the wall behind his head.

'Bit late for that now, surely,' the elf said, then she too ducked as six or seven more followed it. 'Like buses, really,' she muttered. 'You wait and wait, and then they all come along at once.'

'*YOU IN THE HOUSE!*' The bullhorn voice made the surviving windows rattle. '*SURRENDER THE PIG AND NOBODY GETS HURT. EXCEPT THE PIG, OF COURSE,*' it added, '*OR THERE WOULDN'T BE MUCH POINT. YOU HAVE THIRTY SECONDS.*'

'Oh Christ, it's Desmond,' Julian wailed. 'Remember, you said you wouldn't tell.'

'That's okay,' Fang replied. 'We'll just explain that this is nothing to do with us and quietly go on our way. I'm sure they'll understand.'

He opened the door a crack and actually got as far as 'Excuse me,' before another volley of arrows spitted the door. Before retreating he carefully plucked one out of the door, unpicked a white feather from the fletchings and handed it solemnly to the elf, who was cringing under the table with a waste-paper basket over her head. 'You wanted one of these,' he said.

'All right,' she snarled back, 'point taken. Where are those other three clowns when we need them?'

'*IN CASE YOU'RE WONDERING WHAT'S BECOME OF YOUR THREE FRIENDS,*' the voice went on, '*PERHAPS I SHOULD MENTION I HAVE THEM HERE. IF YOU EVER WANT TO SEE THEM ALIVE AGAIN, YOU'D BETTER DO AS YOU'RE TOLD. GOT THAT?*'

'Incentives just aren't his strong point, are they?' Fang sighed. 'Well, we might as well make ourselves comfortable, because it looks as if we're going to be here for quite some time.'

'You reckon we should stay put?' the elf said doubtfully.

Fang shrugged. 'Not much option, really,' he replied. 'At least while we're safe in here, there's not a lot they can do to us.'

'True.'

'*ALL RIGHT, THAT DOES IT. TIME'S UP. EUGENE, START THE GENERATOR.*'

Fang didn't particularly like the sound of that; so he crawled to the window and cautiously peered out. In the distance he could see two pigs setting up a huge, diabolical-looking machine, something that looked like a giant mutant vacuum-cleaner. 'Jeez,' he muttered under his breath. 'What in hell's name is that?'

'Let me see,' Julian said, and he crawled over and had a look. 'Oh,' he said. 'That's bad.'

'Really? What is it?'

'It's a heavy-duty compressor,' Julian replied nervously. 'Used to generate an exceptionally powerful jet of compressed air. If I know Desmond, he's proposing to huff and puff and blow our house down.'

'But he can't!' Fang exclaimed. 'That's my . . .' He remembered who he was talking to and broke off.

'Your what?'

'Oh, nothing.'

'Didn't sound like nothing to me. And how the hell did you know my name?'

Julian stared at Fang with a curious expression on his face, but before he could say anything further, the compressor started to rumble, making further conversation impossible. Fang took one last look, then dived for cover.

'Anyway,' he growled to himself, 'it'll never work.'

Wrong again.

CHAPTER
TWELVE

'**Y**ou can run,' Snow White rasped, slashing at random at the bushes with her sword, 'but you can't hide.'

Souris, the former-blind-mouse-turned-mainframe-turned-fairytale-princess, knew better. Perfectly possible to do both, simultaneously even, so long as you did the running part in dense cover, such as a forest. No mere theory, this; she'd been doing it for seven hours, while Snow White followed her chopping the heads off saplings and skewering dead trees. Odd, then, that Snow White should still be trying to convince her of the truth of a hypothesis they both knew to be false. Maybe it was a human thing, this apparent ability to believe propositions one knows to be fallacious. It'd explain a lot, including the popularity of soap opera and the fact that humans still vote in elections.

'Sooner or later,' Snow White went on, 'I'm going to find you, mouse, so why not make it easy on yourself and come out where I can see you? I'm not going to hurt you, I promise.'

Not necessarily a lie; the sword in Snow White's hands looked so sharp that she probably wouldn't feel a thing.

Thinking back, the farmer's wife's eight-inch Sabatier hadn't hurt very much, or at least not at the time. There are worse things, however, than mere pain.

Souris tucked herself under an elderberry bush, painfully aware that she was a whole lot bigger than she was used to and that her concealment instincts hadn't yet recalibrated themselves enough to guarantee her security, and consulted her database. Help, she said.

Running Help, please wait.

Time is a purely relative thing. Measured by one set of criteria, the Mirrors system had a response time that made light look like a twelve-year-old with an impending maths test getting out of bed in the morning. From another viewpoint, such as that of a defenceless ex-rodent barely an arm's length away from three feet of razor-sharp high carbon steel, it moved like an hourly-paid Amstrad. Souris had just enough time to mutter *comeoncomeoncomeoncomeon* under her breath before the answer came through.

Are you sure? she asked. The database confirmed. She stood up.

'Over here,' she said.

Snow White yelped with relief and swung round, the blade raised above her head. 'All right,' she said. 'Now, here's the deal. You do exactly what I tell you and you might just live to see the dawn. Well?'

Souris shook her head. 'I don't think so,' she replied. 'You see, if you kill me, bang goes the network. Not just your access to it, the whole thing. So you aren't going to kill me. And if I know you aren't going to kill me, why on Earth should I do what you say? Besides,' she added, as Snow White tried to work through the equations in her head, 'I wouldn't let you kill me even if you could. I'm the operating system, remember. In this domain, I can do *anything*.'

By way of a demonstration, she snapped her fingers and at once the sword flew out of Snow White's hands and vanished.

'And before you ask,' Souris added, 'the wicked queen is the fairest of them all. Don't ask me how I know, I just do. Okay?'

Snow White took a few steps backwards, until a tree got in the way and made her stop. 'All right,' she grunted. 'But you need me. You may have the data, but you haven't got the savvy. You're not gladewise like I am. Without me, you wouldn't last five minutes.'

Souris felt like pointing out that without her she'd already lasted over seven hours, and that was with a crazed swordswoman hot on her heels. This, though, was no time to score cheap debating points. 'Please explain,' she said.

'You need to know the plot,' Snow White wheedled. 'Like who to watch out for and who you can trust, what's the best way of going about things. Human nature. That kind of stuff. Come on, we can work together. Be a team. It'll be so much better for both of us that way.'

'Really? Why?'

Snow White fished about in the depths of the handbag of her resourcefulness, among the credit card slips, solo ancient peppermints and bits of chewed-up tissue. 'It's too complicated to explain,' she said. 'Like, if you could understand, you wouldn't need me.'

Souris' face twitched rapidly as she subconsciously tried to waggle whiskers that were no longer there. 'What you're saying is,' she said, 'trust you implicitly and take your word for it. Yes?'

'That's the idea,' Snow White replied. 'And as the absolute clincher, I'll give you my word.'

'Fair enough,' Souris said. She gave her new colleague a friendly smile, then looked round to see exactly where she was. It was at this point, or to be precise a second and a half later, just after clobbering the back of her head with a large branch, that Snow White gave her the word she'd promised earlier. It was 'Sucker!', and Snow White put a good deal of feeling into it.

*

Interestingly, the sharp blow to the back of Souris' head had roughly the same effect as the well-aimed kick applied by a skilled electronics engineer to a recalcitrant piece of high-tech gear. A connection closed, or a relay pulled in, or something happened, and the Mirrors network inside the ex-mouse's skull began quietly running a couple of programs.

One was a simple search; and a nanosecond later, Mirrors came up with the following result:

CASTLES: (p2/2) ... From which it can plainly be seen that all castles are in fact the same castle, and the only thing stopping people who have business in castles from meeting each other and spilling over into each others' stories is CastleManager™ For Mirrors, a complex sorting-and-stacking utility that allows an almost infinite number of stories to take place in one castle simultaneously by virtue of a series of spatio-temporal shifts. In plain language, CastleManager™ ensures that for as long as Story A is taking place in the main hall, the narrative requirements of Story B will confine it to the dungeons, while Story C stays in the kitchens and Story D deals with events in the gatehouse.

The few niggling little bugs found in early versions of CastleManager™ have all been corrected, and the utility now operates with the absolute reliability for which all Mirrors products are justly famous. In previous versions, however, it was theoretically possible for the so-called 'Chinese walls' separating different stories to be ruptured by a number of otherwise routine and unimportant systems malfunctions, leading to situations where, for example, two heroines or two assistant villains could be present in the same part of the castle at the same time. This occasionally had the unfortunate effect of triggering the CHARACTER-MERGE.EXE program. CHARACTERMERGE speaks for itself. EXE stands for EXECUTE, an unfortunately ambivalent command in the context of a royal residence well supplied with armed guards.

Sis opened her eyes and quickly turned away. She'd been down in the tunnel for so long that the light scalded them, and besides, they had clearly developed some sort of abstruse technical fault, because as soon as she'd opened them she'd imagined seeing what looked like a scene from an old horror movies, with Boris Karloff and – who was the other one? Bela Lugosi? Something like that. Anyway, her eyes were clearly on the blink. She rested them for a moment –

'Igor? Igor! Don't just stand there gawping. Get those people out of my laboratory.'

This time, Sis's eyes opened wide, and to hell with the brightness of the light.

Igor?!

'Oh bugger,' mumbled Rumpelstiltskin, his nose poking through the thin gap between frame and door. 'Back the way we came, quick.'

But Sis wasn't moving. Instead she was staring at someone; not the Baron, in spite of his colourful language and impressive range of angry gestures; not at Igor, although he was hurrying towards her with a big hammer gripped in both hands. She looked straight past them, or through them, at the figure sitting up on the table.

'Carl?' she said.

'Sis?'

'Where the hell have you been?' they both asked at once.

A lifetime devoted to the study of the art of inter-sibling bickering had given Sis instincts that could override even the most severe shock, so she got her reply in first. 'Looking for you, moron,' she said angrily. 'I could've got killed, chasing round among all these loonies. Of all the thoughtless—'

'Hold it.' The Baron thumped the bench so hard that it shook. 'Shut up, both of you. That's better.' He took a deep breath, then went on, 'Do I take it that you two know each other?'

'Of course,' Sis replied, annoyed at the interruption, 'he's my brother. Who are you?'

'Your *brother* . . .'

Sis nodded. 'I know,' she said. 'People often don't believe we're related. I can understand that,' she added, 'because *he's* got a face like a prune. Who did you say you were?'

'I . . .' The Baron's jaw flopped open, like the gangplank of an exhausted car ferry. 'Never mind who I am,' he rallied, 'who are you? You can't be his brother, for pity's sake, I've just built him. Out of bits.' He stared at Carl for a moment, then back at the table. 'Or at least,' he amended thoughtfully, 'I built *something*. But the one I just made had big clumpy boots and a bolt through his neck. This one . . .' Words failed him, and he pointed. Sis nodded gravely.

'Agreed, our Carl would look much better with a bolt through his windpipe,' Sis replied, observing out of the corner of her eye that although Igor was (still) bustling towards them at a great rate with his hammer raised like a battleaxe, the amount of ground he was actually covering was negligible. 'Real improvement, that'd be. If you could find some way of turning off the voice box, that'd be ideal.'

Carl stuck his tongue out, revealing the neat row of stitching that held it in place, and for the first time Sis realised that Carl didn't look in the least like Carl; he looked, in fact, just like Boris Karloff. More so, in fact, than Mr Karloff himself ever did. But it was definitely Carl, no question. *Whee-plink* went the falling penny, and she realised.

'Did you do this?' she asked.

'Me?' Carl tried to look indignant, then grinned sheepishly. 'Not really,' he said. 'It just sort of happened.'

'*Just sort of happened!*'

Carl stopped being defensive and scowled, a time-honoured tactic he'd used since he was three. It meant he was in the wrong of course, but where else would a younger brother ever be? 'Yeah,' he said, 'it just sort of happened. When *you* started messing about with things. It's all *your* fault really.'

'It is not my—'

'And because *you* started mucking around, *I* got stuck, and the only way I could get unstuck was this. So I did. No thanks to you.'

'But Boris Karloff—'

Carl pulled a face. 'It's a *joke*,' he said. 'Carl/Karloff. Joke. Funny. Ha Ha.'

'Carl, your joke's just about to brain us both with a big hammer.'

Carl clicked his tongue impatiently, turned round and glowered at Igor, who vanished.

When the Baron asked him what the devil he thought he was playing at, he vanished too.

'Joke over,' Carl said, and folded his arms. 'Satisfied?'

Sis gulped, as if trying to swallow a very large live goldfish. 'How did you do that?' she asked.

Carl shrugged. 'I can do anything I like,' he said. 'It's only make-believe.'

'What?'

'Make-believe. Pretend. Like virtual reality or holosuites in *Star Trek*. Just computer stuff, that's all.'

Sis thought about that. 'Then how come I can't do it?' she demanded.

'Because you're thick,' Carl replied, with the air of Einstein crafting the inevitable solution of a quadratic equation. 'And you're only a girl. Girls don't understand computers, everybody knows that.'

He could live another eighty years and earn his living defusing bombs, and still Carl would never be closer to death than he was at that particular moment. But it passed.

'Oh, shut up,' Sis replied wearily. 'And get us out of here. I've had enough. And Mum'll be worried sick.'

'No she won't,' Carl replied, as he systematically erased

the rest of the Baron's laboratory until there was nothing left but four bare stone walls and a flagstone floor. 'We haven't been anywhere in real time,' he explained, 'only in cyberspace. I'd have thought even *you'd* have realised that.'

'Excuse me.'

'The day I understand your gibberings is the day I have my brain replaced,' Sis replied haughtily, ''cos then I'll know I've gone as barking mad as you. And I don't *want* to understand computers,' she added quickly. 'Only very *sad* people understand computers. Only very sad people who haven't got a life . . .'

'Excuse me.'

'Shut up,' Sis commanded, and Rumpelstiltskin immediately pulled his nose back through the trapdoor. Then Sis turned slowly round and stared in his direction. 'Just a minute,' she said. 'Carl, did you do *that*?'

Carl frowned and shook his head. 'Never seen him before,' he replied. 'I thought it must be your new boyfriend. You know, the one you don't want Mum to know about . . .'

Sis made a strange, high-pitched noise, rather like brass foil shearing under enormous pressure. 'You know who that is?' she demanded. 'That's bloody *Rumpelstiltskin*. That's a character from a fairytale!'

Carl shrugged. 'So? For once you got lucky. Well, when I say lucky, compared to some of the freaks you've brought home—'

In order to explain her reasoning, Sis made use of the old dialectic technique of grabbing the other guy's ear and twisting it. 'He's *imaginary*,' she yelled. 'Can't you see that?'

'So you got yourself another imaginary friend. Big deal. Hope he's got a better appetite than the last one, because Mum got really pissed at having to cook dinner for him and none of it ever getting eaten. Ouch, that hurts!'

'Carl. Listen to me. He's a little pretend person from the *Pink Fairy Book*. Make him go away.'

With a well-judged jink and swerve, Carl pulled himself

free and put an arm's length between himself and his sister. 'I didn't make him up,' he said, 'you did. So you've got to make him go away. Nothing to do with me.'

'Excuse me.'

Sis whirled round and pulled the trapdoor open, revealing Rumpelstiltskin cowering behind it. 'I thought I told you to shut up,' she said.

'Yes, but—'

'But?'

'But,' Rumpelstiltskin said, pointing, 'I was just wondering, had you noticed? Sorry to have bothered you.'

'What are you—?' Sis looked over her shoulder. 'Oh,' she said.

The laboratory was slowly fading back in. The workbenches were already there, and the retorts, alembics, Bunsen burners, circuit boards, generators and other clutter were gradually taking shape. Everything was where it had been, right down to the pool of green fluid that had seeped out of the beaker Igor knocked over just before he disappeared.

'Just thought I'd mention it. Bye for now, then.'

Before he could escape, Sis grabbed his collar and pulled. 'Oh no you don't,' she said. 'You're going to stay here and talk to them. They're your kind, not mine.'

A door opened. No need to look to know who it was. 'Igor!' he was shouting. 'Call the guards!'

'*My* kind? I didn't send for them!'

This time, Sis realised, there was something subtly different, even though everything was apparently the same. Something that hadn't been there before. What could it be? Ah yes, the guards, with their body armour and machine pistols. That was what was different.

'That was always your trouble,' she hissed to her brother, who was standing as still as a rock and gazing at the troopers as if they'd just appeared from out of his own nose. 'No imagination.'

'I didn't send for them,' Carl said. 'I thought it was you.'

'*Me?* What would I want with . . . ?'

'This is silly,' Carl said loudly. 'Delete guards, enter!' Nothing happened. 'Control, delete guards, enter!' More nothing. 'Control, Alt, Delete!' he barked shrilly. 'Oh come on, you useless thing, stop mucking about and do as you're bloody well told!'

Somehow, that didn't inspire Sis with a great deal of confidence, since she'd heard him shouting more or less the same words up in his bedroom on the not-too-infrequent occasions when he'd contrived to crash his computer. And Carl's computers, she recalled with a heavy feeling, tended to crash about as often as a blind rally driver.

'I don't think they can hear you,' she said softly. 'Or they aren't particularly interested.'

Nor, on the other hand, were they getting there all that fast; like Igor a few minutes ago, they seemed to be running on the spot. 'Restart,' Carl howled. 'Return to DOS. Mummy! Help!'

Whoever or whatever it was that Carl was yelling at didn't seem to be taking the slightest notice; which was, of course, completely normal. All computers *expect* to be yelled at. There's not a single computer in the whole world that hasn't been sworn at. Even the discreet little VDU with the crossed keys monogram on the keyboard that sits on the Pope's desk in his office in the Vatican has in its time heard language that'd make a Marine blush.

'I don't understand,' Carl confessed, as the guards continued their racing-stalagmite rush towards them. 'It shouldn't be doing this. I think someone's been playing with it, and it's gone haywire.'

'I have an idea,' Sis said. 'Let's run away.'

'Don't be silly,' Carl replied contemptuously. 'It's just software, it can't—'

One of the guards racked back the slide of his machine gun. He made a pantomime of it, and the sound effects were both overdone and unrealistic. And when he fired, the row of bulletholes in the wall above their heads was far too straight and unwavering.

However . . .

They ran.

'I dunno,' sighed the elf, gracefully sidestepping a falling roof-beam. 'Before I got mixed up with you, I used to go days at a time without having houses fall on me. But now . . .'

'Shut up.' Fang grabbed a chair and threw it through a window. 'After you.'

'You're too kind.'

'I want to see if they're still shooting at us.'

As it turned out, they were; but both arrows missed by at least an eighth of an inch. The elf made a peculiar noise, two parts rage to three parts terror with a pinch of cayenne pepper and a cocktail olive, and darted away in the direction of the nearest bush. A couple more arrows narrowly missed her, persuading Fang to jump back out of the way of the window. Then he jumped forward again to avoid a manhole-cover-sized chunk of falling plaster.

'Hey, you,' he yelled at Julian, 'you know about this sort of thing. What should we do?'

Julian, sensibly crouched under a stout oak table with a paper bag over his head (he'd picked up that tip from a government leaflet), beckoned with his front right trotter. 'Under here,' he said. 'It's what I usually do, and it hasn't let me down yet.'

Fang joined him, just as a rafter landed right where he'd been standing. Not long afterwards, what was left of upstairs and a representative sample of the walls followed suit. Despite several direct hits, the table stayed in one piece.

'Thanks,' Fang muttered, when the bombardment was over. 'I reckon I owe you one.'

Julian took off his paper bag. 'Just who are you?' he said. 'I'll swear the voice is familiar.'

'Ah.' Fang thought quickly. There were the three little

pigs. There were the dwarves. There were also, apparently, the samurai, though what harm he'd ever done them he hadn't a clue. Virtually everybody he could think of at the moment was fairly radically anti-wolf.

On the other hand, Wolfpack's fundamental and highly cherished Prime Directive demanded that its officers tell the truth at all times, regardless of the consequences. Along with justice and the Fairyland Way, truth was what the Pack stood for. It was what made them a force for good in the world.

'I'm a handsome prince,' Fang replied. 'What does it look like?'

Julian shrugged. 'Fair enough,' he said. 'Now let's get out of here quick, before those nutcase brothers of mine come looking for me.'

Having shifted sundry bits of dead architecture out of the way, Fang and Julian crawled out from under the table and looked round. The dense clouds of dust were just beginning to settle, and in the distance there were shouts of 'There he is!', followed by the twang of bowstrings.

'Which way?' Fang shouted.

'No idea. Hang on, though, what about that castle over there? Good strong walls, high towers, moat, portcullis; you never know your luck. Come on.'

As they ran, Fang could have pointed out that in his quite extensive experience, the average castle could be razed to the ground with less puff than it takes to blow up a party balloon; but his burgeoning diplomatic instincts prevented him. They made it to the gatehouse in remarkably good time.

'Here,' Julian called out, 'let us in, quick!'

A small sally-port in the main gate creaked open, and a long, thin nose appeared in the opening. 'Why should I?' squeaked a high, thin voice. 'Get lost.'

'We're in mortal danger, that's why,' Julian replied urgently. 'Haven't you people got any respect for the concept of sanctuary?'

'No.' The nose withdrew, and the door started to close.

'Stop,' Fang barked out. 'Wait. Don't listen to my friend, he's just kidding. What we are in fact is, we're double glazing salesmen.'

The door didn't open ' ut it stopped closing. 'Double glazing salesmen?'

'That's right,' Fang panted. 'We also sell brushes, useful gadgets for the kitchen and complete sets of the Encyclopaedia Gigantica.'

'That's more like it,' the voice behind the nose grumbled. 'Still . . .'

'Also,' Fang added desperately, 'we're fully accredited evangelists of the Church of the Divine Revelation, and if you'd care to spare us a moment, we could show you some really interesting pamphlets.'

'Pamphlets,' the unseen doorkeeper repeated, with barely contained excitement. 'Tracts? You got tracts?'

'We got more tracts than you could possibly imagine. Not just religious ones, either. For discerning people like yourself, we also have a wide selection of canvassing leaflets to help you decide who to vote for in local elections.'

The door swung open. 'You'd better come in,' said the doorkeeper. 'Got any Referendum Party videos? I *love* Referendum Party videos.'

Once inside, Fang and Julian quickly knocked the doorkeeper out and tied him up with a piece of rope they found hanging on a hook near the gate; it was just the right length, and presumably kept there for the purpose. 'Now,' Fang muttered, 'we need a couple of guards. Ah, here they are.' He reached for a thick billet of wood that was lying conveniently close; then he frowned. 'I don't believe it,' he said. 'Talk about inefficient. Here, you.'

'Who, me?' said one of the guards, coming over.

'Yes, you. What's your inside leg measurement?'

The guard thought for a moment. 'Twenty-nine,' he said.

'Waist and collar size?'

'Thirty-six and fourteen. Why?'

Fang sighed. 'Go away,' he said, 'and send me one of your mates who's thirty-one inside leg, thirty-two waist and a number sixteen collar. Go on, jump to it. Your colleague,' he added, pointing to the short, fat guard who was standing a few feet away, 'can stay. Go on, jump to it. We haven't got all day.'

The guard trotted off, and a minute or so later was replaced by another one who was the right size. Fang bashed them over the head and stripped off their uniforms. 'Here,' he muttered, passing Julian the short guard's boots. 'I don't know,' he complained. 'I mean, off-the-peg guards are one thing, but do I look like a thirty-six waist to you?'

Someone was hammering at the gate. 'Desmond,' Julian groaned. 'Look, why don't you buzz off, see if there's a back door or something you can sneak out of before they start tearing the place down? It's not you they're interested in, and there's no point in you getting hurt too.'

Fang was tempted. After all, he still had a wicked witch to find, and this didn't seem like the sort of place witches frequented. On the other hand, he noticed, there were quite a few tall, pointy-topped towers, of the kind inevitably inhabited by crazy old wizards. There might even be a wicked queen . . .

'Wouldn't dream of it,' he replied. 'Don't you worry, they won't get in here. And even if they do, they'll never find us. A place this size, there must be millions of nooks and crannies we could hide in. Or a secret tunnel under the walls leading to a ruined priory. I heard somewhere there's more miles of tunnel under the average castle than the whole of the Circle and Piccadilly Lines put together. No, you stick with me and you'll be just fine.'

As soon as they'd put on the captured uniforms, they crossed the courtyard, climbed a short flight of steps and opened the door to the chapel. It was empty, and the light passing through the stained glass windows threw bizarrely garish pools of coloured light on the polished stone floor.

'It's odd, about the nooks and crannies,' Fang said. 'They must be put there on purpose, because they're no earthly use for anything except hiding in, but you take a look at an architect's floor-plan for a castle and show me where it says *Nook here* or gives the dimensions for a cranny. It's almost as if they grow of their own accord.'

'Or else something makes them,' Julian replied. 'You know, like woodworm holes and places where moths have been at the curtains.'

It was bleak and cold in the chapel, and on all sides the grim faces of dead knights and bishops, lying on the lids of their stone coffins like so many malevolent fossilised sun-bathers, seemed to be staring at them. It felt like the inside of Medusa's freezer.

'Somewhere around here,' Fang muttered, 'there ought to be some stairs leading down to the crypt. Plenty of places to hide in a crypt. Assuming these cheapskates haven't turned it into a pool room or a wine cellar, of course.'

'I don't think I like the sound of a crypt,' Julian replied with a shudder, as he did his best to avoid the eye of a particularly sinister-looking marble crusader. 'Crypts have Things in them.'

Fang bent down, grabbed hold of an iron ring in the floor and pulled, revealing a trapdoor and some steps going down. 'Depends on who you're more afraid of,' he said, 'Things or your brothers. You know them better than I do.'

'Good point,' Julian answered. 'All right, after you.'

Fang duly led the way, reflecting as he did so that a good industry-standard Thing, with the usual level of regulation magical powers, could have him back in his nice warm fur coat and running about on four feet quicker than you could say H.P. Lovecraft. 'Mind your head,' he called out as he disappeared down the steps, 'the ceiling's rather *ouch!*'

'Thank you. I'll bear that in mind.'

It was, of course, as dark as strong black coffee in the crypt, and for a while the only sound was Fang's muffled swearing as he stubbed his toes on what turned out to be large marble sarcophagi. But of Things, amazingly, not a sign.

'I don't know,' he grumbled. 'A place like this, you'd expect it to be lousy with Things. Huh. I've been in creepier bus stations.'

'Have you?'

'No. It's a figure of speech.'

'Oh.'

'It's a pretty poor show, though,' Fang went on. 'I suppose it could be something to do with the cock-ups, but it doesn't feel that way to me.'

'I think you're right.'

Fang sighed. 'I reckon it's just good old-fashioned sloppiness,' he said. 'That or the cuts.'

'Could be.'

'And stop agreeing with me.'

'Sorry.'

'Excuse me,' Julian interrupted from the other side of the crypt, 'but who exactly are you talking to over there?'

There was a moment of utter stillness, during which the fall of a pin would have had the neighbours phoning the environmental health people to complain about the noise.

'I think that's a very good question,' Fang croaked. 'I thought it was you.'

'No it wasn't.'

'Yes it was.'

Fang took a deep breath. 'Excuse me asking,' he said, 'but are you a Thing? Not you,' he added quickly, before Julian had a chance to reply. 'Him.'

'Me?'

'Yes, you. The one who lives down here, not the one I brought with me. Are you a Thing, or just waiting for a bus or something?' He clicked his tongue impatiently. 'God, if only it wasn't so dark in here . . .'

'It is rather, isn't it? Just a moment . . .'

There was a disconcerting flash of blue light, which faded

into an aquamarine glow that revealed, among other things, a spider.

'Actually,' Julian admitted, 'what I'm *really* terrified of, most in all the world, is spiders.'

'Tough.' Fang took a step closer to the web in which the spider hung. Web, he thought. No, surely not. The spider didn't move; there, in the very centre of the fragile, lethally efficient environment it had created for itself, there wasn't any need for it to stir, only to wait for the gullible and the clumsy to come blundering through. Web, Fang thought again. Imagine there was a spider's web that stretched right across the known world . . .

'It's you, isn't it?' he said.

The spider lifted its front legs and waggled them.

'Yes, very nice,' Fang said impatiently. 'Great symbolism. Now, would you mind turning back into whatever you really are? You're giving my friend here the horrors.'

The spider began to spin. It quickly spun a huge ball of gossamer, so large that it could easily have concealed a human being. Just as Fang was about to lose patience (gossamer being spun, paint drying; you pay your money and take your choice) the cocoon split open and out fell a short bald man in rimless spectacles and a threadbare towelling robe bearing a monogram on the pocket that suggested that it had been stolen from the Grand Hotel, Cardiff. 'Watch it,' muttered Fang. 'You nearly trod on my foot.'

'Sorry,' the short man apologised. He was sitting on a tomb whose lid was carved into what looked uncomfortably like an effigy of himself. 'Problem with the encryption software. I'd try to fix it, but I can't understand the code.'

'Code,' Fang repeated.

'Code. Computer language. You know,' the man added, 'the stuff the programs are written in. What you get when you open one of the system files, and the screen looks like someone's eaten too much alphabet soup and been sick. Code.'

'I haven't got a clue what you're talking about.'

260 • Tom Holt

'What? Oh, of course, I forgot. Sorry.'

Fang took a deep breath. 'Forgot? Forgot what?'

The man grinned a forty-watt grin. 'I keep forgetting that I'm the only one of you, or rather us, who knows about the operating system.'

'Operating system.'

'That's right. What makes this whole domain work.'

'And you know all about it, do you?'

The man nodded. 'I ought to. After all, I built it.'

Counting up to ten usually worked, but not this time. 'You'd better start explaining,' Fang growled. 'And it'd better make sense, too. If it hadn't been for those tricks you just did I'd assume you're as crazy as a barrelful of ferrets; but you aren't, are you?'

The man shook his head. 'Not to the best of my knowledge,' he replied, 'though after two hundred years down here all on my own in the dark, maybe my own assessment of my mental health isn't all that reliable. I could be stark staring mad by now and not have noticed. Anyway,' he went on, as Fang made an involuntary flexing movement with his fingers, 'what it all comes down to is, I created this domain. Does the phrase *computer-generated imaging* mean anything to you? No? Well, never mind. How about Mirrors?'

'The things you look at yourself in?'

The man shook his head. 'I'd better start at the beginning,' he said. 'Now then, once upon a time . . .'

'Hey!'

'You want me to cut the traditional preamble? Very well. I used to be what we call where I come from a software engineer, and I was playing about one day when I found a way to break into alternate universes using computer simulations as a gateway . . . This is all gibberish to you, right?'

'Yes.'

'I wrote all this,' the man said. 'On my old Macintosh. At least, I wrote an operating system that would make all the hundreds of different fairystories and folktales and nursery rhymes and what have you actually exist in real time, rather than just floating about in the human imagination. It was just a question of protocol compatibility, really. Once I'd got that sorted out, it more or less wrote itself. Anyway, I called it Mirrors, and it all works through the magic mirror belonging to the wicked queen; you remember, Snow White's stepmother.'

Fang nodded. 'At last,' he said, 'something I can under-stand. You're the magician who cast the spell that gives the mirror its power.'

The man blinked. 'Isn't that what I just said?' he replied. 'Sorry. You'll find that's a common failing among com-puter people, saying perfectly simple things in an utterly incomprehensible way. And before you ask, a computer's just another word for a magical thing that does spells. All right?'

Fang nodded. 'I follow,' he said. 'So then what?'

'Actually,' the man went on, 'the wicked queen was my pupil. Nice kid, hard working, quite good at it whenever she managed to apply her mind to it for more than a minute at a time.'

'And she locked you up down here, did she? To make you tell her the secret of the magic?'

'Oh no. Tracy wouldn't do a thing like that.'

'*Tracy?*'

'That's right. She used to be my secretary when I was still running Softcore Industries. That's in the real – I mean, in the domain I originally came from. Tracy Docherty, her name was. She'd been with Softcore for years.'

Fang closed his eyes and concentrated. 'And Softcore was the name of your – what did you call it? Your domain?'

'Oh no.' The man laughed, and there was just the slightest fleeting hint of cold, hard authority in his voice; a faint smear on the glass, no more. 'No, when I was running Softcore the whole *world* was my domain. Or at least I was the richest, most powerful, most widely respected –' The little old man stopped, and smiled. 'I *was*. Never really liked it much, either.

It all happened so fast, or at least that's how it seemed to me. One minute I was sitting in my squashy little apartment in Aspen playing about on my computer, and the next there were all these deputations from world governments offering me honorary doctorates. Anyhow, where was I? Oh yes, Tracy. Nice kid. Did I mention she was a nice kid?'

'Yes.'

'Ah. Sorry. Actually, it all started because every time I looked round, it seemed as if she had her handbag open and one of those powder compact things in her hand, and she was looking at her face in the little mirror. And every time I saw that I used to say to myself, "Who's the fairest of them all?" And that sort of set me thinking.'

Fang decided that concentrating on what the little man was saying was probably counterproductive and might even eventually fry his brain.

'Anyhow, when I wrote Mirrors she became the wicked queen, and I was teaching her to run the system by herself. Then,' he added with a sigh, 'came the accident with the bucket.'

'Accident. Bucket.'

'Well, more with the mop than the bucket. She tried my cleaning-up program, but it sort of went wrong and created one of those Groundhog Day loops, the kind that run the same program endlessly over and over again until your hard drive falls to bits. In this case, the whole castle got filled up with self-propelled mops and flooded out with soapsuds. I got trapped by the flood and ran for it, and then I got lost, ended up down here and found I couldn't get out again. Because of the loop, I think. I've had plenty of time to think it over, and I suspect what happened is that two mirrors some-how managed to end up facing each other, with me trapped in the middle . . .'

Fang had no trouble visualising that. He shuddered.

'So basically,' he said, 'you're a wizard, right?'

The man nodded. 'That's what they used to call us, computer wizards. I think it was meant as a compliment, but I'm not sure. Ambiguous term, really.'

'So.' He took a deep breath. 'You can, um, turn people into things, right?'

'Oh yes, piece of cake,' the little man replied. 'I can turn you back into a wolf, no trouble at all.'

Fang stared. 'You *know*—'

'Like I said, I wrote the code. Shall I do it now?'

'Yes. Yes *please*. I can't—'

Pfzzz.

'–Woof.'

'Better now?'

Fang, a large grey timber-wolf with a lolling tongue and staring red eyes, wagged his tail furiously. 'Woof!' he said; and then paused and listened to what he'd just said. 'Woof?' he queried.

'Oh, play fair, please,' the little bald man protested. 'You said you wanted to be turned back into a wolf, so that's what I did. And when you're a wolf, you're not *supposed* to be able to talk. It was only the mess-up in the code when the system crashed that gave you the ability. Can't you remember what it used to be like? Before the crash, I mean?'

'Woof. Woof.'

'But that's silly,' replied the little man. 'You were Fang the non-talking big bad wolf for ages and ages. You must be able to remember *something*.'

'Woof. Woof woof. *Woof!*'

'Honestly? Well, you surprise me, you really do. Obviously the problem's more serious than I'd guessed. If only I could get out of this place,' he added with a deep sigh, 'I could get it fixed.'

'Woof?'

'He's right, you know,' Julian added, coming out from behind the granite coffin where he'd been hiding just in case the little bald man really was a Thing (or, worse still, Desmond or Eugene in a latex mask). 'You should be able to get out, if we could get in. Maybe whatever's been keeping you down here was wiped out along with the rest of the system.'

'That's –'The little man peered at Julian over his spectacles. 'You're one of the Three Little Pigs, aren't you?' he said. 'Julian?'

Julian nodded.

'And you seem to understand something about how the system works,' the little man went on, 'which is why, though they don't know it themselves, your brothers are trying to kill you. They think you've gone so dreadfully mad that you've got to be stopped at all costs.'

Julian shivered. 'And that's all because of the mix-up, is it? What you called the crash?'

The little man shook his head sadly. 'Not that simple, I'm afraid. You see, on top of the original crash – which I strongly suspect was no accident, by the way; did you happen to meet a couple of strangers in grey suits earlier on? Hm, thought so. It's depressing when you think that actually they're my employees. Still, that's corporate politics for you. Sorry, where was I? Quite apart from the original crash, there's several other rather tiresome people fiddling about with the system, and that's been causing all sorts of further problems. Quite simple to put right,' he added, 'if only I could get out of here.'

Julian shrugged. 'Maybe you can. Have you tried?'

'Have I tried?' the little man repeated. 'Have I tried? Well no, now you come to mention it. At least, not since the crash. You know, it might be a rather interesting experiment, don't you think?'

Julian tried to imagine what it must have been like; two hundred years trapped in a dark crypt, when you knew that it was all just a fairytale anyway. 'You could say that,' he replied. 'How will you know if it's stopped working?'

The little man smiled. 'When I walk up the stairs and actually manage to get to the top,' he replied. 'As simple as that. In this business,' he added, 'things are rarely difficult.

They're possible or they're impossible; no grey areas where things like difficulty can breed. Shall we go?'

'All right.'

'Woof.'

'Fine,' said the little man, standing up with an enormous effort and nearly collapsing again. 'Let's go, then. After you.'

Although it's open to the public (in roughly the same way as a spider's web is open to visiting flies) there is no readily available guide-book to this castle. Which is not to say there isn't a guide-book; it's just that it's twice as big as the castle itself.

If you were to get a crane as high as Kilimanjaro and a winch capable of pulling the moon down out of orbit, you could turn to page 254,488,057,294,618 of the guide-book, where you'd find a plan showing the corridor that leads from the back of the chapel to the minstrels' gallery above the door of the great hall. Twenty-seven thousand-plus pages further on, you'd find another plan showing the secret passage from the great hall that comes up through a trapdoor in the woods a mere five yards or so away from the spot where Snow White clobbered the ex-blind-mouse, Souris. From there, turn back 908,415,012 pages and you'll see a diagram of the Baron's laboratory, clearly showing the passageway that connects it to the great hall. They are all, of course, the same passageway. There's only one passageway in the whole castle.

First came Snow White, dragging the unconscious body of Souris. She dumped her burden on the steps of the dais on which the high table stood, straightened her back and used some coarse and unimaginative language. Then she heard a shuffling noise, looked over her shoulder and saw . . .

A wolf, a pig and a doddery old man with a bald head and round glasses. They didn't notice her at first; the old man was making a beeline straight for a place on the wall where a rectangular outline marked in discoloured whitewash and grime showed where a large mirror had once been. He took in the absence of mirror, sat down on a bench and used coarse and unimaginative language, until the sound of running feet, angry shouting and distant gunfire made him turn his head and see . . .

A blonde girl and a scruffy-looking boy running out of the archway where the corridor came into the hall, closely followed by quaintly costumed halberdiers with assault rifles, who were just about to catch up with them when they ran lickety-split into the small knot of samurai who were chasing a beautiful but dangerous-looking young woman in the opposite direction . . .

But before any serious mayhem could get under way, a side door burst open under the weight of a battering-ram swung with great enthusiasm by two pigs, who were followed by a motley collection of dwarves and Brothers Grimm, their hands securely tied behind their backs with a length of rope lashed to the carriage of the ram . . .

While at opposite ends of the gallery two doors opened, to admit a flustered-looking elf and another, extremely bewildered-looking dwarf with cobweb in his beard . . .

At which point, everything froze.

CHAPTER
THIRTEEN

The accountant sat up.

He'd been dreaming again; a most bizarre dream, in which a substantial number of his clients had gathered together in the great hall of the wicked queen's castle and then vanished in a cloud of glittering pixels. He shook his head, as if trying to make the dream fall out of his ear. Usually, his dreams dealt with profit and loss accounts, quarterly statements, double grossing-up of advance corporation tax and other relevant issues. He enjoyed his dreams. Quite often they were so specific, he was able to charge his clients for having them. This sort of thing was as unwelcome as it was unfamiliar.

In the top left-hand corner of his office, he noticed, there was a cobweb. It wasn't a particularly fine example of the genre, more of a wispy mess that looked like the sort of candy floss you might expect to eat in the house of Lucrezia Borgia. It wasn't the sort of thing any self-respecting fly would be seen dead, let alone frantically struggling, in, obviously produced by a spider who didn't take much pride in its handiwork (spiders don't weave gossamer with their hands, but delicacy of expression forbids a more apt choice of words). It was quivering, vibrating even, as if in tune with a million wave-patterns that rushed into it from every side (*and a fat lot of good that'd be to a hungry spider; can't eat radio signals, can they?*) and were caught and held in the threads until they solidified into tiny droplets of water that slid down the micron-thick wires and fell, like small, fat shooting stars, to join the rapidly growing pool that was collecting in the accountant's empty coffee-cup.

There's a thought, the accountant mused. A web that catches messages from all over the world. A world-wide web. What possible use could it ever be, though?

Hello. Hello? HELLO!

The accountant reached for the nearest file and opened it.

For pity's sake, Grimm, switch your bloody modem on! Though why I'm telling you to switch it on when you can't hear me, because if you could hear me it'd mean you'd already have switched your modem on . . . Oh God, just listen to me, I'm starting to babble. Has anybody in the building got a stamp I could borrow?

The web shuddered a little, though there wasn't a draught. A young bluebottle, who'd just passed his flying test and was really stretching his wings for the first time, hadn't quite slowed down quickly enough. Bugger, it thought, as the foul sticky stuff refused to let it have its legs back; then, since flies are fatalistic creatures, it stopped struggling and hung upside down, waiting for the main event. Nothing happened. Just my luck, the bluebottle reflected, first time out on my own and I run smack into the bogies.

Curious; it was almost as if it could hear voices – some people called Softcore in a place so far away it couldn't possibly ever matter were apparently trying to talk to two friends of theirs called Grimm, to ask them why they hadn't reported back yet, and also what the explanation was for the unusual activity they were monitoring on [some technical stuff that the bluebottle couldn't and didn't really want to understand] and did that mean the Crazy Old Bastard was up to something?

All very peculiar, the bluebottle thought; and it'll never replace the blindfold and last cigarette. You can't beat the old ways at a time like this.

Below, the accountant's head began to droop again. It slid forward and hung from his neck like an over-ripe pear on a thin branch. His eyes closed; then opened again. He could see a tiny reflection of himself in the pool of condensation that had gathered in the bottom of his cup.

'Running DOS,' he said. 'Please wait.'

We've been waiting long enough as it is, you idle bloody – Hang on. You're not Neville Grimm. Who the devil are you?

'Bad command or fi—'

Don't give me any of that crap, please. I write this garbage, remember? Save it for the customers. And listen; I need to talk to Neville Grimm, urgently. Can you pass on the message?

The accountant's eyes glazed over, then blinked seven times. 'Channel now open,' he said. 'Please transmit now.'

Neville. Neville, you dozy . . . Hey, you. I thought you said you'd put me in touch with Nev Grimm. All I'm getting is static.

'Drive Nevgrimm:\ is not ready,' the accountant droned. 'Please try again or restart Mirrors.'

Oh Gawd. You can tell we designed this crap, can't you? All right, transmitting as text-only files for later retrieval. Don't lose it, okay? Here goes. I'm sending through the update, that's Mirrors 2000 1.1, with this message. We've fixed it so it'll overwrite all existing files, repeat, all existing files, which means we'll be able to control the whole box of tricks from back here. Your priority one is to make sure that the Crazy Old Bastard, the woman Tracy Docherty, the girl Sis and the boy Carl do not, I say again do not, leave the Mirrors domain. That way, we can seal the whole thing up tight as an actuary's bum, throw away the key and get on with running this company the way it ought to be run. And before you start panicking, there's two outshots reserved for both of you under filename THREEPIGS.EXE, so you'll be able to get out before we

close the domain up for good. Just make sure you get the right one,
or you'll find yourself buried under a load of useless fonts before
you can say Clive Sinclair. You got all that? Why am I asking,
when you can't bloody well hear me? Oh . . .

The accountant's hand shot out and knocked the cup over,
spilling the water on to his desk, where a thick pile of papers
quickly absorbed it. The accountant opened his eyes.

'Bugger,' he muttered, 'now look what I've done.' He
scooped up the papers, tried to mop up the water with his tie,
then hit the intercom button.

'Nicky,' he barked, 'bring me a J-Cloth, quick as you like.
And another coffee.'

'Right you are,' crackled the voice at the other end.

Presumably she didn't mean it.

'Tracy?' said the little doddery old man.

The wicked queen looked round, did a double-take
and stared at him. 'Mr Dawes!' she shrieked. 'Oh my God. I
thought you were . . .'

Mr Dawes shook his head. 'Well, I'm not,' he said. 'Obviously.'

Neatly sidestepping a pair of samurai, the wicked queen
vaulted over a bench on to a table and down the other side,
patted Fang absently on the head, ignored Julian and gave
Mr Dawes a hug that would have squashed a grizzly bear.
'Mr Dawes!' she repeated. 'Oh boy, am I glad to see you!'

'Are you? That's nice.' Mr Dawes disentangled himself
from the wicked queen with the ease of a bullet passing
though a sheet of wet blotting paper. 'Is there a mirror anywhere in this tiresome place? There's some things I think I
ought to sort out.'

'Hey!' Carl's voice, loud and piercing with all the abrasive
clarity of youth. 'You're Ben Dawes! You run Softcore! Wow!'

Mr Dawes gave him a sweet, sad look, the sort that's worth
a million of the sort of words that are usually immediately
followed by *off*. 'Yes, that's right,' he said. 'And don't tell me,
you want to be a software engineer when you grow up.

My advice is don't. Either of them. And now, if you don't mind . . .'

It occurred to Sis, as Carl stopped dead in his tracks and went red in the face, that if this was really the celebrated Ben Dawes, then of course he'd have had plenty of practice in making bumptious young computer freaks shut up; still, it was quite an awesome exhibition. It would be nice, she reflected, if he could make the same technique work on armed guards and Japanese warriors. Assuming it really *was* the great Ben Dawes. She remembered something.

'Excuse me,' she said.

Mr Dawes turned to look at her. For a moment she was afraid he'd loose that awful stare on her; but for some reason he didn't. He looked even more like a kindly old uncle than ever. 'Well?' he said.

'Excuse me,' she repeated, 'but are you sure you're Ben Dawes?'

The old man smiled; it was a very sad smile. 'Last time I looked,' he said.

'Ah. It's just – you're rather older than I expected.'

Mr Dawes nodded. 'Young lady,' he said, 'I'm twenty-nine.'

'Ah.'

Mr Dawes nodded. 'It's the climate in these parts,' he said. 'I'm not sure it agrees with me. Now then, where was I? Oh yes. A mirror. Any mirror will do,' he went on, and he was speaking to – yes, confound it, it was the wicked queen, although a moment ago Mr Dawes had called her Tracy, which seemed improbable. 'Polished metal'd do at a pinch,' he added. 'Or even a bit of wood with a good beeswax shine on it. Surely that's not too much to ask, is it?'

'Sorry, Mr Dawes,' the wicked queen replied awkwardly, as if she'd negligently brought him a cup of warm blood instead of his morning coffee. 'Usually there's any number of mirrors around the place, but just now we seem to be right out of them.'

'Marvellous. Well, there must be *something*—' Just then Mr Hiroshige, who'd got his sleeve snagged on the corner of the table, managed to free himself and advanced on the wicked queen, brandishing his sword in the approved, highly ceremonial and utterly symbolic manner. He'd just, in fact, accidentally sliced through a bowl of wax fruit and a table lamp; and as he swung the shining *katana* around his head, the light flashed on the immaculately burnished steel of its three-foot blade.

'You there,' Mr Dawes barked, and at once the samurai stopped brandishing and stood on one leg looking extremely self-conscious. 'Stop fooling about with that thing and give it to me. Hurry up,' he added, snapping his arthritic fingers, 'that's the way. Now then,' he added, as he took the sword from Mr Hiroshige's unresisting hand, 'let's see what we can see. Tracy, I'd be ever so grateful if you could stop those buffoons with guns clumping up and down. This is rather delicate work, you know, especially under these conditions.' As he spoke, an oppressive weight of guilt and shame seemed to encompass the Baron's halberdiers, as if they'd been called up to the front at morning prayers and told off in front of the whole school. They shuffled back out of the way, holding their assault rifles behind their backs and trying to look inconspicuous. For beginners, it was a creditable attempt.

Mr Dawes held the swordblade up to the light; then he laid it down again, took off his glasses, rubbed them on his sleeve, put them back on his nose, breathed on the sword, rubbed that with his sleeve and held it up again, squinting at it. 'Not used to bright light, you see,' he explained. 'Now then. Mirror!'

For a heart-twistingly anxious moment, nothing; then the face of a very old and venerable Japanese monk appeared in the steel.

'Mirror,' Mr Dawes repeated.

The monk stared at him impassively for about three-quarters of a second; then he bowed slightly from the neck and opened his lips.

> '*Fleeting, like the snowflake,*
> *Fragile as the cherry blossom,*
> *DOS is now running.*'

'What?' Mr Dawes frowned. 'Oh, right. Never mind all that now. Select Setup, quick as you can.'

The Japanese gentleman bowed again and vanished. Mr Dawes made an exasperated noise with his teeth and upper lip and sat down on a bench, tapping the fingers of his free hand on the table. Everybody else seemed to be watching, and also (Sis realised) trying to avoid being noticed by Mr Dawes; even Fang had curled up under the table with his tail between his legs. She wondered why this was; after all, he seemed a nice enough old man, not to mention being the rich and famous Mr Dawes; then she remembered the effect that a very slight brush with his displeasure had on Carl (he was under the table too, and the only reason his tail wasn't between his legs was that he didn't have a tail). A nice enough old man, she decided, but also formidable; kindly old Uncle Darth.

And then she noticed someone who wasn't respectfully cowering: a cute, fresh-faced blonde girl, a year or so older than herself, with pigtails that came down to her waist and cheeks as rosy-red as the bruises on the face of someone who's just been done over by a Glasgow dope gang. *Snow White*, she deduced, *and she looks ready to commit mayhem.* As yet, though, she didn't look as if she was about to do anything more aggressive than mere savage pouting (*she's got the lips for it, God knows; she's what you'd expect to see if Frankenstein had gone to work for the Disney corporation*), but it crossed Sis' mind that she ought perhaps to warn Mr Dawes; and then she thought of what might happen if she interrupted Mr Dawes when he was busy, and decided that he was probably old enough and avuncular enough to look after himself. She looked away –

At precisely the same moment that Snow White made her move; which is why the first Sis knew about it was the ear-splitting shriek as Snow White snatched Mr Miroku's sword out of his fist, leapt up on to the table and aimed a ferocious slash at Mr Dawes' head. Fortunately, she missed; but the blow knocked his sword clean out of his hand and sent it flying across the hall. It hit a wall, rebounded and fell with quite remarkable precision on to the rope that still attached Dumpy, Tom Thumb and the Brothers Grimm to the battering ram, cutting it in two.

The Grimms had been fidgeting nervously for some time; now that they were suddenly and unexpectedly set free, they didn't hang about. Grimm #2 hurled himself under the table, but #1 lowered his head and charged at Mr Dawes, yelling something inarticulate and managing to head-butt the poor old man without actually having to look him in the eye. At this point Fang sprang up from his crouch under the table. Perhaps it was because he'd been human for so long he'd forgotten what size his true shape was, or maybe it was just a freak outbreak of clumsiness. Whatever the reason, he stood up too fast and too tall, nutted himself on the underside of the table and flopped back to the floor with his eyes shut.

With Mr Dawes's restraining influence temporarily removed, the gathering became a trifle disorderly. Desmond and Eugene (who'd been utterly paralysed by the sight of Mr Dawes, though they had no idea why) caught sight of Julian and went for him like a pack of hunt saboteurs in pursuit of a Range Rover. Julian didn't hang around; he scrambled up on to the table in a flurry of clattering trotters and galloped along it at a speed you'd normally expect to be far beyond the ability of even a souped-up Formula One pig, until he had the misfortune to cannon into Dumpy, who'd wanted to hit one of the halberdiers in the eye (because he was there, presumably) and had climbed on to the table so as to be able to reach. At this point Fang came out of his table-induced swoon, caught sight of two little pigs, and instinctively took a deep breath. The pigs saw him, recognised him and stopped dead.

'Hey, you!' Eugene yelled to Dumpy. 'Leave that and get this bastard wolf off us. That's what we're paying you for, isn't it?'

Dumpy blinked; his head was still full of breathtaking indoor fireworks after his collision with Julian, but a remark that finally makes some sort of sense after you've been living in a world with severe continuity problems has power to penetrate even the wooziest skull.

'Darned right you are,' he whooped with all the satisfaction of a short but fierce warrior who finally knows what he's supposed to be doing; at once he threw himself at Fang and would undoubtedly have knocked the stuffing out of him if only he hadn't missed and gone rolling across the floor like an out-of-control snowball. 'Dammit!' he yelled, as he trundled towards the door, ''Stiltskin, Thumb, do something!'

Rumpelstiltskin, of course, was still up in the gallery. He'd been hoping very earnestly that whatever it was that was going on could manage to carry on going on without him, and he was just about to plead a bad cold or a severe attack of conscience or a grandmother's funeral when he observed that Fang was now more or less directly below him, and that on the parapet of the gallery, just nicely handy and conveniently balanced, was a large potted fern. He nudged it and it fell.

'Wugh!' said Fang as the pot hit him; then he closed his eyes again and went back to sleep.

Dumpy, who'd pitched up against the doorframe and rolled back on to his feet, punched the air with his fist. 'Yee-hah!' he shrieked. 'We done it! We done nailed that old big bad wolf!'

Snow White and the wicked queen, who'd been having a little private wrestling-match to decide who was to have Mr Miroku's sword, both looked round simultaneously. Then they looked at each other.

'Something went right,' said the queen.

Snow White growled like an angry dog, let go of the sword and belted her with a cut-glass fruit bowl, causing her to lose interest; then she picked up the sword and advanced along the top of the table towards Mr Dawes, who did a fine impression of a crab in reverse gear backing round a tight corner.

'It won't work, you know,' he said.

'You reckon?' Snow White lunged, missing Mr Dawes by the thickness of a cigarette paper. 'We'll see.' She feinted to his left then, as he dodged, brought the blade whistling down, snipping a button off his jacket cuff with a degree of precision that'd have been the envy of half the surgeons at Guy's Hospital. 'I'm the fairest, and that's how it's going to stay,' she snarled. 'Now keep still while I kill you.'

She swung again; but this time the blade bit an inch and a half deep into the oak of the table-top, and while she was struggling to twist it free, Mr Dawes ducked under her arms and made a Warp Two dodder for it. He got up quite a respectable turn of speed, but it didn't get him very far, because Grimm #2 reached out from under the table and tripped him up. 'Get him,' he yelled to his brother; and to be fair, Grimm #1 wasn't far behind; the only reason he didn't get there earlier was because he'd stopped to pull a bell-rope clear from the wall. He pounced on Mr Dawes and started tying him up.

'Bugger that,' Grimm #2 shouted. 'Kill the old sod.'

Grimm #1 swivelled round, his hands tight on the rope. 'I can't do that,' he shouted back. 'That'd be murder.'

'Nah. Aggravated pesticide, top whack.'

Grimm #1 scowled. 'Look, we tie him up and get out of here, and that'll have to do.'

Then both of them were shoved out of the way as Snow White charged through, still gripping the sword. 'This is between him and me,' she warned, carelessly letting the tip of the blade pass no further than a thirty-second of an inch from the tip of #2's nose. 'Stay out of this, unless you fancy going home salami.'

#1 opened his mouth to object, but #2 got in before him. 'Fair enough,' #2 said. 'You do it, we don't mind. Equality of opportunity is one of the things Softcore takes most seriously.'

Sis looked round in desperation; but the samurai didn't seem as if they were interested in intervening, while the halberdiers were standing there like book-ends. The pigs and the dwarves just seemed out of it all, somehow, as if their storyline was over and someone had switched them off to save electricity. She looked away . . .

And saw the doors that led up to the gatehouse tower fly open, and a great torrent of what looked very much like thick soapsuddy water come flooding into the hall, with three or four frantically struggling mops riding the crest of the tidal wave like surfers as depicted by L.S. Lowry. A fraction of a second before the flood caught her up and swept her away, she thought she might just have seen a tiny elfin female and an equally diminutive male clinging on to the bolts that had held the doors shut; though whether that meant they'd deliberately opened them or were just clinging to something to keep from being drowned in the suddy deluge, she neither knew nor (*Help! I can't SWIM!!*) particularly cared.

It's a terrible way to go, drowning in a sea of soapsuds. The assurance that, once the flood has subsided and your sodden, swollen body pitches up somewhere among the driftwood and other assorted flotsam, your clothes will be whiter than white and free of those hard-to-shift stains is little real consolation.

Most of the hapless victims trapped inside the great hall

when the deluge broke through coped remarkably well, all things considered. Fang, for instance, swam round in circles until his strength was just about to fail, whereupon he was rescued by the three little pigs, who had improvised a raft out of an upturned table (complete with a tablecloth sail and serving spoon oars) and were arguing among themselves as to which of the three chandeliers pointed north when Fang floated by.

'Let him drown,' said Desmond. 'For pity's sake, he's the big bad wolf.'

'Shut up,' Julian argued, reasonably enough. 'And help me get him on board.'

'On table, surely.'

'You can shut up as well. Come on, jump to it. Or do you want to spend the rest of your lives on this contraption?'

It was remarkable how quickly their differences had been put aside, once it became apparent that Julian was the only one with a clue as to what to do.

'All right,' Desmond grunted. 'Eugene, get his ears. Now then; one, two, and *heave*!'

Fang landed in the well of the table with a bump, too exhausted to do more than wag his tail feebly. Julian, however, was in a hurry.

'Now listen,' he said, grabbing Fang by the scruff of his neck and lifting his head. 'You see that archway over there? Good. Now that's the way out on to the battlements – we're floating level with them right now. If we can get this raft over there before the sud level rises much more, we can get out on to the ramparts and shin down the drawbridge ropes. Piece of cake. All you've got to do is blow in the sail, right? I said right?'

'Wf.'

'I don't care. You used to be bloody good at huffing and puffing and blowing things down when it was a real pain in the bum. If you need an added incentive, how about if you don't get huffing and puffing before I count to three, you're going to be breakfast, lunch and dinner until further notice? You like that idea? Okay then. Get huffing.'

Quickly, with his ears right back against his skull, Fang huffed. Then, more from force of habit than anything else, he puffed. And then the raft skimmed across the surface of the great hall like a speedboat, cutting a huge wake of froth and bubbles as it went and spewing out a tidal wave that turned the great hall into a jacuzzi.

'Too fast!' Julian screamed, as the raft shot towards the archway like a torpedo. 'Too *fast* . . . !'

His words dopplered away into nothing as the raft shot through the arch, bump-bump-bumped down a flight of steps and slid off through another archway and over the parapet like the crew of the *Enterprise* doing warp nine back to the nearest starbase in time for Happy Hour.

'We're flying!' Eugene shrieked above the scream of the wind all around them.

'In a sense,' Julian yelled back.

Fortunately, and at odds somewhere in the region of seventy million to one, they touched down on the moat, bounced like Barnes Wallis' celebrated bomb, and skimmed along the lush grass of the castle foregate before coming to a gentle, civilised stop in the middle of a cesspit. Almost immediately after stopping, the table submerged with a loud and flatulent *glop!*, leaving Julian and his brothers struggling out of the smelly mire, happy as pigs in muck (which is to say, not very).

'Don't say a word,' Julian warned, as they scrambled out of the pit and collapsed on the grass. 'I'll just mention this. If the Wright boys had made a nice soft landing like that at their first attempt, they'd have been hugging themselves with glee.'

'Yes,' Desmond muttered, after spitting out a mouthful of cesspit. 'Well. I think the basic idea was bad and getting that bloody wolf to blow in the sail was about as daft an idea as anybody's ever had in the history of the world. On both counts . . .'

'What's he's trying to say,' Eugene interrupted, 'is that two wrongs don't make us Wrights. So what. We're still in one piece. I say we forget about the whole thing, and . . .'

'Hang on.' Julian held up a trotter for silence. 'Where's the wolf?'

The three little pigs looked round. Sure enough, there was no trace of Fang to be seen anywhere. The pigs exchanged glances and stared at the bubbling, glopping surface of the cesspit.

'May he rest in peace,' said Desmond, after a long while. 'And whatever else is in there, of course.'

'Maybe we ought to try to fish him out,' said Eugene reluctantly. Julian shook his head.

'Nice thought,' he sighed, 'but he's been under – what, forty-five seconds? A minute? He's huffed his last puff and that's that. What a way to go,' he added with a shudder. 'Apt, but nasty. Come on, let's find a stream or a pond or something, before anybody sees us.'

Desmond nodded thoughtfully. 'Forgive and forget, huh? Oh well, why not? It's no skin off my snout, provided it's guaranteed he's not coming back.'

Julian stared at the billowing mere, then shrugged his sloping shoulders. 'One thing's for sure,' he said with a sigh. 'If the bugger does manage to survive, we'll never have any trouble about him creeping up on us unawares. Not unless the wind's in the other direction and we've all got really bad colds.' He shook his head, then pulled himself together. 'Move it, you two,' he said. 'First a bath, then we've got a house to build. It so happens I was reading the other day in *Scientific Gloucester Old Spot* about a way to make high-tensile breezeblocks from straw. Game, anybody?'

'At last,' muttered Tom Thumb. 'Now I understand.'

'Understand what?'

'Why it's such an unfair advantage being small.'

The elf grunted. 'Good for you,' she replied. 'Now it's your turn to bail.'

As well as being magical and containing a simultaneous translator/amplifier unit that'd have most terrestrial electronics manufacturers sobbing themselves to sleep from envy, Tom Thumb's hat was watertight and therefore suitable for bailing soapsuds out of an up-ended floating contact lens. It had been Thumb's suggestion that they name the lens the *Nelson*; something to do with being temporarily blind in one eye was the reason he gave, and the elf was too busy sloshing suds over the side in a soggy hat to object.

'Anything to report?' he asked, as he took the hat and stooped to dip it in the suddy bilges of the lens.

'Just listen to yourself, will you?' the elf snarled back. 'Ye gods, it'll be *splice the mainbrace* and *make it so, Number One* in a minute. No, there's nothing to report, just a lot of damn great big soapy bubbles as far as the eye can . . .'

The lens lurched alarmingly, and if the elf hadn't had reactions like a caffeine-addicted rattlesnake, Thumb would have been lost over the side for sure. As it was, the lens was only a degree or so of tilt away from capsizing.

'What the hell . . . ?' Thumb spluttered, through a mouthful of soap.

The elf craned her neck to see. 'Styrofoam cup ahoy,' she replied. 'What careless maniac left that there, right in the middle of a shipping lane? And why are you talking in that funny voice?'

'I lost the hat over the side,' Thumb wailed. 'It's no good. We're shipping too much soap, and without the hat I can't bale out. We're going to sink. All we need is a string quartet in full evening dress, and we could do an utterly authentic *Titanic* re-enactment.'

'You're the captain,' the elf snarled back, one leg over the side. 'If you insist on going down with your lens, that's your business. I'm going to jump for it.'

'Wait for me!'

There was a tiny plop, followed shortly afterwards by another, similar. Not long after that, a wee small voice cried out, 'heeelblgblgblggbgbgggbbbllgb!'

'Hang on, I'm coming!' the elf yelled, kicking frantically. 'Don't you dare drown on me, you big sissy, not after all I've . . . Just a minute,' she added, standing up. 'You clown, it's only knee-deep.'

'You sure about that?'

'Stand up and try it for yourself, idiot.' The elf grunted, and wiped suds off herself. 'Marvellous,' she added, 'we're standing on top of the gallery rail. Here, give me your hand, I'll pull you out.'

'Just a minute, I think I can see the hat. That's better,' Thumb went on, scrambling on to the rail with the hat pulled lopsidedly over the back of his head. 'You know, I really thought we'd had our chips that time. You know how you're supposed to have your whole life flash before you when you're about to drown? Well, it's true. I saw it, the whole thing; us getting married, the reception, with your Uncle Terry getting drunk and falling down the back of the chair, little Tom junior's first day at medical school . . .'

'Just a second,' the elf interrupted. 'That's your future life, you idiot.'

'Oh? Oh,' Thumb repeated, as the implications hit him. 'Oh, right,' he added pinkly. 'It's a pity I didn't notice how we get off this rail, then.'

'I could push you back over so you could have another look,' the elf suggested.

'That'd be cheating,' Thumb said firmly, 'which would tend to corrupt the validity of the data. How'd it be if we just walked along the rail and climbed out through that window over there?'

The elf looked where Thumb was pointing. 'I dunno,' she said. 'You're sure it's safe?'

'Well, the alternative is staying here and drowning. You choose; I'm biased.'

'I'll tell you one thing, for sure,' the elf said, as they tightrope-walked towards the open window. 'If we do get out of this alive, I've had it with fairytales. No more fooling about with big bad wolves and homicidal woodcutters and wicked witches with machine guns and psychotic pigs for me. No more Miss Nice Girl. We're going to move right out on to the outskirts of the forest and open a video library.'

'Sounds good to me,' Thumb replied, in a rather wobbly voice. 'Happily ever after, and all that jazz.'

'Certainly not,' the elf replied severely. 'Miserably and fighting all the time, like *real* people. That way,' she added, 'ever after might get to mean longer than a week.'

He was a single star in an infinite blackness, a tiny speck on an endless ocean, one solitary spectator in an otherwise deserted Wembley Stadium. On all sides there was nothing but an eerie expanse of white bubbles, like some bizarre Antarctic seascape shrouded in low fog.

'Go on,' Dumpy growled. 'Git.'

'I'm going as fast as I can,' replied the mop plaintively. 'Properly speaking, I'm not obliged to carry passengers at all. I'd be well within my rights . . .'

'Shut up.'

'Witches, now,' the mop continued, taking no notice, 'we've got to stop for witches, 'cos they're entitled, provided they've got a current brush pass and all. But it doesn't say anything in Regulations about giving lifts to passing dwarves. I could probably get in serious trouble for this, you realise.'

'Keep swimmin'.'

'It'd be different,' sighed the mop, 'if you appeared to have the faintest idea about where it is you actually want to go. But we've been cruising round in circles for hours now, and my handle's starting to hurt something awful. I'm going to have to insist that you either specify a valid destination, or . . .'

'Over there,' Dumpy broke in urgently. 'Quick.'

'Now you're sure about this, aren't you?' said the mop. 'Because if you suddenly decide to change your mind . . .'

'Quit complaining,' Dumpy said. 'That's my partner over there.'

Sure enough, on the bubble-thronged horizon, a bedraggled figure was clinging desperately to a floating baguette. 'Hang on, 'Stiltskin,' Dumpy roared. 'I'm a-comin' to get you.'

'Now just you hold on a moment,' the mop objected. 'One of you's bad enough, but if you're suggesting I stop and take on another one of you freeloaders—'

'Do it or I'm gonna stick your head down a toilet full o' Harpic so fast you won't know you're born. And that's a promise.'

'Vulgar beast. All right then, if you absolutely insist. But you're taking full responsibility.'

'So sue me. Hey, you sure you can't go no faster'n this?'

The mop drew up directly alongside Rumpelstiltskin's baguette, and Dumpy quickly pulled him aboard. For some time he could do nothing except spit out water and swear, with the outraged mop keeping up a running commentary of protests while he did so. When at last he'd finished with all that, he heaved a sigh that seemed to come from deep down inside his socks.

'Serves me right,' he groaned, 'for turning my back on a perfectly good scam to go trailing and paddling about playing Heroes. What I wouldn't give for a nice cool dry cellar with a spinning wheel and a big heap of straw.'

The mop shuddered under them like a nervous horse. Frantically, Dumpy grabbed a handful of mop-strings and pulled. 'Whoa there,' he commanded. 'Ain't no call to be in such a gosh-danged hurry. You just bide there quiet and let me think.'

'Honestly,' muttered the mop darkly, 'is this the time to go trying entirely new experiences?'

'Shuttup.' Dumpy looked round, but there was nothing to see except the billows of white, eye-stinging foam, and he had to admit that he didn't know what to do. That troubled him; a dwarf, surely, ought to know exactly what to do at any given moment. He should be in command, in charge of every situation, proud, self-reliant and brimming with self-confidence. A dwarf should walk tall.

'Looks like this is it, then,' mumbled his colleague beside him. 'The end of the chapter. For you, the story is over.' He sighed. 'Well, there's probably worse ways to go, though I'd be surprised if there's many that are more bizarre.'

'That ain't no way to talk,' Dumpy replied, shocked. 'Dwarves don't quit, boy. That jes' ain't the way.'

'Oh, put a sock in it, please!' Rumpelstiltskin exploded. 'God, you should listen to yourself for a minute, you really should. It's enough to make a cat laugh.'

Dumpy narrowed his eyes. 'What you sayin'?' he demanded.

'Quite simple,' Rumpelstiltskin replied, turning his back. 'So simple, in fact, that even you shouldn't have too much trouble getting your head around it. Ready? Then I'll begin. You – do – not – talk – like – that. Nobody – does. Got that? Or would you prefer to wait for the novelisation?'

A surge of fury set out to cross Dumpy's face, but it was overtaken by a flood of bewilderment. 'What kind o' nonsense you talkin' now, partner?' he groaned. 'You done bin out in the sun with no hat on, and that's fo' sho'.'

'You see?' Rumpelstiltskin cried, whirling round so fast he nearly upset the mop. 'You can't even do it *properly*. It's just what Thumb was saying a while back, only we didn't listen to him. *You're not you*, get it? I can remember now, you see. For some reason, when the water came up to my chin and I thought I was just about to drown, all the memories that'd somehow been locked up in a cupboard in the back of my mind came busting out, and I *remembered*! I used to know you.'

Dumpy blinked at him. Somewhere at the back of his own mind was a tiny voice yelling *Help! Let me out!* 'You did?' he queried.

'We used to work together,' Rumpelstiltskin replied. 'That's if you can call it work, of course. There were seven of us, and we lived in a real dive of a place out the west edge of the forest. All the neighbours used to refer to us as Dwarves Behaving Badly.'

'I . . .' Dumpy raised his voice to yell a rebuttal, but somehow didn't. 'I remember,' he said.

'Thought you would. We used to go off to work every morning down the sewage plant, then troop back of an evening, send out for pizzas, open a couple of cases of beer, put a dirty film on the video . . .'

'We used to dry our socks in the microwave,' Dumpy interrupted suddenly. 'Once a month, regular as clockwork, we'd take 'em off, sloosh them down with the garden hose, then bung 'em in at Defrost for ten minutes. Very good way of doing them, too. Efficient.'

'That's it, you're right,' Rumpelstiltskin said. He'd noticed that Dumpy's accent and vocabulary were completely different as well, but he didn't mention that. 'I remember that. And then *she* came along and said we mustn't do it any more.'

Dumpy winced. 'Snow White,' he said.

'Yup. Dear God, how could I ever forget *her*?'

'Takes some doing, I agree,' Dumpy concurred with feeling. 'You remember the newspaper she used to put down all over the furniture?'

'The pink velvet curtains with brocaded tiebacks.'

'Having to iron the dishcloths.'

'That godawful picture of happy kittens playing with a ball of wool she made us hang in the bog. Where the peanut calendar used to be.'

'The little frilly lavatory brush holder in the shape of a cutely grinning pig.'

'And none of us daring to say a thing. Which was fair enough, because you had to be as brave as two short planks to say *anything* when she was in one of her moods . . .'

'That's amazing,' Dumpy said quietly. 'And to think, I actually managed to forget all that. I'd have thought it'd have taken three hours with a chainsaw and a jemmy to get all that stuff out of my head.'

Rumpelstiltskin nodded. 'It's all been very . . .'

'Quite.'

'And . . .' Rumpelstiltskin sat up as if someone had just jabbed a needle up through his trousers. 'Dammit, we were Japanese.'

'I don't remember that.'

'We were, straight up.' Rumpelstiltskin frowned, as if he was trying to grip elusive memories in the folds of his brow. 'At least, part of us was. About the time the rest of us was playing cowboys. Something suddenly went wrong, and we were . . .' He shook his head. 'No,' he said, 'forget that. Must've been imagining it. For a moment there, though, I could have sworn – OH, JESUS, LOOK OUT!'

'Look out!' is, of course, a particularly useless form of warning, because it's so vague. It can even be counter-productive, since your immediate reaction on hearing it is to look round. If the source of danger is in front of you and closing in very fast, it can be absolutely disastrous.

'NOOooo!'

In retrospect it was all Mr Nikko's fault. At a time when young Mr Akira should have been concentrating a hundred per cent on steering the long wooden bench they were using as a makeshift canoe, Mr Nikko had been telling him all about the hypothesis that so long as you're truly as one with the boat, the direction you actually point the rudder in is irrelevant, since in the higher reality all places are one and the same anyway, and what really counts is not arriving but being in a state of harmonious travel towards (or away from; makes no odds) one of the infinite aspects of the place you'd wanted to go to. In consequence the bench hit the mop and nine people (seven samurai, two dwarves; calculation based on a simple head-count rather than being by weight or by volume) were catapulted into the foam.

Far away, something went Click*crinklecrinkle*whirrrr.

CHARACTERMERGE.EXE was doing its stuff; reintegrating that which had been delaminated, slotting back together the thin strips of what had been blown in all directions. It was like watching one of those shown-backwards sequences of a mill chimney falling down, where the long heap of scattered bricks suddenly seems to pull itself together and stand up as a solid tower once again.

So that was all right; except that where there had been seven samurai and two short plains drifters who couldn't swim thrashing wildly in the soapy water there were now seven dwarves who couldn't swim thrashing wildly in the soapy water and, not to put too fine a point on it, drowning.

'Igor!'

Oh Jesus, now what? 'Yes, boss?'

Treading suds like an up-ended paddle-steamer, the Baron raised his arms above his head and pointed in the direction of the laboratory. 'Igor, did you remember to switch the power off?'

'Me? No, I thought you . . .'

Zap.

At this point, with half the protagonists drowning and all of them, drowning or not, suffering the effects of a million volts getting loose in a hallful of soapy water, Mr Dawes decided that enough was enough.

When he'd set up the domain, he'd guessed that something like this might happen: a combination of a systems meltdown and a virus infection, quite possibly deliberately introduced by his enemies in the company, very likely exacerbated by further mutations from within the domain itself. It can be rough in virtual fantasy. In cyberspace, nobody can understand you when you scream.

So he'd built in a last-ditch save-all defence mechanism, a digital equivalent of the system that floods a ruptured compartment in a submarine or an airliner with instantly drying foam. That's where the suds motif had come from, in fact; at the time it had struck him as a piquant little play on themes.

He hadn't planned on being trapped inside when it went off.

But that wasn't a serious problem. All he had to do to get out of trouble was what he in fact did –

Which was to reach out four inches to his left, feel for the power socket and pull out the plug.

'That's it, is it?' Carl said, clearly disappointed.

Mr Dawes sighed. His definition of suffering fools gladly was giving them a little wave of commiseration as the man in the black hood kicked away the stool from under their feet.

'What were you expecting, exactly?' he said. 'Lethal feedback? All of us trapped the wrong side of the screen and looking for something big and heavy to break the glass with? Grow up, son; and while you're at it, get a life. It's only a game.'

'But . . .' Carl held his peace, albeit unwillingly. Not all that long ago, he was sure, he'd been a little wooden puppet, and then a huge humanoid monstrosity with a bolt through his neck; he could remember it all as clearly as if it were yesterday; except that he'd been up all the night before last and had spent yesterday fast asleep. Now he thought about it hard, he couldn't remember a thing.

They had rematerialised in an office. It was a nice office. It was the sort of office God would have liked to have if only He'd had as much money as Mr Dawes. The Seven Years War was fought to decide who owned an area rather smaller than the square of carpet under Mr Dawes's desk.

'In fact,' Mr Dawes went on, as he lit a cigar the size of a giant redwood, 'it's all quite simple.' Back here, he was quite definitely twenty-nine; a youngish, shortish twenty-nine, the baby-faced sort that gets exceptionally good value out of each razor-blade. Such a small man behind such a big desk;

the bizarre incongruity of it made some of the special effects Sis'd seen on the other side of the looking-glass seem positively mundane. 'There were these guys. They used to be on the board of Softcore till quite recently.'

'How recently?' Sis interrupted. Mr Dawes grinned and glanced at his watch.

'About three minutes ago,' he replied. 'Anyhow, they had the same dumb idea about how the domain works as your kid brother here. They thought I could be stranded there permanently.'

'Gosh,' Sis said. 'How silly.'

The door opened, and a secretary brought in the coffee. A jug and three cups.

'Quite,' Mr Dawes said. 'So I stranded them there instead.'

Sis spilt hot coffee down her front. 'But I thought you said it was all just a game,' she stuttered. 'Not for real at all, you said.'

Mr Dawes shrugged. 'There's real,' he replied airily, 'and then again, there's *real*. You want to know how real it is, you go down to the ninety-eighth floor and look for Eileen Suslowicz, George McDougall and Neville Chang. If you can find them,' he added, stirring his coffee, 'I'll give you the company.'

Sis thought for a moment. 'Snow White,' she said.

Mr Dawes nodded. 'That was Eileen. George and Neville were the Grimm boys. You run across them?'

Sis nodded. 'The wick— sorry, Tracy said they weren't from inside the, um, domain.'

'Tracy's a good kid,' Mr Dawes said, with a faint hint of fondness in his voice; the sort of slightly mellow tone you might expect from the head of Strategic Air Command talking about his favourite warhead. 'On reflection – sorry, no pun intended – maybe I should have told her more about what was going on inside the corporation. But then she'd have been worried, afraid she couldn't handle it herself. Much better she thought they were only pretend people.'

'I see.' Sis made a quick inventory on her fingers. 'So there's the three bad guys—'

'Not bad,' said Mr Dawes. 'Misguided.'

'The three misguided guys,' Sis corrected, 'and Tracy, all still stuck down there. That's four real people—'

'Five, actually. There's also our chief accountant. But he *prefers* it down there. Reckons he gets far more work done. He's a very sad man. You met him, yes?'

Sis nodded. 'Five people,' she said. 'And they might as well be dead.'

Mr Dawes made a vague gesture. 'Let's call it living in a world of their own. Remember, with the best will in the world, they started it. What else would you have me do?'

Sis frowned. 'You could go back and rescue them. And don't say it's not possible,' she added sternly, 'because I don't believe you.'

Mr Dawes stood up and walked to the window, from which you could clearly see the curvature of the Earth. 'Maybe I haven't explained it clearly enough,' he said. 'It's a fault I have, I know. Especially when I'm talking to people who aren't in the business. I can't go back there,' he said, leaning on the windowsill, 'because there's no there to go back to. It's a computer simulation, that's all. And all I had to do to leave it was pull out the plug and switch off the machine.'

'But that can't be right,' Sis protested vehemently. 'You said yourself, this Eileen woman who was Snow White, and the other two—'

'Snow White,' said Mr Dawes quietly. 'The Brothers Grimm. One's a girl from a fairystory, the other two have been dead for a hundred years. That's why they don't exist, kid. Don't you see that?'

'But we were there. And we exist.'

'Ah.' Mr Dawes's smile was reflected in the glass of the window. 'But we're real people.' He drew on his cigar, and the smoke obscured the reflection. 'Neat, huh? So much better than having them buried in concrete or dumped in the

Bay. And so simple, you could say it was child's play. Hey, kid,' he added, turning to Carl, who'd gone an unwholesome shade of green. 'You don't like coffee? I'll tell Evette to go fetch you some milk.'

'You arranged it all,' Sis said, very quietly. 'You set it all up just so they'd try and get you, and you could get them. That's . . .'

'Business,' Mr Dawes replied. 'And pleasure too, of course. I *like* squashing bugs.'

More than anything else in the entire world, Sis wanted to go home. Mum'd be going frantic for one thing; for another, there was something about Mr Dawes and his office and his soft, quite pleasant way of talking that made her want to hide under the bed, probably for the rest of her life. But there was still one question she badly needed the answer to.

'I still don't understand,' she said. 'They were real people, just like you and me. When you pulled the plug, we all just found ourselves back here, in this building . . .'

'My building,' said Mr Dawes. 'Which you and your brothers broke into. But I'm not going to call the police or anything, even though you did make things a little hard for me back there.'

'All right,' Sis said. 'We're sorry. We didn't mean to make such a mess. But if we're all real and it was all just a computer thing, how *can* they still be there, like you said? It's just not . . .'

Mr Dawes sighed. 'You want to know the answer, don't you? Okay, you want it, you can have it. Follow me, and on your own head be it.'

He led the way down a long corridor to a service lift that went either up or down (there was no way of knowing) for a very long time; and then the door opened and they were in a large, bare room with a concrete floor and no windows. In the middle of the room was a trio of free-standing computer workstations surrounded by three chairs. In the chairs sat three people, a woman and two men: Snow White and the Brothers Grimm.

'George and Neville you already know,' said Mr Dawes. 'And you saw Eileen briefly back in the great hall. You know, the resemblance is really kinda striking.'

All three were dressed in white surgical gowns; they had black plastic helmets and goggles on their heads, wires connected up to various parts of their bodies and plastic tubes going in and out of them like an Underground map. 'They're alive all right,' said Mr Dawes, matter of factly. 'And perfectly real. Well, as real as they ever were. Trust me, I'm a computer bore. I know about these things.'

Sis didn't want to look, but she found that she had to. 'They look awful,' she said at last.

Mr Dawes nodded. 'I know,' he said. 'But it's cheaper than litigation and more legal than murder, and the joy of it is, they did all this themselves. I'm not sure I even have the legal right to unplug them. I shall carry on paying their salaries,' he added. 'It'll just about cover the cost of keeping them like this.'

A spasm of something like pain flitted across Snow White's lovely face. Fairest of them all, no question.

'She's alive,' Sis protested. 'And she's here, in real life.'

'Yes,' agreed Mr Dawes, 'but *she* doesn't know that. Maybe it's all a matter of opinion, anyway. I mean, it all really comes down to what you're prepared to believe.'

'Can we go now, please?' Sis said. 'I'm truly sorry I asked now.'

She turned her back on the three of them (three little chairs, three little computers, who's been climbing about in *my* head?) and walked quickly to the door.

'Really,' she said, as Mr Dawes keyed in the security code, 'really and truly, they're dead, aren't they?'

Mr Dawes looked at her with no discernible expression. 'Let's just say they're away with the fairies,' he replied gravely. 'Time you were getting home.'

CHAPTER FOURTEEN

Once upon a time there was a little house in a big wood. It was a dear little house. It was adorable. The glass in its small, leaded windows was so old and distorted by age and authenticity that light stood about as much chance of getting in through them as an unemployed Libyan has of getting into the United States, and the sheer weight of the climbing roses on the front elevation was threatening to pull the house's face off and dump it around the front door in dusty heaps. It had been photographed so often you could almost see it hold its thatch back with both hands and show the cameraman a bit of basement.

And in the cottage there lived a cute little girl called Snow White, along with seven dwarf samurai. And three bears. And three little pigs. And three blind mice. And a cross-dressing werewolf. And that was just the downstairs parlour.

Ask the residents of Own Goal Cottage (such a pretty name, even if nobody has a clue why it's called that) about the reasons for the overcrowding, and if they'll admit that the place is a wee bit cramped (which is by no means certain) they'll be sure to tell you about the great flood; the flood in which all the other cottages in the domain were washed away, leaving only this place and Suckerbet Castle still standing. Just don't bother asking when this flood was, because they won't remember.

On the wall of the parlour there hung a big mirror in an ornate gilded plaster frame; and it had a crack in it that ran diagonally across the face. Even before it was broken it hadn't been much good, of course, for it was a distorting mirror, bought by Dumpy the dwarf from a travelling circus for the sole reason that it was cheap.

In front of the mirror one fine sunny morning stood Snow White, in her prettiest gingham dress, with her brightest and most cheerful pink ribbons in her hair. She smiled at it, wedged her face into a demure smile, and asked:

'Mirror, mirror on the wall, who's the fairest of them all?'

In the cracked mirror there appeared a rough impression of what her face might look like if it was inadvertently put in a blender. One eye was six inches higher than the other, the two halves of her nose made her look as if she'd been drawn by Picasso and then got in a fight with a barful of marines, and her mouth was a fat red slug trying to climb a ladder.

'You, O Snow White,' said the mirror, 'are the fairest of them all.'

Snow White preened herself like a contented cat, even though she knew the mirror said exactly the same thing to everybody who asked the question. It had worried her for a bit, until nice Mr Hiroshige had explained to her that since all things are, cosmically speaking, One, all reflections are the same reflection and so everybody is by definition the fairest. Although she was somewhat disappointed, in the end she came to the conclusion that that was probably the best way to deal with the matter. After all, where there is no competition there's no conflict, and where there's no conflict there's peace. Except in this case, when the flying pigs swoop too low and the sonic boom breaks all the glass in the greenhouse. Fortunately, that only tended to happen once in a blue moon; say, on average, every sixty-two days.

'Doesn't necessarily mean beautiful, either,' Eugene whispered to Julian behind his trotter. 'It could mean all sorts of things besides that. Could just mean the one with the most mouse-coloured hair.'

Julian made a noise that eloquently if somewhat vulgarly communicated his scepticism by blowing air through his snout. 'Just because she's the fairest,' he muttered, 'I still don't see why that gives her the right to boss us around. That's twice this week she's stopped my choccy bicky allowance for treading mud on the carpet, and it wasn't even me that did it.'

Eugene drew his trotter along the point of his chin thoughtfully. 'You know what,' he said, 'I've been thinking, wouldn't it be nice if we had a place of our own? You know, a nice little house just for the three of us.'

Julian considered the proposition, then dismissed it. 'Face facts,' he said. 'With none of us working we'd never get a mortgage.'

'I wasn't thinking of buying,' Eugene replied. 'How'd it be if we built it ourselves?'

'What, us? Just the three of us?' Julian's nostrils twitched. 'What the hell do we know about building houses?'

'We could learn,' Eugene said. 'Can't be all that difficult, can it? We could build it out of – oh, I don't know, how about straw?'

'Straw,' Julian repeated, a thoughtful expression on his face. 'Actually that's not a bad idea. I mean, it's cheap, it's good insulation, it's no bother to move about. And if hayricks and stuff stay up, why not a house? The only problem I can see is spontaneous combustion in the hot weather, when the residual moisture content starts to ferment. I gather that's the cause of seventy-nine-point-three per cent of all hayrick fires.'

Eugene chewed his lip. 'All right,' he said. 'How about sticks? Sticks are really cheap.'

'True,' Julian said, as he unearthed a truffle. 'And you avoid the spontaneous combustion problem quite neatly. But then you run into your strength-of-materials hassles. You'd have to get the equations just right, or you'd end up with the whole lot around your ears.'

'Okay,' Eugene said, with just a hint of exasperation. 'Forget straw *and* sticks. What about brick? Plain, honest-to-God bricks and mortar? You can't go wrong.'

Julian shook his head. 'Don't you believe it,' he replied. 'The ground's way too soft around here, you'd never be able to get proper foundations. You'd come home one evening and find the whole thing on its side, like a stag beetle that can't get up again. Sorry, but bricks are a definite no-no in these parts.'

Eugene closed his eyes. 'Just a minute,' he said. 'Dammit, the answer's as plain as the snout on your face. How about straw *and* sticks *and* bricks? Thatched roof to reduce weight, wooden rafters, lintels and floorboards, the rest of the fabric in brickwork? Though I say so myself as shouldn't, it's bloody brilliant. Well?'

Grudgingly, Julian nodded. 'Can't see much wrong with it myself,' he replied. 'Taken at face value, of course. We'd have to draw up proper plans, do the maths—'

'You could do that. You're ever so good at that sort of thing.'

Julian nodded to acknowledge the self-evident truth. 'And I reckon I know where I could lay my trotters on a supply of brick, definitely at trade, maybe cheaper.' Already he'd started tracing sketches in the dust with his nose. 'Of course, we'd have to get someone in to lay the damp-proof course . . .'

While he was talking, something moved away in the distance, nearly out of sight of the cottage, over by the patch of marshy ground where the old cesspit had been. At first it was just a quiver on the surface of the slime; then there was a deeply resonant glopping noise, and a long, thin canine muzzle forced its way to the surface into the air. It sneezed;

then the rest of a wolf's head followed it, and finally the rest of the wolf. It was, of course, filthy dirty, its fur plastered to its skull with creamy black yuck, and the smell was somewhat distressing.

'Woof,' muttered the big bad wolf; then he sneezed again.

How long he'd been down there, he had no idea. Fortuitously, he had fallen into a large air-pocket, just enough to keep him going while he gathered his strength for the monumental effort of forcing a way out. Now he was hungry and thirsty, he felt horrendously squalid and he had a doozy of a cold. His priorities were revenge and a nice hot bath, in no particular order.

As soon as he'd shaken the loose stuff out of his coat he looked round and saw the cottage. It looked good. There'd be all sorts of useful commodities in there; things (or people) to eat, hot water, clean towels, maybe even a basket lined with an old blanket where he could get a good night's sleep. And what was more, someone had been up on the roof putting back a fallen rooftile and had left a ladder leaning up against a wall. It'd be a piece of cake, climbing (*a-a-a-CHOO!*) up on the roof, sliding down the chimney, in like Flynn before you could say pork teriyaki. Having wiped further crud out of his eyes with the back of his paw, he set off across the clearing at a loping run.

Inside the cottage, an argument was raging. Mr Nikko was trying to get Baby Bear to understand that no, he hadn't been sitting in her chair, it was too small for him and he simply wouldn't fit; Mummy Bear was complaining loudly that the damned mice had been nibbling the cheese again and since there were seven grown men with blasted great swords around the place, couldn't something be done about it, because if not she was going to commandeer one of said blasted great swords and cut the little perishers' tails off. Dumpy the dwarf, meanwhile, was protesting that his back was killing him and there was no way he was going off to work today, not for all the cocaine in Nicaragua. The only sound that could be heard above all these discordant voices was Snow White, announcing that she wanted a nice warm bath and it was Mr Miroku's turn to light the fire under the copper. This did at least have the effect of ending the civil disturbances like a volley of rubber bullets; and Mr Miroku, grumbling softly under his breath, got up out of his comfy armchair and did as he was told.

'And mind you make sure the water's piping hot,' Snow White added. 'And then the lot of you can clear off and let me have a couple of hours' peace and quiet.'

Alone at last, Snow White pulled the cork out of her bottle of bath salts and poured copiously, until the tub overflowed with foam. She was just about to get undressed when there was a frantic scrabbling from somewhere up the chimney. A cloud of soot came billowing out, engulfing Snow White to the extent that her name suddenly ceased to be even remotely appropriate. Then there was a colossal splash, and the hot tub was suddenly and unexpectedly full of large, mucky wolf.

'Woof,' sighed Fang contentedly. '*Woof!*'

For once, Snow White was utterly speechless. Forget the soot for a moment; the whole of the living-room floor was awash with suds, scores of cubic feet of the stuff. Obviously she'd put in too much bath salts, because the foam was still oozing out over the sides of the tub, glugging across the floor like a self-propelled predatory carpet. At this rate, it wouldn't be long before the whole room was flooded in the stuff . . .

In consequence, she was not pleased; and when she wasn't pleased, she tended to express herself freely. This occasion was no exception.

For all that he was back in lupine form again, Fang had been a human being for so long that, when he suddenly became aware that he was lying in a bathtub with no clothes on in the presence of a young girl, he immediately began to feel markedly self-conscious. As it happened, there was a change of clothes handy; true, they'd once belonged to the wicked witch, and consisted of a thick, baggy black dress, a shawl and a bonnet that looked like something left over from the last BBC Dickens serialisation; but Fang was scarcely spoilt for choice. Quick as a flash (as you might say) he was out of the bath and into the clothes and out of the door and up the stairs, a part of the house that had the all-important feature in his eyes of being Snow White-free.

Even before he'd reached the landing, he was aware of the nature of his dilemma. He couldn't stay upstairs indefinitely, but going downstairs wasn't currently a viable option. He was standing there in an uncharacteristic state of dither when he heard footsteps. He took stock of his position, namely that he was a wet, wretched wolf in women's clothing in a strange house, and that if word of any of this ever made it back to the 77th Precinct, the rest of his career in Wolfpack was going to be very, very wearing.

He saw a bedroom door, slightly ajar. He bundled through it, closed it carefully behind him and turned the key, drew the curtains, dived into the bed and pulled the covers up over his muzzle.

Not a moment too soon; the door flew open and Snow White burst into the room. Somewhere along the way she'd picked up Mr Nikko's *katana* and a handful of razor-edged throwing stars. She stood for a moment in the doorway while her eyes adjusted to the dim light; then she made out the figure in the bed and raised her right arm as if about to let fly. Fang braced himself for a race with a speeding missile that he knew he'd lose; then Snow White's arm seemed to relax a little, and she lowered her hand.

'Grandma?' she said. 'Is that you?'

'Wf,' Fang mumbled, trying to make it sound like a sneeze.

'Oh.' She sounded disappointed. 'Buggery. Look, you haven't seen a wolf roaming around the place, have you? Probably wringing wet and covered in soot and soapsuds?'

'Wf.'

'Well, if you do . . .' Snow White narrowed her eyes and peered. 'Are you all right?' she said. 'You look awful.'

'Wf,' Fang replied, and added a yawn for good measure. He was halfway through it when he realised how bad a mistake it was.

'Shit a brick, Grandma, what big teeth you've got,' Snow White observed. Then she did a massive doubletake. 'You!' she snarled.

As the first throwing star split the wood of the headboard, Fang was already out of the bed and halfway out of the window. The second star shaved off the last few split ends of his tail-hairs. He landed in the flower-bed below with a heavy thump, rolled down a slight slope and found himself up to his neck in a goldfish pond.

Suddenly there was activity everywhere; dwarves, little pigs and samurai coming at him from all directions with a curiously diverse selection of garden implements, builders' tools and traditional Japanese weapons. As he tried to make a run for it away from the cottage, an arrow from Mr Akira's bow missed him by the thickness of a hair split by a top-class lawyer, sending him scampering for the back door. But the way was blocked by Rumpelstiltskin, who was wearing a red hood and holding a garden fork, so he turned in his tracks and sprinted for the front of the cottage, where Julian was lying in wait for him with a twelve-pound sledgehammer. He managed to dodge the blow, but the only safe direction open to him was up. He sprang as hard as his hind legs could manage and was just able to get his forepaws into the tangled branches of one of the climbing roses that clustered (inevitably) round the cottage's door. There were ever so many thorns in the rose entanglement but somehow, in his moment of direst need, the thought of Julian's sledgehammer inspired him with the will and determination to keep on going. If there was an award for scrambling up climbing roses and he'd won it, no doubt the sledgehammer would have been properly thanked in his acceptance speech.

So far, he said to himself, so good; because all the psychopathic loonies are now *outside* the house, which makes being inside the house a viable, not to mention preferable option.

With the last scrapings of his adrenaline reserves he hooked a thorn-lacerated paw over the sill of an open window and dragged himself through. Now all he had to do was run downstairs and get the doors bolted and the windows shuttered before the psychos could get back in; then it'd be a simple matter of sending a smoke-signal to Wolfpack HQ for reinforcements. Piece of –

A stray fragment of cobweb brushed against his catarrh-blocked nose, which started to tickle. A bluebottle, which had been trapped in it, managed to struggle free.

Oh hell, Fang thought.

The first spasm he was able to smother, so that all that came out was a muffled noise, something like *hf*. The second one nearly got away from him, but he pulled it back at the last moment and managed to hold on, while puffing out briskly through his nose. The third and most convulsive tickle, however, was more than lupine flesh and blood could stand. He sneezed.

To start with, the building merely stirred, like a heavy sleeper gently shaken by the shoulder. Then plaster dust started coming down from the ceilings, which Fang took as a fairly heavy hint. The first football-sized gobbet of falling masonry missed him by a few inches as he jumped through the scullery window without bothering to open it first; in consequence, he was well and truly clear by the time the roof caved in.

On the other paw, he found that he'd landed directly between Desmond and Mr Hiroshige.

Not surprisingly Mr Hiroshige was the first to react, and he'd have cut Fang into two equal halves if his slicing sword-blade hadn't collided with Desmond's flailing pickaxe. As it was, the two instruments met in a shower of sparks a few inches above Fang's shoulders, giving him plenty of time to dart between them and head for the trees, which were at most some forty yards away. Desmond was momentarily distracted by a direct hit on the head from a falling rafter, leaving Mr Hiroshige to take up the pursuit alone.

Easy, Fang muttered to himself as he ran. A race between a wolf and a middle-aged man in heavy armour; no problem. He put his head down, accelerated, and ran full tilt into a tree.

When he came round, he found himself sitting in a huge cauldron full of water, on the surface of which floated a few thinly sliced carrots, some parsnips, a few leeks and other sundry vegetables. The cauldron was tied with thick hairy rope to a couple of stout posts that had been driven firmly into the ground, and below it lay a large and tangled pile of junk timber, mostly salvaged from the ruins of Own Goal Cottage. Around him in a ring stood the pigs, the dwarves, the bears, the samurai, even the three blind mice. Snow White was just inside the circle, and she was holding a burning torch. All in all, he got the impression that he wasn't here to receive an honorary degree from the University of Fairyland.

'Woof?' he murmured, in a very small voice.

Snow White was grinning at him. She was bending forwards. She was touching the torch to the wood—

'That'll do,' said the wicked queen.

She walked out of the trees, passed through the cordon of spectators and up to Snow White. 'Now then,' she went on, grabbing the torch in Snow White's hand, 'I thought I told you to play nicely.'

'Get lost,' Snow White replied. 'This is none of your business.'

The queen smiled. 'Oh yes it is,' she said. 'I'm the queen, remember? Which means everyone's got to do as I say. Including you.'

'We'll see about that,' Snow White replied furiously. 'Miroku, Nikko, Hiroshywashy-whatever-your-name-is, get up here this instant.' She waited. Nobody moved.

'Hey,' she shrieked, 'that's a direct order.'

Mr Hiroshige, whose attention appeared to have been elsewhere, looked round in mild surprise. 'I'm terribly sorry,' he said. 'Were you talking to me?'

'Yes. Now get your mystic arse up here and—'

'Although,' interrupted Mr Miroku, in a calm, soothing voice, 'looked at from the point of view of the true adept of the Way, how can anybody hope to be that specific? A call to one is surely a call to all. Are we not all blossoms from the same jasmine bush, after all?'

Snow White ground her small, pearly teeth. 'All right, then,' she said. 'All of you. Come on, move.'

Mr Akira rubbed his chin. 'Surely in this context,' he said, 'all of us means not just those of us who are gathered in this particular clearing in this particular wood, but all samurai everywhere. Indeed, all human beings, regardless of race, creed or caste. All living creatures even, since all living things are part of the universal matrix.'

'Good point,' muttered Mr Wakisashi. 'I like that.'

'Which means,' Mr Akira went on blithely, 'that, much as we'd like to help, it's simply impossible. There's not enough room in this forest, let alone this rather cramped little clearing.'

Snow White's eyes were starting to bulge out of her head. 'For the last time,' she growled. 'Are you going to come up here and kill this bitch for me, or aren't you? Well?'

There was an awful silence, and the dwarves, bears, mice et cetera took a few steps backwards. Eventually, Mr Hiroshige spoke. He said:

'*Softly, the east wind stirs*
Dried leaves of autumn.
Go and get knotted.'

At once the rest of the crowd burst into furious applause; and in that split second, Snow White knew she was through.

She could see it in their faces; no more fetching and carrying, no more taking their boots off in the hall, no more running errands and being at her beck and call. Her power was broken. It was time to move on.

'Oh, all right then,' she said, and her voice was almost cheerful. 'See if I care.' She let go of the torch, skipped lightly away through the cordon and off into the darkness of the wood. She knew where she was going; there are always places you can go when you're cute, sweet and utterly ruthless. In a few months' time she'd be trying on the glass slipper or taking a thorn out of the Beast's paw or thanking some poor sucker of a knight in shining armour for rescuing her from a dragon the size of a small Jack Russell. She didn't even look back. Her kind never do.

The crowd started to drift away, chattering in quiet but excited voices about the cottages they were going to build, the evenings they were going to spend with takeaways and videos, the pink frilly curtains they weren't going to have in the living room. For the first time since she'd come to this domain, the wicked queen sensed the absence of something; it was like the moment when the pneumatic drills that have been digging up the road outside for the whole of the past week suddenly stop.

'Woof,' muttered Fang.

'That's all right,' the queen replied. 'Sorry I took so long getting here.' She cut the ropes, the cauldron hit the ground with a bone-jarring thud and Fang poured himself out of it, brushed a few slices of potato off the top of his head and curled up in a ball. 'After all,' the queen continued, 'what's the point of being a *wicked* queen if you can't interfere with the true course of justice? If I were you, though, I'd take a hike. Better still: get a haircut and a collar, pack the wolf business in for good and start over as a cuddly dog. Waggle your tail a bit and sit in a shop window. There's girls in Amsterdam who do that for a living.'

As Fang wobbled unsteadily away into the trees, the

wicked queen sighed and shook her head. She had her doubts about this, even now. Starting all over again from scratch was all very well in principle, but there was going to be an awful lot of this sort of thing; old habits dying hard, deeply rooted narrative trends to get rid of, happy endings to untangle. At times it made her wish she was back in real life. No, belay that thought. However hairy it might get here sometimes, it was never that bad.

She walked home, let herself into the castle by the back door and went upstairs to her dressing room. On the way she passed the great hall, where the Brothers Grimm were busily, if hopelessly, occupied with mops and buckets. It was possible, she told herself, that one day they'd manage to clean up the mess, and if that day came then in theory they'd be free to go back. But somehow it turned out that for every bucketful of soapy water they tipped out of the window into the moat, another two or three would ooze up out of the waterlogged rushes. Served them right, she muttered to herself.

'That's right,' she called out as she passed. 'Remember, if you can get your chores done in time, you *shall* go to the ball.'

The Grimms looked up at her and muttered something under their breath. It had something to do with the ball, or balls in general, but the queen was too far away to make out what it was.

She reached her dressing room, closed the door and sat down in front of the mirror. She took a deep breath and said the words.

'Running DOS,' replied the face in the glass. 'Please wait.'

When the moment came, she felt unaccountably nervous. True, she had no reason to do so that she could think of; she'd saved the big bad wolf from the lynch mob, the Grimms had been dealt with, she'd broken the power of Snow White and set everybody free. Not a bad start, she told herself.

'Path *fair* not found,' said the face. 'Define *fair*.'

'Just,' the wicked queen replied. 'Even-handed. Amenable to reason. Equitable in one's dealings with others.'

The face remained impassive.

'You, O queen, are the fairest of them all.'

The wicked queen nodded politely, said thank you, and closed down the mirror. 'So that's all right then,' she said aloud. 'And now I think I'll go and have a bath.'

Once upon a time there was a little house in a big wood.

No roses round this door. No white picket fence, no neatly trimmed flowerbeds, no cheerful chintzes at the windows. This place is a pigsty.

Which is as it should be, because three little pigs live here. As far as they're concerned, it's just the way they like it, even if it can be a bit of a nuisance crunching your way across a carpet of empty styrofoam pizza boxes every time you go for a pee.

It's solidly built, of thatch, timber and brick; but there are no more wolves to huff and puff in the forest now, so it's largely academic.

No more Snow White, no more wolves; you'd be forgiven for thinking this might constitute a happy ending. That would be premature, of course; it's never the happy ending until the master of ceremonies calls out 'Let's hear it for the fat lady' and they start bringing on the bouquets. There'll be other pests, be sure about that: road-widening schemes, local byelaws about keeping livestock in residential areas, RSPCA inspectors, weekenders from the city who move in and start complaining about the noise or the smell. But this is Make-believe Land, where the wicked queen can be relied on to come and chase the nuisances away.

It'd be nice to be able to say that everyone gets to live happily ever after, here in Mr Dawes's rose-tinted Gulag; but that would be taking fantasy a bit too far. The happiest the ending is likely to get is probably the small diner that Tom Thumb and the elf are running these days, out by the

Hundred Acre Wood by-pass; or the noisy, dirty engineering works where the dwarves go during the day, endlessly churning out precision-machined grommets and drinking tea out of cups that never seem to get washed up. It may even be somewhere in the Akira Integrated Circuits business park, where Mr Akira (president and managing director), who gives a fair day's pay for a fair day's work and tries not to screw too many people while he's about it, applies to the production of high-quality electronic components absolutely none of the principles he learnt back in the days when he was an earnest young student of the True Path of Enlightenment.

Handsome is as handsome does; ask any mirror.

VALHALLA

Tom Holt

As everyone knows, when great warriors die their reward
is eternal life in Odin's bijou little residence
known as Valhalla.

But Valhalla has changed. It has grown. It has diversified.
Just like any corporation, the Valhalla Group has had
to adapt to survive.

Unfortunately, not even an omniscient Norse god
could have prepared Valhalla for the arrival of
Carol Kortright, the one-time cocktail waitress,
last seen dead, and not at all happy.

Valhalla is the sparkling comic fantasy from a writer who
can turn misery into joy, darkness into light, and water
into a very pleasant lime cordial.

'A riotously funny read, told with a cracking and
inventive wit and the best similes since Douglas Adams.
Buy it, for heaven's sake!'
SFX

NOTHING BUT BLUE SKIES

Tom Holt

There are very many reasons why British summers are either non-existent or, alternatively, held on a Thursday. Many of these reasons are either scientific, mad, or both – but all of them are wrong, especially the scientific ones.

The real reason why it rains perpetually from January 1st to December 31st (inc.) is, of course, irritable Chinese Water Dragons.

Karen is one such legendary creature. Ancient, noble, near-indestructible and, for a number of wildly improbable reasons, working as an estate-agent, Karen is irritable quite a lot of the time.

Hence Wimbledon.

But now things have changed and Karen's no longer irritable.

She's FURIOUS.

Praise for Tom Holt:

'Brilliantly funny'
Mail on Sunday

'Wildly imaginative'
New Scientist

'When Tom Holt's on form, the world seems a much cheerier place'
SFX

WISH YOU WERE HERE

Tom Holt

It was a busy day on Lake Chicopee. But it was a mixed bunch of sightseers and tourists that had the strange local residents rubbing their hands with delight.

There was Calvin Dieb, the lawyer setting up a property deal, who'd lost his car keys.

There was Linda Lachuk, the tabloid journalist who could smell that big, sensational story.

There was Janice DeWeese, who was just on a walking holiday but who longed for love.

And finally, but most promising of all, there was Wesley Higgins, the young man from Birmingham, England, who was there because he knew the legend of the ghost of Okeewana. All he had to do was immerse himself in the waters of the lake and he would find his heart's desire. Well, it seemed like a good idea at the time.

OPEN SESAME

Tom Holt

Something was wrong! Just as the boiling water was about to be poured on his head and the man with the red book appeared and his life flashed before his eyes, Akram the Terrible, the most feared thief in Baghdad, knew that this had happened before. Many times. And he was damned if he was going to let it happen again. Just because he was a character in a story didn't mean that it always had to end this way.

Meanwhile, back in Southampton, it's a bit of a shock for Michelle when she puts on her Aunt Fatima's ring and the computer and the telephone start to bitch at her. But that's nothing compared to the story that the kitchen appliances have to tell her . . .

Once again, Tom Holt, the funniest and most original of all comic fantasy writers, is taking the myth.

'Tom Holt stands out on his own. . . If you haven't read any Tom Holt, go out and buy one now. At least one. But don't blame me for any laughter-induced injuries'
Vector

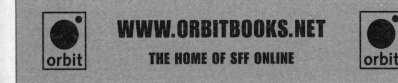